D0131293

Top ten bestseller Louise Bagshawe is published in more than eight languages, including her latest *Sunday Times* bestsellers *Glitz* and *Passion*. She lives in Northamptonshire with her family.

Visit www.louisebagshawebooks.com for all the latest news on Louise's books and much more!

DESIRE

Lisa Costello has it all: expensive clothes, exotic vacations and all the perks that come with dating a rich man. But Lisa's relationship with Josh Steen is a sham. Yet nothing could have prepared her for what she wakes up to the morning after their decadent but disastrous wedding in Thailand. Josh is dead — and it looks like Lisa killed him. As Lisa escapes, ex-FBI trainee turned journalist Sam Murray is on her trail. Suspecting a set-up, both Lisa and Sam face a race against time to uncover who is really behind the hit. With a professional assassin moving in for the kill, the clock is ticking fast . . .

Books by Louise Bagshawe
Published by The House of Ulverscroft:

A KEPT WOMAN
THE DEVIL YOU KNOW
MONDAY'S CHILD
TUESDAY'S CHILD
SPARKLES
GLAMOUR
GLITZ
PASSION

LOUISE BAGSHAWE

◆

DESIRE

Complete and Unabridged

CHARNWOOD
Leicester

First published in Great Britain in 2010 by
Headline Review
An imprint of Headline Publishing Group
London

First Charnwood Edition
published 2011
by arrangement with
Headline Publishing Group
London

British Library CIP Data

Bagshawe, Louise.
  Desire.
  1. Motion picture producers and directors- -
  Crimes against- -Fiction. 2. Fugitives from
  justice- -Fiction. 3. Romantic suspense novels.
  4. Large type books.
  I. Title
  823.9'2–dc22

ISBN 978–1–44480–612–0

Published by
F. A. Thorpe (Publishing)
Anstey, Leicestershire

Set by Words & Graphics Ltd.
Anstey, Leicestershire
Printed and bound in Great Britain by
T. J. International Ltd., Padstow, Cornwall

This book is for my brother James.

Acknowledgements

Michael Sissons is, as ever, my agent and rock. I could not do any of this without him. I'm so pleased to be working with Gemma Hirst at PFD and my thanks are due to Fiona Petherham and Jateen Patel. At Headline, I'm truly fortunate to have Marion Donaldson as my editor; her notes are brilliant and immensely improved this book. Marion Works with a great team: Sarah Douglas, Louise Rothwell, Clare Stacey, Sarah Jane Coleman, Rosie Gailer and Kate Tindal-Robertson. My thanks to all of them. It's very comforting to have Headline's legendary sales force behind me; I'm grateful to James Horobin, Barbara Ronan, Jess Fawcett, Diane Griffith, Ross Hulbert and Nigel Baines, and of course the whole team abroad especially sales and marketing at Headline Australia and New Zealand where I had such a wonderful time last spring!

Prologue

'Dangerous,' the client said. 'His wedding. There will be hundreds of people. Reporters, photographers. It'll be high profile.'

Felix smiled thinly. Did this fool think he was an amateur?

'The higher the better,' he said. 'Whenever we do this, there's gonna be press. At any wedding, people are distracted. Distraction is good.' He ticked off the advantages. 'Foreign resort. So no police — not thorough ones, anyway. No forensics. Tired wedding guests who need to get back to the States. It's perfect.'

'You can get in?'

Felix was silent. He never discussed his methods.

'I suppose nobody will know *all* the staff.'

'That's right. They won't.'

The client looked at him with an ugly mix of longing and desperation. That was how they usually looked in his business.

The sun beat down on the terrace. They were looking over the smooth green lawns of the golf course in one of Malibu's most expensive country clubs. Felix was sitting drinking mint tea and watching his client fret.

He was enjoying the moment. The last six months had been journeyman stuff for him, small fees. He was not one of the major players, the world's greats. This job came off a

1

recommendation, for a client who didn't have connections, from a cocaine dealer he'd paid handsomely. A good investment. Once he was hired — and he was about to be hired — a high-profile job like this might kick him into the big league. The client was a meal ticket, a game-changer.

'I want the money in advance. The full amount, wired to Switzerland,' he said. You treated them mean, just like a lover. Let them know who was in control.

'In advance? You might run away with it.'

This customer was nervous. But then Josh Steen, millionaire producer, was obviously a major hit. This was the high end of the target range. Usually Felix took out South American drug barons, sometimes a minor judge or politician. They were small fry, a piece of cake. Beneath him, really. Josh Steen was risky. He was famous. Not a foreigner, or a nobody. There would be heat on his killer, and the assassin would be risking his own life.

The job was only worth doing for the money. Big money. And the prestige that came with it. A big-league hit took a big-league payday.

So Felix wanted his cash. All of it. Right now. Whereas his client was needy, and emotional, and wanted Steen dead.

'If I ran away with your fee,' he said, 'my reputation would be destroyed. How do you think you found me? Reputation. The business works on word of mouth. Don't be dumb, OK?'

'OK. Fine. I'll wire you the money.' Of course. Like there was a choice. 'But there'll be a lot of publicity if you do this at the wedding. Josh is famous.'

Felix inclined his head. 'For a businessman, yes. Which is why the wedding is so perfect. You don't need to take the usual precautions, fake a death that looks natural, like it comes from disease or accident. That's getting riskier. The FBI would investigate a victim like Steen, and police forensic techniques get better every month. Amateurs are often too smart for their own good.'

'I don't understand,' the customer said, leaning forward. 'If Josh is killed, and it's obvious, won't that lead back to me?'

'No. That's the beauty of it,' Felix said. 'You can never have a perfect kill. But you *can* have a perfect suspect.' He grinned at the client. 'And at this wedding, it's going to be the bride.'

★   ★   ★

Lisa lifted her face to the sun.

God, it was beautiful out here. The lush, subtropical vegetation of the private estate. Sunlight, spilling from the sky and flooding their whole reception. Everywhere she looked, this party was immaculate. The grounds of the exclusive hotel, reserved for her and Josh, just the two of them. Wait staff, flown in from America, mingled with their well-dressed guests. There was enough Dior and Chanel, enough Louboutins and Manolos, Piaget watches and Hermès Kelly bags to stock the whole of Rodeo Drive. The guests included princes, senators, ambassadors, starlets, and half the moguls from the entertainment industry. In all her quiet, unassuming life, she would never have imagined she'd end up here . . .

Where was Josh? For a moment, she felt a sudden rush of warmth towards her new bridegroom. After all was said and done, he had provided this for her. Regardless of the fights, the controlling, the misery she'd felt, he'd stuck by her, even when the tabloids decided they didn't like her image. And now they were married, truly married, in spite of it all: Josh's bitchy sister, the catty wives of his work colleagues. Josh had gone ahead, put his ring on her finger. And here they were in Thailand, under the glorious sun, with an exquisite antique four-poster waiting for them on their wedding night . . .

Perhaps she should give him another chance. At least make this *try* to work. They hadn't always been such strangers to each other. Josh was her friend, her rescuer, back in the beginning. If she owed him enough to go through with the wedding, didn't she owe him enough to give the marriage a chance too?

Lisa took a tiny sip of her champagne and gathered her custom-made Vera Wang gown about her. She wanted to go and find him. Some of the Artemis Studio wives waved at her. They were giggling to each other. Lisa shrugged it off; she wasn't about to let them spoil her good mood. She wanted to talk to Josh, hug him. Maybe even kiss him. Their wedding night should be the kind of sex they hadn't had in months . . .

Where was he last? Oh yeah, talking to Peter Mazin, his business partner, over by the gazebo where the string quartet were playing. She walked across the lawn, and guests melted to let the bride past. The pleasant sounds of the musicians, some of the finest in the Los Angeles Symphony, floated above the crowd. The gazebo was tucked into a little corner, out of sight. Josh hated talking business in public. She didn't resent it if he had his head together with Peter on their wedding day. Workaholism was a part of who he was.

Lisa craned her head. She couldn't see Peter Mazin, but Josh was there; she could hear the low-pitched sound of his laugh, something she'd relished in the beginning, when he shocked everybody by starting to date her. She walked around the edge of the musicians' tent, picking her way across the ropes to the little corner of shrubbery where she'd seen the two men last . . .

And stopped dead. Peter Mazin was nowhere to be seen. But her bridegroom was all right. He was leaning over Melissa Olivera, one of Lisa's girlfriends, wife of Josh's deputy. Melissa had her expensive gown pulled down around her waist. Her tits, perky and plastic, were exposed to the hot Thai sun, and Josh's mouth was sucking on her left nipple. Lisa blankly took in the spreadeagled legs, his tailored pants loose at the waist. They'd been married for two hours.

And Josh Steen was already fucking someone else.

1

Lisa Costello woke up next to her husband's corpse.

Her nightdress, originally a yellow Chinese silk with delicate embroidery, a priceless heirloom of his mother's, was soaked with his blood, reddish-brown where it had oxidised. Blood caked everything: her hair, her skin, the diamonds of her engagement ring. It was on the Aubusson rug and the tapestries on the wall.

And of course, it was all over their marriage bed.

Lisa stared blankly. At first she was too shocked to take it in.

She was still coming to. Her head thudded with the relentless pain of a serious hangover. She was dehydrated; her temples pulsed, blood pumping loud in her skull. Her mouth and tongue were wretchedly dry. So dry she couldn't even scream.

The last thing she remembered was slamming the door in his face, stumbling towards the bed. She'd been drunk — but not *that* drunk, surely. She was just drowning her sorrows, against the farce of a marriage over before it had even begun.

But this sight was quite real. She was looking at Josh's body. His carefully styled salt-and-pepper hair flecked with his own blood; his lower body soaked in it. He'd been stabbed, several

6

times. There was a horrible wound at the side of his throat.

Lisa tried to sit up.

That was when she realised she was holding the dagger.

She glanced down, almost unable to release her fingers. A wedding gift from that local aristocrat Josh's company was dealing with — Prince Samyan, that was his name. It was antique, made of pure gold and decorated in the Thai fashion: a smooth ivory handle, slightly curved. It had been kept very sharp. Sickened, she threw it on the bed, but her fingerprints were still on it, reddened against the white bone.

Desperately, Lisa tried to remember. Something, anything after the fight. No dice, it was all blank. Jesus. An alcoholic blackout. She panted in terror and looked around, her brain screaming in protest as she turned her head. No broken windows, the doors were sedately in their frames. No burglar had busted in here.

She had murdered Joshua Steen on their wedding night. She had got drunk, and she had killed him. Stabbed him, tried to slit his throat, with one of their wedding gifts. She didn't remember any of it, but that didn't matter, did it?

She stumbled from the soaked satin sheets of their ornate four-poster bed and headed to the bathroom, where she vomited, dry-heaving. Almost nothing came up. She had a blurry memory of being sick the night before, after Josh started shouting at her. Maybe she'd emptied her stomach then. She gulped some water from the tap and instantly retched again. Even though she was hideously thirsty, the toxins in her stomach would not even allow her to drink.

She sobbed with confusion and terror. Joshua was a rich man, and he had powerful friends. His family was connected in society.

And they all hated her.

Nobody could understand why one of America's top movie producers, with thousands of gorgeous, accomplished models and actresses to choose from, would marry a waitress practically half his age. OK, Lisa Costello was pretty, but hardly able to play in the California league. Her mother, who had come from a small English town, was dead, and her father had left the family when she was ten and not been heard of since. Lisa was no match for a man who had dated Oscar winners, athletes and the Vice-President's cousin.

The American tabloids loved to hate her. They stalked her at the supermarket, took long-range photos of her on the beach. Her non-model's face, her normal curves, everything was lit in the worst possible way. They ran unflattering pictures of her next to Josh's ex-girlfriends. THE MOUSE AND THE MOGUL, one of them screamed. JOSH'S JOKE. Lisa wasn't worthy. And the press never let her forget it.

She'd stayed in the relationship partly to spite them. Because Lisa was stubborn. She wasn't a quitter. Even when it was clear it was not going to work. Even when she knew she would have to bail out sometime.

She was trapped by the massive fiasco of this

wedding, the millions of dollars it cost, the private beach resort, the chartered jets, the society columns and photographers. To cancel at the last minute would have made Josh look like a fool. And she cared about him enough to spare him that, at least.

What was the answer? She'd go through with it, give him his day in the sun, then push for a quickie divorce six months down the line.

How stupid. What a mistake.

She wished to God she had just walked away. Let the celebrity magazines crow how they were right. Who cared? Why did she care? Her younger self wouldn't have given a monkey's. But Josh's universe was seductive, of course it was. Lisa wasn't a saint. To go from struggling with the rent to this opulent fantasy — yeah, sure it was hard to give that up. And she'd learned habits from her dead bridegroom, like the importance of clothes and caring about what the press said.

Josh hadn't much approved of her friends, and to her shame, Lisa had dropped them. In truth it was hard to stay friends with your mates from the surfer bars and the part-time job at the diner when you suddenly acquired a mansion, a chauffeur and two bodyguards. She had paid the price for her selfishness, for being disloyal and dazzled. As she discovered the bargain she'd made, as Josh's control-freakery, cruelty and faithlessness became clear to her, she had no allies to back her up. Just some future in-laws who despised her and told her constantly how fortunate she was to be in this man's life. How

9

amazing it was he'd chosen her for his bed.

Lisa was *planning* to call it off. But she never pulled the trigger. So the wedding juggernaut rolled on, and she let herself be flattered, and bullied, and bribed into submission. The celebrity florists, the spread in *People* magazine, the Vera Wang dress, the epic diamond ring. Lisa Costello was a star of the show, and trapped in a glittering cage. Locked into marriage, no way out . . .

Until she saw Josh with Melissa. Actually on her wedding day. Two hours after they'd exchanged vows.

Then — the row. The start of which at least fifty of their guests had seen.

Lisa had stormed up here, to the honeymoon suite, for privacy, to get away from her sniggering bridesmaids and the whispers of the guests. She'd been screaming at him . . .

She lifted her head from the sink. Her reflection was haggard. Her hair was matted, her eyes bloodshot, with dark circles underneath. She was still wearing the ruby-rimmed platinum Blancpain watch Josh had given her; local time was coming up to nine in the morning.

A surge of panic welled in her throat.

Housekeeping.

Any minute now they'd be knocking on the door.

She limped to the doors of the suite and hung a 'Do Not Disturb' sign outside. Then she locked and bolted them. She moved to the telephone, rang reception, and said they were enjoying their honeymoon and were on no account to be disturbed until noon.

She made herself sound calm. Oh God! She was terrified.

This was Thailand. There was an extensive guard of Thai police around the estate, a private hideaway owned by Josh's partner, Peter Mazin. Five members of the royal family had attended this wedding, along with two government ministers and a US senator. Thailand was a death penalty state. Christ!

The sadness and the guilt would come later.

Her husband was dead, and she could see his mangled body, but right now, all she could feel was fear. A white wall of terror blocked everything out.

She had to think. She had to think *now*.

She forced herself to get back into the bathroom, where she ran the shower, watching the warm water sluice the blood off her body. There was no way to dispose of her nightdress; she just left it. More nausea rose in the back of her throat, but her stomach heaved dry. There was no time to be ill. How far away was the airport?

She washed her hair, her fingers fumbling to gain some speed. She towel-dried it, then ran to the vast closets, ornately carved from cherry-wood. Her clothes had been unpacked and placed on hangers. Instantly she found what she was looking for: her Escada jeans, her Nike sneakers, a plain black cotton T-shirt from Marks & Spencer, one of a few relics from her old life. She picked out a Hermès scarf and her Ray-Bans and hastily pulled them on.

Her wallet was there, Joshua's too. She took all the cash. There was more than two thousand US dollars and thirty-five thousand Thai baht. Her passport and his were both downstairs; security had collected them all before the wedding.

But Joshua had a key to the safe. Gingerly she approached his body, trying not to look at his face. It was in his trouser pocket. Her fingers trembled as she investigated. She knew she was depositing DNA, but what the hell; there weren't going to be any other suspects, were there?

Thank God, there it was. She fished it out and took it to the sink, rinsing off the blood. Then she crept to the door.

The corridor was silent; Joshua had rented the entire floor. His sister was up here, sleeping it off, but Lisa could hear no sound from her. The hotel staff were keeping their distance.

There was no other way out anyway. She had no choice and no time. She opened the door and slipped into the corridor. It was empty and silent, apart from the pounding of her own heart. Softly she pulled the door back shut. It closed with a heavy click anyway, but nobody came.

She would not risk the elevator. There was a stairwell, and she ran down that, as fast as she could manage, moving against the wall to steady herself at times. She was dizzy, sick, dehydrated. But she could not afford to pass out.

She exited the stairwell on the leisure floor. Here they had a gym and pool. She could hear the sound of the machines; some health-nut Californians, colleagues of Josh's, were in there exercising already. Her blood was racing around her skin without the slightest need for aerobics; there was someone in the locker room, and she needed to go in there.

She walked in, ready to spin some line of bullshit, to smile and make conversation, talk about the wedding night that never happened, whatever was needed. But no, the woman was wearing slippers and the brown dress of the estate staff; she was cleaning, and her look at Lisa was blank. She didn't recognise her, didn't care.

Lisa moved to the safe next to the lockers and inserted her key. There they were, a neat row of passports, stacked and ready to go. She flicked through them till she found what she was looking for: Janet Parks, an English actress. She was roughly the same build as Lisa, and last night she'd been very drunk, passed out in the fountain by the ornamental temple. Lisa had watched two of the wait staff carry her away to her bungalow. She'd be up later than anyone else, miss her passport after everyone else. Lisa picked up her own too, as cover, although the police were bound to block it.

A side door led from the locker room out to the grounds. Lisa let herself out and sheltered for a minute under a thick golden bamboo bush. She tied the scarf around her wet hair and slipped on the sunglasses. She was in a back part of the hotel garden, and she could see the road through the estate; it led down to each bungalow and guest house, and then out towards Phuket City. She felt ill enough to faint, but she made herself jog. Each step, each pace took her further

13

away from that horror, from Joshua's lifeless body, that bloody dagger. She ran, tense, always waiting for the shout, for a siren, a shotgun, guards running towards her, but nobody came. And suddenly she was running past the hotel's sign, and she was out, and there they were, the little group of taxis, beat-up and battered, the drivers waiting for wedding guests to emerge, to strike out on their own, those precious Westerners with all their money.

She made herself slow to a walk. The taxi drivers smiled at her. The guy at the head of the queue tossed down his cigarette, stubbing it out with his shoe, and climbed into his car, joking with the men behind him. To Lisa, his every movement took an age. They would knock on Josh's door soon; they would be coming. She would rot in a festering Thai jail until they hanged her.

She smiled as briskly as she could and slipped into the back seat. The cab stank of smoke, maybe enough to mask her sweat and fear. 'Phuket airport,' she said clearly.

The driver pulled away and switched off the meter. 'Thousand,' he said.

A thousand baht. Thirty dollars. Lisa nodded and put the notes on the passenger seat. She held up another thousand to the mirror.

'If you get me there fast,' she said.

He grinned and stepped on the accelerator. Had that been necessary? He'd remember her now, when the police came asking. But speed mattered more than secrecy. Getting out of here was more important than anything.

★ ★ ★

Felix rolled over in bed, checked his watch. He had slept well, as he usually did after a kill. The shower he'd taken in the hotel bathroom had been wonderful; it was short, but he never liked to leave a crime scene with blood on him. He had folded Lisa's slack fingers around the dagger — great touch that, the antique dagger, the royal wedding gift — and then allowed the fragrant hot water to blast the arterial blood off his skin. His clothes were splashed, but that was one reason he always wore black.

It was the middle of the night when he left the hotel bedroom, a lock of Josh Steen's hair in his pocket as a souvenir. He would visit Lisa again, in jail, when she was waiting to be executed, in the guise of a counsellor or a cleric, and get some of her hair too. That would be a thrill. He liked to keep those little surprises in his pocket for later.

It would be good to see Lisa Costello like that. His cock stirred at the thought of it. She had looked so goddamn hot on that bed, passed out cold in her little nightdress. Great ass, tight but real round, sticking out from that small waist. Good tits too. Natural, generous. The kind of body that promised a man a fuck he would never forget. She'd been his willing little helper all along. It would have been a simple enough kill if nothing had gone wrong at the wedding. Nobody liked Lisa; she was easy to blame. But that fool Steen had gotten himself into a fight. A giant, public, screaming row. And Felix's curvy little

15

alibi had been knocking back those drinks and causing a scene before he even got himself into the picture.

It was just so beautiful. If he'd paid her she couldn't have played her part better. Nobody would look anywhere else for the killer now. Absolutely nobody. He'd enjoyed thinking about what a stupid, gorgeous, curvaceous little bitch she was when he was standing next to Steen's warm corpse, playing with himself, looking at that lovely ass, her legs spreadeagled over the marriage bed.

Mostly clean, he had exited the hotel through the staff entrance in the back, behind the gymnasium. One of the managers shouted at him to join the clean-up crew in the reception tent. Before dawn came, the Thai and Filipino staff would have made the entire elaborate edifice disappear; not so much as a flake of confetti would remain on the ground.

How carefully Steen had planned it all, like a military operation. Felix grinned at the thought. And it would go on just fine without him.

Felix had ignored the manager and gone home to bed in his flat outside the complex, the little place he rented in town. By the time one of the other workers complained he was shirking, he would be long gone, on a first-class flight to Manhattan, where somebody had a beef with a bent congressman who took bribes but didn't deliver.

He glanced at his watch. Late morning. The drug would still be in Lisa's system; she would be out cold. A perfect time for him to stumble upon them, raise the alarm.

He rose and showered again. That would cause a delay for a couple of minutes, but he liked to be clean. Psychological, no doubt, to do with being a killer, but he didn't care about any of that crap. Didn't see a shrink, didn't want to. Being fucked up from this life had to be normal. He just got on with delivery.

He pulled on his staff uniform and prepared to get back to the house. Room service . . . the deferential waiter, the knock on the door . . . then a cry of horror, an alarm raised . . .

Brilliant. He didn't normally play games like this, but the set-up was too perfect. She'd wake dazed and sick, confused, glance at the bed, try to take it in, notice her own hand . . .

By then the staff would be in the room. She'd be in custody, probably hysterical. He loved it when they cracked up, right in front of him. Pleading innocence while she was soaked in her husband's blood.

They would summon the local police and Lisa would be flung in some festering jail to rot, and nobody, not the British consul, not some high-powered defence lawyer, would be able to help her. She had no friends anyway. Nobody cared. His bluntness with the weapon, the chloroform, the slow, brutal stabbing, the blood everywhere — none of it would matter. The arrogance of taking a shower right in Josh Steen's bathroom, leaving his hair and cells everywhere — Felix had a free pass. It was an obvious murder. And he had the perfect alibi.

Lisa Costello. Guilty.

He slipped from the apartment, smirking, and into his car. Ten minutes later he was in the hotel, yawning as though he'd been hard at work all night.

'Manuel.' The manager, Newton, a Canadian, was snapping his fingers, reading Felix's metal name tag. He was posing as one of the catering crew, mostly Americans, flown over to ensure that Josh Steen's guests got the ultimate white-glove service. The local Thais were used for set-up, cleaning, background stuff. Steen had gone with a major, expensive US company to run his party, and he'd willingly paid for the charter plane.

Nice of him to be so profligate. Made blending in a piece of cake.

'Get out to the terrace and check for any broken glass fragments.'

'*Si, señor.*' He had perfected the whiny, subservient voice; if asked, Mr Newton would recall Felix as pounds lighter and much shorter than he actually was, due to his meekness. It was psych stuff, and you could take it to the bank. 'But first the champagne, yes? The room service.'

'Who ordered room service?'

'Oh, *si*. Mr Steen and Mrs Steen. Shall I take up now?'

The boss stared at him. 'When did this happen? Mrs Steen rang us. Don't disturb till noon.' He grinned and made an obscene gesture. 'Guess he's getting laid. Marry for money and you earn every cent, right?' He laughed.

Felix's pulse quickened. Years of practice kept his face steady; his hangdog expression didn't change. But this was bad. How the hell . . . She should have been out still, unconscious. The dose he had administered was more than enough.

He ran through the possibilities in his mind. He'd got the wrong drug, administered it incorrectly to the wine. She hadn't drunk that wine after all, had put the glass down and picked up someone else's . . . but nope; the girl had fainted on to the bed in a classic symptom of toxicity. More likely she had drunk some but not the whole dose, plus she had the constitution of an ox.

She must still be up there, panicking. Smashing windows maybe, or trying to hide the sheets.

'How long ago did she call? Maybe I got message wrong.' He gestured vaguely towards the kitchen. 'Bellhop tell me.'

'Couple of hours.'

'Maybe I make mistake.'

'Hold up. If they want champagne, we mustn't keep them waiting.' Newton was reaching for the phone on the wall, punching in the number of the honeymoon suite. Felix hovered. He was greedy for information. This was always his favourite part of any kill; the discovery, the drama, the screaming . . .

His boss hung up after a few minutes. 'No answer at all. I'll go check on them. Get the champagne anyway, bring it up just in case.'

Felix hurried to the fridge, fetched the champagne and ice bucket, picked two crystal flutes out of the dishwasher and set them on a silver tray. He hated every second's delay. Within moments, he was bounding up the stairs after Newton, the tray barely moving on his outstretched hand; he had a gymnast's balance, came in useful on a number of jobs. When he reached the corridor to the suite, the door was closed; Newton was knocking on it, hard.

No response. Perhaps she had killed herself. Yeah, that would be a nice neat way out. Nobody looked twice at a murder-suicide. It wouldn't be so much fun as a trial and execution, but it would work.

He had the money already. So that was cool. But the more spectacular the kill, the bigger his fee on the next job and the one after that. High-profile cases were worth more. He shrugged mentally. If Lisa had taken the easy way out, there was no point crying about it.

'Señor Newton, maybe open door just a little peek, check if they OK,' he suggested.

His boss already had the skeleton key in his hand and was turning it in the lock. Felix moved forward, champagne tray at the ready, straining eagerly to see his work.

The door creaked open.

'Holy shit!' said Newton. 'Oh my God! Jesus!'

Don't bother Him, Felix thought, smiling. He had nothing to do with it.

Newton had run inside the room and was standing there, gulping for air like a fish, his chest heaving. Felix put on his concerned face and moved inside with him, letting the champagne tray drop to the floor for effect.

'Santa Maria!' he gasped.

20

Josh Steen was pretty much where he'd left him. The dagger was on the floor by the body. His gaze scanned the room, real quick: closet door was open — so she'd taken a few clothes. He checked the bathroom. That was ajar too. She had showered and run. Jeez, he didn't think she had it in her, that little Limey nothing. Why did she bother? There was no point. She'd be stopped at the airport, or picked up by Thai police if she tried to stay on the mainland. But people weren't logical, not in this state.

Man, Lisa Costello must be feeling sick. And she must think she'd killed her meal ticket. Sucks to be her.

Still, Felix wasn't pleased. Until Lisa was caught, it would be an open loop; it would bother him. The client might try to fuss about it. He was going to call, just to make sure. In fact he would call right now.

'Mistah Newton — I can't take this, I going to be sick. She kill him,' he gasped.

His boss spun around. 'Manuel, go call the police! Have everybody look for Mrs Steen! Call the owner! Tell the family! Get people out of the hotel . . .'

'Si, si — then I go home, yes?' Felix sobbed. He withdrew from the suite. Go fuck yourself, old-timer, you can do all that shit. His presence in the room was now explained, should they find any hair or DNA — not that he thought it was likely. Yeah, he'd call the police. And he'd call the FBI in LA and he'd call CNN. Nice anonymous tip-off.

After that he was getting on a plane. It was fun

21

to be around the scene of the crime, but you didn't want to overstay your welcome. He would call his client from the airport. He decided not to track Lisa. As long as the media convicted her, the trial was just a formality. Felix's commission was fulfilled, right? Josh Steen was dead.

Besides, he had a strong feeling that his client would get somebody else to do the tracking.

Felix went downstairs to use the phone. After that, he had a little date with Congressman Louis Cantor.

★   ★   ★

The road to the airport was dusty and hot. There were a thousand cars, she was anonymous. Lisa dared not lean back against the seat and close her eyes. If she did that, she might be sick again, or try to. Maybe the driver would throw her out. She had to keep it together. The cars and trucks streamed past her; he was driving so fast. She kept her eyes on the asphalt, on the signs. Twenty kilometres to the airport. Ten . . .

They were there. He looked around and gestured, asking her which terminal.

'International,' Lisa said, and forced a smile. It was still only half nine. She might make it, she just might. She passed the extra notes across and jumped out of the car, running into the building, fighting her nausea.

It was a big airport; unexceptional enough. Check-in was a large hall divided by pillars, yellow on the bottom half, the floor white with huge pink cross-lines. There were baggage cart

22

displays, ticket sale booths, rows of airline check-ins. She was instantly relieved to see plenty of travellers just like herself, twenty-somethings, carrying just backpacks or even without luggage at all; Thailand was the backpacker centre of the universe.

Her thirst could no longer be denied. She was forced to waste precious time at a Dunkin' Donuts stall. She bought water, a coffee and a large chocolate doughnut; try to raise her blood sugar levels after the alcoholic crash. With trembling hands she passed over some more of her precious baht notes, and unsteadily unscrewed the cap off her water bottle. The drink moistened her dry mouth; she could feel her cells sucking up the hydration, pleading for more. Her gorge rose, but she told herself to calm down; mind over matter; she had to get on a plane, and they don't let drunks fly.

A quick look at the departure schedules. There were flights to lots of places, some safe, some not. Finland — Milan, even. God, how she longed to board a flight to Milan. But she dared not do it. They would discover Josh soon, and some time after that, find out Janet's passport was missing. They'd put out a stop on it at the airport. How long before they checked all the guest passports, not just her own? This would be a celebrity case, lots of pressure. If she took a long-haul flight, her little ruse would be found out before she landed. Police would be there to arrest her before she got off the plane. They would turn her around; she'd probably never even get through immigration to claim asylum.

Breaking for freedom too early would be a death sentence.

A short-haul flight was the only answer. She had to be off the plane before they found out about the passport.

But the closer destinations offered little comfort. Singapore. Mainland China. Hong Kong . . . every one of them could extradite her back to this hellhole. All these Asian countries had the death penalty, didn't they? The lot of them! But she had to make a choice anyway.

Before she could be extradited, she'd have to be caught.

And a little chance was way better than none at all.

Dragon Airlines was flying regularly to Hong Kong. Lisa had an old friend from school who lived in Hong Kong, or used to. They hadn't stayed in touch. But that was more than she had anyplace else in south-east Asia. Maybe she could repeat the trick, borrow Alice's passport. Steal it if she had to. Alice had shorter hair, and she was dumpier, and a brunette. But she was at least the same age, and British. Maybe Lisa could figure something out.

A slim chance. But a hell of a lot better than nothing. Lisa had no idea if Alice was at the same address, or still lived in Hong Kong at all, but she had to try. She walked up to the ticket counter and got in line, trying not to let her stress show as the couple in front of her asked about upgrades and vegetarian meals. She nibbled a little on the doughnut. It gave her sugar, and something to do. Each second took an age to pass.

24

'Can I help you, miss?' the agent said.

Lisa tried for her most brilliant smile, the one that had landed Joshua Steen.

'I'm thinking about going to Hong Kong for the weekend. Wondered if you had anything on standby.' She forced a chuckle. 'Coach of course.'

'Let me see.' The woman did not respond to her humour, but that was OK. She was brisk and looking right through Lisa. 'There's an open seat on the next flight if you hurry. Luggage?'

Lisa shook her head. 'Kind of an impulse thing.'

'OK. Then you should make it. How you like to pay?'

'I have cash,' Lisa said. 'US dollars OK? I only want one way. I might go see a girlfriend in Sydney after that.'

The agent nodded, uninterested. 'Standby one hundred eighty dollars.'

Lisa counted the money out. She had hundreds; the agent did not care. She passed back the change in Thai baht and gave Lisa a boarding card.

'Gate 122, boarding now. You hurry.'

She sure would hurry. Lisa rushed upstairs to the metal detectors and passport control. She was fortunate; it wasn't too busy. When she came to the passport desk, panic almost overwhelmed her, but the surly man sitting there barely checked her photograph; she was waved through and nobody cared that she was running to the gate. When she got there, passengers were filing into the plane. Lisa offered her boarding card; it was placed in a machine, the stub given to her. She had a middle seat, way in the back, and she was grateful for it.

She buckled herself in and sipped slowly at her coffee, nibbling on the doughnut to settle her stomach. Each moment the plane sat on the tarmac was torture. Each minute was torture. The whole flight would be an eternity of terror.

Finally the plane moved from the gate, taxiing out on the runway. Thirsty, sick, her heart thumping and her head pounding, Lisa watched with utter relief as the wheels lifted from the tarmac and the plane moved into the sky. It was nine forty-five. She'd asked the hotel to back off until noon; would the maids knock then, or wait a few hours? Would Josh's sister, or his mother, interrupt them early? Her heart crunched in pain as she thought about that. God, but she had hated those women, so petty towards her, so cold to Josh, greedy for his money . . . but they were his family. Miriam had given birth to him. She tried to imagine their horror, the wail of grief that would rip through them when they saw him, found him, poor Josh, the master of the universe a cold, helpless, blood-soaked corpse on that bed. The moment would scar them both, as it had scarred her, for life. Whatever quarrels or fights . . . how small those things seemed now, how very little they mattered. Horrible waves of guilt and pity and fear raced through her. She dug her nails into her palms, distracting herself with the pain, trying not to be sick, to push the image away, concentrate on her survival. Once those poor women found him dead, how quickly

26

would they assume she had done it?

Everything depended on the passports. The estate guards would call the police. Rumours would sweep the hotel, the wedding guests. The selected, hand-picked journalists Josh had chosen to attend — tame poodles, permitted to report on the big society wedding — would suddenly find themselves, celebrity hacks though they were, in the middle of the story of the year. What the Thai police did not think to do, the paparazzi would suggest to them.

Lisa didn't know how long she had. This flight was three hours and forty minutes. She would also have to get through Hong Kong immigration. None of what happened now was in her control.

The fasten seat belt sign was switched off. An air hostess was coming round with a trolley full of drinks. Some louts, British holidaymakers, were already asking for alcohol. Lisa would join them. She never wanted to drink, not ever again in her life. But the hangover was brutal, and she needed to be whole, to cope with the forward journey, the escape. She knew enough about drinking to understand that hair of the dog was real. A little alcohol now would attack her liver, her poor, bruised liver, but while it dealt with the fresh assault the toxins besetting her would lie low; the symptoms would be masked; like a miracle from Lourdes, she'd feel better. And Lisa needed to feel better.

The trolley arrived, and she asked for a white wine, although she blushed as she did it. It was passed to her without comment. She poured the liquid into a little plastic glass and swallowed, feeling her sanity return with every slug, not able to care about the internal damage it was doing. She was sorry she had killed Joshua. Sorry she had seen him with Melissa. Sorry she'd been dazzled by him in the first place, sorry she'd gotten drunk at her own wedding. But she dared not cry or make any sort of scene; the hole in her heart would have to do for penance this morning.

Lisa Costello was sorry for a lot of things. But she did not want to die.

The wine flowed down her gullet and into her body. For the next few hours, life was out of her control. She put her head back against the synthetic leather seat, and started to pray. What else could she do? She didn't want to get caught. She didn't want to die. Right now, nothing else mattered.

2

Sam Murray wondered just how far he could go.

The party had lived up to expectations. It should do, he guessed, for the reported two-million-dollar price tag. He thought it had cost more than that. The cocaine alone must have run Josh Steen a hundred grand. And Beluga caviar another fifteen. His back-of-an-envelope calculations suggested three to three and a half.

This kind of bash was manna to *USA Weekly*. His was the new trash celebrity mag on the block, and they prided themselves on being first with the exclusives and the glossiest pictures. His editor walked the fine line between the exclusive, scurrilous stories of the *National Enquirer* and the Eurotrash puff pieces of *Hello!* and *OK!*. They hinted darkly at marital rifts, they ran blind items, they suggested and prompted and sniggered, but they covered it all with the first pics and the official photo shoots. And they paid very well. Half a million for this party, which would cover the coke *and* the caviar.

He had great copy for them, too. A stand-up fight between the gilded lovebirds at the actual reception party of their wedding. Gossip sweeping this glittering crowd that the new-minted bridegroom had indulged in his first affair less than one hour after tying the knot — and with an ex-fiancée, too! The sister-in-law

29

openly insulting the bride! All that wealth — and no happiness.

He'd seen Kevin's pictures, and they were gorgeous, if you liked that sort of thing. Sam's editor did. Lisa Costello, looking good enough to eat in her Vera Wang gown with the real South Sea pearl tiara, and a ten-carat flawless diamond glittering on her hand. She was a naturally pretty girl, but the artifice of some of Hollywood's best make-up magicians turned her into a stunner. Then there was the wedding itself, on the beach, by the Buddhist temple; the extravagant fireworks, the private jets, the hired estates, Atomic Mass, the giant rock band, performing a private concert, drugs and champagne, an imported casino and every kind of wild excess.

His own guest bungalow might be the most luxurious place he'd ever stayed in. Its quaint woven bamboo roof belied the comforts within: jacuzzi big enough to swim in, goose-feather bed, cool marble floors, a private kitchen stocked with Beluga, Krug, Evian, lychees and other fruits; a cinema-sized big-screen TV, ultra-fast wireless, and in the back yard, screened by a lanai against the local mosquitos, his personal eternity pool, complete with fountain and swimming current.

The assignment was over, but Sam Murray did not want to leave. To do what? To fly back to his one-bedroom apartment in the Hollywood Hills, the only thing he had to show for a lifetime's work? To get back to his computer, trail a few more shallow celebrities, discover who'd had plastic surgery this week, which box office hero was banging the nanny? It was no life for a man. But it was his life. It paid the bills, and he went along with it.

While guys like Josh Steen, tanned and well groomed in their designer suits, over fifty and overpaid, ran the businesses that made his copy. They had the money to throw the parties where he was just another guest, just another leech.

They walked away with girls like Lisa Costello.

Josh Steen hadn't cared about Hollywood's judgement, not at first, and that was because he was a judge of quality. Big enough to have taste. So Lisa Costello wasn't Hollywood attractive, not obviously blonde and petite-nosed and manicured up to her eyeballs. But she had something about her. It didn't come over on the TV cameras or in photographs. She was real, she was un-plastic; grounded, independent, feisty, pretty. The girl next door — but with ferocious guts, and a mind of her own. The kind of woman a man could partner with.

Lisa Costello was still standing. After two years of tabloid abuse and pillory. Some of which Sam had thrown at her. No drug problems, no alcoholism. Not even a retail addiction. She just got on with life, no excuses and no crutches. Sam admired the girl. She was gutsy.

It was a tragedy, really. She could make him happy, if he'd let her. But somehow Steen had slipped into conventional thinking, got Lisa all groomed and taken in hand, booked the big wedding, flattened her spirit. It wasn't Lisa whose nerve had failed. It was Josh.

Sam knew it. One thing that made him what he was, made him so good at this shitty job. He could read people. If he got close, he could read characters, strip them down further than their therapist or their rabbi. He'd met Lisa now, knew already how wrong her image was. What a strong girl she was. He hated that he'd never have the chance to go any deeper with her, see what made her tick.

Sam checked himself. He was thinking about her *way* too often. One chance encounter, one short conversation, and Sam Murray, divorcé, man about town, breaker of hearts, relentless womaniser — Sam Murray was transfixed. He understood immediately why Josh Steen had made that choice. His own past copy on Lisa Costello was instantly revealed to him to be so much junk. This was no gold-digging bimbo playing out of her league. Lisa Costello was something very special.

And Josh Steen, not Sam, was marrying her.

But maybe not — after that little display at the reception last night.

The thought cheered him. Surely he was watching the newlyweds break up. Surely she couldn't have gone to the honeymoon suite after that — not to make love to him, anyway. Josh Steen, apparently, could not buy her. Lisa Costello was willing to throw it all away. Half his readers would think she was the dumbest broad in the world.

Sam was unreasonably glad to be proved wrong about her.

Anyway, the fight gave him a wonderful excuse to stay on. Josh Steen's hospitality would end at first light tomorrow, and there was no way the magazine would stump up for these ultra-exclusive digs, but perhaps he could get a room at a nearby hotel. He'd taken care to generously tip every cleaner, guard and waiter he met, too, with his editor's money; there were now half a dozen people who would let him back on to this estate, even if he was no longer an official guest.

Kevin would want to stay too. He was going through a divorce. At least the guy had somebody to lose. But Sam didn't want to do this with Kevin, he wanted to do it solo.

Sam was a loner. When he was young that was OK, but he was getting on now, thirty-seven and no serious relationships. His marriage had lasted longer than the Steens' was going to, but not by much — an impulse thing in Vegas with a fun-loving girfriend who immediately metamorphosised into a nagging wife. She'd cut and run after two weeks, and he would have called it off if she hadn't.

No woman had lasted more than six months with him.

Sam moved to the living room to make the call — landlines were a necessity; his cell phone was patchy out here at best — and felt the familiar pang of self-disgust. Every time he went cap in hand to them for anything, he loathed himself. What was he doing, writing pieces on puffed-up nonentities who nobody would remember in fifteen years, maybe not in five?

Collecting your fat paycheque, Sam told himself sternly, the one you need for the girls and the casinos and the property taxes and the stupid toys and the fast car. It was amazing how much cash he could blow in a month and have nothing to show for it afterwards.

He knew he was better than this.

His editor did too, and that was why he bound Sam's hands so tight with the golden cuffs. Sam got good pay, but he also got just enough excitement to keep him happy — assignments like this in exotic locations, tickets to the best premieres, a slot at *Vanity Fair*'s Oscar party. Because he offered something none of the other overpaid celebrity hacks could.

He could get close.

Closer than anyone.

Sam was a man of talent, even brilliance, but no discipline. He'd applied to the FBI and graduated their training with honours. Unfortunately, that same training had revealed to him how easy the corrupt had it in this world, and what a lot of danger for shitty pay he'd be getting in the FBI. So he quit.

There followed a few unhappy years. It wasn't as easy as he thought to make it happen. He was rejected for investment banks and lost money in property. The jobs on offer seemed worse than the FBI, which at the very least promised excitement. He drifted, and he started to like himself less and less. The Bureau wasn't interested in having him back, and he doubted he could take the discipline of the army. So he became a private investigator, renting a small office in Beverly Hills and offering to tail anybody if paid enough cash.

At this he was an instant success. He could

prove he'd been in the FBI, and errant husbands or trophy wives looking for a younger guy on the side were easy enough prey. Word spread. After that, *US Weekly* came calling. They wanted to know if a certain film star was cheating on his terminally ill wife.

He was; and the sarcastic, witty report that Sam wrote about it got him hired.

Within two years, Sam told his asshole landlord that he could stuff his rent cheque. He bought the smart little place in the Hollywood Hills. He was finally steadily employed, and doing well at his job. It was how he'd ended up in Phuket, watching how the other half live and sharing a cigarette last night with Lisa Costello, this month's Girl America Loves to Hate.

Lisa Costello. If *she* was really going to jack it all in, walk away from luxury and a hundred million dollars, then Sam could leave his mid-six-figure salary. I'll do it, he promised himself. Just as soon as I get home. Just as soon as I can figure out what else I want to do with my life. And who will hire me to do it . . .

He shook his head; he was already making excuses. Damn, snap out of it.

He picked up the phone and dialled.

'Rich Frank's office.'

'Sarah, it's Sam, can you put me through?'

'Hey.' His boss, a sluggish two hundred and eighty pounds, sounded unusually excited. 'Sam? You still there? You on this thing?'

He must have heard about the possible divorce already. Sam cursed; he liked to be first with the news, it was why he got the big bucks.

'The fight? I'm an eyewitness.' Yeah, think about that angle.

'Fuck the fight. The death.'

Sam tensed as a surge of adrenalin pulsed through him. He drew back the white chiffon curtains of his bungalow and looked up the manicured lawns and tropical gardens towards the main hotel. There were flashing lights there, the unmistakable blue and red of cop cars.

'The murder,' Rich was saying. 'He's fucking dead and she's fucking gone. She killed him! The stupid bitch killed the guy!'

No need to ask who. His heart started to thump. Lisa Costello had killed Josh Steen? She was a hundred and thirty pounds, tops. Steen was nearly two hundred, and he worked out. Sam did not believe it.

'I'm on it. I watched them fighting . . . '

'Lots of the networks had that already. CNN and Fox are already scrambling their jets. But you're the only journalist on site right now, this second. This is going to be the new O.J. Simpson case, Sam, for fuck's sake, and *you're there first*.'

His head was spinning. He wanted to get the hell off the phone and get up to the hotel.

'Is my credit card extended?'

'I took the limit off it. But don't screw me, Sam.'

'OK.'

'Look.' Rich Frank was using that earnestly passionate voice he brought out only in times of extreme stress. Sam read people well, and he paid attention when Rich used that voice. 'This is going to be the biggest story of the year. If we get lead exclusives on it, it will *make* this fucking magazine. We'll eat the *Enquirer*'s lunch for them. You were *there*. They don't know where she is. Find her.'

'Find her?' he repeated dumbly.

'You were FBI. Find the girl or find her body if she offed herself. If it's a corpse, get pictures.'

Lovely. But Sam understood the magazine business. This story was worth multiple millions to their publishers, and he knew it.

'What do *I* get if I break this, Rich?' It was his opportunity; this whole thing was his once-in-a-lifetime chance, and Sam was determined that he was going to take it and run with it. 'This is massive for you. I want fair compensation.'

'You find her, you'll win a Pulitzer.'

Sam rolled his eyes. They didn't give out Pulitzers for celebrity crime stories. 'That's nice. I want cash. Lots of cash.'

There was a pause.

'OK, hotshot, here's the deal. A million dollars.'

Sam closed his eyes briefly, letting the words sink in. One million dollars. Enough to go somewhere and have a fresh start. A complete new life. Enough to solve all his problems.

'Half when this assignment's done, or if you're the guy that finds her. And the other half I'll pay you on the road, but only piecemeal. Each story gotta be worth it. Twenty-five grand a pop.'

He ran the sums in his head. 'What if there isn't twenty weeks in it?'

'If you find her, you get it all. Come on, Murray, what did I hire you for? Cops don't know shit. If she's good, they won't find her. If she's just some dumb bitch and they catch her tomorrow, then you lose. I ain't giving you a million bucks as a birthday present. Fair?'

'Yeah.' It was. And now he was on the manhunt of his life. For a moment, a rush of sympathy for Lisa Costello overwhelmed him; if he found her, dragged her to court in Thailand, tried her there, wouldn't they kill her? She'd be lined up for the execution O.J. never had to have.

What the hell, don't be so soft. He was no bleeding-heart liberal, after all. The woman stabbed Josh Steen to death. Being obnoxious didn't merit his execution.

He glanced down at his watch. Three p.m. local time. If they hadn't caught her by now, she was likely well away, clear of the hotel and the area.

'Yeah, it's fair. I got to go, Rich. Get you something for that first twenty-five grand.'

'Then go,' his editor said, hanging up.

Sam looked round the bungalow. Kevin was still sleeping, and he did not intend to wake him for photos. This was Sam's story, his game. He slipped out of the front door, closing it gently behind him, and started to run across the neatly clipped grass towards the hotel. Time to see if his generosity would pay off.

Something unfamiliar stirred in him. Excitement. Sam was on the story of a decade. And now he was on a second chance, for life, his life, a chance to be somebody, to start all over again.

The marble façade of the luxurious hotel rose before him. The Thai police were already there, their cars parked out front; they'd taped the building off. Luckily there were no TV cameras. Sam could still be first. He looked to see if the old man was there, the one he'd tipped so generously.

Yeah. There he was — Bhumibol, the porter, standing forlornly by the side of a police car, in front of the tape. Party guests were hanging around; some were crying, although to Sam the tears looked theatrical. He couldn't see any family members. They had to be secluded somewhere else.

Sam palmed his camera and subtly photographed the scene. He was skilled in doing this without holding it up; there was a knack to it. When he'd got enough shots, he sidled up to his contact. No point in pretending to be devastated with grief. Bhumibol knew he was a journalist. When they'd arrived here on Thursday, he'd tipped the guy a hundred American dollars. Now he would see how much goodwill this bought.

'I can't believe this,' he said quietly.

The man shook his head. He had excellent English; the staff at this place were all educated, and most of them spoke several languages.

'Very shocking,' he said.

'And bad for business?' Concern was written on the porter's face. The billionaires and minor princelings who used this little Shangri-la, rap moguls and overpaid athletes, they would shun this sort of publicity. The Jade Dragon Estate traded on its privacy. Would he soon be out of a job?

Bhumibol nodded. 'Yes, it is not a good thing.'

'I heard the wife is missing. Are they searching the hotel for her?' Sam craned his neck. 'They won't even let you inside, huh?'

'Yes, they are taking fingerprints, bringing special dogs.'

'Sniffer dogs?' Sam liked that detail. Who knew the Thai police had such things? Maybe he was the typical Yank, assuming the local cops were rubes. He mentally adjusted.

'If that is what you call them.'

'So no staff are inside at all?'

'Some — they are asking many questions of the workers. If they saw her last night, if they saw him.'

He needed more.

'Did you see it — where he was killed?'

The porter's eyes narrowed, and he looked steadily at Sam.

'Maybe I shouldn't tell it to you.'

Sam understood. 'I want to know. I'll pay you, Bhumibol, and I never reveal my sources.'

The older man's eyes widened in surprise. 'You remember my name.'

'I'm not one of these guys,' Sam said, gesturing at the overdressed crowd of super-rich gawkers. 'I'm here on sufferance, to make Mr Steen look good. They put me in a bungalow but I might as well be serving the drinks. You know this story will be in all the papers. It'd be good if it was in mine first.' He drew the porter to one side and carefully peeled off another hundred from the roll in his pocket; Bhumibol took it carefully.

'She killed him in bed.'

'The marriage bed?' That was sensational. They'd be going to press in an hour back home. He'd give them something worth a last-minute rewrite.

Bhumibol had an audience now, and he was rather enjoying Sam's shock. Sam could play that up to good effect. It made the speaker want to go on surprising you.

'Yes, and with the royal dagger. You understand?'

He did. Sam licked his lips, now dry with excitement. 'You're kidding. The one the prince gave them?'

'Yes,' Bhumibol hissed. Like most Thais, he took royalty very seriously indeed; parts of the country still regarded the royal house as close to divine.

'If she's not there, how do they know it was her?'

The porter raised his eyebrows. 'Come along, mister,' he said. 'Room service go into the room when no answer. Man dead, lady gone. No window broken, lots of blood. Her clothes also gone, shoes too, and police have her fingers on dagger.'

'Open and shut,' Sam agreed.

'Excuse me?'

'Just an expression.'

'She will not get far away,' the older man said, with grim satisfaction. 'Her passport gone, but police stop it. On computers at airport. They have police looking in Phuket town. Villages too. Family gives already big reward. Three million dollars US. Everybody will looking for her.'

41

Sam nodded. 'Thanks, man. I might be back for more.'

'No more.' He had that slightly sick look, the way interviewees often did when they thought they'd said too much. 'I want job more than hundred dollars. Understand?'

'Yeah,' Sam said. He peeled off another bill. 'Have two hundred anyway, man. And thanks.'

It felt wrong to leave the scene, but he had to. He turned around and sprinted back to the bungalow. The gods were with him, because his magazine was going to bed tonight; for once he could beat even a print newspaper. He called his editor and breathlessly dictated the copy.

'Fucking hell, Sam, that's great. It's going in.'

'I want my twenty-five.'

'Check your bank account in ten minutes.'

Sam felt a surge of satisfaction. Now the basic facts were out there, he could chase up more around the hotel.

'And Sam, get me those pictures.'

His phone had wireless internet, and the cabin was equipped with it, so lack of signal was no problem. Sam didn't leave home without all the latest toys. Today they would even be useful.

'Done and done,' he said.

'So she's on the run. That's even better. Take longer to catch her, we sell more copies.' A greedy pause as Rich figured out what this little scandal would do for his career. 'You think you can do it?'

His tone was almost pleading.

There was a million dollars at stake. And Sam's mind, trained to hunt, had already started to imagine what he'd do, how he'd get away from the rest of the press pack. He had met Lisa Costello, and he understood one thing. The girl was not stupid.

'Don't worry, boss,' he said. 'I'm on it.'

★ ★ ★

Sam walked back up to the hotel. He'd got a few more ideas. Definitely have to bribe a cop. He could get in trouble that way, if he picked the wrong guy. He was gonna ask Bhumibol who he should talk to. It worked like a referral; get the guy you bribe to recommend another guy who'll take a bribe.

But before that, he wanted more. The guests; these were Josh Steen's family and friends.

Josh's, not the happy couple's. Staggering how few people Lisa had there. She was a friendless girl. He warned himself not to misjudge her, not to be a sucker for a pretty face. The chick couldn't help having no family, but no friends? What did that say about her? Most killers were loners.

And you're a loner, too, said the voice in his head.

He shoved that aside. He wasn't the issue.

Outside the hotel, more people were standing in a crowd, waiting to be interviewed maybe. He saw Melissa Olivera and her husband Paulie; Melissa had been crying, Paulie stood apart from her. Sam filed that away carefully. Lisa Costello thought her husband had screwed Melissa yesterday.

43

She certainly looked upset.

He could not see the mom and sister. The cops must have taken them aside. There was Fiona Greenberg and her husband Stan; Fiona was shaking her head, looking shocked, but he could not see tears. She was talking to a few of the other women, their voices low, murmuring about the scandal.

Yeah. They were not upset. He wondered how many of this crowd truly loved Josh. A quick glance told him a few of the men, colleagues perhaps, were genuinely sorrowing.

Sam moved up to the group of women, a sombre expression on his face. It was always simpler to get women to talk. And after going to this wedding, he knew just how to do it.

'I can't believe this,' he said to Fiona Greenberg casually, like he had a right to start talking to her and had known her for years. 'Lisa Costello seemed like such a sweet girl. Who would believe she could do it?'

'Sweet?' Fiona said tartly. 'You didn't know her.'

He looked humble. 'I guess not.'

Hannah Mazin tossed her hair. 'She was a bitch. She never supported Josh. No interest in his work at all. I mean, Peter hardly even talked to her.'

Peter . . . right, that was Peter Mazin, Josh's business partner. They'd had a prickly relationship lately, fights over movie royalties. Didn't seem that unusual if Lisa hadn't socialised.

'I don't think Josh loved her at all.' A third woman, in her forties, her mouth wearing too-red lipstick, chimed in. Sam flicked through his mental Rolodex. This was Emma Greenberg, Fiona's sister. 'She was demanding. Nagging at him. We all knew he wasn't faithful . . . '

Sam swallowed a grin. Demanding, nagging? That didn't sound like the girl he'd met. Ms Greenberg meant that Lisa Costello hadn't rolled over for Josh. That she'd put up a fight, maybe, tried to stop him turning her into a clone of these overgroomed, Botoxed Hollywood bitches. Wives in this circle knew their place, three steps behind their meal ticket. If Lisa Costello had rebelled, tried to be herself, they would condemn her as a vicious harridan. You conformed, or it was social death. Lisa Costello's crime was not giving a damn.

'Melissa is such a slut, though,' Fiona added.

'I bet Paulie gets a divorce,' a younger woman said with relish. 'Why put up with that? He'll be a laughing stock.'

'Yes, and Melissa doesn't have Josh to protect her now,' Hannah added. 'She's not getting Josh and she'll lose Paulie.'

'She deserves it. Poor Josh, to get himself involved with such awful women,' Fiona said, with a big fake sigh. 'And now he's dead . . . '

They don't care, Sam thought. Not really. None of them. It had been a lonely life for Josh Steen, when you thought about it. He was unhappy with Lisa, and all these vultures simply used him. Could you feel sorry for a billionaire? Poor little rich boy?

'Lots of rumours flying around,' he said. 'They were drunk, all that stuff.'

'She was drunk. She killed him in a drunken rage,' Fiona said. 'What a lush. Did anybody see how she spoke to me?'

'Oh, that was awful,' Hannah Mazin sympathised. 'You poor girl . . . '

Sam looked at them, his gaze darting from one to another. They despised Lisa Costello. She'd killed a man; they hadn't. Yet he didn't think he could stand to be in their company one more second.

'Josh asked me to write the story of his wedding,' he said. 'Name's Sam Murray. I work for *USA Weekly*. If any of you ladies want to talk about Lisa, on the record I mean, give me a call.' He handed out business cards. The women looked askance, but they all took them, of course; they were as publicity-hungry as the next Hollywood chick. Wives were the worst; they lived a life in their husbands' shadow, and most of them did nothing themselves. Gossip and bitching turned into a way of life.

'Will people be interested in this story?' Fiona asked innocently, as though she wasn't slavering at the prospect of seeing Lisa vilified across America's newsstands.

'Sure they will. At least until they catch her.'

'Well, that won't be long,' Hannah said. 'She's got no money, and she's a stupid drunk. Where's she going to go? She won't get away.' A pinched smile. 'Not unless she grows wings.'

The other women tittered, and Sam walked away. He noticed Stan Greenberg and Paulie Olivera were both staring at him, and there was rage in their eyes. Time for him to go.

★ ★ ★

'Please remain in your seats until the aeroplane has come to a complete halt.'

Lisa smiled at the incongruity of it all. So normal, so boring. And here she was running for her life.

The last seconds of the flight were the worst. She had nursed herself through every wretched minute, fighting the bile that rose constantly in her throat. It seemed like the worst hangover she'd ever had. Rehydrating was a battle. Her body was screaming for water, but her stomach still did not want to keep it down, even hours later. She had to sip slowly, and then use all the concentration she could manage to stop herself from vomiting.

The skies were cloudy; Lisa stared past the head of her snoring neighbour at the window, and a blanket screen of white and grey. Her own memories were just as foggy. She tried, desperately, to recall something of what had happened. But there was nothing. The fight — that hadn't been physical; she was too sick, too weary to do something pathetic like slap him. Rage, drink, stumbling into their room. Then nothing. When had she lost her mind? When had she taken that golden dagger and sliced through Josh's throat?

Tears prickled in her eyes. Angrily, she dashed them away. If they caught her, she could cry all she wanted. Right now, nothing about her could attract attention. She needed to get through. The next ten minutes might be the most important of her whole life.

Mercifully, the seat-belt light snapped off. Lisa jumped to her feet; the passenger on the aisle seat, a dumpy woman in a sweatshirt, was still plugged into her headphones.

'Excuse me,' Lisa said, shoving past her. The woman grunted in protest, but Lisa didn't care; loads of people rushed to get off a plane, she wouldn't be marked out for that. Most passengers had hand luggage, kids, magazines; but she was standing by the door, behind a handful of businessmen and ready to disembark, within twenty seconds.

Her hand slipped into her pocket. Janet Park's passport was in there. Adrenalin surged through her, making her palms moist and her heart pound again. The door opened, and the men pushed out of it. Lisa was wearing sneakers; it would have been easy for her to run past them. But she did not. Arriving first in immigration, not a good idea; first was always noticeable. And she knew she looked anxious. She slowed to a walk and pasted a slight smile on her face, hanging back just behind the first passengers, even letting others pass her. Every step was torture. The urge to run was so great. But no, she was still trapped, still behind the barrier; and here was the immigration hall, with the Chinese agents ready to interrogate her.

The clinical expanse of Hong Kong airport was before her. A vast domed roof made out of thousands of panels of glass, floor shining white like a hospital. It was clean, architecturally pure. Lots of light. No place to hide. The immigration agents had computers and pressed uniforms.

48

They didn't look as though they missed much.

Lisa's pulse was racing; she was covered in sweat. She wasn't James Bond, she was just a girl in trouble, and she felt her body start to shake, the fright surging through her. Paralysed with fear, she let a family of four get in front of her; their baby was crying his head off, the parents were distracted . . .

The sobbing kid was clawing at his mother. Lisa watched the immigration officer wave them forward, his face creasing with annoyance at the sound. She breathed in, hard, calming herself. You've done all you can, she thought. There is nothing else you can do.

He was done with the raddled holidaymakers. He nodded briskly to Lisa. She moved forward, past the yellow line, trying to smile.

He flicked through her passport, looking at her.

'You OK?'

She was white-faced; she could see it in his eyes, assessing her. She shrugged, trying to explain her pallor. 'I'm just tired, and I hate that sound. Why can't she just give him a bottle?'

He nodded, snapping her passport shut. 'Exactly. Baggage claim that way.'

Christ! She was through! A rush of blood flooded to her head, and she realised she was blushing. Quick, get out, before he sees . . .

'Thank you,' she said, and moved off where the agent pointed.

Customs — the last throw of the dice. Her luck could not hold, surely. There was a bureau de change inside baggage reclaim, but Lisa simply could not wait another second. She had no luggage. She rushed through the green channel, her heart in her mouth; but nobody came forward to challenge her, and now she was through to the arrivals hall.

It was beyond glossy. Stores for luxury goods were everywhere. Coach luggage, Hermès scarves and bags, a Gucci, a Chanel. The scent of freshly brewed coffee around the cafes. Moneyed Asian businessmen and women in chic little skirt suits. This airport was clinical, beautiful. There were long people-carrying motorised walkways everywhere. Enough space to cope even with the teeming airport crowds. For a second, Lisa was paralysed. The money, the brand names — it was almost like being back home, before the nightmare started, bored, shopping on Rodeo Drive . . .

But she wasn't home. And she wasn't a rich Hollywood wife, not any more. She was a fugitive on the run. For murder. In a public place that was doubtless crawling with cops and security cameras.

Think, she told herself amidst the waves of relief. They could call the alert in any minute. You're not through yet. You can't walk out of here, not unless you want to get mugged.

She needed a cab, and that took money. Local money. There was another bureau de change right in the corner, next to a Starbucks. Go — don't think about it, she told herself. The more you dwell on this, the more shifty you'll look.

She made herself march up to the window.

50

'I'll change this for dollars, please,' she stammered. Her voice was quavering now; she was so close.

'You OK, miss?' The teller was looking at her curiously, his head tilted on one side like a bird's.

'Some trouble with my husband,' Lisa said, and a small, hysterical laugh escaped her. It was true, wasn't it? Her nerves shifted to anger; this man was the last thing between her and safety. Or at least less danger. 'Please, just give me the money.'

He sighed at her rudeness but busied himself in the till.

She changed all the rest of the baht. That gave her four hundred Hong Kong dollars, and as soon as the notes were in her hands, her legs trembling, she started to run. She fled out of the pristine, glossy airport into the muggy heat of the day, looking for a car, for a way out.

It was no good. She had no discipline left. She ignored the stares of the passengers and baggage handlers. There were a lot of people lining up for the official cabs — plenty of vehicles, but she could not join another queue. A shady-looking guy asked if she wanted a car — he was a rip-off merchant, the kind the terminus signs implored you to ignore. Lisa had never been so glad to see anybody in her life.

'OK. Yes, cab.' She nodded and he beckoned her to follow, off the arrivals platform, round a corner, and there it was, his beat-up vehicle with a hubcap missing. He jumped in front and she slammed the door; old leather seats that had

51

been slashed in several places, the reek of sweat and smoke, a plastic Buddha on the dashboard.

It was perfect.

'Where going?' he asked.

Good question. Where was she going? With Josh, it had been the most luxurious hotels, the exclusive gentlemen's clubs. She would not go to those again in a long time, maybe ever. She was incapable of thinking that far ahead. She would go to her friend Alice's house, when, if, she remembered her address.

She was looking for anonymous and safe.

'You know a hotel, very cheap?' she asked, summoning up a smile. 'I don't have too much money.'

He shrugged. 'You can go to youth hostel. Christian for girls on Kowloon. Cheap.'

Christian for girls. YWCA? Sounded good right now. Sounded real good.

'Yes please,' she said. 'I'm tired, I need to sleep.'

He wasn't listening. He pulled into the stream of traffic, and now they were away from the airport and Lisa had done it, she had gotten away from the blood and the police and the death, at least for a few moments, a few hours.

The tension and fear overcame her, and she put a hand over her eyes to shield her face while she wept.

★ ★ ★

He dropped her off by the City Road market, in the East Kowloon corridor. It was a total

52

contrast to the pristine airport; this was hot, humid, the fetid-sweet smell of food and human sweat hitting her as soon as she stepped out of the car. The market was located under the pillars of a road bridge. Red awnings from tatty shops leaned over to cover the temporary stalls, their wares lit up by gaudy coloured paper lanterns.

Shops, not tourist ones, crammed along the sidewalk. Little groceries and pharmacies, signs in Chinese script. There were narrow apartment buildings with signs done up in peeling paint. This was a cheap area, crowded and a little desperate. But the sign for the YWCA was clear, and Lisa didn't object; it was teeming with humanity, and a backpacker with no money would fit right in. She took a deep breath and walked up to the front door.

The hostel was cramped and overbooked, exactly what she'd expected. The desk clerk, a rail-thin older Chinese woman, looked at her without interest.

'Sorry. Hotel full.'

Hotel? That was a stretch. Lisa forced a smile.

'I understand, ma'am. I'm just really tired, got in from the airport. Maybe there's an extra bed in one of the dorms?'

'No bed. Full.'

'If you could check, I'd really appreciate that. Obviously I'd pay extra. For your trouble.' Lisa slid twenty dollars across the counter. The woman shrugged, but she took the twenty.

'OK, you wait.'

She marched up the back stairs. Lisa glanced around. There was no kind of security here, but the place did look clean, at least from the inside. There was a reassuring chemical smell of disinfectant. She didn't think she could deal with bugs crawling on her face in the night, not now.

The woman came back to the counter. 'One bed in shared dormitory, extra charge, thirty dollars the night.'

'Oh, that's great.' She was being ripped off twice, but she didn't care. She handed over the money, trying to ignore the anxiety she felt. It was so strange, worrying about cash again after all these years. How would she ever get more? But getting away was more important. 'Thank you.'

'Follow me.' The receptionist led her upstairs to the dorm.

It wasn't safe; open plan, like an English boarding school. Anybody could come up while she was sleeping and steal her money. But it was what there was, and it would have to do. Her bed was jammed next to a grimy window. At least on one side she was protected by a wall.

Once she was sitting on the allocated bed, and the receptionist had left her alone, Lisa tried to clear her head. They had not caught on to the stolen passport, but they would soon, and they would know she was in Hong Kong. And they would come looking for her.

The nausea was still oppressive. There was no urgency right now, no need to act happy and healthy to fool cops or flight attendants. Lisa rushed to the bathroom, locked the door of the stall, and crumpled to her knees, puking again until her stomach was empty. None of the other girls asked if she was OK. They all had their own problems; nobody cared.

It was perfect.

She ran her tongue around her dehydrated mouth, trying to talk herself out of a panic. There was no use giving in, going back to her bed and sobbing her heart out. They could easily get her here, in a city with thousands of cops and Chinese security agents. How long could she stay in Hong Kong? Where was there to go? It was small, and she was Western and didn't know a word of Chinese; and soon her face would be truly famous, not society-column famous. She'd be on every TV screen in the city. And of course Miriam Steen and her godless bastard family would put up a reward. She's in Hong Kong, they'd say, and you have to find her and you'll win a million dollars. Hunting Lisa would become a spectator sport.

Her breath caught in her throat; she was terribly frightened. The relief of getting out of the airport evaporated. As it stood, she'd bought herself just a couple more hours.

Think, Lisa, think, dammit, she told herself. OK. OK. She had to get out of Hong Kong. Get to somewhere they did not have the death penalty. Like Europe, or Canada. Somewhere they'd never extradite her.

Life in a godforsaken jail was bitter enough, but from where she was sitting, it sounded like a good option. Through all the fear and depression, and the loss and the panic, she held tight to that one thing: she did not want to die. She had enough hope, enough love of her life, to want to

55

keep it, to fight this, fight what an alcoholic blackout had made her do.

So fight. They were looking for Lisa Costello, blonde society butterfly. She opened the door of the stall and ran a little water in the sink, splashing it on her face. Her hair was buttercup yellow with platinum highlights, applied at seven hundred dollars a time by one of the best colourists in Beverly Hills. Her nails were long and scarlet, like Josh preferred. She could do something about that, maybe. They would identify what had gone from the closet, so the clothes had to go. Anyway, she needed to shop. She had nothing with her, not even toothpaste and mouthwash to clean her mouth after the vomit. Yes; there were things she could still do.

Lisa left the bathroom and went out of the hall, until she had landed on the street. Shops and storefronts were everywhere. She walked north, randomly, looking for a chemist. OK, there was one on the corner, CVS Pharmacy, just like in America. The air was humid and muggy, and a sea of humanity thronged every inch of the pavement. Fighting her way through the crowds, Lisa felt like she was swimming, swimming through bodies. She'd forgotten how much she hated it here; too much neon, too many people, stinking air, that dreadful feeling of rush and pressure. Josh had mainlined on the adrenalin. Lisa thought Hong Kong made Manhattan look like a Somerset village. It was too much for her, and now she was trapped here.

Being in the store gave her some momentary relief. Yes, most of what she needed you could buy. She hurriedly chose some hair dye, scissors and fake tan; her skin was exceptionally pale, Josh had liked her to stay out of the sun and wear block; that English rose look, he called it. There were travel-sized bottles of shampoo and conditioner, cute little deodorants; she tried to shop slowly enough to think: what was the well-dressed fugitive wearing these days?

A hysterical giggle bubbled up, but she suppressed it. Tweezers — stop herself growing a moustache or a unibrow; razors; they even sold multipacks of underwear and soft cotton bras. She went and paid for everything. A side door led into a small shopping mall. Thank you, God, Lisa thought. There were cheap, nasty-looking clothes stores, food stalls, toyshops, souvenir tat peddlers — everything you'd need for the non-discerning traveller on a budget. Gratefully she purchased a cheap nylon holdall, several T-shirts, sweatshirts, jeans and socks; what you might wear if you were a backpacker on holiday, a skeleton wardrobe she could wear, wash and change.

Now all she needed was to change back, to move away from what Josh Steen had wanted her to be. He'd turned a moth into a butterfly; now she had to become a moth again.

Back in the hostel, Lisa waited to get in the shared shower while a drunk student freshened up. She'd chosen cheap dye, the kind that worked in ten minutes; as it sat on her head she shaved her leg and armpit stubble, tidied her brows and cut her nails. When that was done, she sluiced off and then covered her body with fake

57

tan, slathering it all over herself, rubbing it hard into the skin. At least she could be a sun-baked brunette backpacker, instead of a pale, blonde trophy wife . . .

Lisa paused suddenly, her hands kneading her slim flesh. Something was wrong, something was nagging at her consciousness. She couldn't quite put her finger on what it was, but her subconscious was insisting, this isn't right, *look*, it's not right . . .

She got it, suddenly, with almost a gasp. Her skin . . . her carefully maintained, pale English skin. It was white as mother-of-pearl, shot through with pink. It was scrubbed and smooth.

It was perfect.

What it was not was bruised.

She stopped at once, her palms pausing mid-stroke. There was no mirror in this dingy little room, but she twisted in the dry shower cubicle, examining herself under the ugly fluorescent light. No. Nothing. No marks on her collarbone or around her throat. Nothing on her ribcage, where Josh might have grabbed her. She stared at her upper arms; surely he would have shaken her there, grabbed at her; but there was no mark on her body, however slight, however small. She'd already covered her legs with the tan cream, but it took a while to develop; through the white layer on her skin she couldn't see anything wrong. Even if she'd missed it, she thought with rising excitement, would he have grabbed her there?

How could she have killed him?

Josh was older than her, but he was still in his

prime; he worked out; his horribly wounded chest, when she'd stared at it, terrified, in their bed, had been muscular enough. He would have fought her, hit her back. How could she have killed him?

Don't be stupid, she told herself. You killed him. You woke up next to him and you had the knife in your hand.

So what had happened then? He'd fallen asleep, OK, and she had been awake and slit his throat . . .

The wound was awkward, though, not clean. Why would she have done that and then stabbed him again, over and over?

Who knows why you did it? You just did it. If you weren't such a stupid, drunk idiot maybe you could remember why, said the accusatory voice inside her head. At least stay out of sight until any bruises would have faded, then you can say you had them once and it was self-defence. Because if they see you like this, without a scratch . . .

Hold on, though. Hold on just a second. The brutal pain in her head was only just starting to subside. Yeah, OK, she'd seen what Josh had done, and she'd been angry and got drunk, ready to make a scene, ready to do her worst to him. But 'do her worst' had meant *embarrassing* him, not stabbing him to death with a gold and ivory antique dagger in the middle of their honeymoon bed. Was she that drunk? How could she have been that drunk?

She was starting to feel something she hadn't felt since she woke up. Hope — a tiny sliver of it.

What if she hadn't done this?

Come on, Lisa, you're an intelligent girl, she commanded herself. Work it through. Work it out.

She tallied up what she *did* remember. The handsome, weary American journalist, talking too much, smoking again. Two glasses of champagne and then Josh and Melissa, and that had turned into a double Jack Daniel's and Diet Coke, then another, and lastly a Napoleon brandy right in front of his mother and the goddamn prince, and then it turned into a screaming match and they were storming upstairs, she'd thought to finish it, right in the honeymoon suite . . .

And then it was black.

So that was a lot to drink. But not enough for this pain, not enough for a blackout. She must have had lots more. But . . .

Lisa sensed her excitement rise as the questions poured into her brain. She must have had more to drink, OK. But where did she get it from? Not Josh; he'd been pleading and begging with her not to make a scene, then yelling at her, cursing her for a tramp and a drunk, even though *he* was the one who cheated. He wouldn't have given her more. There was no minibar in the suite. He said he hated alcohol, and hated women who drank alcohol. Would she have ordered room service? He would never have allowed that. He'd have told the hotel not to bring anything, and he was the guy paying the bill.

So could she have left the room and returned

later? But she did not remember that. If she was so drunk, how would she have walked there? For that matter, if she was pass-out drunk, how could she have wielded the knife and killed Josh before he could lay a finger on her? How could she have killed her healthy, strong, sober husband?

Impossible — impossible, Lisa thought, elated. *She hadn't killed Josh.* She hadn't! She'd been drunk — maybe somebody had drugged her. Perhaps that was why this hangover was so bad.

But somebody out there *did* murder Josh Steen. And tried to frame her. Everybody hated her, everybody. She'd be an easy target, wouldn't she? The media would love it, the police would have a nice neat case all wrapped up, some district attorney would make his reputation. Who the hell would believe her — especially after she'd run?

But Lisa knew there'd been no choice. Run or die. Those were her two options. And she'd chosen to run.

Her new hope made her bold. She wanted out now even more desperately. Maybe dyeing her hair wasn't enough. She needed to change her look as much as possible. Vanity could not be allowed to trap her.

Back in the dormitory, a cotton towel wrapped around her head, Lisa reached for the scissors she'd bought. Then she returned to the bathroom, and pulling off the thin white cloth, hacked off all her hair, all her gorgeous, thick, tumbling hair. God, it had taken her ten years to grow it that long, and Josh had spent a fortune

61

on it once he'd found her.

He'd be furious to see her getting rid of it all. Any other day she'd be traumatised. This afternoon, she couldn't give a monkey's.

She scooped up all the hair in both hands, poured water on it to make it stick together, then wrapped it in loo roll and flushed it away.

Then she stared at herself in the bathroom mirror. So they weren't going to offer her a gig as a top stylist at Vidal Sassoon. But it wasn't all bad. She was now tanned and glowing, and the rough cut of the scissors had given her a young, punkish look. Better for a backpacker anyway. It wasn't plastic surgery, but she wasn't immediately obvious as Lisa. A large pair of sunglasses, and she thought she might pass through some of Josh's friends' houses and not be looked at twice.

Satisfaction at doing something pulsed through her. She wasn't gonna get out of this by rolling over and surrendering. If she was right, somebody had slaughtered her husband, her bridegroom, and she had business with them. Yeah, Josh was a controlling, cheating bastard, but she didn't want to see him dead. They had been happy together at one point. He deserved to be avenged.

And the same somebody had tried to kill Lisa too. By the bullet or the hangman's noose, after a show trial and months spent rotting in some south-east Asian jail.

Hell no, she thought. I'm not going out like that. I will get out of this, and nothing is going to stop me.

She looked around the hostel bathroom with a

pang of regret. It sure would be nice to stop for a few minutes, lay her head down, go to sleep. But she knew in her gut that every second, every minute counted.

She wanted to get back to the West. And that meant stealing another passport.

It was time to go see her old schoolfriend. The one person she knew in Hong Kong.

Alice Kennedy.

She moved back into the dormitory, packed up her pathetically small amount of clothes and put them in her new nylon holder. Then she slipped out of the front door and walked down the crowded street, hanging on to her bag for dear life. There were buses to the Peak, but she wasn't sure exactly where Alice lived; she'd recognise it if she saw it — maybe.

She was going to walk. At the very least the climb would improve her fitness.

With each step, Lisa strained to remember what Alice looked like. Dumpy, chestnut-brown hair, a little shorter than her, but that wasn't something she could help. It had been eight years since they'd last seen each other face to face. Was her hair now red or blond? Was she thin? Had she been aged by children? Wasted by anorexia . . . all the things that could happen to a person. The likelihood that she would still be suitable, still be OK for Lisa to impersonate — what was that?

In the end, it didn't matter, of course; Lisa was a twenty-eight-year-old alone in Hong Kong, and this was the only choice she had left. Would Alice even be living there, in that same old house? That was the first thing. If she was, but her hair was a different colour, Lisa could change her look again, her hair wouldn't fall out . . .

The ascent was steep in the humid air. Lisa's T-shirt was sticking to her now, and she was grateful for her neutral-coloured Hanes bra; anything else in this weather and she would be advertising her lingerie choices to any passing stranger. Imagine if she'd chosen red. You'd be able to see it through her wheat-coloured T-shirt like she was starring in a wet T-shirt contest. In future she'd save the beige Ts for Europe and stick to black out here. But it was no use complaining. She was halfway up the mountain now, and clothes changes were not possible.

Lisa breathed hard, trying to regulate her heart. The road was steep and she was moving quickly. God knew why, because if Alice wasn't here, she was all out of ideas. Maybe she'd go down to the docks, try to find some Triad guys who would ship her in a crate to Australia, except they'd frisk her and take all her money, maybe rape and kill her too . . .

Holy shit. *Holy shit.* There it was. Lisa's breath caught in her throat. That was it, that was the house. She actually remembered. Now that she was standing in front of it, the memories rushed back at her, shocking her with what the brain filed away. This was Alice's old house, where she'd stayed that one time, for a week, when she was fourteen, and hated every minute of it.

But that hadn't been Alice's fault. Lisa

couldn't stand the heat, the smell, the people packed in every store and on every pavement. Alice had tried to show her a good time, taken her to Ocean Park, the giant aquarium, the zoo and a little bird market . . .

They had parted civilly enough. Thank God, because all her hopes rested on that.

She looked at the door. Number thirty-four. The house rose on stilts, its foundations propped up on logs carving it a space on the mountainside, hung round with green creepers; there was a garage in the space underneath, unheard-of luxury round here, Lisa thought. On the front of the house were wooden boards painted a brilliant reflective white, visible from miles away. It was a prosperous house for a well-to-do family. Hardly the spot someone like her should be right now . . .

Lisa couldn't be nervous; she was sweating too hard, breathing too hard. That was the good thing about exercise, it didn't give you any time to think. She climbed up the stone steps carved into the mountainside and rang the bell.

It took an age. The sound faded inside the house. She waited; there was nothing else to do. At last she heard footsteps, pad-pad-pad. Alice? Lisa's mouth was dry. She hadn't had a decent conversation with another human being since the night Josh Steen was murdered. Now she was here, what exactly did she say? It was a hell of an icebreaker, face it . . .

The door opened.

It was not Alice. It was a Chinese woman in a black dress with a white apron. A maid, somewhere in her late forties, heavy-set and unimpressed.

'Yes?' she said, looking Lisa up and down, her lip curling.

'Is Alice Kennedy in?'

What the hell would she do if the answer was no?

'Miz Watson now.'

Right, so Alice had married. But she'd always be Alice Kennedy to Lisa.

'Who is asking, please?' the housekeeper demanded. Slightly more politely. At least the visitor knew her employer's name.

What should she say? Lisa was frightened to give her own name. She was news now; her blonder, paler self had made the TV screens, even if they didn't realise where she was.

'Susan Wilkins,' she said, in a burst of inspiration. Susan, a petite redhead with a passion for ballet and smoking behind the rhododendron bushes, had been Alice's closest friend at school.

'Just a minute,' the fat woman replied, shutting the door in her face.

Lisa tried to breathe deeply, to steady herself. Alice and she had been friends — kind of. They socialised at parties and went to each other's houses. But they were hardly best chums, and after that one invite to spend half-term out here, they had not kept up after school. Lisa had no idea how Alice would react when she saw her again.

But she could already hear the footsteps, and now her heart gathered speed again, and the

66

door opened and there *was* Alice Kennedy, her brown hair still short, thank God, and artificially straightened, and she had put on thirty pounds but it was well distributed, and her skin was permatanned from the subtropical heat . . .

'Susan!' Alice exclaimed joyously, but of course it wasn't Susan. She stared at Lisa for a moment, uncomprehendingly, and then let out a great gasp, partly fearful, partly shock. Lisa could see the fat housemaid behind her look sharply at her mistress.

'Alice,' she said, tears in her eyes, and she didn't have to act it. 'Alice, hon, *please* . . . '

And the grovel worked; Alice pulled herself up straight, and nodded to Lisa and said, 'Susan — how nice to see you. Come in,' and then, even better, she turned to the nosy maid lurking behind her shoulder, ears pricked, and said, 'Miss Wilkins and I will have tea upstairs.'

The housekeeper padded away on her slippered feet, and Lisa was left staring at her last hope, a woman she hadn't seen or spoken to for years.

'You'd better come upstairs,' Alice said, and Lisa was so grateful she could have kissed her.

★ ★ ★

The room made Lisa smile. It was so Alice; weird how people didn't change. It was all pink, pale pinks and dusty mink shades, not the bubblegum brights of her youth, but there they were; she even had a couple of kitsch Hello Kitty lampshades. It was Alice, fifteen years on and

67

girl-made-suburban-good. Lisa somehow knew that this lifestyle was provided by a husband. Alice Kennedy had never been the career type, never been ambitious. Not like Lisa. Once, Lisa had wanted more for herself, but she'd settled when a rich man picked her out of the rat race. Maybe she ought to have been stronger. But it seemed so ridiculous, fretting over a raise that might have got her another ten grand in salary when her man was worth over a hundred million.

Too late to regret that stuff, Lisa thought.

Alice carefully shut the door. There was something about the set of her back. Lisa knew she was angry and frightened, but she sensed that her old classmate was also a little thrilled. Alice had never been one of the cool kids in class. This was her opportunity to have an adventure.

'What are you doing here? Why did you come? The police are looking for you, Lisa. You've got to turn yourself in.' Alice was red-faced and clucking like a hen. 'My husband has a respectable job, you know. He's a pilot on Cathay Pacific . . . '

Oh God, she was starting to get hysterical. That wasn't good. Lisa wanted her to embrace the adventure part of it. She put one hand gently on Alice's plump arm.

'Al, I came because I needed someone to talk to — and you were always the cleverest girl I knew. I need your advice.'

The brown eyes widened. Advice! She hadn't been expecting that — more a plea for money or a hiding place. Lisa instantly decided that she had to seem confident, at least a little bit.

'I've got plenty of money,' she said, trying to sound relaxed. 'And places to stay. I just don't know if I should go back to England or stay here and fight this. I didn't kill Josh, but of course you knew that . . . '

Alice's face said she didn't know that at all — but at least she was listening, her breath coming quicker now.

'Who did kill him then?' she asked.

'I don't know. He had a lot of money. Lots of enemies too, I expect.'

'He did have loads of money,' Alice admitted, admiringly. 'Who'd have expected you to wind up with somebody like him?'

Lisa sighed. 'You're not the only one to think that.' She was looking around the room while she was talking; there was a neat little Samsonite suitcase, hard-case, in peach by the side of the bed. 'Are you going somewhere?'

Alice blushed, obviously pleased to be asked. 'Actually Roger, that's my husband, he gets these free tickets so we fly off at short notice quite a lot. I like to have a suitcase packed.'

'You're so organised,' Lisa said, flattering her. 'Does he keep your tickets and passports? Josh always looked after mine.'

She held her breath. Was that too obvious? But she had to at least broach the subject. That passport could be anywhere in this house. Alice had opened the door talking about free flights. But Lisa's luck was holding: her old schoolfellow wasn't suspicious; her round face was proud, she wanted to talk. A lot of the girls at school had assumed that Alice would wind up a spinster. She wasn't pretty enough. But here she was, married, and to a glamorous, jet-setting pilot. Lisa sensed she relished boasting a little.

'He gets the tickets. My passport's just there in my bedside drawer. We fly off all the time.' Alice preened. 'When we got married, he sold his place in Canberra to live here with me, and he's doing quite well with the airline. He always treats me. He's very romantic.'

Just there, in the bedside drawer. Fantastic. Thank Christ for that. Lisa smiled flatteringly. 'Oh, Alice, that's wonderful. What a life! Always ready to go!'

She reached for the drawer; the passport was there, lying face down. She flicked through till she found Alice's photo; a younger, slightly less dumpy girl stared out at her. Even better. The resemblance wasn't great, but people were often different from their passport photos. Their hair colour, nationality, style, age, those were all the same. That might work. She hoped so.

'This looks like it was taken this morning. You haven't aged a day.'

Alice flushed, pleased with the compliment; Lisa made a show of returning her passport, face down again, to the drawer.

'Do you have children?' she asked, trying to show an interest in Alice's life, get her off her guard.

'Not yet.' Her old friend blushed. 'We're trying. It's harder than you'd think. They're going to put me on some special drugs.'

'I bet it'll happen, Alice. You've just got to relax about these things.' Lisa felt like Judas Iscariot. The longer she sat here, the clearer it became to her what she would have to do. And yet she was chatting away to Alice and watching her shoulders untense, her guard drop.

'I hope so,' Alice murmured. 'I really do . . . ' Her expression cleared, and she focused on Lisa again. 'But Lisa, if you're innocent, how can you prove you didn't kill him?' she asked.

Lisa shook her head. 'I don't know that yet. They drugged me, Alice, they put the knife in my hand. I would never hurt Josh like that. I can't let them get away with it. Do you think I should go back?'

Alice tilted her head, the way she had done when she was a girl. 'But they might try you . . . Do you have a Thai lawyer?' She was anxious, and that concern cut Lisa to the heart. Poor Alice.

'I can get one,' Lisa said with false bravado. 'Look, Alice. Why don't you take me to the airport.' She fished around inside her backpack and produced her own passport. 'This isn't cancelled yet,' she said. 'I could get a flight to Sydney . . . hire a decent English-speaking lawyer . . . '

'Yes,' Alice said with relief. 'Australia — it's practically like home, when you think about it.'

God, she had no idea, did she? Lisa hated this. She mentally prepared herself. Gotta do it to the girl, simply got to.

'Alice,' she said, 'do you think you could drive me to the airport? And tell your maid to take the

71

day off, come back tomorrow? If she comes in here with the tea, it could be really awkward for me. She might recognise me. I have to get that lawyer . . . '

'I don't know,' Alice said, shaking her head. 'I mean, if the police find out I helped you . . . '

'They'll never guess. You're entitled to give your own staff some time off, aren't you? Please, Alice.' Lisa folded her hands together and fluttered her eyelashes. She felt stupid, but that was what they'd done at school. 'A lift to the airport, that's not much. And if you send the maid away now, she's only seen me one time, she could hardly be sure who I am . . . '

'You do look different,' Alice admitted. She paused, but Lisa could see the spark of excitement in her eyes. She was being offered a risk-free thrill. 'OK. Just a ride.'

'And you'll go and talk to the maid?'

Alice got up purposefully. 'On my way. You stay here, I'll come back when she's left the house.'

She walked out of the bedroom, and Lisa was alone. Quickly she reached into her backpack, drew out Janet's passport and put it in Alice's drawer, face down, taking hers instead. Could she do this? Alice was heavier than she was. But bored, in LA, with no friends of her own, Lisa had concentrated on fitness, including self-defence. And now she was about to put it to the test. If it went wrong and Alice got away, at least she'd be able to outrun her.

She sat on the bed and waited. Alice was a little while; she came back ten minutes later.

'OK, she's gone. Let's leave now, before the police come calling.'

Lisa shivered a little. 'Is she really gone, Al? Has she gone out of the front door?'

Alice moved to her bedroom window, hung with chiffon curtains and affording a fabulous view of the Peak and the city-island spread out below it. 'Look! That's her car driving down, the red Datsun.' She turned around, holding up her keys. 'Ours is the Mercedes — come on, we should go right now if you want to do this.'

'Thanks, Al, really,' Lisa said. She meant it. 'Hope I can pay you back one day.'

'Doubt it,' Alice replied, 'I'm not planning to kill anyone.'

Me neither, Lisa thought. Well, those years of self-defence classes at her Beverley Hills gym had cost enough. Now she would see if they were good for anything.

She got up from the bed, walked over to her friend and opened her arms as though to hug her. Then she brought her elbow sharply down on the inside of Alice's neck, at the base of her skull, and as her friend gasped in pain and fear, Lisa delivered a round kick hard to her temple, knocking her to the ground and putting her out cold.

There was some pink notepaper on her desk. Lisa wrote a note and put it in Alice's jeans pocket: *Alice, I'm sorry, I had to. I didn't kill Josh.* Now all she had to do was drag her friend's heavy body and put it somewhere safe. She left the bedroom and looked around the house. There was a secondary wing and what looked like a guest room. She found some tights and a scarf and bound Alice tightly, hands and feet; she gagged her too. She hated doing it, but her friend didn't even stir. Most likely she was concussed. She'd need medical attention, but Lisa was going to ensure she didn't get it. Guilt coursed through her; but Alice was alive, and so would Lisa be. And right now that was all she could think of.

Alice was heavy, a dead weight, but Lisa was getting used to exertion now. She hauled her with all her might, far away from the main bedroom, into the guest area and then into the closet. It would be terrifying for Alice when she woke up. But it was Lisa's only option.

She ran back into the bedroom, picked up her own backpack and Alice's car keys, then walked out of the house to the garage. It was an expensive one, opening with a click. The fewer people Lisa had to see, the better. She opened the car, started it, no problems. Once she was safely in Europe she would call, let poor Alice out. Her husband worked for Cathay Pacific. That was enough, plus Lisa had the address.

She told herself all this. It didn't make her feel any better.

★　★　★

Felix lay back against the soft-grain leather of his imported Italian couch. A copy of *USA Weekly* was on the leather beside him; he had flicked through it, impressed by the work.

On the wall in front of him, his cinema-sized TV screen, on mute, was tuned to a rolling news

74

channel. They had talking heads on the screen, discussing Lisa Costello — the 'Brit Bride Killer', as they were rather amusingly calling her.

The story had been the same for hours. They varied the talking heads, they had reporters outside Steen's home and his office in Artemis Studios, and more reporters out in Thailand. In an hour, they might give over five minutes to sport, five to the financial crisis, and another five for weather and headlines. Otherwise, it was all Lisa, all the time.

Any jury in America would hang her out to dry.

Felix was thinking. He looked around, taking in the sheer luxury of his surroundings. This was his American base, one of four that he owned around the world, along with the flat in Venice, the Mayfair townhouse, and the farm in the Dordogne.

In the States, he chose to live in Colorado. Mountains agreed with him: the clear air, the views for miles outside the bulletproof floor-to-ceiling windows that marked his modernist designer pad; they were tinted ochre on the outside only, so were completely clean and safe, and free from prying eyes. But from inside, next to the wooden log furniture covered in down cushions, the Red Indian art, the real cowhide logs, those windows placed him almost outside, on the slopes down to the plains, under the Rockies' big sky.

He loved that. The sense of freedom. No assassin liked to be hemmed in.

It was a risk, a base in America. If they ever

caught him, they'd kill him. The Europeans were far more squeamish. He liked that about them.

But Felix enjoyed risk. It gave him a thrill. And right now he was thinking of another one.

He did well enough. With his real estate and stock portfolio, and that nice emergency account in the Caymans, his net worth was coming up to ten million dollars. But Felix was not a big killer, not one of the top names on the scene. He earned well enough, and was known to be reliable. But for those key jobs, the ones that made you a legend in a tiny crowd of people, the big clients went elsewhere.

He wanted that to change. He was greedy. There was much further for him to rise.

Perhaps he'd been hasty in the matter of Josh Steen.

So, a producer was just a producer. But the publicity — he'd underestimated it. This was now a huge deal in America. Not quite the Kennedy assassination, but a juicy, celebrated slaying. Just as he'd promised his little piss-ant client, they were all blaming Lisa Costello. She was now more famous than she'd ever dared to dream of.

But she was still out there.

He'd had the opportunity to kill them both, murder-suicide it, and chosen not to. Hell, nobody paid him to kill the *wife* — why should he work for free? He had promised to lay the death on Lisa Costello. Nobody was looking anywhere else. Not at Felix. Not at his customer.

Yet Lisa was still on the run. They were reporting that nobody had caught her, her passport had not been presented at any airport.

Felix didn't like it. There was a small alarm buzzing in his brain. Faintly, perhaps, but it was there. What if Lisa Costello thought she was innocent? What if she actually made the argument in court? There were fantasists and conspiracists on the internet for any little thing. There would be for this case too. Trying to prove her innocent, just because they could.

He'd expected her to be caught. Within hours.

It was still less than one day since she would have awoken in that bed, soaked in blood. Plenty of time for her to be brought in. But Felix hated loose ends.

He reached for his remote and turned up the TV. The caption said 'Rich Frank, Editor of *USA Weekly*'. A squat, jowly little man in a very expensive suit was sat in the newsroom, beaming while an earnest newsreader asked him questions. He was smirking like the cat who'd got the cream.

Felix fingered the edges of his own copy. This magazine was everywhere now, in supermarkets, bookstores, even the little delis that normally only took the *Enquirer*. He imagined the Sam Murray exclusives were very good for trade.

'Your magazine has the hot story this week,' the pretty anchor purred at Frank. 'Tell us about that.'

'Yeah, that's right, Ellen.'

'Emma,' the girl said, smile frozen.

'Our reporter Sam Murray was an actual guest at the wedding when these fatal events occurred,' Frank said with obvious relish. 'Not only that, but he actually talked to Ms Costello, the killer — '

'Alleged killer.'

'Right. Alleged,' Frank added, waggling his eyebrows. 'Anyway, he talked to her the night before. Saw her fighting with her husband. This special edition of *USA Weekly* has the whole story.'

'And I gather it has sold out?'

'We've reprinted four times.' He looked like he was about to have an orgasm. 'I can tell people out there, the team is working real hard to supply all the extra copies.'

'Well, now you have the exclusive pictures of the murder scene for the next issue. They're pretty gruesome. Lots of blood. We can't show that on TV.'

'No, folks will have to buy our magazine. Not suitable for kids,' he added, putting on a sanctimonious face.

'This means big money for you.'

'The money's nice, but our mission is to expose the truth,' Rich Frank lied. 'And Sam Murray's just the man to do it.'

'His previous exclusives included the Tom Cruise story and that Christian Bale telephoto lens thing?'

'Uh-huh. Obviously this is far bigger. And I can tell you, Ellen, Sam isn't finished yet.'

This time she didn't bother to correct him. Felix watched, fascinated; the woman was evidently as gripped by this as the rest of her audience.

'Well, you hit the streets before anyone else, and got the reward,' she coaxed, 'but now CNN,

Fox have their cameras there, and every major paper in America is on the case. What other exclusives do you think you're gonna get?'

'We're saving some of it for next week's special edition. Sam has a major lead on the whereabouts of Lisa Costello.'

The presenter actually gasped. 'Are you serious, Mr Frank?'

'Totally serious,' he said, and tilted his double chin up proudly. 'A second, midweek edition of the magazine will be on newsstands tomorrow. We have details no other organisation has. So look out for that.'

She tried to rally, but Felix could see this was a killer blow. Her bosses in the newsroom would be screaming at her through her earpiece — get details, get a location, anything!

'Surely if you know anything, or Sam Murray does, he has to go to the authorities. Otherwise wouldn't that be obstruction of justice, or . . . or concealing a fugitive?'

'Oh, honey, you can be sure that Sam's sharing his information with the FBI. *USA Weekly* always operates to the very highest standards,' Frank managed, with a straight face. 'We just ain't sharing with you guys.'

Felix smiled. They already had the Breaking News graphic up on the screen. So this Sam Murray wasn't just lucky, he was also good. That was helpful.

'Sam Murray was once in the FBI training programme,' Frank was saying. 'He has experience with law enforcement. He'll do whatever he can to help in the investigation.'

79

'And now he writes stories for your magazine?'

'Yeah,' said Rich Frank shamelessly. 'Great, huh?'

'Well, I'm sure we'll all be looking out for that news tomorrow. An awful lot of people want to say hi to Ms Costello . . . '

Damned right. And I'm one of them, Felix thought.

He flicked off the TV. This was a situation. If he didn't take her out, there was a remote chance she might discover the truth. And if he did take her out — then he would be the one that found the girl every cop was looking for. It would be a suicide, and the whole Josh Steen murder would be put away for ever. Especially after he persuaded the girl to make a full confession in her suicide note.

Felix wasn't a tracker. This was one reason he'd never made it to the very top. Clients showed him the target, he slew them in untraceable ways. That was his deal, and he was good at it. If you wanted somebody offed who was in the witness protection programme, or some retired CIA agent who'd gone off grid, then you paid more, and you went further up the chain. He shrugged his shoulders at the thought. He was a killer, not a goddamn detective. His client had hired him because he'd killed Jack Stone, another Hollywood mogul, and framed the wife for it. That was known to a small segment of the Hollywood underworld. Like the drug dealer his customer used.

Word of mouth. So important in business. He grinned.

But once Lisa Costello was in police custody, she would be impossible to kill. The world would have to wait for the trial. Bent cops were a lot rarer than anybody thought. He was interested in getting to her before that happened, before she could talk to a judge. Yeah, this job was spiralling. But Felix had to roll with the punches.

No time to learn the tracking skills the big boys used. He would take a short cut. He was a big fan of short cuts.

This Sam Murray was ahead of the pack because he used to be FBI. Following Lisa would be hard; following Murray, a lot easier. For a start, he was probably using a corporate credit card.

Felix wasn't interested in tomorrow's hot edition of *USA Weekly*. He wanted to go wherever Sam Murray was right now. He flipped through the magazine, looking for the masthead, the name of the company. It would take him a day or so to establish a safe link at a credit agency, one that would give him access to Sam's data. But it could certainly be done.

The blood began to race around his veins — he was ready for this, ready to hunt again. There was a job waiting on a banker in Zurich, but he would pass. It didn't hurt to be a little unavailable.

Felix had money in the bank. He wasn't hurting. It was time to do a job for glory.

3

Kowloon airport was thick with passengers, and there were plenty of Western girls travelling alone; at least that gave her some cover. Lisa looked around carefully at the ticket counters. She needed to get this one just right. By now they were looking for her. Not Alice Kennedy, her; but they'd have her photograph right in the computer terminals.

It had to be a flight to Europe. Australia was no good; Lisa wanted to keep moving, keep going, in and out of countries and police jurisdictions. There were flights to London, but that was far too obvious, and she was a bigger story over there, the latest WAG they loved to loathe. It had to be the Continent.

She scanned the desks for the most stressed-out-looking agent. Perfect; there was an Air France counter with a heavily made-up forty-something booking in some kind of school trip. They appeared to be German kids, and they were fighting and shouting and snapping at their teachers. Lisa got in line, her gaze travelling to the departures board. Air France flew to Paris; that was cold, expensive, not a friendly city to get lost in. But they went to Rome, too. Lisa had been too long in California; she had the sunshine bug under her skin. Rome was a better choice. That was where she would go. She'd been the summer before she met Josh, when she was romancing that broke Italian ski bum, gone there to meet his family in the off-season, decided he wasn't for her. But the city itself had been wonderful. She'd had no money then, and she remembered how hospitable it was. Laws that forced restaurants to give you a glass of water and let you use the bathroom. Plenty of youth hostels. Tiny dark trattorias in the side streets, with the menus all in Italian and a half-carafe of rough house red already set on the table. You could buy a square of thin, crisped pizza and eat a scoop of fresh pear sorbet and still have change from five euros. And the local police seemed to have a commendable lack of interest in doing any actual police work.

Maybe it would be different now she was properly on the run. More expensive, that was for sure. The dollar had collapsed. Even Josh had grumbled at European prices when they last stayed in Paris at the Georges V. And she was no longer on that kind of budget. How long would her cash last her?

The last of the kids had straggled off towards the check-in counters, cursing in German, and Lisa approached the ticket agent, who looked ready to cry.

'I'd like to get a standby ticket to Rome, if you have one,' she said, handing over her passport. 'But I've run out of cash, so I only have US dollars left.'

Tap-tap-tap . . . Why did airline computers take so bloody long? She'd never noticed it before, but now it was right in her face.

'Dollars are OK. Luggage?'

Something about the tone told Lisa to beware. Maybe they'd put out a warning for a girl her age without bags.

'Of course,' she said, patting her backpack. 'I've been all over the world with this.'

The ticket agent unbent slightly, flicking through Alice's passport. 'Yes, I see, Egypt, Paris, Cuba, Miami . . . '

'I just love to travel,' Lisa said, as jauntily as she could. She was starting to sweat. Jesus, let me on the plane, would you? 'Next year I have to settle down. Get a real job.'

But the agent had blessedly lost interest. 'Last-minute tickets are available, economy class is five hundred dollars US.'

She reached into her wallet and peeled off the bills. She hated how fast they were going. What about when she was done? What kind of a life could she have, what could she do? Work as a waitress like an illegal immigrant, off the books and under minimum wage? How long then before her boss realised who she was? Then he'd try blackmail . . . rape, maybe . . .

Ugly scenarios flashed before her, but that was the great thing about fleeing for your life; there really was no tomorrow if you didn't get through today.

'There you go. Where's check-in?'

'You only have the backpack?'

Lisa nodded.

'I can do that for you,' the agent said. 'Did you pack this bag yourself?'

Bought it, packed it, ran with it, Lisa thought. She went through the security questions, trying to sound as bored as any other traveller. Finally it was hauled behind the agent's desk, a security sticker on it, and the boarding pass was handed over. The woman told her she should get to the gate. Lisa didn't have to be asked twice. There was no quick passage through this airport. The queues for the metal detectors were long; they made her take off her shoes, and she worried there might be white flesh left under her instep, that she could have missed a spot when she was using the fake tan, but if there was nobody noticed, and the secondary passport check was brief, and now she was running for the gate, and the crowd were already starting to filter through.

Lisa forced herself to go to the newsstand and buy a novel. This flight was eighteen hours, it was important she have something to do. Staring into space would attract attention. She purchased a John Grisham thriller, a Harlequin romance, some mints and a large bottle of water. No alcohol this time, however much she was tempted. She didn't trust herself. She would never drink again.

She handed over her boarding pass, received a stub, and made her way into the aeroplane. It was night-time now, and she hadn't slept a wink since she'd woken on the worst day of her life with Josh's blood all over her. She couldn't see how she could have killed him, but she still wasn't sure; and she was afraid, and exhausted.

Her seat was all the way down the back of the plane, and miraculously it was a window seat. That was perfect. Nobody would have to climb over her to get to the lavatory, or stretch their legs. She strapped herself in and extracted her thin red airline blanket, forcing herself to stay awake while the stewards checked on the seat belts and tray tables. There was a Chinese couple sitting beside her, and they nodded and smiled and clearly spoke no English, so that was perfect too. Lisa made a show of pretending to read her novel while the plane groaned and strained its way out on to the runway. How did the law work? she wondered desperately. Was she in French control once the plane was in the sky? How far out from Hong Kong did they need to be? Could the police phone in to the flight, force them to turn back?

She did not know, and she couldn't keep worrying about it. She thought of Josh, brutally stabbed, lying there lifeless, and his mother and sister, and she thought of Alice, who'd tried to help her a little when she most needed a friend and who would wake up in pain from the tight binding, alone and in the dark. Lisa had no family, no friends she could trust, and not much of a future. She had gotten herself on this plane with no idea if she could ever make it off it — or what would happen if she did.

Twenty-four hours ago she'd had everything.

Now she had nothing.

The plane banked and steadied at cruising altitude and the little ping of the seat-belt light going off sounded over her head. She found her elasticated blindfold, pulled it over her newly cropped hair, and turned her face towards the tiny plastic window, out of the view of the airline staff, the thin blanket covering her. It was somewhat cold in the cabin, but she would not ask for another blanket. She would not draw attention to herself in any way.

Lisa was out of ideas, and out of energy. She shut her eyes, and let herself drift off to sleep.

★ ★ ★

The lieutenant's name was Prem Songakul, and he enjoyed being interviewed by the big American with the pleasant manner and the open wallet.

'We don't understand where she go. No credit cards gone.'

Sam nodded sympathetically. He slid a hundred-dollar bill over to Prem's coffee cup.

'I don't take bribes,' the lieutenant announced unconvincingly.

Sam soothed him. 'Of course not, and I'm not allowed to offer them. This is a legitimate expenses payment, Lieutenant; your time is very valuable.'

Prem put it in his pocket, appearances nicely dealt with.

'Cigarette?' Sam said. He pushed an entire packet over the table. In his long experience, smokes were one of the world's most reliable forms of currency. 'Please, take them. I'm trying to give up.'

That was even partly true. He was always trying to give up lots of things. Never managing it.

'Thanks. So she kill him with the royal knife.'

87

His readers already knew that part. 'Can I photograph it?'

Prem shook his head. 'In evidence already. Body in morgue,' he added, before Sam could ask for that. He hadn't really expected anything else.

'I understand, that's all sensitive stuff. The crime scene's been photographed, dusted for fingerprints?'

'Of course,' Prem said, with a flash of annoyance. 'Just like America. *CSI.*'

Sam doubted that highly. But they probably had dusted for prints. Maybe. And photographed it.

'Then it's not so important to the investigation. Hey, Lieutenant Songakul, you think I could at least see the crime scene?' He emphasised *at least*, making it seem like this was nothing, that Prem had driven a hard bargain. 'Your guys have already been through it.'

'I don't know. Maybe it's not allowed.'

'My paper was the honoured guest of Mr Steen at his wedding,' Sam said piously. 'He chose us over all other outlets. You really would be fulfilling his wishes by allowing us to take those pictures. Of course we would pay for your time and trouble.'

Songakul shrugged.

'I would only need five minutes. You can time it.' Sam gestured to the policeman's watch. 'You'd be protected as a source, and I'll give you five hundred dollars in cash.'

A broad smile. 'One thousand.'

'That's too much.'

'OK then. Maybe CNN pay one thousand.'

Sam exhaled and shook his head. 'Goddamn it, Prem. OK, you win.'

It was so important to let these guys think they'd beaten you. His patsy smiled triumphantly, and beckoned for Sam to follow him inside. He stuck close to the cop, his gaze travelling round the sumptuous fittings of the hotel, forlorn now, all the guests still being questioned in batches in the dining hall. News choppers were buzzing overhead, the other journalists in the rat pack were massing at the borders of the estate. But only Sam Murray was on the inside.

That was the benefit of being first. His story would hit the newsstands tomorrow. By the time it was leaping off the shelves, the rest of them would have muscled their way in here, threats or bribery, whatever it took. By then Sam would be long gone. The story wasn't here, after all. She had already moved somewhere else. After he got these snaps done, he would figure out where.

'Here,' Songakul said, pushing him into the room. 'Be quick.'

Sam didn't need telling twice. His camera was already in his hand, and he fired off shot after shot, the bed, the bloodstains on the curtains, the draperies, the antique rug. He went into the bathroom and photographed that; there were flecks of vomit on the side of the bowl. Who had been sick? The little murderess?

Turning on his heel, ignoring the hisses that Songakul was sending his way, calling him to come out, Sam methodically started to photograph the non-sexy stuff: the unbroken windows, the sealed doorways, her clothes still hanging in the open closet. You didn't try to investigate at a time like this, you gathered evidence and went through it later. Something was already prickling in his mind about this, something he didn't understand. But he would figure it out later.

'You has to go *now*,' Songakul insisted. Sam switched his camera to movie mode and shot a little forty-second panorama of the entire room, slowly, sweeping over the bed, moving into the bathroom, then the closets, and back again. He clicked the camera off and went over to his contact, who exhaled, glancing warily behind him.

'My money,' Songakul demanded. Sam produced his wallet and counted out ten hundreds. He could tell the guy was surprised, as they often were, when he actually paid up. Lots of journos didn't bother, once they'd got what they wanted. But Sam Murray was good for a promise. People were short-sighted. You got that good reputation for paying up, more sources gave you info in the first place. He might need to come back to Lieutenant Prem Songakul.

'Hey, thanks,' the Thai said.

Sam handed him a card. His mobile number was scrawled on the back. 'You get anything good, you ring me. There might be more where that came from.'

Prem nodded. 'OK, mister. But you leave now.'

'I'm going. I'll find my own way out,' Sam said.

He let himself out of the side door. That was where she would have run, surely, because it led to the stairs, and you wouldn't risk an elevator ride, nowhere to go. He walked Lisa's route slowly, staring at everything, trying to drink it in, snapping a few shots of the interior of the hotel, Steen's fantasy wedding setting, just for luck.

So the stairwell came out on the ground floor, near the gym. He passed by the locker room — empty, of course; nobody had been allowed to work out since they found the body, the same way nobody had been allowed to . . .

. . . get their passports.

A wash of adrenalin prickled through his skin. The passport safe was here, in the gym locker room. He'd asked security where his was going to be, when they took it. Not that anybody had seriously worried. If you were a guest of Josh Steen at this exclusive resort, nobody was going to steal your passport. Sam had only asked because back then, he was hoping to get out of this assignment, to file some shitty copy on yet another gala wedding and then get the hell home and play some poker.

He was used to cutting and running. He needed his passport for that.

He moved inside the locker room and to the anonymous metal chest they kept the passports in. It had been locked, and only Mr Steen had the key, Bhumibol had told him. Fine, but it wasn't locked now. The key was in the lock. He tried it — it was open.

She had taken the key from the bedroom.

91

Sam photographed the safe, his heart accelerating, taking a shot of the key in the lock. The Keystone Cops around the building had not even checked the basics. When the FBI got here, they'd put that right.

He wanted to take the key, but dared not. It would be interfering in a criminal investigation. He could report it to the police and be a hero, but at what cost?

Sam ran the facts through his mind, processing them like a computer. Lisa had run and she had run with her own passport. But she wasn't as stupid as they thought; she'd come to this locker, taken somebody else's passport, and run with that. Once they figured out whose, they would know how to find her.

He pulled the edge of his cuffs down, over his fingers, and knocked open the door of the safe, spreading out the passports with his elbow. They were neatly stacked, face up, so you could read the names. He photographed them closely, then carefully put them back and knocked the door shut. They'd be looking for Lisa Costello, but he didn't intend to leave any of his own prints. If he got as close to her as he planned to, things were going to get awfully muddy.

His dealings with the law had not been that great. Cops despised guys like him. If they had anything, anything at all, that they could stick him with, they'd do it. Obstruction of justice. Withholding evidence. Interfering in a police investigation. There was no point tempting fate.

He heard footsteps in the corridor outside. Quick — what was the best way out? There was a door in one wall of the locker room. It led to the lawn outside. And it was ajar.

If he was right, Lisa Costello would have walked out of that door.

Sam slipped through it. He glanced down at the grass, to see if he could make out footprints. But there were none, at least not to an untrained eye. The blades had sprung back from the time she had passed across them. It was late afternoon right now. When had she left?

He started to jog away from the building, thinking hard, putting himself inside her head. When you did his job, you were half a shrink. You had to think like the people you were investigating. You had to anticipate where they'd go, who they'd sleep with, the drugs they needed, their favourite strip club. It had been a long time, for ever really, since he'd investigated anything worse than fraud or possession. How did killers think . . .

Wrong question. How did a runner think? How did a frightened girl who wanted to get away think? Somebody with brains — his brief conversation had already convinced him of that. She was no dumb blonde.

Sam had a handful of facts. He brought them out to the front of his mind, going through them like a poker player reading his hand. Lisa had gone to bed drunk, after a big fight. He, Sam, had gone to bed convinced he'd be writing a juicy story about a twenty-four-hour divorce, so yeah, the fight had been pretty major. She had killed Josh. That was one surprise, based on her character so far; Josh Steen was the most exciting thing that had ever happened to Lisa Costello. Sam had already done the tedious legwork on her past: not much of a family, bright at school but rebellious, didn't want to go to college, had planned to start a small business after her mother died. That hadn't worked and then she'd done the one thing that changed her life. She'd been desperate for a new start, and she'd come to America.

There were no stories of drug use or hookerdom or anything juicy the readers would have enjoyed, and plenty of tabloids had looked. This would be the first violent attack on her record.

So maybe it had been self-defence?

Except no cries for help, and no marks on the victim, his Thai informants had told him.

Something didn't fit, but no time to analyse it yet. On the road, on the hunt, there was always plenty of time. Just the facts right now. So she'd gone whacky from the fight, killed him. Presumably she must have passed out, because she called reception in the morning and put on a cheerful voice to ask them not to come to the room.

That had bought her crucial hours.

It required smarts, a cool head under extreme pressure. She'd passed out, because she would have run right after she killed him instead of waiting until the morning and calling downstairs.

He nodded to himself, slotting the pieces around like a jigsaw puzzle. Events were starting to play in his head, like a movie.

As he jogged, he saw where he was headed: to

94

the edge of the estate. Lots of cars out there now, local reporters, tourists, sightseers, news media. When she got here this morning there would have been none of it, just a cab rank.

He slowed and turned, away from the gates. He would walk out a different way, around a jogging path, and emerge some little distance up the road, then walk back to the gates from behind, like the rest of the crowd. If he just emerged from the estate there would be a forest of cameras in his face, microphones under his nose. It was important not to become the story yourself.

Besides which, he'd thought he recognised the silhouette of Neil Gatins from the *National Enquirer*. Gatins knew Sam pretty well and was eaten up with jealousy over his stories. He might tail Sam to glom on to the inside track.

Nobody was going to ruin this. It was the million-dollar dream.

There were plenty of cabs still, ferrying the journalists and gawkers in and out of town. Sam moved along the jog path till he was a respectable distance from the throng. There were several cars lined up. He went up to the head of the queue; nobody looked twice at him.

'Where going?' the guy said, as Sam slid into the back seat.

Somebody had asked Lisa Costello the same question. She'd taken a passport and she wouldn't have thought too much. In Thailand they executed people. She would have been desperate to get off the peninsula.

'The airport,' Sam said.

The client waited at home and started to sweat.

It had been a mistake, a goddamn mistake, all of it. Not that Josh didn't deserve it, the dirty bastard. And not that anybody gave a damn about some gold-digging Limey waitress who cut their friends dead at parties. She could go to hell. The money was gonna be theirs, not hers — the revenge was going to be theirs too. This hit was for both of them.

They'd both worked for this money all their lives, in different ways. And big bad Josh Steen had skimmed it off the top. Getting rich from other people's work. *The family's* work. That was theft. So fuck him. Fuck him with a golden dagger. The client sniggered.

Yeah, but none of that changed this clusterfuck Felix was in now, right? The freaking English whore had run away and the cops hadn't got her yet. And the TV — they were all over it like a rash. The client was prepared for that, but not to this extent. That goddamned hitman had been so sure of himself . . .

The cops were blaming Lisa, but that wasn't enough. The worst thing was that the case was still in the news, always in the news, every fucking minute, in the car on the way to the office, in the house, on the cell phone news updates. The client didn't believe in God, or ghosts, but damn, it was like fucking Josh Steen was fucking *haunting* them.

Their house was a gorgeous three-acre mansion in La Canada Flintridge, one of LA's most expensive neighbourhoods, and not obvious and brash like Beverly Hills or Bel Air. They had central air, central vac, three maids, a cook, and a pool boy — and the studio provided a chauffeur. Their kids were at the exclusive private schools, there were the country club memberships, designer wardrobes. But the family was deep in debt. The money was big, but not big enough to support their tastes. Josh's will was locked in probate. The girl was running around. The story was all over the news. The client couldn't sleep right. This fucking thing was causing a rash.

The girl should be dead, the case closed. Then maybe there would be some sleep. Once the fucking story was off the news.

The client fretted. Maybe if somebody was hired to kill Lisa and Felix. But no, that was gonna be too complicated. If one more person knew who was behind Josh's death, that was one more to blackmail you. Plus, if the next killer failed, Felix would come after them. And Felix didn't miss.

Better never to speak to Felix again, but there was no choice. The client went back inside the house, trembling a little, and picked up the phone.

★ ★ ★

Sam made his decision. He'd call Kevin in the bungalow and tell him to pick up the computer and ship his stuff home. There was no time to go back. Those American media giants were fast;

they'd be inside the complex within the hour, and Sam had to stay ahead of the pack. He had his passport, his credit card and his phone. Anything else he could buy.

Kevin was awake.

'Where the hell are you, dude? You know what's going on?'

'All sorted while you were asleep. Go get pictures,' Sam said, and relayed his instructions. Kevin snorted, but he was used to being Sam's dogsbody. He knew what kind of a story they were in.

'OK. On my way,' he said, when Sam was done.

'Wait. Not yet. I want a couple of things emailed to my phone.'

'You got it.'

'Send my notes on Lisa Costello as an RTF file. And send me the complete guest list, it's right there on the desktop. All the names.'

'Done.'

'And tell Rich I'm going to the airport and I want the open limit on my credit card maintained all month.'

'You lucky bastard,' Kevin said.

You don't know how lucky, Sam thought and hung up. He didn't feel guilty, though. Kevin had an ex-wife, kids and a girlfriend back home, a nice little house in Pasadena with swings in the back yard and a Mercedes in the garage. His life had some purpose, some meaning. Sam's did not.

He was not going to miss his chance to change that.

As the cab hurtled towards Phuket International, Kevin emailed through the data. Sam read the list, mentally separating out the women, trying to recall names. There were about twenty to thirty she could actually have used, women roughly her own age. And he guessed she would have wanted a British or Australian passport, to avoid questions about her accent. Now he had sliced a guest list of hundreds down to about fifteen names.

A pen and a piece of paper would have been good, but there was nothing to write on. He would have to do this in his head, like mental arithmetic. Kate Wilson, Emily Berry, Penny Chisholm . . . all had dark hair; Lola Sanchez would look too Hispanic; how about Janet Parks, though? She was English and Lisa's build. Her hair was a little dark, but she'd been drunk, and he knew Lisa had seen her drunk. Drunks woke up slowly and didn't notice they'd been robbed. At least not until it was way too late. Janet's thoughts wouldn't have turned to her passport for several long, painful hours.

Of course Lisa would have wanted to get out, but there were a couple of things she'd have been forced to think through. Like what she took with her, like ringing the hotel reception. And which passport to steal.

He tapped on his screen, pulling up his photo album. There were the passports, fanned out in rows. Another couple of taps and he had blown up the pixel sizes, and now he could read the names.

Janet Parks's wasn't there.

He looked again. It was definitely missing.

They were pulling up outside the airport now. It was sleek and rich-looking, delightfully anonymous and Western. She would have been relieved to get here. He climbed out and paid the driver, then walked inside the terminal, his phone already to his ear, calling a number he hadn't had to use in years.

'Craig Gordon,' his contact said, sounding half asleep.

'This is Sam Murray.'

'What the hell do you want?'

The weariness, the contempt in that voice stung him. Craig Gordon had been one of his closest friends in the academy. When he'd dropped out at first they'd stayed in touch. Later, Craig grew sick of Sam's degeneracy, the drinking, the whores. Sam was gambling away more in a week than Craig earned in a month. And Sam was tailing celebrities with a camera, while Craig was tracking drug dealers and terrorists and risking his life.

But they used each other intermittently, all the same. Sam had good info on prostitution rings and drug buyers; and in return for calling him whenever he needed to, Craig sometimes gave him a car registration or a flight manifest, all strictly illegal, and very common.

Sam had not made use of Craig for quite some time, all the same. He could no longer bear the sound of repulsion when he spoke to him. Because Craig thought Sam could have been a hell of a lot more. And his was one of the few opinions Sam still cared about.

'Flight data,' he said.

'Forget it. You can't have it.'

Sam sighed. 'Craig, it's me.'

'I know who the hell it is. Airport security is much tighter now, and that includes flight data. We don't give it out unless it's for a legitimate investigation.'

Sam knew better than to offer money. Craig Gordon would have had him arrested.

'This is a legitimate investigation.'

'Not unless you've joined LAPD. It's late here, Sam, I'm going back to bed.'

'Craig, no. Wait.' He needed this; the chase was going to get stuck without it. 'I'm on the trail of Lisa Costello, I know you've heard what happened here.'

'Yeah,' Craig admitted. 'Not just heard of her. We're on this case.'

Sam blinked. 'The FBI?' This was a murder committed on Thai soil. It would be way out of Craig's jurisdiction.

'The Thai police are going crazy. She kills her husband, it's all over the news, then she's on the run. They want her caught. They asked us for assistance, the vic being an American. We agreed. It's a real high-profile case, she's America's Most Wanted right now. What you got on her?'

'You need to do a deal with me.'

'No deals. I'm FBI.' And you're not, he didn't have to say.

'Well, if you want to be the one that catches her, you need to deal with me. I know what she did to get out of the hotel complex and I need a search on a name. You give me the search and

101

you guarantee this information will stay out of the media for forty-eight hours.'

Hesitation. 'I don't know, Sam.'

'Yeah, well, you do know me and who I am, and you may not like it, Craig, but you also know I'm good at this shit. What I have for you is a solid lead. And I've been to the crime scene and the Thai police don't have the first idea. Plus, they're open to bribery, and you know that means the whole place will be crawling with journalists in about another hour and the evidence will be hopelessly compromised.'

His ex-friend had not hung up, at least. That was something.

'I'll find her and I'll tip you off.'

'And what's in it for you?'

'Money.'

'Of course. I should have guessed.'

'There's nothing un-American about money,' Sam replied, and hated how defensive he sounded. 'Look, this is going to be my last job. And I will help you catch her. Which makes it legitimate.'

'If I like what you got to say, I'll co-operate,' Craig Gordon said.

'She took two passports. Her own and a guest's. They blocked her passport but she didn't use it. I think she's using the name Janet Parks. My guess is she rode straight to the airport.'

'Not totally dumb, then.'

'Don't believe everything you read.'

A grunt. 'You should know.' He heard a rustle; Craig was getting out of bed. There was a sound of footsteps. He was going downstairs, to the computer.

'Got any more, Detective?'

'I got plenty more. But you give me that data. If Janet Parks took a flight out of Phuket this morning after eight a.m. local. British national.'

'I can see your cell number. I'll call you back.'

Sam hung up and moved over to the Starbucks counter. He ordered a large black coffee and a Danish, the closest he was going to come to real American food. He felt a moment's stupid homesickness, thinking about the cheerful little diner at the foot of the Hollywood Hills, with the giant plastic Coke bottle outside. They made a fantastic cheese and bacon omelette, which you could have with coffee strong enough to stand a spoon in, and find your hangover would be half-done when you'd finished.

But coffee and a pastry would do. He swirled his little stick in his paper cup and thought about Lisa Costello. She'd managed the first, most important thing, and most people didn't. She'd been able to get away.

Away from the body, away from the crime scene. Away from the cops. He hoped for her sake she had got on a plane. Anyplace was better than here.

He turned around, enjoying the caffeine and sugar, and studied the large arrivals and departures board. He knew in a heartbeat where she had gone.

His phone rang; he picked it up instantly.

'Hong Kong, right?'

'Right. I thought you didn't know where she was.'

'I worked it out.'

103

English-speaking, short-haul flight, big city, good place to get lost in. Cheap food, cheap clothes. Connecting flights to lots of places, boats too.

'You're a regular psychic.'

'I was right, though, wasn't I,' Sam snapped back, then passed a hand across his forehead. He had no wish to attack somebody like Craig. It was just tiresome being reminded of his own inadequacies. He didn't really need help in that department.

'You were. Look, Sam, we'd like to catch this girl. Lots of media interest, but you know that.'

'Sure.'

'Good for the Bureau. Good for me.'

'I'll help. I'll give you what I've got, Craig, only it has to be later than I get it. If you guys scoop her up first I might not get this bonus, and I need it.'

'You got bookie trouble again?'

'No.' He wondered why he was telling Craig Gordon all this, like Craig was his rabbi or something. 'It's enough cash for me to quit the stupid celebrity stuff and start over. A new life somewhere else. I know I messed up. I'd like enough money to be able to figure out something else to do. Maybe get a family like you, or something.'

Craig laughed, surprised. 'Get married? You? I don't think so.'

'People change.'

'Not in my experience, pal, no they don't. If they get sober, that's a win. Other than that folks stay the same. Almost all.'

104

'Well I'm gonna be in the 'almost' part. When did she fly to Kowloon?'

'On the nine a.m. flight. And she disembarked no trouble. She's still there, unless she left by boat. I already blocked the passport.'

'Then I'm going to go and find her.'

'Give me your leads.'

'Soon as I'm done with them. Talk later, Craig.'

He hung up and put his phone on silent, in case Craig called back. Then he went over to the British Airways stand and booked himself a business-class seat on the company's credit card on the next flight out.

★ ★ ★

'Champagne, sir?'

The stewardess bending over him was very pretty, if you liked that tight, manicured look. He smiled back at her.

'Sure. Thanks.'

There was no point being abstemious about this. He'd get a good hotel in Hong Kong, not the priciest, like the Peninsula or the Mandarin, but somewhere good and tucked away; the Hotel Jen, he thought, in the heart of the old city, with clean modern rooms and a nice rooftop pool. The only place in Hong Kong you felt calm was swimming against the sky. He was not going to find Lisa Costello tonight. He was certain of that much. She wouldn't be using the passport again. If she had planned on a second flight, she might just as well have flown direct from Phuket to

105

Europe. She'd picked short haul so that she could land before they stopped the passport.

Probably she was still in the city. His job was to go there and sleep, and then figure out what a smart Limey girl on the lam would have done next. He should be capable. She didn't have credit cards, at least not her own nor Josh's, and he'd tracked her this far. He wanted to buy some new clothes and an overnight bag, a toothbrush and a razor. Oh yeah, and swimming trunks.

One thing he did do for himself was exercise. Other than gambling and sex, it was the only activity in which you could lose yourself totally. And when your life consisted of flying and driving and hanging out in nightclubs, you could either work out or give up. Sam had zero intention of turning into some fat, drink-sodden old newspaperman like his boss. He wasn't doing a man's job, but he made damn sure he had a man's body. Wherever he went, he packed a pair of trainers and some jog pants; you could do push-ups and tricep dips in your bedroom, using whatever was there. Fitness was available wherever there was a road.

His body ached to be used. And he wanted to do it. If you were trying to catch a person, you had to clear your thoughts of fog. Working out and sleep were the best two ways to do that.

He wondered how Lisa Costello had spent this flight. Not up front, being offered a flute of champagne and her meals on a china tray. That would be conspicuous, and he thought she was working from cash. She would have been very

106

frightened. Caught at this stage, and she could face the death penalty.

She'd have been hungover, so thirsty at the very least. He doubted she would have wanted to eat. He sipped absently at the chilled drink, allowing the bubbles to burst against his tongue and the softness of the alcohol to blunt the edges of his day.

None of this told him facts, not like the passport thing. But it helped him to crawl inside Lisa Costello's head. And that was going to be very necessary. Whoever wrote 'London is an anthill' had never seen Hong Kong. It was some of the most crowded real estate on Planet Earth, a place where somebody with survival skills could stay, perhaps for ever.

Only he did not think Lisa Costello would want to stay. Their brief conversation he replayed, over and over again. She had seemed then, to him, to be straining against the leash, like a dog desperate to be let out in a field for a walk, pulling against the tether so hard it might strangle itself. She was fighting against the couture Chanel suits, the glossy blond hair, the expertly plucked California eyebrows, and the million-dollar wedding where the bride had no real friends.

It was why he'd liked her; why he'd been so surprised by her, at last, in the flesh.

She was like him. Claustrophobic. Prepared to give it all up rather than be married alive. A free spirit in a world where you thought they no longer existed.

And now here he was, hunting her down. Only

unlike the bumbling police and the imagination-free security agencies, he really would find her, and then they'd try her, and they'd kill her.

He found the thought depressing. Which was ridiculous. She'd stabbed some poor schmuck to death. He'd be a fool to start mooning over a chick with a drinking problem and a mental block that made her give up a life of luxury in favour of the electric chair, or whatever they used out in Thailand.

Lisa Costello was not his problem. And he wasn't about to give up a million dollars by going soft.

★ ★ ★

The hotel had a vacancy, which did not surprise him. Even the cheaper places were finding it hard to fill their slots these days, with the recession biting deep all over the world. Funny thing was, trash like his sold perfectly well even in times like these. When they were down, people loved to read about the troubles of those richer, sexier, privileged stars who seemed like they had everything.

They were glad to take his money, and offered a discount when he demanded it. In fact, when he produced his press credentials, the smiling woman at the front desk smiled just a little wider, and her supervisor appeared as if from nowhere and upgraded him to a junior suite.

It was tough out there. They needed all the good reviews they could get.

Sam knew Hong Kong well enough. He was

out of the hotel, room key in hand, before he even went upstairs, and eight minutes' walk brought him to a tourist shopping area. There were plenty of stores that sold clothes and sports goods. He hated shopping, loathed it with a passion, and as such had learned to recognise his size on the peg. He bought fast, selecting some Nike Airs, because as far as he was concerned they had never been beaten, some cheap socks and workout shirts, swim trunks and a towel; then toiletries, which he was without often enough to know exactly what basics he needed; and finally a plain wardrobe: fresh underwear, suit socks, two blue shirts, two ties, and two pairs of trousers; some jeans, T-shirts and a good thick coat. It was ludicrously hot and muggy here, but he didn't know where he was going.

All that done, he headed back to the hotel, past the receptionist, who by now was staring a little, and finally went to his room. It was luxurious, but he resisted the temptation to flop on the bed. Once you did that, you were finished. He poured a glass of tap water, drank it, and changed into his new gear. Then he went upstairs to the gym, where he ran hard for half an hour on the treadmill then forced himself to get on the machines and lift the weights. Finally he changed into the swim trunks and did fifty laps.

God, but it felt good. Every stroke in the water felt like he was washing the blood he'd seen this morning from himself. He loved the fitness area in this hotel; the machines were right up against the window, and you could see the harbour while you worked them. Sam wanted to run, to run from Rich Frank, to run from the dead body of Josh Steen, to run from his crappy life, somewhere else, anywhere else, and pounding the treadmill till his heart thudded and his breath was ragged helped, just a little bit, to get him through.

He let the aerobic exertion blank out his mind. It was better than meditation; hard to concentrate on anything bad when you were working on keeping going. He towelled off and slipped on his T-shirt and sweatpants, and then returned to his room where he luxuriated under a blissfully hot shower.

He was ravenously hungry. He dressed in his jeans and a sweatshirt and ordered room service: a burger and fries, with mineral water, a side salad and half a bottle of red. They brought it to him fast. He tipped the guy generously with Rich Frank's money, then sat down and started to eat, trying to stop himself wolfing the meal. It was piping hot, and too good. He needed salt and he needed protein.

He drained a tumbler full of fizzy mineral water choked with ice, and then poured himself a large glass of red. The food and the alcohol relaxed him, his blood was singing from the workout; he felt momentarily great. At last he allowed his thoughts to return to Lisa. He took out the free writing paper and the biro they'd left in the drawer of his bedside cabinet, and started to make some notes.

Would she try to travel again on that passport? No. Coming here meant she was going to ditch

110

it. Would she stay in Hong Kong? Hmm. More difficult — he might have hung out here for a while, but you'd have to figure they'd catch the passport trick eventually and know where she was. And China would have no problems extraditing her back to Thailand.

No, if he were Lisa he would want to get out. And he knew the mentality. Once you started to run, you did not stop, not until you could, or you had to. What did that mean, then? A fake passport? Nothing in her background said she knew the seedy underworld, or would have the first idea how to go about it.

Her background . . .

He reached over to the bed and picked up his phone, pulling the email off it that Kevin had sent. There were his notes, his file on Lisa, her past, her schooldays. She hadn't been to college, but her little private school was known for taking pupils in from all over the world.

Lisa Costello wasn't a good correspondent. She was essentially a loner, he thought. She did not keep up with people.

But when you were desperate, where would you go?

He was exhausted. Nothing was going to happen tonight. Besides, he thought, maybe part of him wanted the girl to run. Wanted her to get to Europe, someplace at least where they wouldn't kill her.

He was going soft in his old age. No, more likely it was because he actually needed her to get away. The thought suggested itself, and Sam relaxed a touch. Yeah. He needed Lisa to keep running, at least at first. If they caught her right now, there was no story. Well, there was the trial story, but he'd have nothing to do with that and did not get paid on death-watch cases.

That million dollars was conditional. He needed the chase to be just the right length. Too short and he'd only get the fee for his current stories. Which was nice, sure, but no cigar, no new life.

So let the girl run. Tomorrow would be soon enough to see who she was talking to.

He moved back to the phone and opened an email, typing up another article. Rich would get his twenty-five grand's worth and then some, from the reporter who had the FBI tracking down Janet Parks's passport.

* * *

'We are now on our final approach to Rome Ciampiano airport,' said the soothing mechanised voice. 'Please fasten your seat belts, and return your seats to the upright position . . . '

Lisa did as she was told. She was drained, almost numb from the dizzying length of the flight. She had been forced to get up and walk around the cabin; you could die of blood clots, or something, if you didn't do that. But at least she had slept. Blessedly, the ordeal had left her more drained than she cared to remember, and she had fallen asleep pretty easily, without the need for drink or drugs, and stayed that way for at least seven hours.

And now they were here. In Rome. She

112

desperately wanted to get off the plane. Rome was Europe, where nobody got executed. She wished to God she knew the law. What was the deal if they stopped her at immigration? Wasn't she still on Italian soil? She would claim asylum, claim anything, ask for a lawyer. It was a Catholic country, they wouldn't send her back to Thailand to be hanged, surely . . .

Only the worst was, she wanted more. Now she was here, she wanted to survive, be free, keep out of jail. She hadn't killed Josh — she hoped; that meant she ought not to spend the rest of her life in a sunless room.

It felt like a joke. But it was not a joke. It was real, and it was happening to her.

★   ★   ★

In the end, there was no problem getting through immigration. Lisa raised up her head and laughed, supremely relaxed — it was easy, she was so tired — and the guy let her through; and she was standing by the baggage carousels, wondering whether to run and deciding not to.

Her money was dwindling. She couldn't go around just buying everything afresh. Her backpack would be here soon, and it had all the basic things she needed. Besides, they weren't coming for her, at least not yet.

The carousel started and spluttered, and suddenly Lisa was watching a horde of suitcases tumble down, and she was actually ready to pick up her backpack and move, get out of here, to freedom . . .

There it was; and she moved to get it, and slung it on to her shoulders and walked through customs. Nobody stopped her, and nobody stopped anyone else. She was in Italy. A country that had banned the death penalty. She was safe, and she thanked God. Only a few steps outside and she'd be free . . .

But Alice . . .

Lisa hesitated, the weight of the backpack heavy on her shoulders. What about that, her friend, terrified and sweating? The maid would be back in twenty-four hours and would hear her. That extra time could let Lisa run far, far away. Before they knew about the passport, before anything.

But she just could not do it. What if there was a problem? If the maid didn't come back? If the maid had a heart attack, to take it to a stupid extreme? In that case, Alice might die, and a horrible death too, thirst and starvation.

It sounded unlikely, but maybe it was true. Lisa couldn't say if Alice had lots of friends — and even then, who amongst them would drop by and go into the house if it was shut up?

There was a bank of payphones in the arrivals hall. They took coins, but she didn't have euros, and anyway it would be expensive. She went to the bureau de change and switched her money. Thank God for the EU; she could stick with euros now for a little while, wherever she went.

There were a few kiosks, and they all spoke English. Just as well, since she only had a few words of Italian. She bought a phone card for thirty euros; she could have got more, but maybe

114

they could trace those things. She had written down the airline and police numbers before she left Hong Kong. The police were easy enough.

'Hi,' she said. 'I'm calling to report a robbery on the Peak. Ms Alice Kennedy.'

'Excuse me? Address please?'

She gave the address twice.

'The householder is bound and gagged in a closet in her second bedroom.' What could she say to make them believe her? 'Her husband is with Cathay Pacific, a pilot.'

'Who is speaking?'

'Somebody who knows. And who is telling Cathay that the police were informed.' She hung up. She was under no illusions; they'd have her voice recorded now, and they'd know exactly where she was. As soon as possible she had to go to ground, and dye her hair again. But none of that mattered. It was about getting Alice free.

She could not trust the police. The passport in her pocket had a number for Cathay Pacific, an emergency number to reach Alice's husband. That was good. With a stab of fear, Lisa dialled the country code and the number.

A computer replied.

'For quality and training purposes, your call may be recorded.'

Lovely — of course it may. She waited for a human.

'Cathay Pacific.'

'Hi, I'm calling to reach Ronald Watson, a pilot of yours. It's a family emergency.'

There was a pause on the end of the line.

'Is this about his wife?'

Lisa breathed in sharply; the pit of her stomach crunched and her entire body prickled with adrenalin.

'Yes,' she said, in a half-whisper. 'She was assaulted — '

'Her journalist friend notified the airline already, thank you. Ronald's on his way home.'

'Oh, she did?'

'He did — it was Mr Murray. He seemed to know Lisa Costello would go to see her.' Another pause. 'I didn't get your name, miss.'

The voice was starting to change tone, get suspicious. Lisa replaced the receiver and ran blindly out of the airport. There were cabs everywhere, buses too. She fished in her pocket for a few euros and caught the bus, shoving them at the driver. He was used to tourists; he gave her change and waved her to a seat. It was packed already with students and families, and a few seconds later pulled blessedly away.

Lisa watched the city as it rolled past her windows, trying to bring back the experience of being here as a poor girl; where she'd been, what she'd done. How long would she be the story if she stayed on the run? How long would it take them to forget her? The temptation was to make for some little nowhere place, a village in Umbria or a hilltop town in Lazio, rent a minute studio and try to get a cash-in-hand job. But it wouldn't work. In small towns not much happened, and you got noticed. She didn't want to be noticed, to be the conspicuous Englishwoman. In that situation, she would soon be rotting in Regina Coeli jail.

So what, what now? Stick in the anonymity of tourist-trap Rome? They would get round to the call to Cathay Pacific, and anyway, they'd know she had Alice's passport. So they would be looking here. But she thought she might stay anyway, for a little while, move around until her money ran out; maybe by that time they'd have forgotten her, and she could get a job.

It was bad, all of it. Lisa longed to be free, but now she was in Europe, the future rattled down on her like a runaway train; the best she could hope for a long, grubby existence of grinding poverty, working tables for less than minimum wage, with no identity, no way to open a bank account or buy a house. It was not a good life. Was it better than taking her chances in jail? Yeah. But not by much.

The bus pulled in to the Colosseum. There was a stand right next to the giant monument, full of tourist info. Lisa asked for the address of a cheap albergho, someplace she could stay on a budget. There was one in Monti, she was told, safe and clean but with shared bathrooms.

She hoisted up her backpack and walked there. It wasn't as clean as all that, but it was twenty euros a night and would do for now. The door to her room seemed heavy enough and had a key chain. She wanted a shower, but someone was using the bathroom in the hall. She wanted a lot of things. She bolted her door, slid the chain on, and flopped on her bed, fully clothed.

Alice was safe. But they knew she'd been there. Somebody apparently knew she would come. A man, a Mr Murray. She could not

117

remember anybody by that name right now, but it would come back. Right now she needed to sleep. She put down her head, and surrendered to darkness.

★ ★ ★

When she woke, the shadows were long outside her small window. It was still light, though, maybe late afternoon. Nobody was around the hotel. She took a fresh set of clothes and the small, scratchy towel they provided and went to the shower room. It was cramped, and the tiles were cracked, but the hot water was utterly blissful. Gratefully she shaved and washed her hair, cleaned her teeth, even washed her face with the small, functional bar of cheap soap they provided. She was awake now, the fog of tiredness gone from her. Time to think, time to plan. She pulled on new clothes and went back to her room, running a cheap plastic comb through her wet hair.

What the hell had happened with Alice?

Somebody had found her. Somebody had told Cathay Pacific, but not the police. Mr Murray . . .

Oh God. The comb stopped in her hair. *Sam* Murray. That was the guy. The journalist from that trashy tabloid, the one Josh had insisted on inviting.

It came back to her then, all in a rush, a flashback from just days ago, but a world away from her new life, a person she had been a million years before, when she was still rich, still

118

married to Josh, and he was alive, and her future was golden . . .

There they were. Her bridegroom of a couple of hours, and one of her bridesmaids. God, the ultimate cliché. They were in the bushes, having sex. And Josh's hand was cupping her ass and his other hand was on her shoulder, and the tip of his tongue was teasing her earlobe. He was doing to that bitch Melissa Olivera what he'd always done to Lisa, and she had loved it, that possessive way he had of taking her, fondling her like a chattel. It was sexy, until he started to treat her that way out of the bedroom too.

Not that she hadn't suspected. How could you not, when his bitchy family made remarks all the time, and the press went on about Josh Steen marrying beneath himself, and magazines like Sam Murray's ran those cute photo-spreads comparing mousy little Lisa to the golden California butterflies Josh had dated. Josh was away on set more and more frequently, and Lisa was left behind with the ladies who shopped, bored out of her mind, buying things she didn't need or want on Rodeo Drive and spending hours in the gym or at the beauty parlour. Why wouldn't he get bored with her? He had fallen for her because she was different, then spent all of his very considerable energies making her exactly the same.

And when that happened, he wanted a challenge. The safe, easy lay of a married woman. The thrill of screwing one of his wife's friends — nominal friends, anyway, a girl she hung out with, because Lisa had no true friends in America, certainly none amongst Josh Steen's circle.

But still. Even though it was all over before their private jet touched down in Thailand. Even though she'd only gone through with the marriage to spare him embarrassment. Even though Lisa had been planning a divorce, it still hurt to see him with Melissa, on their wedding day.

Funny how much it hurt.

It was his final act of control, perhaps, his statement that he was everything and Lisa was nothing, that he was never going to change, not for her, not for anybody. Josh Steen loved his mafia movies, didn't he? He thought of himself as a real Michael Corleone, with the goomah in the rented apartment giving him wild sex and getting paid in Bulgari necklaces, while the wife and kids stayed home and provided a respectable backdrop.

He'd had everything in Phuket: the pliant English wife with no past, no scandals; and the sexy-as-hell American girlfriend who'd say yes to anything, even a highly charged fuck on Lisa's wedding day.

So then there had been nothing to do but go away. And she had done, stumbling backwards, not letting Josh see her at first, grabbing a flute of champagne from a passing waiter, and then doing the thing he hated most of all.

She'd made a scene.

Her bridesmaids were all from Josh's side of the altar, with only her fat friend Lilly dredged up from home to stand for her. Lilly had played with her as a child, and had been happy to take an all-expenses-paid trip out to the Far East to be at this wedding, but they were hardly close. Lisa smiled as she remembered seeing Lilly in her bridesmaid's outfit of sage and cream chiffon and silk; she'd insisted on sleeves, in an attempt to spare her embarrassment, but the girl still looked like an overdone Christmas pudding.

Lilly was outside smoking while the other girls went through their choreographed rehearsal.

'Wotcher, Lisa,' she'd said, dragging deep on her cigarette. At the time Lisa thought it was the best thing she'd heard all week.

But Lilly had retired to her bungalow after the reception dinner, saying foreign food didn't agree with her. So Lisa was out there alone in the lush tropical garden, and she wasn't the only one who'd seen Josh's paws all over Melissa. Lots of young trophy wives, and their catty mothers, were putting their heads together as Lisa walked past by herself. Some of the single women even sniggered aloud. Guess they saw this marriage being stillborn. Josh Steen would be a prize catch, out on the market again where he belonged, instead of stuck with this bitch . . .

She'd heard the whispers, and the sniggers. And she'd tossed back the glass of champagne, telling herself she didn't give a damn any more, and if he wanted to blow up this wedding that was fine with her.

'Hey, Lisa.' It was Fiona Greenberg, Josh's cousin and another of her bridesmaids. 'Maybe go easy on that, huh? I mean, you did have wine at dinner.'

There was a cruel little smile playing around Fiona's mouth. Like she was determined to add to the humiliations this day was heaping on the bride. Lisa glanced around and saw several knots of wedding guests staring at her. By a palm tree, lounging casually, observing her, there was a man by himself, wearing a relaxed suit with an ice-blue shirt, tanned, with five o'clock shadow round a square jaw. She remembered it clearly, because she hadn't seen him before, and Josh had forced her to make small talk with most of his boring little friends.

'Hey Fiona,' Lisa said, loudly and clearly. 'Why don't you just get lost?'

The older woman drew back. 'Excuse me?'

'No, I don't think I will. This is supposed to be my wedding. It's not for you to tell me what to drink. Look at you,' she said, gesturing to Fiona's pudgy arms and double chin. 'I didn't tell you not to eat the ice cream at dinner. Maybe you'd like yourself a little better if you didn't stuff your fat face every other second. And then you wouldn't need to snipe at me.'

'I can't believe you!' Fiona said, going red-faced with fury. 'You'd speak to a member of Josh's family like that?'

'Hey, you got no trouble speaking to his wife like that.' Lisa stared her down. 'Why are you still here? I thought I told you to fuck off.'

There was a chuckle, and she looked past the stumbling form of Fiona, tripping on her heels and chiffon, one hand over her pudgy mouth, to see the stranger by the palm tree grinning broadly at her.

'Waiter,' Lisa said, snapping her fingers. Somebody immediately materialised with a silver tray and more champagne; she chose rosé this time, and slugged down half of it, right on the spot. Wedding guests were staring. She laughed. Some of her other bridesmaids hurriedly withdrew. They were looking for Josh, she knew, looking to give him the bad news: Lisa was making a scene; Lisa's mask was slipping; Josh was going to look very bad indeed, and his million-dollar wedding was about to turn into a farce . . .

Should have thought about that before you decided to bang Melissa, Lisa decided, and laughed again. The alcohol was surging through her body, making her feel light-headed, damn the consequences. She didn't have to take it. Maybe that was Josh's belief, that she had to take whatever he threw at her, whenever he threw it.

Only it wasn't going to happen. She looked defiantly around her wedding, at all the well-dressed people she didn't even like, and silently said goodbye to them; first thing tomorrow she'd be on a plane on her way home, and Josh Steen would be getting an annulment. Because God only knew, she wasn't about to consummate this union.

'Hello,' said a male voice. Lisa looked up; it was the guy by the palm tree. 'Want to talk?'

'Depends. Who are you? Another of Josh's slimy friends?'

He grinned again, and she quite liked the smile.

'Yes to the slimy. No to the friend.'

123

'Intriguing,' Lisa said, and she couldn't help smiling back, just a little. 'I don't recognise you.'

'You wouldn't. Want to go for a walk? They're staring at you out here.'

'Yeah? Well sod the lot of them.'

He crooked an eyebrow. 'Brit expression, but I can guess what it means. I don't think your husband will like it.'

'I hope it doesn't look like I care,' Lisa said. But she allowed herself to take a walk with him, past the palm tree, down one of the estate's little gravel paths. They were in some kind of shrubbery garden now, with a little ersatz Italian fountain, and shielded from the prying stares of the guests.

'I'm a journalist. Hand-picked by Josh to cover the wedding of the century. Except it doesn't seem like you're all that enthused by it.'

'A journalist. Society columnist?'

'I do celebrity puff pieces for a mass-circulation tabloid,' he said, honestly enough, and she liked that about him too, and she laughed.

'Lisa Costello.' She held out her hand.

'Sam Murray,' he said, and he was very handsome, but she knew she was buzzed from the wine. She wasn't going to do anything stupid. Her judgement with men was not that great, obviously. 'USA Weekly. Anyway, isn't it Lisa Steen now?'

'No. It's not. And it's not going to be.'

'Getting divorced, or keeping your own name?'

She didn't answer him; he was a journalist,

124

after all, and she at least owed it to Josh to have it out. She'd spent five years of her life with him, and some of that time had been happy.

'I wish I had a cigarette,' she said. She took another pull at the wine. *Fuck* Josh for doing this to her, seriously. She didn't care if she was behaving badly in front of a journalist. She was tired of being a show girl, another of his trophies, and she was going to get good and drunk.

'You smoke?'

'Used to. I gave it up. I gave up everything fun.' She drank some more, then looked at Sam Murray. 'What about you? Your life ever take a wrong turn?'

'More than one. That's why I'm here.'

'It must pay well.'

'It does,' he said. 'I still hate it. I could say the same thing to you, I suppose.'

She drank some more and felt the euphoria being replaced with anger. How dare Josh — seriously, how dare he — go bang someone else on her wedding day? How dare he treat her like one of these anonymous servants he paid to wait on his wedding party or fly his jets or clean his pool? It was like he'd given her a job description, girlfriend, with promotion to wife, and she was here just to shut up and obey his orders.

'You mean because Josh is so rich?'

'That's exactly what I mean. You seem angry at coming into a home where you'll be able to spend millions of dollars on whatever the hell you want.'

'Money's nice,' Lisa said. She was slurring a

little now, but she didn't care. 'Freedom's better. I'm only twenty-eight. I could do things, lots of things. I never tried hard enough to stick at anything.' She looked at the older man, and his eyes were on her, assessing her, like he was trying to figure her out.

'And are you going to stick at this marriage?'

'You'll see,' she said, delighting herself with her own mysteriousness. 'What about you, Mr Slimy Reporter? If you hate your job, why don't you just get out? It's not jail, you can leave when you want, I guess.'

He sighed, a long, deep sigh that seemed wrenched out of his body, and even though she was a little drunk, Lisa felt sorry for him.

'Why don't any of us do what we know we should do? You tell me. Life. It gets in the way sooner than you'd think.'

She held his gaze. He was right, he shouldn't be a celebrity hack. There was something different about him. Maybe he should be a spy, or a soldier.

'Well, things can change. I'm going to change things. For me,' she said, and she stumbled because she was unsteady, and he caught her. He was thickly muscled, and very strong, and she enjoyed that second's contact, that feeling of his hand on her elbow . . .

'Lisa!' The shout came from the path behind them. It was Josh, and he was bellowing with rage. Fiona must have spoken to him. 'Hey! Lisa! Where are you?'

'I think that's your cue,' Sam Murray said. 'Good luck, Lisa Costello.' And he melted away just before her bridegroom came charging through the bushes and proceeded to yell at her some more, and she tossed down the rest of her drink and stormed away from him . . .

The memories dissolved. She sat there on the single bed with the hard mattress, her wet hair dripping on to her thighs, and tried to collect herself, tried to think.

So Sam Murray had somehow found Alice Kennedy — and he'd known she was going to go there.

How?

She couldn't have told him and blacked out the memory. Because she hadn't even known she was going to do it. Would she have mentioned Alice in some other context? No — she had just remembered the whole conversation. She shook her head, hating the lost time. What if she had gone back to find Sam Murray later, if she'd got up after passing out on the bed and discussed Alice Kennedy with him, and an alcoholic blackout had concealed that memory . . . And what if pigs flew over the Colosseum, she asked herself. It was all too stupid. She'd thought of Alice when she had to, and not a second before.

Think, Lisa. You're not dumb. Think!

She tried working backwards. So he knew she was going to find Alice. Meaning . . . he already knew that Alice and she were at school together. OK. How would he know that? Well, he was a journalist; hadn't lots of them crawled around her old schoolfriends for their stupid little gossip-column pieces? Maybe Sam Murray had something of the cop about him after all, something that she'd guessed that night. Maybe he did more than write puff pieces. Hell, perhaps he actually *was* a cop. Lisa only had his word that he was a journalist.

Except, as she replayed the conversation, she didn't think he was lying. Was that naïve, to go with her hunches? Maybe not, if it was all she had.

Think. She stood up and towelled her hair a little. Soon she would go out for food. Maybe something else as well.

So Murray had a yearbook perhaps; certainly records of her schoolfriends. Which meant he'd looked around for somebody she knew in Hong Kong. And as she was a loner, with few friends anywhere, let alone in Hong Kong, that pretty much cut it down.

But he'd known she would come. That suggested he understood why. The pieces were falling into place for Lisa now, and despite the fear, she found she was impressed. The guy had brains and cunning. As far as she could tell, no state agencies had tracked her this far yet.

Sam Murray knew she had Janet Parks's passport. It was the only explanation. How else could he be in Hong Kong? Lucky guess? And he'd also worked out that she wouldn't try two flights on the same document. So he figured she'd repeat the pattern . . .

And that had led him to Alice.

It would also lead him to Rome.

Her heart pulsed with emotion. Sam Murray *understood* her. That was something, wasn't it?

The authorities would track her to Rome; that

128

was going to happen anyway, since Lisa herself had tipped them off about Alice, bound and gagged in that closet, and Alice would tell them what happened, and they'd find her passport missing and run the standard trace. Being tracked was inevitable.

But the authorities hadn't had the chance to find out yet. Sam Murray had got there first. He must have moved very fast, she thought, with a thrill of admiration. And he must have thought hard, to work out not only that she'd run, but how she'd run. The Thai police were probably still scouring every two-bit hostel in a hundred-mile radius of the estate.

Sam Murray had caught the scent. And her new best friend from that disastrous wedding night, the guy who had seen her drunk and sloppy, was hunting her.

Would he hand her over?

Come on, Lisa, one conversation doesn't make a friendship, she told herself. He's hunting you. What else do you need to know?

Only she did need to know. Badly. She needed to talk to Sam Murray. Because if he was that smart, then maybe he could help.

4

Alice Kennedy, Sam thought. It had to be. She was the only contact he could find who still lived in Hong Kong, and he'd been through everything. There was one other chick from Lisa's school days, named Rebecca, but she had left Hong Kong for Sydney when they were still in the fourth form, and Lisa would know that. So Alice Kennedy it had to be. Plus, her husband was an airline pilot. That had to be helpful, if you were looking to get the hell out of Dodge.

The Kennedys had a nice place on the mountain at the heart of Hong Kong, the Peak. From his research Sam knew that it had been in the family for some time. He arrived early, seven forty-five in the morning, because he wanted to get the woman before she left for a job, or to shop, or whatever it was that suburban Westerners did in the post-colonial city.

He knew immediately that something was wrong when he got there. It was the garage: open, but only half so, like somebody had forgotten to close it after driving out. He was able to stick his head inside pretty easily, and there was no car in the bay.

People like Alice Kennedy and her husband didn't leave their garage doors ajar. They were far too safe and respectable to take risks. It smelled off, and Sam had learned to trust his nose.

He mounted the steps and rang the bell. No answer. Nothing. They had no maid, apparently, no kids or nannies. He looked up at the windows; several lights were very clearly on.

He had to get in, and he was prepared to talk his way out of a burglary rap. They had a tiny back yard behind the house, sloping up the mountain as Peak houses' gardens usually did. He clambered up there and examined the house from the back. Lights were on in random places, but nobody seemed to be home.

He knew she had been there. He could feel it. Maybe she'd run away with Alice Kennedy; maybe she'd been recognised and they'd had to leave fast. He needed to know. By clambering up on the side of the conservatory, he got himself on to the flat roof of the kitchen. From there he could see the window of an internal corridor.

He stripped off his jacket, wrapped it around his elbow and smashed the window. Then he kicked in the rest of it until the hole was big enough to crawl through, and clambered inside.

'Hello?' he shouted. 'Anybody home?'

Hell, if somebody *was* there, it would be better to portray himself as a concerned citizen than encounter the lady of the house coming out of the shower.

There was no answer. Sam started to move through the corridors of the house. They were covered in a thick silver-grey carpet, the walls a muted shade of peach. All very comfortable, very middle class. Not Lisa Costello at all.

Then he heard it. A rhythmic thumping, and tiny snuffling noises, like the mewling of a cat.

Sam had heard noises like that before, although not often. That was a human being, bound and gagged. A woman or a child, from the pitch of the voice.

'It's OK,' he called out. 'I'm here to help. Keep making noise, I'll find you.'

The mewling rose to a screech. It was coming from his left. He ran down a small set of stairs into some kind of guest wing. She was in the bedroom. Already he could smell the stink of urine; the poor woman must have been there for hours.

He flung open the closet doors. There was a young woman in there, dark hair, hysterical, her gag soaked with tears. She had a bruise on her forehead, a nasty one, shades of purple and brown.

He moved to her and tugged down the gag.

She started to cry, as though she couldn't say anything.

'It's OK, ma'am. My name's Sam Murray. I'm going to cut off these ties. When the blood comes back to your limbs it'll probably hurt.' He glanced around him; there was an open door to an en suite shower room on the other side of the bedroom. It was smallish, probably for guests. 'Lean on me and I'll assist you into the bathroom.'

She nodded, still crying, and he ripped off the ties that were holding her arms and legs. They were tight, and she wouldn't have been able to loosen them herself.

'You're Alice Kennedy, right? Did Lisa Costello do this to you?'

'Yes,' she sobbed. 'She's mad . . . ah . . . '

She gasped in pain as Sam lifted her to her feet, holding her elbow. A small piece of paper fluttered down from her chest to his feet. He picked it up. Alice didn't say a word; she was staggering next to him, her limbs spasming with the agony of her circulation returning, her bound muscles screaming. He slipped the paper into his pocket and helped her into the bathroom, sitting her down on the lavatory while he gently pulled the door half closed.

After a few minutes he heard the sound of water running. She was drinking; she must have been gasping with thirst.

He looked around. There was a bathrobe hanging in the closet where she had been bound. He slid it gently through the door.

'Hey, Ms Kennedy. If you need this.'

'Thank you,' she wept. 'Are you police?'

'No, ma'am. I'm a journalist who's been tracking Lisa since the murder. I figured she would come see you.'

More sounds of water; she was getting undressed, washing herself. He sat on the bed and waited.

The paper was in his pocket. He fished it out and looked at it.

A note.

Dynamite. He photographed it quickly. A wash of adrenalin swept through him. Wait till Rich Frank got this instalment; he would struggle to believe it. Sam was proud of himself. This might be a shitty, demeaning job, no job for a man, but goddamn, he was good at it.

While the sounds of the shower came from inside, he moved to the closet and photographed it extensively.

'Ms Kennedy? You OK in there?'

'I want my husband,' she said. She sounded a little calmer now. 'He's a pilot with Cathay. The number's programmed into the phone in our bedroom; that's right down the hall.'

'OK. I'll bring it to you.'

'Thank you. What's your name?'

'Sam Murray, ma'am.'

'Thank you, Mr Murray,' she said. She was still crying a little bit.

'I'll — uh — shall I call them for you and let you get dressed?'

'That would be kind.'

'OK. Sure.' He was pleased; she was actually asking him to enter her bedroom. He found the phone, and saw the coverlet was halfway off the bed — this must be where Lisa had attacked her. Quickly he took a picture, and noted the suitcase. While he rang Cathay, he opened drawers and the bedside cabinet.

There was a passport in there, face down. He took more pictures, flipped it over — yep. It was Janet Parks's all right. Man, I'm good at this shit, he thought.

Cathay assured him that Captain Watson would take the first flight home. She's more ruthless than I expected, he thought; got to give her credit. If that was the right word.

He would call Craig later, when he got up. For now, this baby was all his. He walked back towards the spare bedroom, and knocked

134

politely on the door.

'Ma'am — are you ready?'

She opened it in a pair of slacks and a baggy sweatshirt. Classic defensive dressing, what rape victims typically chose. She looked shell-shocked.

'My legs still hurt.' She rubbed at her wrists.

'Your husband's being notified; they said they'd have him on the next plane home. Can you tell me what happened?'

She sat down heavily on the bed. 'What day is this?'

'Tuesday.'

'She came to see me yesterday afternoon. We talked. She said she didn't kill her husband, John Steen.'

'Josh. She denied it?'

'Yes, and she said she wanted me to tell her what to do and would I give her a ride to the airport. I said she should go to Australia. I mean, I don't know if I believed her, but this is China here.'

'So she was afraid of being executed.' He'd got her right so far. But then that was something that would likely occur to any fugitive for murder in this part of the world. 'Did she say anything about who did kill him?'

'No. She didn't know. She said nobody would believe her but she didn't do it. Then she said she wanted a lift to the airport, and when I wasn't looking she *hit* me.' Alice's voice rose to a wail of outrage.

'Did you fight back?'

'I couldn't. I was blacked out.'

135

She must have hit her pretty hard then; she must have some basic skills. Women in fights usually clawed and slapped and pulled at each other's hair. It might be sexist, but it was perfectly true in Sam's experience.

'When I woke up I was tied in a cupboard and gagged. And the worst thing is she made me tell my maid to take the day off today! I could have *died* in there!'

'Not after one day. Sounds like she just wanted time to get away.'

'Are you on her side? I trusted her, like an idiot,' Alice said, and burst into tears again. 'I was so thirsty and so frightened. I thought I was going to die. I went to the bathroom on myself!' She shuddered. 'That poor man, she stabbed him to death . . . '

Sam wrestled with himself. What did he do now?

'Excuse me — can I use your phone? I need to call the police.'

'Yes, go ahead,' Alice said, twisting her hands.

'Walk around if you can a little,' Sam told her. 'Get the blood flowing.'

He pulled out his cell and dialled Craig's number. This time it was answered on the first ring. Craig would have caller ID.

'You asleep?'

'Not yet. But I'm guessing you didn't call for some male bonding,' Craig replied.

'Not exactly. I've tracked the girl a little further.'

'To where?'

'A house of a schoolfriend in Hong Kong. She

136

tricked the woman into getting rid of her housekeeper, then knocked her out and tied her in a closet. Hands and feet, gagged her too. That's where I found her.'

'Holy shit,' Craig said. There was grudging admiration in his voice. 'She alive?'

'She's fine. She's only been in there about twenty-four hours.'

'What's her name?'

'I need another deal, Craig. For the story.'

'You and your fucking deals. You want to get pulled in on interfering with a federal investigation?'

Sam felt anger surge in him. 'Fuck you, Craig. I'm tired of this. You guys are walking around with your dick in your hands photographing some bedlinen in Thailand and I'm one step behind this girl and giving you everything you've got. You can't compel me to do shit right now. You don't have a subpoena. By the time you get one she'll have completely disappeared. I'll lose the story and you'll lose the case.'

A sigh. 'Go on, man.'

'You deal with this yourselves first and wait twenty-four hours before you call the Chinese police.'

'What if this woman calls the police?'

'I told her I'm doing it. Maybe she will eventually. She's a Brit, though, more likely to trust the Fibbies than the locals. I want Lisa Costello to have a head start on the Chinese.'

'Because they'll send her back to Thailand?'

'If she dies right now, I got no story.'

'I'm sure that'd make Josh Steen's family real

137

sad, that you missed your story.'

'Craig — '

'OK. Deal. But we're going to pursue her with all the resources of the Bureau. They put me on the case, because I got contact with you. I'm flying tomorrow.'

'Well don't fly to Hong Kong.' He grinned at the pleasure of giving the FBI information. 'She left. She dumped the first passport she stole in her friend's house. That's Alice Watson, wife of a Cathay pilot. No doubt she took Alice's passport instead and flew on that. She left a note on her friend saying how she was sorry and she had to get away because she didn't kill the dude.'

'Yeah, sure. And she didn't assault this girl either.'

'Doesn't follow, Craig. Maybe she's telling the truth.'

'This is what you call open and shut, Sam. Don't fall for this girl. She's very bad news.' Craig was smiling a little, Sam could hear it in his voice. 'This is nice work, man. How the hell did you get it?'

'I just know she's not stupid. You guys work on the assumption that she is. She'd know she needed another passport.'

'She can't go round the world boosting passports for ever.'

'I'll put the victim on the phone, OK? She can tell you the rest. I'm going back to my hotel and you're going to call me with the destination that Lisa flew to, and you're also not going to tell anyone else till tomorrow morning so I can get my copy in.'

'Done. Email me a photo of the note.'

'OK. Hold the line.'

He walked back to Alice and told her the FBI wanted to speak to her.

'The FBI?' She blinked. 'They're Americans.'

'They're investigating the murder of Josh Steen. Helping the Thai police out. This ties in, because it's the same suspect.'

'I'll speak to them,' she said numbly. Then added, 'Thank you. Thank you so much.'

He handed her a card. 'If you want to talk. One more thing: can you tell me if she looked different to you?'

'Oh yes,' she said. 'She'd cut off her hair. And it was brown.'

Clever girl. It was stunning how many people didn't bother. Especially women, unwilling to sacrifice their beauty. Plenty of girls would risk jail just to keep looking hot.

'He's on the phone in the bedroom. Oh yeah, and I broke your window, to get in.'

'I'm glad you did, Mr — what was your name again?'

'Sam Murray. It's on the card. When you're through with the FBI, you should really get checked out at the hospital.'

'I will. Thank you again.' She walked off to pick up the phone, and he left the house. The woman was fine, and recovering fast. She would dine out on the story for years, he suspected.

He had to get back to the hotel. There was a cab passing, and he flagged it down, his phone in his hand, already composing an email. Even more sensational stuff; he could imagine how the paper would run this: *SHOCKING NEWS — LISA COSTELLO LEAVES FRIEND TO DIE — DENIES FIRST MURDER — ON THE RUN IN HONG KONG — THE SCANDALOUS PICTURES, THE SORDID DETAILS . . .*

It was the kind of copy that changed a magazine, even a publishing house. You're a sucker, he thought, and rang Rich Frank at home.

'What the fuck, Sam, I'm sitting down to dinner.'

'Tell your wife it's important.' He ran through the story, hearing his boss's breathing shorten. He could almost see him salivating over the details.

'Holy shit. That's fucking great.' Frank's voice turned anxious. 'But we don't go to press till next week.'

'Screw that, Rich, the whole world will have it by then. Put out a special edition.'

'Yeah! Great idea. I will. I'll put out a special edition.' Rich chuckled with sheer glee. 'They're gonna call me a legend after this.'

'Call you a legend? How about me?'

'You too. Plus you get a million bucks. That was the deal.'

'I'm changing the deal,' Sam said.

Silence. 'You can't.'

'Don't worry, I'm not holding you up for more cash. I just want it faster. I'm hot behind this girl, and I'm going to catch her, and I'm not taking a lousy twenty-five K a week for stories that are making the publishers tens of millions.

140

You raise the instalments. I want two fifty a story.'

'Two hundred and fifty thousand dollars a week? You want a thousand per cent raise?'

'What's this 'a week' shit? I'm not mopping floors in the office, Rich. It's a quarter mil a story, and with stories like these, it's a fucking bargain. You know it and I know it. Besides, I'll have caught her in another fortnight. She's not bad, but she's not smart enough to outrun me.'

'What if it takes longer?'

'When we reach a mil, you get the rest of the stories for free.'

'I only have your word on that, Sam.'

'That's right.'

He could hear Rich chewing his lip at the other end of the line, making little sucking sounds of annoyance. The money was the only thing he had over Sam's head. On the other hand, only Sam could deliver him the story.

'We both know you don't have a choice,' Sam said, just to stick the knife in a little more. 'Come on, let's get going with this.'

'It's evening over here.'

'You got twenty-four-hour banking. I'm on my way back to the hotel. When the money's in my account, email me. You'll get the story by return, exclusive interviews, pictures, the entire thing. It's my best yet, Rich.'

'OK. You extortionate fuck.'

'It's not extortion. It's a goddamn bargain. And you better speak nice to me, or I *will* raise the price. Later, Rich.'

He hung up, chuckling to himself.

★ ★ ★

Rome. It was perfection. An ancient city, full of ghosts. The tumbled ruins of the Forum, the markets and the temples; pillars and remnants thrust up everywhere through the ground, mixing with ornate Baroque architecture and crumbling Victorian palazzos, while the store-fronts that punctuated them were glossy black stone, chic and expensive. The sun warmed everything, three thousand years of history, a place where the slate was never wiped clean but one layer was simply piled on top of another. It was hot, and it was busy. The traffic surged around the city. Cars and *motorinos* were illegally parked everywhere. There was graffiti and abandoned dogs, a lot of money, a lot of dirt, so much beauty that it was hard to appreciate it all. Statues and paintings that would have formed a centrepiece to any other city in northern Europe, let alone the States, barely got a second glance here. Rome sucked Lisa in and did not care. She had the comforting sense that in this city, with its million stories, its world-conquering heroes, the place of Empire, the Church and luxurious dissipation, she was a footnote. Rome and the Romans did not play by modern rules. The pace of life was slow, sunk in sunlight and good red wine, and the grasp of law was pretty lax. It was a city for thieves, a city for fugitives. In that way, she fitted right in.

Lisa was here now, in Rome. The city would do, temporarily. But only a few days into her new role, girl on the run, she hated it already. She

142

wanted a way out. Somebody had killed her husband, and stolen her life. And she was not prepared to curl up and die.

Her hair was still wet, but she tied it back and slipped on her black coat and sunglasses. In a tourist city nobody would look twice at her, at least not in the sense of criminal apprehension. There was the more basic problem of the Italian male, though. It was hard right now to think of herself as a woman, a pretty girl. Her fear was so all-consuming. But those Roman boys just liked the figure, the curves, a pretty face. A girl on her own, she was subjected to catcalls and whistles. They brushed against her and felt up her ass. It was almost like being public property. And if the men hollered loudly enough, the women might pay attention too.

So Lisa dressed down. She let her hair stay damp, she eschewed make-up, she hid behind sunglasses and a coat. You could minimise it, at the very least. Combine that with a fast walk and fewer of them noticed her. There were easier, blonder targets, the students in their little khaki shorts and backpacks, the straps framing tits in push-up bras and tight T-shirts. She enjoyed the sense of being able to disappear.

But she could not disappear for ever. She had to get hold of Murray.

She walked up Via Panisperna towards Santa Maria Maggiore, past the drunks and the prostitutes and more young boys buzzing her with their *motorinos*. At the top of the hill she turned into a side street off the basilica. There she found it, a little shop selling phones. She

143

haggled with the owner in English and French; at least with the euro she couldn't be cheated. They had a pay-as-you-go phone, quite a nice one, with a screen and internet and a little camera. She bought it for seventy euros and loaded it up with a hundred; drug dealer special, she knew, and they didn't ask her any questions.

Outside, in the sun, she fired it up on the battery and got online. The connection was slow, but it was at least live. Sam Murray — *USA Weekly*. That part was easy. Lots of celebrity fluff. Some unflattering stuff about her, nicer about Josh. Not difficult to see why he'd been picked for the wedding.

There was an email button on the website, next to his name. She typed 'From Lisa Costello'. Then thought about it; he probably got a hundred of these. Whackos and fans and other attention junkies. She added, 'Likes to smoke and talk in the bushes.'

Then she wrote in the body of the email: 'Alice Kennedy. Rome. Mobile' and added her number.

After that she walked around the city a little, heading over to the Spanish Steps. If these mobiles could be traced, she didn't want to be anywhere near her digs. If she was right, Sam would call.

She had no idea what she'd say. But it felt like the only option she had left.

She bought a slice of pizza and an ice cream from a street vendor, and sat on the steps around the back of the church, away from the panhandlers and the tourists taking photos. The food was good. Too good. She was hungry, true, but she was also learning to appreciate things again, to taste them and enjoy them, instead of letting everything slide by. A personal chef could numb your senses. Now the most basic things tasted exceptional to her.

It was a balmy night in Italy and nobody bothered her. She was jet-lagged, and the evening felt like morning to her body. She was wide awake now, full of energy. When she was done with the food, she stood up and walked in a circle for a few blocks, keeping moving in case somebody noticed her. You could walk for ever in Rome; it was a friendly city for pedestrians.

She headed, vaguely, down the hill, but away from her hotel. When she was outside the church of the Gesu, closed now to gawkers and worshippers, the phone buzzed in her pocket.

It was him.

★ ★ ★

At the hotel Sam swam another forty laps, to give Rich time to get back to him. The motion calmed him, and he was feeling better anyway. It had been good work, seriously good, to put it together like that, crawl inside her head and find the girl she'd harmed.

He was feeling upbeat for the first time in maybe a year. Craig had offered him some grudging respect. And he'd shaken his boss down for money, real money this time. Maybe he could pull off a double here, catch this woman and get rich doing it. The FBI would love him and so would his bank manager.

He was going to do this, dammit. He was going to get that second chance. Stop living out of a suitcase, go someplace good, put roots down. Part of him wanted to apply to the FBI again, but he was too old. He'd need to do something utterly different. Maybe he'd go back to Texas and buy a ranch. Living in America, but far from the shallow crap of LA. He thought maybe he could make a go of that, outside in the sun. Grow crops, not cattle.

Plenty of other choices too.

He checked his office email. There were several messages. One word from Craig; it said 'Ciampiano'. So, she'd gone to Italy; clever little girl, they wouldn't extradite her to Thailand without a cast-iron guarantee that the death penalty was off the table. Rich was next. The money was there. He called his bank; it was, it was actually sitting there, total available cash, three hundred thirteen thousand dollars.

Sam felt rich. He'd have some champagne to celebrate. Maybe he'd go out and buy some condoms, get a hooker. He wanted a woman, bad. It had been weeks.

Then again, maybe not. This was the Far East; who knew where those girls had been, if they were trafficked or what. The high-class chicks he banged in LA were models and actresses and sometimes bored college girls with their own trust funds. It was easy to lose the guilt that way.

He needed to find Lisa Costello, so he could go home and get laid.

There was a message from his building super

146

about his spare set of keys, and bills emailed from his cell phone company and fitness club. And one more, *From Lisa Costello* . . .

Very funny, Rich — some joker. Unless the readers could access his email from the articles. Was that possible? He'd need to change the settings if it was.

He moved his thumb across to click it open anyway. Just in case.

The full heading said *From Lisa Costello. Likes to smoke and talk in the bushes.*

Holy fucking shit. It was her.

He was glad he hadn't got to the wine yet. He would have dropped it.

How the hell . . . ? Sam was hunting Lisa, not the other way round; how the hell did she find him? *USA Weekly* wasn't even published in Europe. She couldn't have found his byline on a newsstand. Did she have time to scour the internet looking for stories about herself?

He flashed on their short conversation. Had she thought he was a kindred spirit? That he would help her?

Alice Kennedy, it said. *Rome*. And a number.

Alice had called Lisa, told her about Sam? That was galactically improbable. His heart thumped, and adrenalin sweat broke out on his palms and forehead. No way was he giving Craig this little snippet, not yet. If they knew she had a cell phone, they would simply GPS it and pick her up.

Sam would find her first. And that day was closer than he'd ever thought possible. A quarter mil for the story — and half a mil for being the guy to close the case. There might be a book in it too after that, maybe even a movie. Perhaps he'd write the script.

Sam stared down at the email for a few moments. He wanted to get his thoughts together before he called. What was her deal, sending this? Why mention Alice and Rome?

Because she wants you to believe it's her, came back the answer, same as the email title; made you look, made you open it. She's sending a signal . . .

Which meant she somehow knew that Sam had found Alice. Otherwise it would be meaningless.

Sam forced himself to slow down. Reason his way through. How could Lisa possibly know he'd tracked Alice down?

There were only two answers. One, that Alice had called Lisa. He knew that would not be the case. Two, that Lisa had called Cathay Pacific to notify them that Alice was locked up in that closet, and they had told her.

He breathed out. Lisa's character was coming through to him, clearer now, like she was emerging out of a mist.

His pretty young quarry wasn't as evil as she seemed; she'd landed in Rome and called Cathay to tell them where Alice was, and they had responded that Sam Murray had found her already.

Lisa Costello had never intended to let her friend die. She just wanted to get the hell out of south-east Asia. And she'd needed to buy time, because . . . because the flight to safety, to

Europe, took so long.

All this indicated a quickness on her feet that was deeply impressive. She'd worked out that it wasn't enough to steal a second passport; she needed a day's delay, and so she'd gotten her old school pal to lose the maid for an extra day, before she attacked her and dumped her in that closet. Otherwise, armed police would have arrested her on the plane before she set foot on Italian soil and she would have been brought straight back to Kowloon.

She'd called Cathay Pacific. She'd told them about Alice Kennedy. If she had actually let her friend die, or even suffer for forty-eight hours rather than twenty-four, she could have got much further away. Hell, she could have killed Alice, and nobody except him would ever have put the pieces together.

Sam was irrationally pleased by this. Lisa was not the monster she appeared. He knew it. Had she killed Josh Steen? She said she hadn't. If she hadn't done this for Alice, hadn't called her husband's airline, Sam would have been convinced she was a murderer. But the sliver of doubt remained, lingering.

He rang the number she'd put in the email. His heart was thumping. Was hers? he wondered.

'Who is this?'

Christ. It *was* her, it was Lisa. Hearing her voice, live, was a shock.

'It's Sam Murray. Who else has the number?'

'Only you. I just bought this phone. I'm going to throw it away when we're done talking.'

Like he thought, not stupid.

149

'I just got your email. Nobody's seen it but me.'

'You found Alice? She's OK?'

'She's not your biggest fan, Lisa.'

'I called her husband's airline and they told me.' Right again. He congratulated himself on that deduction. 'I had to do it,' she said, and he thought he heard the start of tears. It was a very clear line, like she was standing in the next room. Technology was incredible. 'They could have killed me if I'd stayed, shipped me back to Thailand and put me in a show trial.'

'I found your note. You say you didn't do it.'

'I did not kill Josh.'

He took a breath. 'Are you sure about that? You were drunk and looking to get drunker.'

She breathed in sharply. She was embarrassed by that.

'Maybe you killed him and you can't remember; did you consider that possibility?'

'What else do you think I've thought of, spending hours in the air? Lots of time to think, Sam Murray. I didn't kill him because I couldn't have killed him.'

He didn't say anything. Often the best thing was to let them talk, and then they hanged themselves. But Lisa was too smart for that trick. She waited for him to speak.

'Why did you call me?'

'Cathay said a journalist had contacted them, I said who was she, and they said a man, Sam Murray. And then I remembered you.'

A small jolt of pleasure when she said those words. He had found Lisa to be an exceptionally attractive woman.

'You called me because of one conversation?'

'I called you, Mr Murray, because you found Alice. That meant a lot of things, you get it? You tracked me to Hong Kong, meaning you found what passport I took, and you figured out I needed another, and that there was only one contact I could get it from. You're a regular Sherlock Holmes.'

He was surprised. He wanted to laugh. Lisa was his mirror, right now, sitting there working out what he'd done, and what that signified — the same techniques he was applying to her. They were watching each other in this dance of hunter and hunted, and for a second it was hard to tell who was who.

'Doesn't that scare you?'

She laughed a little, bitterly.

'I'm past scared. I'm past exhausted. I'm stuck in Europe with my money running out and no future and I didn't kill Josh. And I think maybe you can help me. If you're the only one clever enough to find me this far, maybe I can tell you things about Josh, and you can work out who killed him and why they framed me.'

'Did he have lots of enemies?'

'Hundreds, I'm sure. I don't even know most of them.' She paused. 'Have you been talking to the police?'

He wouldn't say FBI; that would spook her.

'Yes.' Who knew what she knew? It was better not to lie.

'I want you to stop.'

'I can't do that. It would make me a suspect too. Interfering in a police investigation.'

151

'You're a journalist. You want the story. And I am the story.' Another deep breath. 'I'll meet you in St Peter's Square, tomorrow, five o'clock in the evening. You promise me that for one meeting you won't bring police. I want your word of honour.'

His word of honour! How English, how old-fashioned. Yet Sam couldn't help it; he was charmed by her, charmed by the concept, flattered that she thought he had honour and would be bound by it.

'Very well. Only one meeting. Why St Peter's?'

He thought he knew the answer, but he wanted to hear her say it, to confirm his opinion of her yet again.

'Because it's Vatican City, not Italy, so if you're a lying scumbag and you do bring the police, they won't be able to arrest me.'

Sam lay back on the bed and smiled at the ceiling. Lisa didn't disappoint. Whatever else happened, she had guts. And brains.

'You're a gambler,' he said. 'I understand that pretty well. I'll be there.'

She hung up.

He dressed quickly, packing his stuff into the small overnight case he'd bought on the streets. He filled out an express check-out card, and was in a car and headed for the airport within ten minutes. During the ride, he cracked the window, and let the hot, muggy air of Hong Kong brush over his face, breathing in the fetid scent of the city that lay underneath everything else, all the neon and the skyscrapers and the noise.

152

All his senses felt charged. Lisa had done that to him. He was alive for the first time in a decade. It was utterly exhilarating, and for tonight, he loved his life.

He couldn't believe how much he was looking forward to seeing this girl. If he was honest, the desire was so fierce, it was almost longing. Sure, it was sexually charged; when wasn't it? If a man met a woman there was always that. But he wasn't some idiot, to be led around by his groin. She'd killed Josh Steen, almost certainly — almost — and he would call the FBI and they'd put her in jail. She'd be alive and well treated, back in Europe. And twenty or thirty years, well. She deserved it for killing that poor bastard. None of his money did a damn thing for him in the end.

But if he was going to hunt her down and put her away, be the hero, get the cash — he wasn't going to do that *this* time. He was going to keep his word, and talk to her once, just once, without police. It was a pass, a free ride. He could be with her, just be with her. Like before. And he was looking forward to it out of all proportion.

At the airport, he checked in with Alitalia and bought a first-class ticket. Hey, it was Rich Frank's money, and he deserved it. For one thing, first class had flat sleeper beds. It would be smart to rest before he had to deal with Lisa Costello.

The cops, the press, Josh Steen and all his friends had underestimated this woman. Sam Murray was damn sure he wasn't going to do the same.

5

The sun was sinking now, behind the dome of St Peter's, the sky over Michelangelo's supreme work streaked with red and gold. Lisa wanted to give Murray enough time to get here, but there was another reason: in the evening, the shadows were long, the pillars set around the basilica casting their fingers across the square; easier to dart in and out, easier to hide.

She didn't know what she was feeling. It had been a weird day. Ever since she'd spoken to him yesterday she had been on edge. She didn't want to be recognised, so she had walked around the city, in the cool of the early evening, her shades on her face, amongst a million other Romans and tourists. Some boys whistled, and she nearly jumped out of her skin, but they were just checking her out, just young kids leering at a girl. It was hard to see herself that way, a girl, an ordinary female. It was good though, and once she'd settled down again, it was wonderful to think that maybe she could pass, be just another woman.

The streets started to empty around half eleven, and she walked back to her cheap digs and locked herself in for the night, hearing other kids leave for the clubs and a drunk vomiting in the bathroom across the hall. All that was how it was in a budget place, and Lisa relished it. She stayed awake until one, then slipped into a fitful slumber. But nobody knocked on the door, and she was safe for now at least.

She woke late, around quarter to ten, showered and left the hostel. It was baking hot outside. She walked around the city until her feet started to ache. Motion seemed safer. When she got tired, she slipped into a church. There were hundreds of them in this city, and most had a few worshippers in the pews, kneeling with their beads, or staring into space. That was good; she could sit quietly, in the darkness, staring at the rich Catholic decorations, and nobody thought to look her way. The flickering votive candles gave off a soft, welcoming light. It was womb-like, protective; she had that ancient sense of sanctuary.

The day ticked by, agonisingly slowly. She wanted Sam Murray to come so desperately, each heartbeat ticking away another second that he might be in the air. There had to be a way out of this nightmare. She tried praying herself once or twice, but those muscles were rusty, and she felt like a fraud. She was dry, like a Californian creek in summer. She could think of nothing else but escape. When the churches started to oppress her, she left for more walking, a cheap gelato from a stand, a panini. It would be good to sit in a trattoria like a human being, but Lisa didn't dare stay still, risk some American tourist recognising her. She had to move until she could not walk and then sit until she could not bear it. It was like a prison. It *was* a prison, only under the good blue sky and the hot sun.

And she wanted out.

At three, she headed to the Vatican. That was better, because she was walking somewhere, not strolling aimlessly. She walked over the Bridge of Sighs and past Castle Gandolofo, and the side streets began to fill with tourists and pilgrims. You had to queue for an hour these days and go through metal detectors, and Lisa kept her head down, bowed as though she were in prayer. It was gone four when she was permitted to walk through the great open doors of the cathedral, and in the vastness of St Peter's she took her time; when she emerged at last, the bright sun had sunk below the horizon, the shadows were safely long, and it was almost time.

She could never remember being this nervous.

★ ★ ★

It was late when she saw him. Twenty past five, and with every minute that ticked by on the clock, Lisa was starting to sweat. His plane was delayed. Or cancelled. Or he hadn't come, or come with the police . . .

She moved in and out of the shade of the pillars, her fingers twisting each other, trying not to look as anxious as she felt. And suddenly, at last, she saw him.

He was running, and looked panicked. There was nobody with him. She checked that carefully. He raced over the yellow lines painted on the cobbles that separated Vatican City from Italy, without looking back or checking with some tail. He was looking for her, anxious that she might have left. She could see his hand over his eyes, shading his face as he scanned the crowd. He walked past the edge of the queue for the basilica, moving around the centre of the square.

And then he saw her.

He stopped dead, taken aback. Lisa's breath stuck in her throat. And then he walked deliberately over to her. It was the first time she'd been confronted since Josh had been killed. A wash of fear and hope together ripped through her body, so strong she thought she might faint. She put out one hand, and steadied herself against the stone of the vast grey pillar. *Try and keep it together.*

Sam reached her and stood in front of her. He was tanned, with brown eyes and disturbingly thick black lashes. Very muscular under that shirt. He had flecks of grey in his dark hair, a strong jaw, and five o'clock shadow that said he hadn't stopped to shave after climbing off the plane.

Lisa became stupidly aware that she was bare-faced. Keeping herself showered and with washed hair had been enough of a challenge. For days she hadn't bothered with make-up of any kind.

Josh had liked her perfectly groomed and professionally made up as soon as she emerged from the shower after her morning workout. And now here she was, her hair cut short, her skin wearing nothing but sunshine. And Sam Murray was looking her up and down with a gaze that said he'd known hundreds of women. Stupidly, she wished for some lipstick, some eyeliner.

Anything to make herself look presentable.

Don't be a fool, Lisa warned herself. He's not here on a white charger. He's here to put you in jail. For the rest of your life.

'Did you come alone?'

He nodded. 'You can see I did.'

She glanced round the edge of the square. 'You might have brought somebody. They could be hiding.'

'Yeah, but you know I didn't,' Murray said, looking straight at her.

Lisa realised she did know it. Her shoulders relaxed. 'OK.'

'Let's go somewhere. We can talk. Are you hungry?'

'I don't want to sit in a restaurant,' she said. 'Too many Americans in this city.'

His dark eyes swept over her. 'You're careful. I get that. But I think it's OK. You look very different already.'

Her hand crept to her head; a pang of loss for her long golden hair hit her, and then she was embarrassed for being so stupid and trivial.

'You look fine,' Sam said.

Lisa blushed.

He looked around, checking the square.

'Nobody's watching. I know a few places in Rome. Out of the way, where they serve the locals and the menus are in Italian. It must be some time since you've sat down and had a meal.'

'OK,' she said, suddenly gripped with longing. To sit and talk like a human being, to be normal, if only for half an hour. 'If you're sure.'

158

'Everything's a risk, as I'm sure you've learned. Follow me.' He led her away from the safety of the pillars and the shadow of the cathedral, out to the taxi rank, where he shoved her inside a waiting car. His Italian was quite good, and the driver ploughed away without speaking.

Lisa stared out of the window as the baroque city slipped past her. It was no good starting a conversation with somebody else there to listen. Small talk was pointless. She smiled a little; she had to, because her life had become so ridiculous.

It was weird to have him sitting next to her. Days of running from people had made her sensitive to company. Murray's body was close to hers on the small back seat, and she felt his maleness as though his heartbeat was pulsing in her own veins. The ochre walls of the palazzi slipped past them, and they drove across bridges lined with statues of angels. Rome crowded in from all sides, the ancient stones almost leaning in to shelter them.

He directed the driver and they moved out of the *centro storico*, past the ancient city and into Trastevere. The cab pulled up in a crowded street and Sam helped her out and paid the driver. Sunset was sinking over the roofs, and warm, limpid light pooled around them, as though the city itself were trying to relax them.

'Down here,' he said. He led her through a little alleyway and around a corner. Washing was hung out to dry high above them, in the narrow gap between the buildings. The modern city was full of superstition and old-fashioned poverty; Lisa had a sense of being lost as soon as she stepped out of the light.

There was a restaurant halfway down the street, not like the tourist eateries with their outside space marked by gleaming metal chairs and topiary in pots. It was small, with an open door and a hubbub of noise. Sam took her hand, as though they were lovers, and pulled her through the door. Lisa ducked her head, and he was talking in Italian, and before she knew it he had pushed her to the back of the crowded bar and into a tiny booth with polished wooden benches, her back to the street, facing him. It was wonderfully gloomy, a bit like all those churches, and there was already a half-litre of red wine in a slightly chipped carafe on the table.

He reached over and poured her a glass.

'Like it?'

'It's perfect,' Lisa said. Nobody could see her at this angle, and nobody was looking. There was loud conversation all around them and incredibly delicious scents from the food. Theirs were the only English voices in the place. 'What's on the menu?'

'They don't do menus. Volume is the key to a place like this. You got two pasta dishes, a fish and a meat, and pastries if you want *dolce*. They cook cheaply and get hungry workers in and out.' Sam took a look at the chalkboard in front of them. 'There aren't too many of these places left in Rome, but this is one of the best. Today you can choose pasta primavera or pappardelle al lepre, and the *secondi* is lamb stew or monkfish.

160

I'd go for the pappardelle.'

'I don't speak Italian too well . . . '

'Pasta ribbons with a hare sauce. It'll be wonderful.'

She was salivating. 'Yes please.'

Sam fired off an order and handed over a twenty-euro note. 'That'll cover us both for wine, water and food. And you won't eat better in the city.'

Within seconds a brawny waiter, his apron splashed with sauce, had set down two enormous bowls in front of them. He said something to Sam she didn't catch, and then vanished.

'You also don't wait for service. They want you to eat well, drink a little and get the hell out.'

For the first time in days, Lisa laughed. 'Suits me.'

He smiled back at her. 'You look good when you do that.'

Lisa put her fork in the pasta and took a mouthful. It was sensational. Her body was craving the protein of the meat. Sitting down with someone else, sipping wine; everything was fantastic. The small pleasures were magnified almost unbearably.

'What do you think?' He grinned at her, comfortable. It was almost like they were back in Thailand, before she got drunk, before the worst happened. 'Good?'

She ate for a little while, holding up one hand. You couldn't talk while you were spooning buttery, rich pasta into your mouth. Finally, gratefully, she took a big slug of wine — it was rough, new wine, but really good, strong enough to cope with the hare — and looked him straight in the face.

'Better than good. Sensational.'

'I'm glad.'

'But you didn't come here to buy me a meal.'

A shadow crossed his face, as though she'd spoiled something, popped a bubble for him. 'True. For today, I came here to talk.'

'So talk.'

'Can I tape you?' He reached into his pocket, drew out a dictaphone. Lisa pulled back.

'No way.'

'Why?'

'I don't know. Voice-print analysis. The police would have me on file. No. I don't trust them, I don't trust anybody.'

'You trusted me enough to come here with me.'

Lisa pushed the bowl of pasta away from her. 'And I'll run straight out of here if you don't let it go. I don't need that, Mr Murray. We talk, only talk, or I run. I'm getting good at running. Maybe I'll scream rape. I guarantee I'll get away from you.'

He held up both hands. 'OK, Lisa. No tape.' He reached for the Dictaphone, but her hand closed over it. Sam lifted a brow.

'I'll take that. In case you switch it on in your pocket or something.' She smiled at his reaction. 'See? You've obviously done it before.'

'I have. But I will keep my word to you, if I give it.'

She noted the 'if'.

'I didn't kill Josh, Sam. I was framed — I had

162

to have been framed. It's clever and I don't know how they did it and I don't know why. But I'm not going to jail for the rest of my life for a murder that had nothing to do with me.' She looked around. 'Christ. I wish I had a cigarette.'

'Have wine instead.' He poured her a little more. 'It's OK, there's not enough here to get drunk.'

'Do you believe me?' she asked, and his answer mattered, very much. If he lied now, she would walk right out of this restaurant. She would never contact him again. She'd run right out of Italy and take her chances in Switzerland.

'No,' Sam said slowly. He held her gaze. 'But I don't disbelieve you. I figure maybe you don't know what happened yourself. You think you're innocent, but you have powerful reasons for wanting to think that. And there's a lot of evidence.' He shrugged, drank some of his own wine. 'Maybe one or two things don't add up, all the same. I'm hoping I can figure them out by talking them through with you.'

Lisa stared at him. He wasn't lying, then. That was something.

'Tell me exactly what's in it for you.'

'By finding you and talking to you, I file a story with our magazine. I get a quarter of a million dollars per story. Once I capture you, and turn you in . . . it's a million!' He put a hand on her arm, steadying her as she prepared to leap from the table. 'Not now, Lisa, not today; today I'm not hunting, I'm keeping a promise. But if you talk and you leave, and I leave, then tomorrow is another matter. That

163

was the deal. Am I right?'

Sam Murray could get a million dollars for locking her away. She must be mad, she must be fucking insane. But she found herself saying, 'Yes. Right.'

'So tell me, Lisa. Tell me why you didn't do it. You were pretty drunk.'

'I was.'

He leaned back against the glossy wood of his bench, and as he relaxed, the knot of tension in her stomach started to unravel. She did desperately want to talk. As much to herself as to him.

'Why were you getting drunk? It was your wedding day. You were angry . . . '

'I'd just seen Josh making out with Melissa Olivera. He actually screwed her.'

Sam nodded. He had heard those rumours.

'It wasn't like he was discreet about it. His damn family were laughing at me. His friends. I was supposed to be grateful I'd finally landed him, just take it and shut up.'

'And you were angry? That wouldn't be a good start point for the defence.'

She ate some more pasta. How could she explain it so it sounded logical? But Sam Murray was listening to her. His eyes were on her, and he was paying close attention.

'I wanted to divorce him. Not kill him.'

'He was stabbed many times, so this wasn't a logical thing. What if you were in a jealous rage?' She looked at him, and Sam inclined his head. 'OK, a humiliated rage? What if you snapped, and you were so drunk you didn't remember?

164

Did you black out?'

'Yes. I woke up in bed with the worst hangover I've ever had, Josh dead beside me, and the dagger in my hand.'

'And remembered nothing?'

'The last thing I remember was fighting with Josh, then we stormed upstairs and I lay on the bed. That's it.'

'OK.'

'Did you see Josh, Mr Murray?'

Sam nodded. 'I came back a little while later to watch you fight. Don't look at me like that, Lisa, I'm a journalist, it's my job. And call me Sam. Really.'

'How drunk was he?'

Sam considered it. 'Not very. Angry with you for making a scene, but I wouldn't think he'd had more than two or three drinks.'

'So riddle me this,' she said coolly. 'How did a drunk bride who weighed about half of what he did, a fall-down-drunk girl, stab multiple times a healthy, strong man who was not incapacitated? There wasn't a bruise on me, not anywhere. I checked that evening in a hostel in Hong Kong.'

'Bruises might have faded by now.'

'Take my word for it, just for the sake of the argument. How would that happen?' Lisa took a sip from the tumbler of the tap water in front of her. She did not want to have too much wine; the telling of this story was putting her in a teetotal mood.

'Forget that for now,' Murray said. 'What else made you think you were innocent?'

'The blackout. At first I just accepted it. But

165

as the day wore on I wondered why the hangover was that bad. I mean, I was drunk, but I've had more many times and nothing worse to show for it than a headache. Not like that day. Total memory loss, pounding head, couldn't keep anything down. I think they drugged me. I don't think I could have killed a cockroach, let alone a grown man.'

'So you could argue all this in court.'

'Right. And I'd really get a fair trial. I went on the run and I tied up Alice Kennedy in a cupboard.' Lisa's eyes teared up.

'Tell me about that.'

'I already did. I needed a passport and I had to make sure she didn't raise the alarm. I hated doing it to her. I was going to call when I landed — I did call.'

'It'll look very bad for you in a trial. She was frightened and hurt, and she wet herself.'

'Don't,' Lisa said. A tear trickled down her cheek. 'It was that or die. Stay in Hong Kong, get caught, get shipped back to Thailand. What would you have done, Sam? Alice will survive. I wouldn't have.'

'Did you think of trying to buy a passport on the black market?'

She shook her head. 'Look, when you start running for your life, you see things very clearly. I knew I had limited time. The longer I was in Hong Kong, the more likely I was to be caught and killed. Get out fast, or get caught. And die.' She gulped more water. 'You think I was wrong?'

'I think you were exactly right.' Sam's expression was strange, and she twisted a little

166

on her seat, under his gaze. 'I think I would have done the same. I also think you truly believe you didn't kill him.'

'Josh was strong. He wouldn't have let me do it to him without fighting back.'

'Then what do you think happened?' Sam Murray asked her.

It was the moment she'd been waiting for; she understood in a flash of insight.

'That's your job,' she said, leaning forward, into his space.

'My job?'

'Yes. It's your story, Sam. That's what you're getting paid for. I called you because you found out about Janet Parks's passport, you figured out my connection to Alice, you understood where I'd go and what I'd do. So if you can do all that while the police are still standing around, then you can work out why he was killed and why they want me dead.' She looked him straight in the eye. 'You can save me. You're the only one who knows I'm not that chick they write about. That girl in the magazines, Lisa Costello the bitch. She's made up. She's fiction. Perhaps you wrote some of that fiction.'

She could see in his face that he had.

'I'm not a detective.'

'You're here, Sam. Where are the police?'

He looked away from her, and she saw a shadow pass over his face. He was wrestling with himself.

'You're worried about the million. Maybe they won't pay it to you if you help me.'

'Try maybe I'll go to jail.' He looked back at

167

her, his dark eyes unreadable. 'I hardly know you, Lisa. You can't even say for sure you're innocent. You don't remember. So why should I take that risk? Why should I give everything up?'

She leaned back and took one last sip of her wine. She'd got him; somehow she knew she had got him.

'Because it's the right thing to do,' she said. 'Because it's an adventure.' She smiled, just a little, and watched the response in Sam's eyes. 'And because you want to.'

He didn't reply. She stood up, and he made no attempt to join her.

'I'll email you with another cell number soon,' she said. 'If you're ready to help, let me know. If not, you won't see me again. Goodbye, Sam Murray.'

And before he could answer, she'd turned on her heel and walked out.

★ ★ ★

My God, Sam thought. He flung money on the table and shoved his way out of the restaurant. She'd gone, though, of course. He would not find her again this evening.

There was a cab for hire at the end of the alley, but he ignored it. It was a balmy night in Rome, good for walking, and he needed to clear his head. He tried talking to himself — *you must be nuts, Sam Murray, you're actually going to blow a new life, a million dollars* — but none of it did him any good. He had to help her. He didn't have a choice.

168

Lisa Costello had him, like a trout on a line. He knew it. So did she. He walked through the city, breathing in the beauty of the old buildings. The air was gritty with traffic fumes and the smell from restaurants, the buzz of the tourists and the young Romani. If he had a million dollars, he could live here full time. Buy a nice apartment with a view of the Forum or the Vatican. He would have total freedom, a new life. And all he had to do was catch an international fugitive. He could rationalise it — he wouldn't be putting the girl in jail; that wouldn't be his fault. It would be a trial, a jury of her peers. Some of the best celebrity lawyers in America would fly to Europe and represent her pro bono, just for the publicity. So she'd get her day in court, get to say everything she'd just told him.

Two problems. And as he looked around the city in the early twilight, he knew there was no way he was going to solve them. One, she would never get a fair trial. They would try the girl in his magazine, the girl who didn't exist, the gold-digging bitch Americans loved to hate. That was who a lawyer would paint and that was who a jury would be primed to see. Lisa Costello would go down to some hole for the rest of her life. And two, she didn't do it.

God damn it to hell. He wished he'd never gotten that email from her. He wished he'd never met up with her. Now he was stuck. The money would dry up, without stories from the trail, and Craig would be after his ass, would slap him with a warrant and a charge. And he probably couldn't do anything to help her anyway. She'd run from the scene and assaulted her friend, viciously enough.

This was really going to suck.

And yet he was going to do it anyway.

Her email came in around fifty minutes later. No preamble this time, just a number. He dialled it immediately, and she answered on the first ring.

'OK,' he said.

She drew her breath in sharply.

'I'm giving up things to do this. You understand.'

'Yes. I can't thank you enough . . . '

He brushed that aside. He didn't want tears, or professions of gratitude. He just wanted to get it solved. 'We do this my way, Lisa. You tell me anything I ask. If you hold anything back, I'm out of here. If you argue with me or fight me, I'm out of here. And then I start after you again. Understand?'

'Yes. Perfectly.'

'Where are you?'

'By the Colosseum,' she said.

'Wait there. I'm going to hire a car. It may take me an hour or so. Do you have stuff? Clothes, money?'

'A little of both.'

'Then go get them. I'll call again when I'm ready to pick you up.'

He took a cab to a rental place just outside the city walls and paid for a nondescript Fiat on the company account. Right now, everything was kosher, it was all in his own name, paid for by the magazine; there was no need to scrimp or hide. He had a bad feeling, though, that he couldn't shake. Like maybe this was not going to last very long. Maybe he'd be on the run soon enough, interfering with a witness, abetting after the fact. That wasn't a capital crime, so he could be extradited, and what fun some piss-ant district attorney would have slamming Lisa Costello's accomplice in jail for twenty-five years. Christ, he'd rather kill himself.

Maybe there was another way out. Maybe he could just help her to get a new identity, then she could be free. Publish some faked stories about the hunt, get the FBI to forget the case . . .

But it wouldn't fly. She was too high-profile. Josh Steen's murder had ensured that.

Whatever, he would think about that later. He called her cell again, and she told him where to pick her up, on a little street away from the Colosseum, Via Panisperna. She was waiting for him with a little rucksack like a tourist. He put it in the back, with his own small case, and they drove off, towards the ring road out of town.

'I don't know what to say to you.'

'Good. I hate driving in Europe. Don't say anything.'

She was very beautiful, he thought, even without her long hair, even bottle-tanned and brunette. Not like a model; he'd written enough stories about how she was no model. But the intelligence, the bravery, the sheer desperate courage of her, all wrapped up in that slim frame; she was stunning, and he tried to concentrate on the road.

What would the public think? For a second he

171

let himself consider her objectively. Yes, she was not plastic, not a TV presenter with smooth features and glossy hair. But the beauty she possessed was real, earthy. She had the kind of looks that stirred men, deep in their groins, not the bland beauty that sold fashion magazines. Her thick, full lips, sparkling eyes, rounded apple cheeks, the narrow waist and flaring hips; she was curves, she was lush. That kind of flesh didn't photograph well. But male eyes peeled the clothes from it. Lisa Costello was made for the bedroom, not the catwalk . . .

No way, Sam, no way. If he was going to solve this, he couldn't think with his dick. That was the surest way to blow everything. Start fucking the suspect. That was if she wanted to, and he doubted she would. He didn't have money like Josh Steen. Steen would have laughed at a million dollars, but Sam didn't even have that. He had three hundred thousand dollars and an overpriced apartment in the Hollywood Hills that had lost half its value but kept up its taxes.

'So where are we going?' Lisa asked. She turned her head away from him, and it was a blessing not to feel those dark eyes on his skin.

'Out of Rome. They know you're here.'

'Who's they?'

'I told the FBI, and Alice Kennedy and Cathay will have informed the police. Air France will have handed the manifest to Interpol. They'll be looking for you, looking hard.'

She swallowed. 'I felt safe in Rome.'

'You were kind of safe, for a little while. The longer you stay in one place, the less the returns.

172

People start looking for you. You were right about that, to leave Hong Kong.'

'So I'm always on the run?'

'Unless we can figure out a murderer. Or you want to turn yourself in.'

'That would be no,' she said, and tilted her chin up bravely. 'Running sucks, but prison . . . forget it.'

'You wouldn't get out of prison,' he said, turning the wheel. Now they were heading north on the *autostrada*, the A24 to Florence, away from the city. 'You're famous, and that means that when you come up for parole, politicians get votes by talking tough and throwing away your key. You'd be an old woman.'

'I'm not doing it. I'll run, I'll steal. People do that,' Lisa said, but her voice was trembling. 'People go on the lam and they disappear and they don't get caught.'

'Not usually such famous ones.'

'First time for everything,' she said, defiant.

Sam liked her. A lot.

'So if not Rome, where?' she asked.

'Eventually, Liechtenstein.'

She turned her dark head back to look at him. 'Liechtenstein? Why?'

'I have a feeling we may need secure banking. Numbered accounts. I know a guy there. And it has a culture of secrecy, loves to keep people out. Tiny state, relies on bank money from a lot of shady people, so they don't love the police.'

'I guess that makes sense. It's a long drive for you.'

'The safest place you can be right now is in a

173

car, on the road. Nobody's going to see you, you don't interact with anyone. Toll-booth guards see thousands of faces every day; for them it all goes by in a blur. They're probably the least observant people you can find.'

'You have this all figured out. Have you done it before?'

He shook his head. 'I've tracked people. And part of that is to work out how they're thinking, what they'll do.'

'Like me.'

'Just like you.'

They were well clear of the city now, driving up the long, wide road that would take them to Florence and the north. The grey asphalt was bleak under the hot sun. He was glad of the air-conditioning.

'We'll stop on the way for lunch and so forth. And I can book us into a motel. Has to be cheap, though, the kind of place that doesn't need passports. I'm going to pretend you're a hooker, so act like it.'

Lisa laughed, then saw his face. 'You're not kidding.'

'No. They need a believable reason that you don't carry ID. But it won't be for hours yet.'

'OK,' she said. 'OK.'

'We got nothing else to do,' Sam said. 'Why don't you tell me about Josh?'

'What do you want to know?'

'Everything. Don't worry if you think I've heard it before. The story that's out there probably isn't your story. How you met, what made him pick up on you. Tell me what he was like. Was he perverted in bed?'

Her face froze. Her head whipped around, and she stared at him.

'Don't give me that, Lisa. What did I tell you? We do this my way or not at all. A guy was murdered. The two usual explanations are money and sex.'

'He was normal.' She was blushing, dammit. How long had it been since he'd seen a girl blush? 'He was fine.'

'Then what? You weren't a likely couple. I want to know about the romance, when it got serious. People who didn't like it, I mean other than the press. I know his family hated you.'

'They wanted the money. I think they'd have hated any wife.'

'Maybe. And anything you knew about his business. Partners, investors.'

She shrugged. 'I wasn't interested in Hollywood. That's one of the things he liked about me, that I didn't try to get cast in his movie in some bit part, or get my name put on a film as a producer. He talked about it, but that stuff washed over me.'

'You're gonna have to try to remember. Have to.'

'OK.'

Night was deepening now. The headlights of the cars flashed past them. He was driving, and nobody knew where they were, and he had a little time.

'Tell me everything,' he said. 'Start.'

6

Lisa was twenty-two when she arrived in America, fresh off the plane with a bit of money from her mother, no degree and no papers. Going to the States was the best thing she'd ever done, she confided to Sam. She'd dreamed about it for years, the sunshine, the fast cars, the tanned men and glossy American girls with artificially white teeth. It seemed so much better than her small, dreary town in Kent. She had no brothers and sisters, and she was a bookworm who liked to read, a bit of a loner. Her favourite stories took her out of her unhappy teen years. They had big gold or silver letters on the covers, and they were set in New York or LA, sometimes Chicago. She chose LA because it was always sunny there, whereas the New York winters were brutal.

She picked up a paper at a bookstore on Sunset Boulevard and found an apartment right away. It was off the Strip, cramped but clean, with a young couple trying to make ends meet by letting out a room. She gave them two months in advance and they never asked to see her papers. She tried to make herself a great tenant by being invisible; never playing music, staying in her room, and being extra quiet if she had to come in late at night. That worked well enough.

She had a great time the first month. She

spent some of her savings on a beat-up car she found on the internet, no expensive rental agreements or trouble with her passport, and drove everywhere, to the beach, to the canyons, to rock gigs and comedy stand-up nights in the cheapest bars she could find. There were new kids to hang out with almost nightly. Plenty of English twenty-somethings, illegals like her, most of them trying to get an acting gig. She tried too for a bit, but half-heartedly. She never wanted to be an actor. Lisa treated LA like an alternative university; she planned to have fun for a year or so, work a cheap job, figure out what she wanted to do in life.

The diner was great. They were advertising for staff, word of mouth, meaning it was illegal, but you kept your tips, ate for free, and there was some money in pocket. Lisa was a catch for them because she wasn't Mexican, and the patrons just loved that cute little English accent. She was also experienced, having served food in a pub back home one summer. She worked hard, got there early, never took time off to drink or do blow, and the customers liked her and tipped her pretty well. The owner didn't do promotions as such, but he palmed her a few extra bills and assigned her to the better tables. Hollywood types sometimes came in when they were craving a greasy burger and fries or wanted to get away from the fancy restaurants their colleagues went to, where they might be overheard. Lisa served them cheerfully. After a couple more months, she was making very nice money. Men asked her on dates; she went, but none of them didn't work out. Sam asked why, and Lisa shrugged and said she was choosy.

That long summer and fall had been one of the best of her life. She partied, she ran on the beach, she hung out with friends, kissed a few boys. It was freedom, it was intoxicating. The sun shone all the time, and after wet, cold England, she felt as though she were wrapped in a cashmere blanket all the time, like the earth itself was looking after her.

She thought about a career. Definitely not Hollywood; the auditions she'd been on convinced her she had no future. She wasn't an actress and she also wasn't beautiful enough . . .

When she got to that point, Sam stopped her.

'Not beautiful enough?'

'Right. Look at me.'

He took his eyes off the road, and did look at her. That heart-shaped face and slim body, the dark hair, the sparkling eyes. She was so vital, pretty, but more than that; clever and brave. He wanted to kiss her, badly.

'You're stunning,' he said. 'I can't believe you don't know that.'

She snorted. 'Don't give me that. Your magazine ran those photo spreads like everyone else. Hollywood's looking for sensational and there are thousands of sensational chicks out there; models with perfect faces, huge boobs and tiny waists, long blond hair, the whole thing. Those that haven't got it can buy it, if they've got the cash. I couldn't compete. Didn't want to try.'

'You didn't have the look they wanted; doesn't mean you weren't beautiful, Lisa.'

'Sam. I've had half the tabloids in America pointing out my flaws for about three years now. So don't try to spin me a line.'

He said nothing further. What would be the point? He waited for her to go on.

Maybe she'd be a writer. Not screenplays; she wasn't interested enough in films. Novels. Lisa smiled bitterly. She'd enjoyed detective stories best, gritty thrillers about American cops. Now she was living one. There were other things she could do. Flowers.

'Flowers?' Sam asked. He was gripped by her story. The woman never stopped surprising him.

'I love flowers. They're a splash of beauty in a bad world, especially if you live in a city. I worked in our local flower shop when I was sixteen and I've never forgotten it. The florist business is badly run, you know that?'

'I know nothing about being a florist.'

'You can do two things with flowers. Wide delivery, like Interflora, or designer ribbons and twigs and stuff. There's a gap in the market for imaginative flowers done cheap. I thought maybe I could fill it. In LA they send a lot of flowers. All those prima donnas, and only half of them are women.'

'I like it,' Sam said. She was impressive, this girl. Not dreaming of becoming an identikit starlet like the rest of them. Concentrate on the road, he told himself.

'Anyway, that's what I was moving towards. I started taking on night work at Madame Rose; do you know it?'

'The florist on Third Street?'

'Yeah, that one. Bunching and tying. I wanted them to give me a real job. Flowers are another area with lots of illegals. Anyway, I wasn't too worried. I was twenty-three and I figured I'd fall in love with somebody and get married, and that would take care of the immigration problem. He'd come with a green card; I'd be safe.'

'OK.' This didn't sound too bad, Sam reflected. Her life so far was different from most of the girls. No drugs, no flirting with hooking, no 'parties' where the chicks removed their tops on a mogul's yacht and got slipped a few hundred. She was normal; only in LA, that *wasn't* normal. Ambitious, grounded, secure in herself.

Maybe Josh Steen wasn't the best thing to happen to her. Maybe he was the worst.

'Go on.'

The owner began to give her work in the front of the store, but Lisa kept up the waitressing. More tips, paid better. And one day Josh Steen came in with his girlfriend. Her name was Elizabeth Cartucci, but Lisa didn't know either one of them. Another waitress had to explain.

Cartucci was an actress with big tits and a bigger ego. Steen was one of Hollywood's top producers, almost as famous as a movie star, like Spielberg, or Jerry Bruckheimer. The cooks and the wait staff murmured when they walked in. There was a jostle, but the manager sent Lisa to the table, like usual.

She hadn't wanted to go. The girl was snapping her fingers for service, and the man was staring at his woman's tits.

180

'You,' Elizabeth said, without looking at Lisa. 'I want an egg-white omelette. Two eggs, make sure they're free range, and capers. I want Pellegrino water and some cinnamon coffee. Absolutely no hash browns, I don't want carbs on the table. Take away the sugar.'

Steen asked for a cheese omelette and some crispy bacon. He also winked at Lisa, which made her smile back. This infuriated the woman.

'And don't stare at my man, OK, honey? You're out of your league,' she added.

Lisa stared back. 'I wasn't.'

'Don't argue with me, missy.'

She swallowed. 'Ma'am, we only have regular coffee here — or decaf. I'll have the cook make up your omelette but our eggs aren't free range. We have mineral water, but we use Voss.'

'I prefer Pellegrino,' she snapped. 'Why don't you have that?'

'I'm sorry, ma'am. Voss is cheaper. Like the eggs.'

Josh Steen chuckled. 'She's got you, Elizabeth. Just eat the damn omelette.'

The woman's eyes glittered, and Lisa knew it was trouble. That aggression, that came from coke. She was mad, and it wasn't about eggs or water. She had some problem with her man, and Lisa was just a convenient hook.

She tried to escape. 'I'll get your order right away, ma'am, sir.' She moved away from the table, but the actress wouldn't quit. She snapped her fingers again, this time at the manager.

'I'm Elizabeth Cartucci,' she said, 'and I want this woman fired.'

Lisa gasped in shock. 'Ma'am?'

'Shut up,' her manager snapped. His name was Tico, and he liked Lisa's work, but wait staff were two for ten cents in this town and he was not going to piss off an Oscar winner. His diner was packed because Joe Public thought they might get to see a star. So you *never* got a star mad.

'Elizabeth. Stow it,' Steen said quietly. 'It's OK, she's fine, she's getting the order.'

There was something in his voice. Even back then, Lisa had thought briefly that she wouldn't like to be Elizabeth when he got her home.

'It's not fine. This woman flirted with my boyfriend and she talks back and she stares. I'm so tired of star-fuckers. I want her out of here.'

Tico rounded on Lisa. 'You can't do that. You heard the lady. Get out.'

Lisa's eyes flooded with tears.

'I said it's OK,' Josh Steen repeated. 'Perhaps you didn't hear me. Both of you.'

'Relax, Josh. You're way too soft,' Elizabeth said, smiling grimly.

There was a pause. Josh Steen glanced from Elizabeth to Lisa, and for a second she held her breath. Then slowly, coldly, he returned his gaze to his date.

'You're right. I should fire people more often. Like you.'

'Excuse me?' Elizabeth stared at him.

'I don't go for breakfast to get into a scene. You can drop your key at the gatehouse. Roberto will pack your bags by lunchtime.' He got to his feet and held out his hand, and Lisa just stared at it, with no idea what to do next.

182

'Well?' he said to her, and at that moment he looked better than any man she'd dated before or since, in his sharp tailored suit, his head shaved, his eyes dark, while Lisa stood there in nothing but her brown waitress dress and a bit of eyeshadow, a tear trickling down her cheek, red-faced with embarrassment and fear. 'Are you coming?'

'Yes please,' she said, and she put her hand in his. She was trembling. He gave her hand a little squeeze.

'It's OK. You have a purse or something?'

Lisa gestured. It was hanging up on a peg behind the till. Josh waited while she fetched it, and they walked out the door together, leaving Elizabeth Cartucci sitting in the booth shouting hysterically after them.

He put her into his car and they drove off. He didn't speak, and Lisa had no idea what to do.

'Thank you . . . sir,' she said eventually.

'It's Josh. I should thank you. I was looking for an excuse to dump her. Way too much drama.'

'I'm sorry if I got in the way.'

'You didn't; you were just there. I guess you're fired?'

'Guess so.'

'Waitressing to pay the bills, waiting for your big break?'

The questions were rote; she got the impression he'd asked them many times before.

'I just want to be a florist,' she said. 'I'm not interested in movies. Sorry about that.'

He'd laughed then, and looked her over properly for the first time.

'You're English. Illegal?'

'Please don't report me.'

'Don't worry, baby, I won't.'

They were headed the wrong way, out of the city towards Malibu. He probably had some kind of complex there.

'Mr . . . Stein . . . could you please pull over? I live on Sunset. I need to get back and start looking for another place.'

'It's Steen, not Stein. You really don't know who I am, do you?'

'I don't mean to be insulting,' Lisa said hastily. 'Sorry, Mr Steen.'

'Josh. I told you. Is every woman going to start arguing with me today?'

'Josh,' she'd said, and smiled. He smiled back, and she decided she liked him.

'You're not going to look for another waitress job. I just took you out of that restaurant; it'll be on Defamer by lunchtime.'

'What's Defamer?'

He laughed. 'Gossip website. You see . . . what's your name, pretty English girl?'

'Lisa Costello.'

'Well, Lisa, I produce movies, and there's a whole bunch that goes into that. Image is a big part of it. I dumped an Oscar-winning cokehead for a Limey waitress, meaning you'll be a story for the next fifteen minutes, and now I got to do something for you.'

'You don't owe me anything — Josh. You didn't let that horrible woman get away with it. I can get another job.' She tossed her hair. 'I don't have an Oscar but I don't do coke either.'

'It's for me, honey, not for you. The town sees me as a mover and shaker. So like it or not, I got to keep up that image and protect you for a while. You want to be a florist, so now you're a florist.'

She gazed at him. 'I don't understand . . . '

He punched a button on his cell phone.

'Mr Steen's office,' came a disembodied voice.

'Penny, it's me. Call Richard Thompson, the guy that owns Lucy's Lilies. Tell him he's gonna be hiring a friend of mine, Lisa Costello, this afternoon. Tell him she starts on forty thou a year and I'm sorting the paperwork.'

'Yes, sir. Right away.'

'He'll get the contract on *Carlotta's Secret* and *Deathtrap*, tell him.'

'OK.'

'Then call Wasserstein and Mensch. Tell them they're representing a new client, my protégée, and I want an alien of extraordinary talent visa for her, an O-1, and I want it yesterday. Tell them they'll have testimonies from five studio heads by sundown. Her name's Lisa Costello and she's an illegal Brit.'

'Yes, sir.'

'Book a short-term rental, furnished, in Park La Brea, six months, two bed, all the extra bells and whistles, pay in advance, Lisa's the tenant.'

'I'll get on to it immediately.'

Lisa gazed at him, her mouth open. 'Josh — I can't let you do any of that. I don't even know you. Please, this is just nuts.'

He grinned. 'You're asking me *not* to do it? This is usually the point where they start

185

squealing and clapping their hands.'

'It's very kind of you, but — '

'No it isn't. My image requires this chivalrous bullshit. Trust me on this. Take the job and the flat; you can always leave later if you want to.'

She shifted in the soft leather seat. They were far from the diner now, heading out towards the freeway and Malibu. She looked him over, and he was handsome and urbane and supremely confident. OK, so he loved himself a little, but wasn't that what made American men so hot?

He didn't like to be crossed. Even on calling him Josh. The woman, Elizabeth whatever her name, she had ignored him back in the diner. Multiple times. And he hated it. He was a man who confused disobedience with disloyalty; maybe that was why he was so good at his job.

Lisa would not want him as an enemy.

But he was here, in the car next to her, larger than life and offering to take her away from everything bad: a free flat of her own, a great job at an executive salary, even a lawyer so she could stay in America. All that was left was for him to wave a magic wand and turn a pumpkin and mice into a coach and four.

'Josh, I just — I need to say something. Please don't be mad.'

'Say whatever you want. No guarantees on whether I'll get mad.'

Lisa swallowed. 'I truly appreciate the offer, but I've made my own money, I pay my own rent and I'm not for sale.'

'For sale?'

She flushed scarlet. 'You're a Hollywood

186

director; I know you know what I mean. I'm not one of those girls who takes presents and . . . and . . . you know.'

'Who takes gifts and screws guys?'

'Yes,' she said, reddening further. She could feel the blush spreading over her neck and her upper chest. 'Whatever you do, I wouldn't sleep with you, not under any circumstances, and I'm not looking for a boyfriend. Sorry.'

Steen spun the wheel of his car and watched the road, but the set of his body shifted, and she could see she had got to him.

'You don't want my money, you don't want my help, you don't want to date. What do you want, Lisa Costello? Other than to sell flowers?'

'I'm only twenty-two. I'm working on that,' she said, and laughed. Josh Steen smiled with her.

'You're a remarkable girl, Lisa. Only now we have a problem.'

'I hope not,' she said, all optimism and naïvety. 'You're a good guy. I like you.'

'Here's my problem. You don't want to date me. But now I actually do want to date you.'

Lisa blushed again. 'You could get a million sexy girls.'

'Could get, have got. You know what the problem is with the Elizabeths of this world? They're all the same. Sometimes I'll call a girl Helen when her name's Marianne. They look alike. They blur into one. Now, no man is going to confuse you with any other chick.' He pressed his foot on the accelerator, and his Maserati picked up speed. 'Lisa Costello, let me do this

187

for you. No obligation. I'll take it as a favour.'

'For your image, huh?'

'That's it. No obligation whatsoever to bang me, kiss me, even hang out with me. But at the same time, I don't promise to stop asking you out.'

She laughed. 'And if I keep saying no?'

He shrugged, hands resting lightly on the wheel. 'Then I look even better, don't I? The mogul who hooked up a young woman and didn't even get to take her to dinner. Every female executive in town will love me.'

'Stop it,' Lisa said. 'You're breaking my heart.'

'So here's the cure. You say yes to all these things. Make Josh Steen look good round town, good in the gossip columns. I come back in a week and ask you out again. You can say yes or no. If it's no, I cut you a break, I don't destroy you, if only on the grounds that it's hard to destroy a florist.'

She really did laugh then. He was cool.

'And if it's yes,' he added, 'then we'll really have some fun. Now is that a deal, Lisa Costello?'

'Yes, Josh Steen,' she said. 'That is certainly a deal.'

★ ★ ★

Sam looked across at Lisa. For the first time since he'd known her, she was crying, properly crying.

'Are you OK?' he said.

'Poor Josh.' She struggled to control her sobs.

188

'I did love him, you know. For years. And then they killed him.'

'Go on,' Sam said. He wanted to stop the car, fold her into his arms, tell her everything was all right. But it wasn't all right. It was all very wrong, and if she did not get him a handle on it, it would never come right again.

He had done this before, just not with anybody he gave a damn about. When they started crying, it was good. That meant it hurt, and they were honest. He let Lisa dive into her memories, and swim around in the blackness.

★   ★   ★

Josh had been as good as his word; better. Lisa found herself transported instantly to another world. One where her landlords were handed six months' rent and were ecstatically grateful; one where she was moved from a cramped walk-up over a store with peeling paint and the constant roar of traffic into a gated community, with her own, hotel-style bland beige furniture. She now had access to a swimming pool and a gym, and there were running trails around the manicured lawns and little McMansion houses. There was no rent; and the florist store, a designer outfit on Rodeo Drive, gave her a nice salary and let her make up bouquets and talk to clients. It wasn't what she'd dreamed of, she told Sam; it wasn't her own firm, just a salaried position, someone else's store, their ideas. Yet it seemed dumb to argue. How else did you get from an illegal immigrant, living on tips, to a middle-class success story in one week?

Josh hadn't called immediately, either. He had waited three weeks. By the third week, Lisa was sweating. She wanted him to call, she was longing for it. She expected an immediate request for a date, but he took his time, and gratitude and curiosity mixed within her; when he did call, she dropped into his hands like a ripe plum, grateful, even hot for him. It was easy to refuse luxury when you'd never tried it. Scary how soon it could get you hooked.

The car ploughed on into the night, past the turning for Florence and straight north to Trieste. Sam wanted to go further before they stopped. The girl was restless, twisting in her seat, but he couldn't help that. She was in the flow of the story, and he wanted to take advantage of it.

Lisa moved faster now. Like she was ashamed, he thought. She told how Josh had swept her off her feet, almost conventionally. Tickets to the best shows, seats behind the plate at a Dodgers game, tickets to movie premieres and award shows. He sent her to Rodeo Drive with his assistant to buy clothes, to sort through her wardrobe. She was guided, gently but inexorably, to a beauty salon, a celebrity hair guy, Josh's private trainer. She tried to resist sometimes, she said. She would try to pay the bills herself from the salary he'd arranged for her. Only he laughed and told her not to be ridiculous.

The way Lisa described it, her new life had swirled around her like a current, sweeping her away. She didn't talk to her old friends from the diner, didn't hang in the old bars, didn't jog on the beach. Gradually she became the mogul's girlfriend, with all that went with it. He would get pensive at times, and that was when she loved him best; he liked to hear her stories of growing up in England, sneaking cigarettes in the bushes and trying to get served in pubs. He loved that she didn't give a damn about movies and came to California for the sun. He loved that her ex-boyfriends had been random dudes from the scene, guys her own age, bass players in failed bands, junior doctors, a lawyer, a surf bum. Lisa had not mixed, ever, in Josh's world. That was obviously a major plus; she was a clean sheet on to which he could project all his fantasies.

As Lisa talked, Sam sensed her weariness. Not just with the drive, but with the story she was telling. What did he want to know? The months turned into one year, then two, and now Josh was asking her to quit the fake flower job and move in. His family and female friends hated her and let her know it. Would they hate any girlfriend? Maybe, she could not be sure. But she was outside the box, even styled by Josh. She ate red meat, she swore and she drank; she was pretty, but not stunning; she was utterly incapable of feigning interest in charity balls or trophy wife fashion shows in aid of the cause of the week.

Josh himself she drifted in and out of love with. At least she thought it was love. Maybe it was just attraction and gratitude. He never denied her anything, and when he started spending time away from home Lisa thought he was just giving her space. The rumours were there, about actresses, hookers, but she chose to ignore them. Sam could judge her if he liked, she said. Life was comfortable and she was settled. It was tough mustering up enough outrage to rock the boat.

Plus, her rebel side had sprung to the fore. The American tabloid press adored her at first, when she was the beat-up waitress rescued by the prince on the shining charger. Only they expected Josh to dump her too. When he didn't, and Lisa wouldn't talk to them, they turned; all of a sudden she was a sponge, a gold-digger, a loser. Why was some no-talent Limey walking off with Hollywood's hottest bachelor? What was wrong with Elizabeth? Or Mariah? Or Elise? Lisa Costello wasn't that hot, and she had no past. They didn't like her. They printed his female friends' comments, off the record, of course, slamming everything about her from her eyebrow wax to her language. And at home, Josh's mother and sister, both divorcees, both living off Josh, made it clear to Lisa that they just wanted her to go away. When Josh was supposedly catting around, they smirked; they waited for her to cry, to flounce out.

So she dug in her heels, even after the relationship was dead.

And two months after that, her mogul actually proposed.

He changed, Lisa told Sam, once the ring was on her finger. It was a heavy rock, an eight-carat flawless diamond set in platinum and white

Welsh gold. Always dominant, he had started to watch her much more carefully, to prescribe her outings, to send his assistants around to chaperone her. It was like marrying into the royal family or something, she said. She was to be Mrs Steen now, the only one he'd actually married, and there was no pre-nup, because to Josh that meant he'd conceded defeat — something he never did. As a result, his control grew stronger, his grip tighter. The things he used to love about her now bugged him. Lisa wasn't to swear, she wasn't to drink.

It threw her. She wanted to marry him — she wanted to be settled, wanted a family. Wanted some standing to back her up with those hanger-on bitches from his family. She'd wanted to stick it to the press. She blushed when she said that, but Sam nodded; it was a petty motivation to marry, sure, but wasn't that what all people were like, how all people thought?

Nobody was pure. And Lisa was honest.

So, she went on, what could she do? She got angrier, and time went on, and now he was having her do interviews and booking the estate in Thailand, and all of a sudden Lisa was scouring her old cell phone to find numbers for friends she'd left behind, all those years back. Just so she wasn't totally alone. It was terrifying, she said, when it came down to it, how she'd dropped all her American friends when she hooked up with Josh and hadn't kept up with the English ones. Yeah, she knew she was to blame. But it wasn't intentional. It just happened. Living with Josh Steen was like falling into a river; you could doggy-paddle a little, do whatever you wanted to do, but the current swept you forwards inexorably.

The wedding was the end, though. His control-freakishness moved into high gear. She felt bullied, harassed and trapped over all the arrangements, from the venue to the minister. She had already decided to leave him. The press interest was nuts; she was turning into a cartoon version of herself, and it sucked. She had even considered going back to England.

'So why? Why didn't you give him back the ring?'

Lisa tossed her head. 'You want a nice pat answer? There isn't one.'

'Try for a complicated one. I need to know. A prosecutor would ask.'

'The wedding got closer, he was spending all this money. Everybody was coming out there. His partners. The studio boss. All his friends, their wives. People like you, hacks on the payroll.'

'Ouch.'

'Cap fits,' she said cruelly. 'And I didn't want to do that to him. I owed him, you know? He saved me, he hired me, he looked after me. He was the only long-term guy I've ever been with. But I knew he was cheating. I was going to go through with the wedding and divorce him, decent interval, let's say six months. Nothing humiliating.'

'That changed on the day?'

'Yeah. It did. He fucked Melissa. And she was one of my fake friends. The wife of a studio exec who did a lot of business with him, so somebody he'd send round to the house to work out with me or get our nails done. Man, I didn't like Melissa. She wanted him and she was blatant about it.'

'But she was married, you said.'

Lisa laughed. 'Sam, she wanted to upgrade. And I was going to leave Josh anyway, so none of it would have mattered. But he did it in the open, on my wedding day, and he let people see and they laughed at me. I don't know. That day I felt I'd have been better off in the goddamn diner. I was enraged. The stupid wedding — I was doing it for him, going through it only for him. And then he pulls this crap.'

'You wanted to hurt him?'

'By making a scene. Nothing in the world he hated more. Hell, remember how he picked me up in the first place. She made a scene, and all of a sudden she was just gone.'

'So no stabbing?'

'Drunk, short girl, one hundred and thirty pounds; tall, sober male, two hundred pounds. You tell me.' Lisa exhaled. 'So that's it and that's all, the saga of my life. Did it help?'

Sam thought about it. 'Yes. But I'm going to need more. Not about you. The mother and sister, the business partner.'

Lisa's shoulders tensed up against the seat.

'Tomorrow will be soon enough,' he said.

He'd have to get more out of her. Somewhere in her life there was the clue. The person who'd hired the killer. Sam was nowhere near finding that guy yet. And the more the whole thing

195

percolated through his mind, the more he sensed the terrible danger Lisa was in.

The assassin had assumed Lisa would take the fall. Only she'd gotten away. And she could make a case that she was innocent. That meant they'd start looking elsewhere. If I was the killer, Sam thought, I'd want her gone. No trial — just execution. Lisa didn't have any of Josh Steen's money or resources. And she was being hunted, right now. By far worse people than Interpol or the FBI.

She was brave, and she was smart. That's how she'd gotten away. But nobody could run forever. If Sam couldn't save her from this man, these men, she was also dead.

It would do no good to hammer her more tonight. She was exhausted, and he was tired himself. He needed to be alert and focused on what she was telling him.

The sign in front of them read Trentino. There were other things in Italian. *Servizio*. She murmured to herself, trying out the words.

'You want to stop?'

'Yes,' she said, and the word was a long sigh. 'We've been doing this for hours. I want to get out, stretch my legs.'

'It's real late. I won't take you over the border. We'll stop, get into bed. There's a motel coming up here.'

'OK.'

'I want you to act sloppy, like you're a little drunk.'

She nodded, and Sam had to stop himself from reaching across the car, putting his hand

196

around the back of her neck, and kissing her, deep and hard. He was sorry for the dead movie guy, but he was one hell of a fool.

'And you have to be all over me.' He laid it out for her, as detached as he could manage. 'Maybe not a hooker, just some drunk chick I picked up on the road. They won't ask questions. Don't be obvious.'

'Be all over you without being obvious. Sure.'

'Smartass,' he said. 'Think about the kind of people they let in the motels. It ain't husband and wife and two point four kids. It's truckers and students and hookers with johns. You want to be just one of them. You do not want to be noticed.' He looked at her. 'You've been thinking about this stuff on the road, am I right?'

'Of course.'

'Then just keep it up.'

The sign for the motel came up ahead of them, bright yellow and neon blue in the darkness. Sam turned the car into the lot easily enough, and got out. He swung his suitcase into his left hand and locked her backpack in the trunk.

'Hookers don't have luggage,' he explained. 'You can borrow some shit from me.'

'OK,' Lisa agreed.

She followed him through the parking lot. Stumbling like a drunk was easy enough; her legs were cramped from hours in the car, and she clutched at his strong arm like he was the only thing that could save her — which, of course, he was.

'Baby,' she murmured in his ear.

197

'*Cara*,' he said, and chuckled. 'Just like that. Great. You wearing perfume?'

She blushed. 'Just the shampoo scent on my hair.'

'It smells great. Come on.'

He led her forwards into the lobby of the motel. It was clean enough, maybe, but the paint was dingy, and the receptionists were smoking, and she could see stains on the carpet.

'*Vorrei una camera, per favore.*'

The night clerk leered at them. '*Matrimoniale?*'

Sam laughed. '*Una doppia, allora.*'

The clerk turned and went to the back wall. Little keys were hanging on hooks, the old-fashioned kind that used locks, not swipe cards; Lisa could already imagine just what this room would be like.

'*Trentacinque.*' He took the notes, then paused, looking at Lisa suspiciously. Her heart leapt into her mouth, her pulse started to race. She could feel Sam Murray's strong hand tighten around her waist; he splayed his fingers across her ribcage, just to calm her, she thought, to remind her of her part.

She had to hide the fear. She buried her face in Sam's neck, licking and kissing at it.

'*Non è italiano?*' the guy was asking. Oh God. He was going to want ID. Her ID. The one that was stopped by Interpol.

'*Sono americano — e ho appena incontrato questa ragazza stasera.*' She could feel Sam fumbling around with his wallet. '*Ho fretta — ecco, dieci per lei.*'

'*Bene.*' The rasp of the metal key slid across the desk.

'Come on, baby,' murmured Sam, 'let's get you inside, get you into something more comfortable. Like the shower.' He was laughing lasciviously, and she stumbled behind him, still kissing, running her hands up his back, afraid to take her face away from his neck and shoulder.

Pity she couldn't hide like that for ever. The thought came to her that hiding away for ever would not be that bad, if she was buried in Sam Murray's skin . . .

God almighty, stop that. She hadn't known the man a day. Last week she was engaged; her husband was a brutalised corpse. Ashamed of herself, she pulled back. They were standing in a corridor, dark brown carpet, torn paper on the walls, heading towards a fire escape.

'It's here.' He stopped outside Room 35 and opened the door deftly. 'After you, sugar.'

Lisa rushed in. Sam was behind her; then he shut the door and put the chain on the lock, throwing his suitcase on the bed. Lisa looked at the chain doubtfully. It seemed very fragile, like it would give with a single push from a strong shoulder.

'You're right. It sucks. But we won't be staying here, and I paid in cash. The only way they know we're here is if you were trailed from Rome. Which I doubt, since then you'd be dead or in jail.'

'Uh-huh.' She sat on the end of the bed and shivered. Sam unzipped his case and busied himself with the clothes; he handed her a T-shirt and a pair of men's boxer shorts.

'Thank you.'

'I'm sorry I don't have any gowns. Wanted to travel light.'

'Me too,' Lisa said, and tried to smile.

'Hey.' He moved around the cramped little room. The double bed took up almost all the space; there was a wardrobe with its door a little loose on its hinges, and a small space between that and the shower room, and that was about all. 'Don't shake like that, eh? I preferred it when you were kissing me.'

She lifted her eyes, but his expression was unreadable. Thank God he doesn't know what I'm thinking, Lisa told herself. The idea that he should read her desire was unbearable.

She ran a hand over her forehead. It felt weird with her long nails cut short; better. At least she wasn't catching her hair any more.

'Sorry about that,' she muttered. 'I got a bit carried away with that whole disguise.'

'Don't be. You were perfect.' He opened his mouth to say something else, then trod on it. What? That she was born to do it? Was Sam Murray scared she'd take offence if he implied she was a gold-digger?

'I'm under a lot of stress,' she said.

He smiled. 'That I can believe.'

'Josh and I hadn't had a good relationship for quite some time.' Why the hell was she explaining herself to this man? 'It wasn't just that he fucked Melissa. There were others . . . I thought. On our wedding day, we hadn't had sex for almost two months. He didn't push it and I

200

was bitter. Besides, I knew he was getting it someplace else.'

'Otherwise he'd come to you?'

'Josh was never shy about that. He loved me, in his way — at first. But in the same way you love your favourite horse, or the best painting in your art collection. He loved me like a thing he owned. Sex was part of what I was for.'

Sam sat on the other corner of the bed and regarded her mildly. She was somewhat impressed. The guy didn't buy a line of bullshit very easily.

'It's part of what every woman is for.'

'Not *every* woman.'

'Not a nun. But every married woman. I don't think you can hang the guy for that.'

'I didn't,' she snapped.

Sam lifted his hands. 'Figure of speech, ma'am. So did you ever go to him?'

Lisa blushed. 'That's a little personal, isn't it?'

'Hey, you started it.' A shrug. 'Want my advice, you should talk it all out. Something might come up you can use to catch who did this. I mean, you're kind of past modesty at this point.'

She swallowed painfully. 'Uh — yeah. OK. No. I never went to him. He did it all.'

'Why not? Didn't you desire him?'

'With Josh, it was always a performance test. I tried not to say no to him. He was a hard guy to turn down, whatever the question.' She paused. 'Maybe I didn't really desire him. His power, his wealth . . . I'd never had a serious boyfriend . . . you know, I felt who was I to turn down the knight in shining armour? Cinderella doesn't get to say, you know what, I think I'll skip the ball.'

Sam laughed aloud. 'You're a funny chick.'

'Thanks,' she said drily. 'I think I'll go take a shower. Quit while I'm ahead.'

She picked up his T-shirt and boxers and took them with her towards the bathroom. There was no question of concealment if you relied on an Italian hotel towel, usually no bigger than a bathmat and just about as scratchy. She'd towel off and get dressed inside. With a sense of relief, she moved into the small bathroom and bolted the door.

It felt dangerous to be in the same room as Sam.

★   ★   ★

He sat on the bed, watching the little white door that she had closed. There was the sound of water hissing into the shower tray, and it was easy to imagine her peeling off those clothes, standing there nude, rinsing away the dust and strain of the journey.

Damn. Think about something else.

It was harder than it sounded. Sam could not get that memory out of his head. Her lips, so soft, round, pressing against his skin. Her slim frame leaning on his back, his arm. Her heart pumping. Fear? Or something else as well?

Was she attracted to him? He was just a beat-up guy fooling himself. This girl was used to the finest of everything. If she did get cleared of this murder, somehow, she'd be famous, a world

202

celebrity; she'd be an innocent victim who could have any guy she wanted.

But his blood told him she wanted him.

Maybe she did. But that was natural. This was a high-octane situation. She was exhausted, and she'd been sick of Josh Steen before he died. If that was the truth about two months . . . wouldn't she be craving a man?

Girls weren't like men, though. They could go without it. He was ready to go down the gym and smash the hell out of some punchbag with frustration . . .

Look, Sam, if you touch this girl, you're a dead man walking. You know what fucking her would do? It would give the cops a motive for aiding and abetting. He shook his head, and winced a little at the idea. Lisa Costello wasn't like that, she wasn't some easy lay, some one-night stand. Men did not forget a chick like her. Sam had dated seriously a few times in his life; various women, always pretty, always clever. He'd blown it every time. They thought it was because he didn't like them; it was really because he didn't much like himself.

If Lisa was feeling the heat from the chase across the world, why wouldn't he be?

None of it was real. He had to get through.

She came out of the bathroom wearing his clothes, and she looked great in them. His T-shirt hung loose around her frame, like a short dress; her legs were toned and went on for ever. Under the T-shirt's thin cotton he could make out her bra and the outline of his boxers. He felt himself stir.

'I'm gonna take a shower too.'

'I guess we're sharing the bed,' she said.

'There's nowhere else. Not even enough floor. So yeah.' He tried to smile, ignore his desire. 'Promise you won't molest me in the night, huh?'

She grinned back. Damn, she was pretty, even with wet hair and no make-up. He wanted to take her into his arms and push her back on that bed.

'I left my dagger in Thailand,' Lisa said. 'You're safe for now.'

He fled to the bathroom, before he stood there and got hard.

★　★　★

When he returned, she was already curled up, her short hair dark against the pillow; her back was to him, the natural barrier against intimacy. He switched out the light. Lisa looked drained, and he thought she needed sleep.

'Tomorrow we'll be in Liechtenstein,' he said. 'You should get some rest.'

There was silence for a few moments. He could hear her breathing, and knew she wasn't asleep.

'Why are you helping me?' she asked in the darkness.

He didn't know what to say.

'I just don't think you killed him.' He hesitated. 'And I like you. It's hard for a man to watch a pretty girl go to jail.'

'Is that all?'

Sam sighed. 'Lisa, you told me your story, because it's part of this. I didn't tell you mine. But I get the feeling I've been wasting my life, and a nice paycheque doesn't fix that for me any more.'

'So if you solve this, if you help me, that means you haven't been wasting your life?'

'That depends if you're innocent. Maybe I'm the biggest sucker in the world.'

'I'm innocent. At least, I'm pretty sure. You know I can't be totally sure.'

'I know. Now go to sleep.'

She obeyed him. After a couple of minutes, her breathing slowed, and he felt her body move as her chest settled into a rhythm. She was out, as quickly as that. She must have been as exhausted as he had suspected.

Sam was flooded with relief. Tomorrow he would call Rich Frank, and get to Liechtenstein, where she'd be a little more secure. The best thing would be to find a safe house and dump her there, then pursue whatever leads he had. She was the suspect, and travelling with her would slow him down.

Besides, if he had to stay too long in one spot with Lisa Costello, he was very afraid he was going to fall for her.

★ ★ ★

The beeper buzzed and Felix looked at it in annoyance. He was in a zone now, a hunting zone, and interaction with customers was forbidden.

But this was the Steen client. Instantly, he knew what they wanted. Felix smiled, suffused with a subtle pleasure. You worked hard for money in this game; it was great when they wanted to give it to you for nothing.

He pulled out his cell phone. It was a military encrypted BlackBerry, as used by the US Government and a few less salubrious types the world over.

'This is Felix.'

'It's me.'

'I hope you've been enjoying the show,' Felix said, smirking because he knew the client had hated it as much as he had. When they paid for a kill, they always panicked afterwards. His clients were a bunch of fucking pussies who lacked the guts and skill to do it themselves. What they wanted was their targets dead and the police's attention elsewhere.

'Not so much. Look, Felix, I know they're all after this girl.'

'Just like I promised.'

'You did, you did.' What a kiss-ass. 'But maybe she says something, like how she didn't do it.'

'She can say what she likes. The dagger's got her prints on it and she's running from the law.'

'O.J. got acquitted.'

'Yes, but you don't see the cops out looking for the real killer, do you? Everybody knows she's guilty. Plus O.J. had lots of fans. Lisa Costello has none of those.'

'Felix, please.' Here it comes, he thought happily. 'I need this to go away.'

'I understand.'

206

'She needs to go away.'

They'd never say the words over the phone. Like the conversation this far wouldn't already incriminate them. But holding hands with the customers, soothing their fears, that was a regrettably important part of this whole thing.

'The job is very high-profile. Right now she's a bigger game than the last one. To persuade her to leave,' there, he'd offer them a nice verbal get-out, 'I want two million, in cash, up front, plus a hundred thou for expenses, up front.'

This time there was no argument. 'The wire is on its way.'

'I'll send a beeper message when it's landed. Then you know I'm going to go meet her. Oh, and by the way, you'll know you have results when you see it on the news.'

'OK.'

'Do not contact me again. There is a limit as to how many contacts can safely be made. There will be no status updates or progress reports. There will only be results. Got it?'

'Got it,' his client said, and didn't sound choked at their parting. 'Goodbye.'

7

Sam woke early. It wasn't yet light outside; the glowing dial of his watch told him it was five thirty local. He slipped into the bathroom quietly, careful not to wake her. Some things needed to be done while she wasn't listening.

A brief two-minute shower, not enough to enjoy it, just time to get clean. He pulled on his clothes, grabbed his wallet and headed out the door, taking the key from his jacket.

Hotel reception was packing up for the day shift. The clerk from last night was still there. He nodded at Sam. '*Com'è stato con lei?*' How was she?

'*Era attraente. E stata brava. Grazie,*' Sam said, returning the leer. She was hot. She was good. Would she have been, with him? If you believed Lisa, she was a little uptight with Josh Steen. A woman who never asked her man for sex didn't enjoy it when he put in for her.

Lisa was not fulfilled, not just with men. He thought he could make her leap. It was killing him not to have the chance to try.

He went into the outer corridor, and out the front door. The parking lot was cold, but he didn't want to be listened to. He punched in Craig's number in LA. Answer machine.

'Hey, Craig. It's Sam. I found her and I spoke to her and the deal is, I don't think she did it . . .'

208

'Sam?'

There was a long beep, and Craig's voice on the phone. 'I heard what you just said.'

In the background Sam could hear Craig's wife swearing. It was night-time there. 'Sorry,' he said lamely.

'It's OK. I want to speak to you bad. Hold on, I'll call this number in one minute.'

Sam snapped his cell shut and wondered briefly if Craig was calling him back with a trace. They could do that — but from his home, late at night? Unlikely. Unless the Fibbies had determined that Sam was wanted, in which case they'd have set it up all ready to go and have three tech goons waiting in a van outside his house, ready to flip a switch.

His cell buzzed.

'You're not seriously giving me the butler did it, are you?'

'Craig, I spoke to her.'

'I saw the pictures. She's pretty and she's got an accent. You were always crazy for that shit. Don't be an idiot.'

'She had no signs of bruising. There was no fight. How could a drunk girl have killed him without a fight? He was sober, I saw him.'

'Yeah? How long before he was killed? You should know you can only be sure what happens when they're in your sights. After that they might burn down Paris, you wouldn't know.' Craig grunted, and Sam heard him drinking, probably a carton of milk from the fridge. It'd be nice to go home. His own fridge was probably stinking out the joint by now. 'And Sam, seriously, how the fuck do you know she wasn't bruised? She strip for you?'

'No, she did not.'

'Tell me you're not banging this girl.'

'I'm not.'

'So where is she now?'

Sam was going to be careful. Nothing he said could be a lie, technically. He trusted Craig, but Craig would do his duty, including testifying in court against Sam if he thought that was what the law required.

'She was in Rome when I met her, at St Peter's. We talked then she left. That was the deal I had with her.'

'We got lots of good prints from Hong Kong; that was smart work, Sam. The guys had everything sent back here, air freight. With the stuff from Thailand they got an excellent case. Ms Kennedy did a video deposition. She'll be a witness.'

'I want you to keep this possibility in mind, Craig. Lisa Costello had to attack Alice Kennedy because she needed a passport, and she had to tie her up because the flight to Rome is eighteen hours and she needed to get through customs the other end. After she landed, she called the Chinese police and Mr Watson's airline. You can check all that with them.'

'So she felt guilty. Doesn't change what she did.'

'China's got the death penalty. She had to get to Europe. Someplace they wouldn't ship her back to Bangkok for execution.'

'Jesus, listen to you. You should be this girl's lawyer.'

'Craig, what motivation did she have? When she married Josh Steen she stepped into millions. Even with a divorce she'd get a settlement. Enough to keep her for life. Why the hell kill the guy in a country where they hang you just for possessing a couple ounces of pot?'

'Because she was drunk. Drunks do stupid shit. I'm sure you can remember. Look, maybe her lawyer will argue temporary insanity.'

Sam looked up at the stars sinking in the east, towards dawn. He was frustrated. Craig was his friend, of sorts. But he wasn't buying this.

'So ask yourself more basic questions. Why does a chick who's a bit tipsy have an alcoholic blackout? How does a hundred-thirty-pound woman kill a two-hundred-pound man when he's sober and she's drunk? Your theory is that her motivation was to get Steen to the altar, and after that he was fair game — as the widow she steps into money — but he was fucking around, he was a big-money player, lots of other people wanted him dead. She admitted to me the blackout, but she says she was drugged. Steen hated drunk women; hell, she was trying to embarrass him anyway. There was no minibar in that room, Craig. Lisa says he would not have let her order more booze.'

'Drunk enough when she got there to have a blackout. Easy.'

'And so if she's that drunk, how does she manage to stab this guy who's twice her size, who's sober, and kill him but not get a mark on

211

her? And here's one more question, Craig. If Josh Steen was stabbed to death in a frenzied attack, how come nobody heard it? His family were staying in junior suites in the same corridor.'

There was silence. That was good; that meant Craig was thinking.

'I'm going to find Lisa Costello,' Sam added.

'Maybe not. We got Interpol pictures, changed for her new hair and all that shit. I got cops all over Europe looking for this girl.'

'None of them are going to catch her. She's too quick.'

'You're sounding to me like you're a little in love with her, Sam.'

'I hardly know her.' That was true; maybe he should remember it. 'Look, Craig, so far you guys have come up with jack-all apart from the stuff I've handed you.'

'Not so, hotshot. We got forensics at the scene, we got hair evidence, DNA from this girl on the body, in the bathroom, on the knife. I have enough for ten convictions.'

'Yeah? Maybe. And if they're ten convictions of the wrong person? Jesus, Craig, you can hear there's at least a possibility. Doesn't the FBI cover all bases?'

He heard the silence on the end of the phone as that shot went home. 'Yes, Sam, yes we do. OK. What do you want?'

'Is the hotel still a crime scene?'

'They pack up tonight. It reopens tomorrow.'

'Then you need to get the fuck on the phone and tell the team to wake up from sleeping, go

212

through it again and this time check stranger DNA. If he was planning to pin it on her, maybe he wasn't careful.'

'You gotta be fucking kidding me, Sam.'

Dawn was breaking in the east now; he could see the first red streaks parting the blackness of the night sky.

'There could have been sixty, maybe more people in that room since then. Wait staff. Local cops. FBI. You, you prick.'

'Go fuck yourself, Craig. Get the samples. You can eliminate every one of those sources. All hotel staff got to give a sample. FBI and police are already in the database. Take the Thai guys' stuff for co-operation, they'll go for it.'

'You really think somebody else did it?'

'I spoke to her. For a while. She's innocent. She's been set up and you can't let her go down because it's the goddamned easy option. Or hell, Craig, if you do that, guess what. You don't get to lord it over me any more.'

'That what you think I been doing?'

Silence hung heavy between them.

'Fuck it, I'll test for strangers. And Sam Murray, if I find you're helping this chick, I will throw your ass in jail for thirty years.'

Sam felt the weirdest mix of relief, fear and pride.

'OK.'

Pause.

'You're doing good so far, Sam. I've told you that before.'

'Yeah. You did.'

'This is what you were meant to do.'

The words hit him like a knife to the chest, in this anonymous parking lot in northern Italy, with the suspect the FBI were chasing waiting back in his bed.

'Don't get too close to the target, Sam. Be a professional. The Bureau would appreciate the assistance. That's all I'm saying.'

'I won't.' He hoped it was true. 'Check for someone else, keep an open eye. Josh Steen had lots of enemies.'

'That much I can promise. Now I'm gonna call Phuket before the cleaners move in with the Lysol, and then I'm going back to sleep.'

Sam glanced back at the motel, lit up still against the pale morning sky. 'And I'm going to find Lisa Costello,' he said with perfect truth. 'Later, Craig. Say sorry to Maria for me.'

⋆ ⋆ ⋆

Felix spoke into his skyphone. The connection was crackly, and it was costing him about ten bucks a minute, but it was worth it. Nobody ever checked these things.

'Come on, baby,' he said. He'd flown up to Detroit last week, where they had a call centre, and he'd picked up one of the supervisors at a bar in town where they all liked to get drunk after hours and forget their shitty jobs. He had worked her over good. Gave her some sob story about his bastard Californian landlord stealing his money and how he just wished he could get back at him, just a little, if he only knew where the sucker was.

214

She'd shaken her head, and oohed and aaahed in sympathy, and then she offered, by herself, to get the asshole's credit history.

Perfect. And he'd told her, never mind about him, baby girl, let's just get down, and then he'd shown the fat bitch the time of her life, and the next morning she was insisting, even begging, to be his partner in crime and hunt this fuck around the globe.

A little more sex, a regretful glance at his watch — he had to be in Milwaukee, because he was a travelling sales manager for a gun show, and if folks like him didn't work then they didn't eat . . . but he'd call her.

Felix watched the shutters come down over those heavily hooded eyes. Guys had promised to call this one before, and never come through with it. He didn't comfort her right there and then. Let her sweat it. So when he *did* ring, halfway to the airport, she was practically gushing with joy. He meant it, you see. He'd be away a few weeks but he'd check in regular. He made plans for the middle of the following month and she was eager to join in. They shot the breeze, phone conversations lasting quarter of an hour to over a half, and only very occasionally did he bring up the topic of his scumbag landlord Sam Murray. Karen was forced to make most of the running her own sweet self.

There was no torturing this one, no blowing out her kneecaps for the combo to the safe. Karen's luckiest break was that Felix needed to track Sam on an ongoing basis, and that meant

215

calling her from various global hotspots, which in turn kind of meant he needed her alive and happy to co-operate.

He blubbed some endearments into the skyphone and chattered about how good it would be to see her the next month. And in return, she told him that Sam Murray had hired a car just outside the centre of Rome, Italy.

'That freaking scumbag,' Felix said. 'Running round Europe on our money. Mine and the other guys in the building. Are you sure?'

'Oh, yes. He's had it for two days.'

'Where's he taking it?' Felix asked casually. Her answers to this set of questions would be crucial. 'I guess you can't tell, honey, can you?'

'Well, nothing yet. He seems to be paying for his gas with cash. Either that or he isn't driving it much.'

Oh, he's driving, Felix thought. He's driving and he's got some smarts. He's close to the chick, at the very least, doesn't want to be caught. There's money in this for him. 'Any other purchases? I'd like to know where he is.'

'There was six euros eighty-five cents on a garage outside of Rome. I can't see what the breakdown is.'

Bottled water, candy bars. The usual.

'Then nothing, honey.' A slight hesitation in her voice. 'You know, he's not worth it, we probably shouldn't be tracking him like this.'

'Hey.' Felix knew better than to sound guarded; he put on his best hurt voice. 'This guy ripped me off real bad and I'd like to find him, that's all. I understand you're uncomfortable, Karen . . . '

'No, it's OK,' she said hurriedly, but it was too late.

'I don't want to make you feel bad.'

'Jack, you're not. I'm sorry if I overreacted,' she said desperately.

'You didn't. I'll call you later, OK? When I get back,' he said, and hung up.

Luckily for Karen, she had no way of contacting him. She would sit in her apartment and cry about being fat and blowing it. Never knowing how death had been breathing down her neck for weeks. Now she got to mourn, and stumble out to a bar, and press herself against another half-drunk dude who was looking for a lay and wasn't too picky about the form it took. Karen's slobbish life would go back to normal. Felix certainly didn't have time to hunt her. But the questions she'd asked meant she was now useless as a source. She had noticed, and that was toxic. Besides, Sam was running, clearly, hiring cars and clamping down on his credit card. That meant she would be of limited use. Did he know he was being tracked? Or was he just taking care?

It was important that Felix find him, and kill him. Sam was the key to Lisa Costello. He would tell Felix where to find her, either directly or under torture, and then the job would be done at last, the loose ends tied together. He was annoyed he'd let it get this far. He was looking forward to seeing them both dead. And this time, no assumptions. Felix would take care of it.

217

★ ★ ★

Sam moved back into the room and watched her for a minute guiltily. There was something personal about this act of trespass. Watching those red lips, open on the pillow, her hair tousled about her, her chest rising and falling with her breath. Lisa Costello, at peace. For a few seconds more.

He bent in close to her, lowering his mouth to her ear. It would be so easy to kiss her, right now, and she wouldn't really understand what had just happened. But he lifted his lips from her skin just millimetres above it. When Lisa kissed him, he wanted her to know what she was doing . . .

He stiffened; yes, he'd had the thought, when, not if. She was so ripe, so hot. Josh Steen had tried to control her, never to fulfil her. She was a woman in need of a man, a true man, but she was suspicious, and would fight it all the way. And Sam acknowledged to himself that he wanted to be in the battle. To fight her emotions and conquer them; to taste her, when she pressed against him, and yielded herself, hot and eager, in his arms. Because she would be eager. Once the fear had gone, she was ready for it.

He glanced down at her sleeping. Her vulnerability made her even more attractive. God, he had to have more control than this. Craig would throw him to the wolves if he fucked her. He was here to solve the mystery, right? Real investigative journalism. Something worthwhile in his life, worth giving up a million

218

bucks for. Sex would cloud it. What if he slept with her, and then she broke up with him? How would that be, on the road together? Impossible. He shouldn't, couldn't have her. He had to keep a clear head.

If Lisa came to him, it should be after this case was done, and she was a free woman. Once some bad guys were in jail and the FBI weren't looking for Sam Murray. That time was not now.

Get to work, buddy, he told himself. He reached down and touched her on the shoulder. God, but her skin was warm, soft. He steeled himself against the surge of desire.

'Lisa.'

She stirred, moaned a little. He guessed she was exhausted, her body still clinging desperately to sleep, but he couldn't help that now. They needed to move.

'Lisa, you got to wake up. Get in the shower.' He shook her harder. She gasped, and sat bolt upright reflexively, flinging the sheets from her. Sam caught a glimpse of long, tanned thigh, and the soft curves of her breasts under the T-shirt as it hung forward. He bit the skin on the inside of his mouth. She was well curved, with a small waist and a flaring firm ass that just sang to him. So different from the lanky LA models with their coke habits. Yeah. Josh Steen had excellent taste.

'God! You startled me.'

'I'm sorry, but we've got to go. They'll be tracking us. Trying to find us. You have to move fast.'

'They who?' she said. She stood up, and it was beautiful. He tried not to stare at her bare legs below those boxers.

'Whoever killed Josh and tried to frame you. Who do you think? If you're innocent, somebody else is guilty. And they want you dead.'

She nodded, her complexion pale. But Sam didn't feel guilty. It was good she should be scared. He didn't have time to waste.

'I'll be five minutes.'

'Be two. Rinse off and dress. You can get fancier once we land in Liechtenstein.'

Lisa didn't argue. She went into the little motel bathroom, and he heard the water running and tried not to think too hard about it sluicing over her naked body, hardening up her nipples. He packed up their stuff, moving fast. It was one way to distract himself.

Within a minute the water had stopped. He heard her brushing her teeth. Good, she was efficient.

'I'm coming out.'

'OK.'

There was a pause. 'This towel's a bit short. Can you turn your back, please?'

He hardened instantly, despite himself. Damm it, get a grip. 'Sure,' he said easily. Thank God he could turn his back to her; he needed to.

The door opened. Sam stared out the window facing the parking lot. He could still see her reflection in that window. Not as clearly as he'd have liked, but look at that. Lisa Costello's fine athletic body, full breasts, narrow waist but not overly thin, terrific round ass, long legs with nicely turned calves. The little rectangular scrap of a white towel did a lousy job of concealing her assets. His mouth was dry.

She was moving around the room, picking up clothes. Jeans and a boxy T-shirt. Unfortunately, he now knew precisely what that boxy T-shirt was covering up. This was going to be tough. She grabbed her panties; he narrowed his eyes trying to make them out. Virginal white cotton briefs. He imagined his hand on them, tugging them down around her thighs . . .

'OK, I'll be right out.' She disappeared back into the bathroom again. Ceasing to torment him for a few minutes. Sam stood there and tried to deflate his erection. He forced himself to think of Liechtenstein, the safe houses he knew of there, wondered if they'd still be active, what Plan B was if they weren't. It worked, a little. He was glad he wore his jeans loose-fitting.

Thirty seconds later, there she was; clean and scrubbed in her nondescript clothes, her damp hair tied back, no makeup, exceptionally hot. She looked young, fresh. Nothing like a hooker.

'We'll go out the same way we came in.' He picked up his small bag of stuff. 'I carry this, and you cling on to me. Try to look hung over. Into me. OK? Just don't get noticed.'

'I can do that.' He opened the door, and Lisa stumbled after him, one arm flung drunkenly round his shoulders, burying her face in his neck. Sam moved through the lobby; Lisa was kissing and licking at him now, murmuring that he was her baby, that she could do him right, he could get her coffee. It was disturbing. The feel of her lips and tongue was too good. But she had it right; his peripheral vision saw the desk clerk giving them no more than a cursory leer, and then glance down at his paper again.

He endured her caresses right through the parking lot, in case they were being watched. Then he opened the car door and half shoved her inside, like you would do with a whore. It was a relief to get her off his neck. He didn't think he could take much more teasing. Fuck, he wanted to drop her somewhere and go get a real hooker. Someone, anyone to ease this torment.

'How was that?' she said, as he turned the key and wrenched the steering wheel, taking them out on to the safety of the *autostrada*.

'Great. Very realistic.'

'You sound angry,' she observed.

'No, I just didn't sleep well. And we have lots to do.' He put his foot on the gas, but no amount of speed would take him away from her; she was right next to him, and the scent of her freshly washed skin was intoxicating. 'I want to get across the border first, then we can find a diner, grab breakfast. I'm gonna need to know more about Josh.'

Lisa sighed. 'Really, I've told you everything.'

'You've told me what you think is important, yeah. But that's not where the killer's hiding. I want to hear about how his family was with you. His mom, his sister . . . '

'Both of them, bitches.'

'Good. So tell me that story. And his business partners, golf buddies. One of them had Josh killed. You're a lead; right now, you're my only lead. You have to go through everything with me

222

and we'll work on finding what you're not seeing.'

She turned her head, and he kept his eyes on the road. He could stare all day long at the curve of her neck.

'Most likely it's nobody I know.'

'Why do you think that?'

Lisa shrugged. 'Josh kept his work away from me. He sometimes talked about it but he was suspicious if I asked, probably because he'd dated so many actresses. One thing he loved about me was that I didn't want anything from his world. So I wouldn't even know about half the guys in his office, the enemies he had. It's bound to be one of them, right?'

'Money's a big factor, yes.' Sam had a hunch, and Lisa was forcing him to articulate it now. 'But so is sex. And jealousy. It's a risk to kill somebody.' He grinned at her. 'Carries the death penalty in lots of places.'

'Yeah. I figured that out fast.'

'The killer would have too. And by killer, I mean whoever ordered the hit. You understand this was the work of a professional assassin?'

Lisa winced, and passed her hand across her temples, as though she could relieve a throbbing head that way.

'Because they set it up to look like I did it?'

'Exactly. Joe Schmoe couldn't have gotten into that bedroom undetected.' He glanced up at the road signs, and spun the car off the motorway, heading into a little side road that took them out through some villages in Aosta. 'We'll go a back route, see if we can avoid the border guards.'

'OK,' Lisa said. She blew the air out of her cheeks. 'Maybe we should dump the vehicle, walk across.'

'Like the family von Trapp in *The Sound of Music?*'

'Don't laugh at me.'

'Sorry. It's a serious thing.'

'I've had enough shit with passports to last the rest of my goddamned life,' Lisa said. 'Getting a new car is easier than getting out of custody.'

'I'm trying to avoid using credit cards. Look, we'll see if we can find a spot to drive over. Getting a car without leaving a trail isn't as easy as you think.' She looked unhappy, but he wasn't about to argue the point. 'Think about how you found Josh's body.'

'I'd rather not.'

'But it's the best place to start, because it tells us about who killed him. You woke up and you thought you'd got a hangover, had a blackout. You were holding the dagger. He was stabbed, his blood was on you. No signs of forced entry. You were positioned like you'd done it. You thought you had.'

'Thank you for the recap,' Lisa said quietly.

Sam was annoyed. 'I'm trying to save your life here, doll. Don't pull me up on everything. You don't have time to be precious.'

She shivered. 'You're right. I'm sorry. I think I get what you're saying. The killer had to have drugged me, without me knowing. Either got into our room without breaking anything or . . .' Her voice trailed off. 'Or have been there all along. In a closet or something, waiting. And

224

then over-powered Josh, killed him, without attracting any attention from the hotel maids . . . '

'Or even his folks. His family was staying on that corridor. It had to have been a real clean kill, with Josh not able to cry out.'

Lisa didn't want to think about that. But it was true: she'd been drugged, out cold, and somebody had been stabbing Josh, right next to her.

'He also framed you perfectly. The dagger was a nice touch, the royal wedding present. That kind of thing makes them mad in Thailand. He got out without leaving a trace, and left you there as the ideal patsy. All of this means professional. So somebody hated your husband, was prepared to risk execution to kill him, and was even prepared to let somebody else in on it — the hired help. That's a big risk to take for just a business enemy. No, I think this was personal, at least in part.'

She was silent, digesting it. 'Yes. I can see that's logical.'

'Money is one classic motivation. Love is another. Josh had an eye for women. He banged Melissa on your wedding day.'

'And you're saying she wasn't the only one?'

'By no means.' He shrugged. 'I'm not trying to hurt you here, but taboid reporter is what I do. Josh Steen stopped seeing other girls for, I guess, maybe the first four months you two were together. After that he hooked back up with his regular madam, and there were lots of rumours about chicks in his circle. His assistants . . . '

'I knew it,' Lisa said fiercely. Her eyes prickled

225

with tears. It was so humiliating, listening to Sam discussing her husband cheating in this matter-of-fact way.

' . . . and the wives of his acquaintances. He could be a real bastard like that, Lisa; he did it for a power trip. Divorce is expensive in Hollywood, and who'd want to cross Josh Steen, with all his money and power? Maybe to one of those jealous husbands, killing him was the perfect answer. And framing you would be the cherry on the cake. You fuck my wife and I'll fuck with yours.'

'Yeah.' She nodded. 'If they felt the anger . . . the shame of it; so dirty. That's how I felt. Trapped. I can see that might make them kill. Contact somebody. So you need me to go over all my so-called girlfriends and tell you which of them were banging my fiancé?'

'Something like that.' Sam looked over, saw her reddened cheeks and the tight set of her mouth. It was interesting to him that she obviously cared. Many a trophy wife in her position wouldn't, in fact didn't, give a fuck. If you had the name and the ring, who cared who the meal ticket was sleeping with? Hundreds of Hollywood wives worked just that way. He knew of some who even encouraged it. If the man sowed his oats in a wide field, he wasn't likely to divorce the wife, who was there for social respectability. A single mistress was much more of a threat than a whore or two in a strip joint or some of the wife's safely married girlfriends. 'Lisa . . . did you really love Josh?'

'At one time, yes. Sure. He rescued me. Any

girl would have loved him.'

Rescued her? From that diner maybe. But Lisa was making a life for herself, training as a florist, working two jobs. He didn't hear reality; he heard guilt.

Never mind. There were tears in her eyes now, and Sam felt horrible. The desire that had clung to him since he looked down at her sleeping finally left him. Poor kid. It had been a rough few days.

'All right, take a break. Enjoy the scenery. We'll get to the border in a little while.'

She stared out of the window at the green fields of northern Italy, with the Alps looming against the sky behind them, but Sam got the impression she was not seeing very much.

★   ★   ★

Craig mopped his brow. Jesus Christ, it was hot. He was used to LA, but this was something else. The humidity stank. It was like walking through soup. He was drenched in sweat; he knew there were patches under his armpits. Should have packed more shirts. Thailand was way out of his comfort zone.

Fucking Sam Murray, he thought.

'How long you be, mister?' A thin local man was looking up at him belligerently. He wore the uniform of the resort. 'We want get place ready. Entire hotel is closed. Nobody working.'

'As long as it takes,' Craig snapped. His men were fanned out through the room, and he'd had to deal with their grumbling already. What was

227

the point of flying out to this hellhole when everybody knew who'd done it? Craig had had to fight with them, with his bosses, now the wait staff. Everybody was a critic.

The man's face fell, and Craig relented. This guy probably made less in a year than he made in a month. It was unseemly to bully him. 'Look, man, we're about halfway through, OK? Couple more hours, it's all yours.'

'OK, OK.' The hotel manager fell away. Craig glanced around the scene and felt his stomach knot. Anxiety, maybe also some excitement.

He had a good hunter's sense. Sam Murray, his old friend, the guy he'd spent the last ten years mad at, had dragged him into this. Murray, the genius who ruined it all by being selfish and lazy. It aggravated him that Sam had thrown away his life for a fast car and some hot chicks; money, basically, nothing more complicated than that. Finally he'd got the one offer of cash that might actually mean something, a new life, a second chance.

And this time he was throwing it away because he thought the girl was innocent.

Craig would never admit it, but he had respect for Sam Murray's skill. The guy was at the top of his shitty, worthless profession precisely because he could read people, he could hunt. That was what brought the exclusives, the fat paycheque and the indulgent editor. It was what made him the guy chosen to cover the wedding in paradise.

Sam's gut told him Lisa Costello was not behind this. It would be real easy to ignore Sam's gut. Nobody would care; the case would wrap

228

up, and he, Craig, would be the intrepid Fibbie agent who had tracked down the tabloids' Bride of Frankenstein. Promotion beckoned. His own fat paycheque, something to make Maria happy. A fast car of his own, maybe. Respect across the Bureau. A glittering future.

He was risking it all. This would piss a lot of people off. Swap one nice neat suspect for a totally unsolved case, for a murderer who'd had a week to get away, who could be one of hundreds of guys. For a second Craig thought about Lisa Costello. She couldn't be better, really, the money-grubbing foreigner the press loved to hate, not even beautiful enough to escape censure, drunk at her own wedding, making a scene in front of some of California's richest people, suddenly the heir to almost a billion dollars . . .

Craig mentally said a regretful goodbye to that nice neat picture. She didn't do it. Instinct told him Sam Murray was right about that.

'You guys got your samples? Got enough?' he called out. He was ready to get the hell out of here, get back to his own cheap motel and change his shirt.

They nodded and grunted.

'Hey, boss.' It was Conchita Sanchez, one of the CSI team, working on the bedlinen. 'Check this out.'

She stood up from her crouch and pushed the ultraviolet goggles off the top of her head, offering them to Craig.

'What are we looking for?'

'Semen,' she said, without a blush. Nothing

229

fazed Conchita. 'There's none on the bed like you'd expect. Just blood. Nothing where the girl was lying. 'But around here . . . by the bedside table . . . '

He tugged the goggles on and let her turn him around, directing his gaze.

'Yeah. I see.'

The telltale white stains, very faded from the heat and the exposure, were splashed across a carved walnut table by the side of the bed, and a little on its ornate headboard. Their height suggested somebody had masturbated standing up. He'd seen it before in crime scenes. The killer jerking off over a corpse. A little shudder of revulsion ran through him.

'Will we be able to get anything?'

It was hot round here. The sample would have degraded badly. He cursed himself for not having sent a team out here before. It was lazy to just accept the obvious. He imagined the press enjoying another orgy of Fibbie-bashing.

'Not much,' Conchita said. 'Maybe a partial.'

'Enough to eliminate Steen?'

That was the key thing, wasn't it? Because degraded or not, you could say one thing for a semen sample. It hadn't come from their prime suspect. Just by itself, this would be enough for reasonable doubt. If they knew it wasn't Josh's . . . and in fact, he thought, chewing on his lip, unless they could prove it *was* Josh's, she likely walked. Because an unidentified semen sample on the bed and headboard . . . Lisa and Josh had rowed violently, she'd been sloppy drunk, they had stormed upstairs shouting at each other in

230

public. Any defence lawyer would argue that Steen was unlikely to have stood over the bed and masturbated at his furiously angry bride.

She shrugged. 'Possibly. I'll get as much as I can for the lab and we'll overnight it.'

'Do that, then pack up. I want to get all our samples off tonight. Photographs and video for analysis.' Craig ran his hands through his hair. His mind had leapt ahead, putting it all together. Goddamn Sam Murray; he was right about the girl. He was actually right. And all hell was about to break loose.

★ ★ ★

They pulled up half an hour later on Via Asilo, in Ronago, a half-deserted border town under the shadow of the mountains. There was a pretty Romanesque church with a square clock tower dominating a large parking lot filled with cheap cars; locals came here, not tourists. It was anonymous, it seemed safe. Lisa glanced around her and relaxed just a fraction. Who the hell would look for her here?

Sam put the car in a space, and she didn't object. Her legs were screaming. She wanted to walk. And she wanted food. Besides, sitting in a car with him was disturbing. The way he talked, so firm, decisive. And his muscles . . . the guy was built. She could see the shape of his biceps, defined under the shirt. He had a confidence, a casual ease about himself, that didn't revolve around money. She thought how insecure Josh had been; maybe that was why he'd cheated so

231

much. Always looking to get one over, desperate for approval, and hiding it all under a curtain of bluster. But Sam Murray was different. He did things on his own terms, and she had to accept those terms.

Sam came across as a man who could handle women. And who had had lots of them, just for being himself. Josh Steen had had tons of women, but then he'd been rich. And would always have wondered if it was for himself or his money.

Sam's presence unsettled her. The flashes of desire . . . a bad idea. He was the only guy who could help her out of this nightmare. Lisa rebuked herself. Why was she thinking like this?

'I'm hungry,' she said, to distract herself from her train of thought.

'Sure. We'll eat.' Sam opened the door and they got out of the car. It was a little cooler up here in the north, but the day was still bright and sunny. 'The food will be excellent.'

Lisa was surprised. 'You know this town?'

He shook his head. 'And nor does anyone else. That's why you can guarantee it. Italians eat here. There won't be any tourist traps or bad food. It'll be cheap and it'll be good.'

Lisa's stomach rumbled, and she blushed. 'Excuse me.'

He grinned. 'We'd better go find someplace. Come on.'

They walked past the church into the centre of town. There was a dingy little train station, and past it a couple of streets full of shops: the *farmacia*, the *alimentari*. The ubiquitous *tabachi*.

It was a modern place, with ugly tower blocks, and nobody gave them a second glance in the street. Lisa exhaled, liking it.

'I wonder if I could get a job here.'

Sam glanced at her. 'Pretty girl like you? Limey? You'd be the talk of the town. Somebody would rumble you in about five minutes.'

She blushed, hearing him call her a pretty girl.

'There's no running from this, not really. You're too famous. We have to solve it. Unless you want to go into a convent or something.'

She smiled. 'I don't think I'm the convent type.'

'Glad to hear it,' Sam said softly, and the way he looked at her could have stripped the flesh from her bones. She lowered her head, unable to meet his eyes. His desire was naked. It was like a wave of heat bearing down on her. Her body warmed in response, lust pulsing between her legs, a merciless point of fire. She swallowed. Her mouth was dry.

'Here's somewhere,' he said, after an awkward few seconds.

'Oh, great.' Lisa was glad he'd broken the spell. At least she told herself that. She tried to ignore her own disappointment.

They were standing at the top of a flight of stone steps, leading down to what looked like a greasy spoon; a little sign outside advertising ice cream and cigarettes. Sam walked ahead and she followed him. There was a group of Italian workers playing cards in a tiny front room; they looked up as she entered, their eyes running over her.

'*E aperto per pranzo?*' Sam asked.

The owner grunted and gestured to a room in the back. This was no tourist trap, Sam was right about that. Strip lights on the ceiling, a couple of shabby posters with ski scenes on them. The tables were aluminium, and there were cheap orange plastic chairs. Not a straw-covered wine bottle in sight.

They were given menus in laminated plastic, written only in Italian. Lisa looked hers over blankly. She didn't speak the language. A bit of schoolgirl French, that was her limit. God, she was suddenly sick of being abroad, being out of control. A wash of weariness and misery seeped into her.

The surly owner reappeared. He had clean glasses and a half-litre of red wine in a stone flask.

'*E dell'acqua minerale frizzante,*' Sam ordered. He looked at Lisa. 'Just water for me. I'm driving.'

Defiantly she poured herself a glass of wine. A large one. She took a big slug of it, letting the alcohol seep into her, relax her, almost at once.

'I can't understand anything on here,' she said.

'Let me translate for you. I'll read you the whole thing.'

Lisa shrugged. 'That's fine. I guess they'll have a pizza I can eat.'

Sam looked at her, considering. 'Do you like mushrooms? They do a pasta with porcini mushrooms in a creamy sauce. It's really good, done well. Or spaghetti with clams. That's great too. And the bruschetta, that's tomatoes and garlic and herbs on little slices of toasted bread . . . '

Her stomach growled again, embarrassing her. 'You pick something,' she said, surrendering. 'You seem to know Italian pretty well. I'll eat whatever.'

'OK.' He smiled, and turned to the waiter, firing off an easy stream of Italian, asking questions. The guy answered, and Lisa watched respect dawn in his eyes. Sam was fluent, confident. She hated that even at lunch she was dependent on him. She hated even more that she found it sexy.

'So.' The waiter returned with a bottle of water, and Sam unscrewed the cap, poured himself a glass and drank deeply. 'We're about ten minutes from the border with Switzerland.'

She felt a shiver run across her skin; the tiny golden hairs on her forearms lifted. 'There'll be police, border guards.'

'We're in the middle of nowhere. I'm going to drive you across the border, avoiding the inspection posts.'

Lisa sipped some more wine. The waiter was back, with plastic plates, some cutlery in a paper napkin, and a dish of bruschetta. Lisa blinked; the scent of the tomatoes filled the entire room. These were not anaemic green things like you might get in London, the colour artificially induced before they were ripe. These were succulent, full, almost like a fruit. She sniffed hungrily at the scent of garlic and herbs.

'Try it.' Sam offered her one. She bit into the toasted bread, and a heavenly mixture of tomato and garlic and drizzly olive oil and crunching

235

toast filled her mouth. It was so good, following the rough, full-bodied wine, that she almost groaned. He chuckled, and demolished a couple himself.

'God.' She wolfed another. 'I've eaten in some of the priciest restaurants in Beverly Hills and never had anything this good.'

'I told you, baby.'

'Doesn't do to be smug,' Lisa said. Trying to ignore how much she enjoyed hearing him call her baby. It was amazing, though; even through the fear, the food and wine lifted her spirits, helped her cope. She wondered if it was being on the run that did it. Made the taste of a good meal so extraordinarily valuable. 'How can you get us over the border in a car without hitting an inspection post?'

He smiled. 'This is farmland round here. Lots of woods. Lots of fields. We go across, dip the headlights. Drive over a field, get back on the road the other side.'

She blinked. 'You have to be kidding. Drive over a field?'

'That's the idea.'

'But the car will stick.'

'It's been hot. No mud. It'll be fine. I know roughly where to go, as well. These days,' he held up his mobile phone, 'this is all you need to get just about anything. Google Earth, and it's as clear as day.'

Lisa stared. 'This is your masterplan? Drive over a field?'

'It'll work,' he said confidently. 'You need to have a little faith. I've done it before. Other borders. You'd be surprised what a car can take.'

She shook her head.

'I'm open to better ideas.'

'I don't have any,' Lisa muttered. The waiter was back, and laid down steaming plates of pasta; Sam had ordered the pasta al funghi porcini for her, and some arrabiata for himself. She lifted a forkful to her mouth, bit down on it, and was transported straight to heaven. The flavours were dense, dark, full mushrooms, the bite of a little cheese, just enough cream sauce to carry it without clogging. It was an intense experience. She closed her eyes for a second, knocked out. When she opened them, Sam was staring at her, amused.

'What the hell's so funny?'

'Nothing.' He grinned. 'I'm just enjoying you. Eating.'

'What about it?'

'You get so into it,' he said. 'You just throw yourself into the experience. You're . . . you're *savouring* it. A woman who really likes eating. That's getting rarer.'

'Depends what I'm eating.'

'This stuff is delicious. It should be enjoyed. I like seeing a girl abandon restraint for this.'

'All I did was shut my eyes.'

He looked at her for a moment, and she had to lower her gaze and busy herself with the pasta.

'Your husband was a fool,' Sam said softly. 'God knows why he bothered with those plastic women. You're sensual.'

Lisa lifted her head. 'Sam . . . '

He made a brushing-aside gesture. 'I don't

just mean sexy. I mean sensual. You enjoy taste. I've seen you get lost in music. It all counts, it's real. You're a woman who takes joy in life. I feel sorry for Steen. He was right the first time about you. And then he lost his guts, and tried to change you into a Stepford wife.'

'You'd never do that, would you, Sam?' she asked. 'You'd never try to change a woman. You like them all for what they are.'

He held her gaze. 'I've never cared enough about any woman to think about it. One way or the other. I haven't wanted a true relationship.'

She stiffened with annoyance. 'So you're some kind of monk?'

He smiled. 'Not exactly, sugar.'

She ate some more pasta. He was already halfway through his giant plate of macaroni, like nothing kept him from his fuel.

'So what? Sleep with them and forget them?'

'Nobody complained. I just never met anybody.'

'It's a little sophomoric, don't you think?'

'Are you passing judgement? You got married to a guy you knew you didn't love.'

Lisa flushed scarlet with anger and embarrassment. It was worse because it was true.

'There's no point in us fighting,' Sam said. 'Nobody appointed us guardians of each other. Right now we need to get you to Liechtenstein. Let's stay focused.'

She nodded, swallowing. 'You're right. I'm sorry. Your private life is none of my business. You're — you're helping me. I'm grateful, I'm very grateful.'

238

Suddenly she didn't want any more wine. She took a long pull of water and finished the rest of her pasta in silence while Sam called for the bill. Sitting at a table, eating a hot meal . . . it might be a while before they could do this again. She made the most of it.

He was handing over some notes and coins. She saw the meal had not been expensive. Just as he'd promised. The guy knew his way around, Lisa had to give him that. She was getting the unfamiliar sensation of being protected physically by a man, and she was finding it very erotic.

Sam stood. 'Let's go. We should keep moving.'

He moved to the door, and she followed him. The thin fabric of his lightweight T-shirt clung to his back, to the muscles there. Sam Murray didn't walk, he strode; there was something about him, a kind of casual confidence. She felt adrenalin shoot through her, her lips part, her palms moisten. *This is because of my situation,* she lectured herself. It's false; it's a high-octane trick.

But his muscles were still there. And this was hard, it was really hard. She stiffened her back, told herself to concentrate. They were about to cross the border.

★ ★ ★

Sam said nothing to Lisa as he put the car in gear. She had slipped on her sunglasses; instinctively cool, he noted, and part of her high level of native intelligence. Shades were very effective against the casual glance, a look

239

through a car window, another driver stuck in traffic who might peer your way. Humans told a lot through the eyes; covering them was a natural disguise.

He wondered if she'd done it against pursuit, or against him.

Her signals were mixed. Sam knew he detected an attraction, at times. Her body betrayed her. He was used to reading women, and Lisa was more vulnerable than most; she loved life, clearly, and her passions tended to be written on her face. She couldn't hold his gaze at times; her head would bow; her eyes would follow him when she thought he wasn't looking.

But then, like at the restaurant, she'd get defensive. Cheated on by her man, attacked by the press. The last few years had trained this woman not to trust. Add in a lousy childhood and it was a toxic mixture.

Maybe she was right not to trust him. Maybe she should be careful. Sophomoric, she'd said, with withering contempt. And Sam Murray flinched to hear it. She was calling him a little boy, saying he wasn't a man. Dilettante, playboy. Selfish. All the same insults that Craig had tossed at him over the years. The suggestion that he could not handle a real woman, one with brains and guts, rankled. It made him want to prove something to her. Prove everything to her.

But there was no time. And he had to get them both over the border. Every day that passed was dangerous for Sam. They'd come looking for the car, for a filed story, for him. Right now Lisa was the fugitive. Soon it could be him.

He drove fast, twisting the car down little side roads, away from the towns. And suddenly, there it was, past Caldi; the edge of a farm, a fallow field, mud baked to a light brown under the hot sun, with a barn of corrugated iron and a single-track half-made road on the other side.

'See that?' He pointed at the barn. She'd been silent. 'That's Switzerland.'

'You're really going to do this?' she asked, but he was already there; he'd floored the gas and with a huge bump rode over a ditch, and the car was bouncing against stones and rocks on the dried earth, the suspension shaking as they hit each sun-hardened furrow of the plough. Lisa was staring around her wildly, looking for a furious farmer with a pitchfork or a gun, and then the car bumped through a scrubby thorn hedge and they were on the white track road, heading out towards a village in the distance, where he could see cars passing on the main road network.

'There you go,' he said. 'Switzerland.'

Christ! Was there a difference? Lisa looked round at the border country. It was neat farms, flat fields, little chalk-white roads, and the mountains rearing up some distance ahead of them. Maps were just that; on the face of the earth there were no lines. They were in rural, bucolic, quiet land, far from tourism and commerce, and yet she was in another country and under another law. Villages and mud and thin hedgerows. And the car driving comfortably along.

Lisa kept her sunglasses on, but Sam could see

the creep of colour in her face and neck. She was obviously impressed, but would die before admitting it.

'Thank you,' she said, and he knew it cost her to say it. 'You were absolutely right.'

'Next, Liechtenstein. Where they don't check passports.' Sam bit the bullet. 'I'm going to have to phone my editor with the next instalment, Lisa, or they'll come looking for me. I'm late. He's bound to be going nuts. The corporation has tens of millions riding on this story.'

She paled. 'Next instalment? What next instalment? I picked her up and we went to a motel?'

'Nothing that exciting. I'll stop at St Peter's Square. Tell them your side of the story this far.'

She started to sweat. 'You can't do that. You promised.'

'I promised to help you. And I can't do that once they work out that I'm aiding and abetting. It's got to be what it always was: the hard-bitten hack on the trail of the killer trophy wife. Because that's what sells copy. You're running, and I'm hunting you down. Unless I file stories that support that, we're both in deep shit. Do you get that, Lisa?'

The excited blush had vanished. She was clearly scared. But he saw her press her lips together, and she said, 'Yes, I do. I guess I do.'

'Besides — something journalists always say when they want a mark to spill — talk to me, get it off your chest; this is a chance to tell your side of the story. Because just about every potential juror in America thinks you're a gold-digging killer. You need to start floating alternative theories, so at least there's debate. Trust me.'

'I have to,' she said. 'Don't I?'

'You don't have lots of options. Other than jail.' He saw the skin on her jawline ticking, and suddenly felt a wave of pity for her. 'Look, *I* don't think you did it. I sure as hell wouldn't be driving this shitty car in the middle of nowhere if I did.'

'Right,' she said, and there was an utter weariness in her tone. 'I know that. And you understand I'm very grateful. If I don't seem it at times, it's just the pressure of the situation. I'm running, I've been running. I don't know where I'll end up or if I'll ever be safe. I don't know who killed Josh, and who paid him to do it, and why they added me to the deal. Sometimes it bears in on me.' A thin smile; she was struggling to make light of it. 'And as you're the only person here, I guess that means it all hits on you.'

'Don't worry about it. Look, go to sleep, if you can.'

Lisa yawned. 'I might be able to. I used to say I could only sleep lying down, totally flat, I was a light sleeper. All that bullshit. Take away those everyday luxuries and you soon find you can do a lot more than you thought.'

'We should be in Vaduz in around three hours, maybe a bit more.'

'OK.' She turned her head, and looked at him through her sunglasses. 'Thank you, Sam. Really.'

* * *

243

Peter Mazin strode the length of his home office, a thirty-foot room with floor-to-ceiling glass walls that looked out over the white sands of his private beach, and the azure waves of the warm Malibu ocean.

It was good to be him. The beach house was one of five properties that he owned. There was the estate in Nantucket, the brownstone in TriBeCa, the chic flat in Mayfair, this glorious mansion in Malibu, and his twelve-thousand-square-foot holiday home in Mustique. That was what you got for being partners with Josh Steen, even a junior partner. And today, he was no longer the junior partner, in the shadow of the big man with the big ego. He was the heir, the only game in town. All of a sudden, no longer the straight man, the backroom boy. Hollywood's eyes were on him.

It had happened before, he thought, watching the waves dash themselves against the puffy white powder of his exclusive acre of beach. When Don Simpson went to that big rehab in the sky, everybody discovered that Jerry Bruckheimer had been the talent all along. And without Don, Bruckheimer went on to be three times as good as the partnership had ever been. That could be me, Peter told himself. It sure could.

The dark, secret joy in his heart he never mentioned to anybody. He tried not to acknowledge it to himself. He'd given a few dignified public statements, mourning the loss of his friend and partner. There would be a service and a eulogy next week at Josh's Bel Air synagogue, and Peter would be reading from the Torah, saying a few words about his dear friend of thirty years.

But what a friend. Josh was younger, handsomer. More famous. More successful. Steen & Mazin had all too often been abbreviated to 'Steen' by the industry. He, Peter, was an afterthought.

But now the company was all his. Not even part of Josh's estate. Josh had the money, the houses, the stock to leave. But they'd set up the company so that the survivor got it all. In fact, looked at in that way, Peter Mazin was one of Josh's biggest heirs.

He gazed over the ocean and smiled to himself.

One of his first acts had been to cancel *Twelfth Night*, Josh's vanity project, the Shakespeare adaptation set on the south side of Boston, starring a young Matt Damon lookalike, the kid Josh swore was headed for Oscar stardom. Well, not any more he wasn't. Peter's movie *Brutal*, starring Louis Ferranto and Gisela Haughey, teenage starlets both, was now top of the priority list. Secretly he felt Josh might have been right about its flaws, but it was important to show Hollywood who was in charge. *Brutal* was the simplest way to do that. Nevertheless, Peter thought he'd hire some new writers, see what they came up with.

Josh had left a mixed legacy. Sure, their production company was thriving. But there were a bunch of husbands around Hollywood who'd be happy to piss on his grave. And Peter was one of those husbands. Only the worst thing was, unlike some of his friends he'd never caught Hannah with Josh. It was just a niggling suspicion, a doubt in the back of his mind. When he looked at his pretty young wife in her low-cut designer jeans, tight lycra T-shirt stretched over those glorious tits he'd paid for, there was that black, fleeting thought: had Hannah, who loved his money so much, ever traded him for a roll in the hay with the big dog, the one guy in the world who could out-bark and out-bite him? It pissed him off that he suspected Josh. Because that meant he suspected Hannah. And right or wrong, that would ruin his life, if he let it.

Fucking Joshua Steen. Still screwing with him, from beyond the grave.

Peter's anger rose in his throat, till he had to swallow the bile. The fucker was dead, and he was glad. Gladder still that they'd pegged his whore of a wife for the deed. Not that he *knew* first hand she was a tramp, but his friends had believed that, so he was happy to as well. Josh had fucked plenty of Hollywood wives. What a fucking irony if his own unsociable Limey piece went away for stabbing him through the fucking heart. And if she didn't do it, all the better. Somebody had just fucked Josh *and* his standoffish woman. Did Lisa know who? Likely she had no idea. He smirked at the thought. He had hit on that chick a bunch of times. Hot accent, looked bored with Josh. Ripe for the plucking, you'd have thought. But she hadn't responded, hadn't even looked his way. And at the same time, he suspected Hannah was fucking

Josh. When exactly, he couldn't be sure. She never stayed away too long, like overnight, or when there might be an obvious window. But there were enough shopping trips, spa days and lunches with the girls that he remained insecure. And whenever he looked at Josh, this ghost reared its head. But Peter dared not confront him. With what? A feeling, a sense? He was the brooding, poisonous presence that loomed over Peter's marriage. And now he was gone, and when Peter looked at Hannah he feared he'd never know.

On the other hand . . . Josh Steen was dead. Fucking rotting in the fucking ground, he thought with grim satisfaction. And his stuck-up bitch of a wife was running for her life. Whether she did it or not, the punishment would be the same.

His mind wrenched itself back to the movie. It was going to be a difficult production. The cost overruns Steen had warned about were already coming true on this film set. He determined to implement Josh's advice, before he'd unilaterally decided to scrap the project altogether: replace the below-the-line producer, get a new director with a focus on the studio's budget and not his artistic expression. This was a teen flick, not Laurence fucking Olivier. It wasn't cancelled. That was Peter's decision. But it would be run the way Josh had wanted.

And it gave him a thrill to be using the guy still.

★ ★ ★

247

Craig went out into the lobby of his hotel, ignoring the drunk hooker and the two johns bothering her under the slow whirr of the giant ceiling fan, and pulled out his secure BlackBerry. He hesitated for a second, the dark phone heavy in his hands. Once he made this call, it was all over. The easy way out, the clean case with the foreign suspect. He was through, and Sam Murray would become the reporter of the decade. Never mind that Craig had collected the evidence to track the real killer; he knew what the press was like. He was the frontman of this operation, and as such he would be blamed for everything. Doing the right thing was about to get him a piece of Lisa Costello's action, whether he liked it or not.

None of that could be helped. She was innocent. Craig knew that, and he made the call without hesitation.

'Hi,' Sam's answerphone said. 'You've reached Sam Murray. Please leave a name, a number, and a time when you can be called and I'll get back to you. Thanks for calling.'

Thanks for fucking calling, Craig thought, with gallows humour.

'What's up, Sam, it's Craig. We found semen stains on the headboard. They're being analysed. Lots of other fibres too. If the semen ain't Steen she's in the clear. Maybe you should get her back here, get her a lawyer.' He paused in the baking, humid Thai heat as something occurred to him. 'If you contact her, remind her that she's a hell of a rich woman. As far as I know she was Josh Steen's only heir. And if she didn't kill him, the

248

entire bunch belongs to her.' He sighed. 'Let's hope she's grateful.'

★ ★ ★

The prop plane banked to the left and settled down towards its descent. Felix found the whirring of the engines soothing. More so than a jet. They were headed to Geneva airport, and the small size of the plane meant his luggage would be out in minutes.

He had no certain knowledge that Sam Murray was going to Geneva, or even Switzerland. But hunches had served him well in the past. That they had hooked up he had little doubt. Sam's silence to his editor — he hadn't called in some time — was just too much with sums this large riding on a story. He'd been tracking her in a highly efficient way; Felix thought Sam Murray might have made a good assassin, with a little more discipline and the right disposition. But that last key factor was something he lacked; he had dropped the pursuit and picked up the girl.

That thought made Felix's lip curl. He had weaknesses himself. Returning to the scene might be prime amongst them. But he never claimed to be the best in the world. Still, he'd never gone so low as to get caught up with a target, or a client. Sam Murray had a good thing going before he went native. How was Lisa Costello? Felix wondered, licking his lips. She must be a great little lay for Josh Steen to have taken up with her in the first place. Didn't have

249

the perfect beauty, the wafer-thin body with plastic tits, or even the connections of his other girls. Felix had run his eye over the target's file. He suspected that Lisa was a hot piece of ass. She had something about her, a fire that the other girls lacked.

He remembered her body, passed out on the bed, while he sedated and killed Josh Steen. Gave him just enough anaesthetic to paralyse him, not enough to make him pass out. Felix liked the look in their eyes while he did it. Helpless, in pain. It was fun disposing of Josh Steen, his wife's hand wrapped around the dagger and Felix's holding it in place while he stabbed. Making sure to stand well back from the spurting blood. Why the fuck should Steen be the one lying next to those rocking curves, in the antique bed and the private luxury estate? He'd waited obsequiously on all those moneyed guests, seen the palatial bungalows some of them were put up in, the obscene wealth thrown casually around that party. Drugs barely hidden. Caviar piled up like it was mashed potato. Vintage champagne, premier cru, flowing freely everywhere. Designer dresses, rocks round the necks of the girls that could have lit Los Angeles on their own power. Platinum Rolexes everywhere.

It made him burn, fucking burn, with resentment. He killed people for a goddamned living, and whilst the money was good, he couldn't play in this league. Why the fuck should these overprivileged trust-fund brats have everything he was working so hard to get?

And all worshipping at the court of Josh Steen and his lackey Peter Mazin. Felix disliked them both heartily. It was great watching the blood bubble at the side of Steen's mouth. All the cash in the world couldn't save him then.

And he'd felt the familiar stirrings in his cock. The sense of power. That he was here, taking the life of somebody who thought he was untouchable. It was a favourite game of Felix's, to try and watch the exact moment they died. To catch the precise second when light dimmed in their eyes, consciousness slipped away. That was it; no way back. But Josh had cheated him. His eyelids shut before he died. That made Felix mad. He'd thought about killing Lisa then; pity he hadn't. But the richness of the joke, setting her up for it, the fear of the squalid, hot Thai jail cell, the mock trial and then the execution . . . that was one reason not to. The other was the publicity. He'd known how America would react to the female O.J. And word would get out in his business whose kill it was . . .

Lisa had lain there, her pretty little antique gown soaked in Josh's blood. Man, that was horny. Like a wet T-shirt contest using blood. Her juicy tits jutting out from under the red, sopping fabric, her limp hand on the ivory dagger. The feelings in his groin deepened and clutched at him. No time to rape her, but he stood by the bed and jerked off. It was an awesome sight, the greedy Steen all messed up, his blood seeping out of him, and his pretty wife, her thighs and half her ass exposed where the nightgown rode up, set up to take the fall. Little

251

gold-digger got more than she bargained for, huh?

When he'd come, he showered, right in their bathroom. Yeah. The arrogance, the confidence. Another job well done. And Felix was right on top of the world . . .

For a few moments he bathed in the glow of the memory. And then it hit him, as the plane tipped down further into its descent, that he'd been wrong. Premature. The job wasn't quite done, was it? Lisa Costello hadn't taken enough of the drug to knock her out long enough. Instead she'd woken up — and she'd run. And to his amazement, she'd run pretty smart.

Now there was trouble. And he had come to Switzerland to end it. No more loose ends. Lisa Costello was not an optional extra any more. She was the main event. He wondered if he'd get to fuck her before he killed her.

8

'We're here.'

Lisa opened her eyes wearily and looked around her. 'Here?'

'Liechtenstein. Tiny sovereign state, ruled by a prince. Run for years on free banking and secrecy.' Sam grinned at her. 'Good place to hang out. I know people here.'

'I'll follow you, then.' She got out of the car, luxuriating in the feeling of stretching her legs. They were standing on a cobbled street under a cliff. She looked up and saw a fairy-story castle looming overhead, perched almost a mile above them. 'Wow.'

'The princely family are billionaires,' Sam said. 'This place may be small, but it's perfectly formed.'

'I guess so.' It was a little cold now, the sunset almost vanished in the sky. 'Now we're here, what's next?'

'I get us into a hotel that doesn't need passports and doesn't ask questions. One where I know the old woman that runs it.'

'Sounds perfect.' She was fiercely glad she had Sam Murray. He was taking care of her. She almost felt safe with him; as safe as she could.

She glanced around. Apart from the castle on the clifftop, they were in a modern-looking slice of middle Europe. Spacious roads, modern hotels and apartment blocks, built in the sixties

253

and seventies, with some of the attendant ugliness. Behind them there were flat fields. The postage-stamp principality seemed prosperous, but not at all quaint. There was money, and farming, and tourism. Lisa turned her attention back from her uninspiring surroundings to Sam. He was a lot more gripping.

'Then I file the story. I'm going to drive back into Switzerland to do it, in case my calls are being tracked. It's safe to say they probably are.'

'OK.'

'I come back. We have dinner. Then we start going through your story, Lisa. We start investigating who did this and why. I'm going to ask lots of questions, some of them a couple of times. Try and be patient.'

'Sure.'

'Patience isn't your strong suit,' he said drily.

She blushed. 'I'll try harder. Sam . . . '

'You don't have to keep thanking me. Let's just get on with it, OK?'

'OK,' Lisa said. She fought the desire to say more, to blurt out why she was grateful, to excuse her snappiness. Sam didn't want to talk, he wanted to move. He was taking command of this nightmare, trying to lift it off her back. The thought made her almost light-headed. She busied herself with her backpack, not trusting her body. Her emotions might show in her face. The last thing she needed was the humiliation of him knowing she wanted him.

'Where's the hotel?' she asked, looking safely down at the cobbles of the street.

'About three streets away. Follow me.'

She walked behind him as he led her into a main road. The buildings here were modern low-rise offices with a couple of flat-fronted churches thrown in, and some hotels and bed and breakfasts in ersatz Swiss chalets. The roads were wide. It was all something of a contrast to the fat round tower and classic castellated walls of the palace perched high above them.

As twilight deepened, rain started to drizzle around them. The headlights of cars reflected in the road. It was soulless, she thought, modern and anonymous. And Sam Murray knew his way around.

'Right here,' he said, stopping. Lisa looked up at the building. It was a small house with wooden shutters painted apple green, and an ad outside in German. 'Frau Vollenhaus owns this place. I knew her from LA, before she came back here.'

'What did she do in LA?' Lisa asked. 'How did you know her?'

Sam shrugged. 'You don't want to find out.'

She stiffened. Was his arrogance infuriating, or erotic? Both, she decided. 'Yeah, I do, Sam. I'm going to be staying here while you drive back to Switzerland for your goddamn interview, meaning I'll be by myself. And so I'd like to trust the person I'm staying with. What was this woman to you? Why do you trust her to keep a secret?'

Sam Murray looked at her, and his gaze narrowed a little.

'She was a madam,' he said bluntly. 'Ran a high-class ring. Clean girls with tests and certifications.'

Lisa blinked. 'Certifications? Like animals at the vet?'

'Exactly like that,' Sam said unapologetically. 'You're paying top dollar. Thousands a night. And for that money, you don't want to worry about disease. AIDS isn't crabs, it'll kill you.'

Lisa bristled, out there in the street, with the cars streaming behind her. Why the fuck did she care? But she did.

'So you're paying for sex?' she said. 'You, the great Sam Murray, playboy, famous journo, man about town . . . and you pay for it?'

He shrugged. 'I don't like hurting women. I wasn't ready for a relationship. I need regular sex. Paying a girl is one way to guarantee you won't break her heart.'

'God, you're full of yourself,' Lisa said. 'If a woman isn't with you, her heart's going to break?'

'Not all of them. Not most of them. But I try not to use girls. Prostitution's an honest transaction.'

She was getting angry. 'Yeah, real honest. Girls who are addicted to drugs, trafficked sometimes. Like they can help it.'

'Ah,' he said, unfazed. 'That's exactly why you go to a high-class madam, see? The girls she works with are certified not just AIDS-free but drug-free too. You don't want a chick who's using needles. They're bored college girls, usually, or actresses who don't want to live on next to nothing. They have prospects and health. Guys will pay good money for that, lots of money.'

256

'Because it takes away the guilt factor?'

'Exactly. She may be sleazy, but she's not desperate and she's not addicted. She's making a clear choice to fuck for money. You know that when you've got her underneath you. And you pay for it. Pure sex, zero emotion.'

Lisa fought for breath. He outraged her. And yet, logically, he made sense.

'But sex should always have emotion,' she said.

'Says a woman.' Sam shrugged. 'That's just not how guys think.'

Lisa shivered. She'd almost asked this guy to fuck her. Lucky escape. 'You're a real prince, you know that?'

He looked her straight in the eyes, like he always did, in that disconcerting way of his. 'Listen, baby, judge away. The difference between me and other guys is that I'm honest. Those girls want to sell, and I want to buy. There's nothing for you to be mad about.'

She could not hold his gaze. The thought of Sam Murray in bed with some eager, greedy little gold-digging college girl was dreadful. And the worst thing was, she actually envied those chicks. It's just curiosity, she told herself. And you should not give in to it.

'So anyway.' She changed the subject. 'You know this woman to be discreet?'

'Exactly. And she'll assume you're my lover. Not a hooker this time, because she knows hookers, and she'll know you're not one. Just on instinct. But my girlfriend, she could buy.'

'What does that involve?'

He shrugged. 'Leaning on me, touching me.

257

Kissing me, at reception. We don't have to tongue-wrestle, but she'll ask the receptionist about us, so you need to be kissing me. Do you think you can fake some passion?'

Lisa nodded, biting her lip. The last thing on God's earth she wanted to do right now was kiss Sam Murray. Yet she was going to have to.

He picked up her bag, along with his own, and she followed him into the guesthouse. It smelled, not unpleasantly, of sauerkraut and meat. She was hungry again. The receptionist was eyeing them up. She was maybe twenty-five, with a worldly air.

Sam fired off some German at her, and Lisa watched, trying not to be too impressed. For an American, he was pretty easy with languages. She found herself curious. Was he really this skilful? Apparently so. And that was more than anybody could expect from a tabloid hack. She understood that Sam Murray was way more than that.

He turned round, and crooked his finger, smiling. 'I think they got a room. Come here, baby.'

Lisa forced a smile. Not hooker-ish this time, just warm. 'Great.' She walked over to Sam and nestled against him. It was much harder to do than it had been in Italy, at the motel. Just a single day later, and she already found herself falling. Fighting it, but falling all the same.

He slipped one arm around her waist, casually. The caress was cruel to Lisa. It burned on her skin. She felt the blood pool in her lower belly and her groin. A hot flush of wanting him ran across her. What the hell is wrong with you, girl? she asked herself. Just minutes ago he'd been casually describing how he used high-class call girls. With such male arrogance, such ruthlessness. How could she want him? Her body was a traitor.

But she did want him. And helpless against it, she sensed herself relaxing, pressing into him, returning the pressure of his arm.

Lisa blushed. Maybe he'll assume it's all part of the act, she thought.

Sam was still talking, but as she moved against him, he glanced at her. And as his eyes made contact, her body stiffened, her face blushed. She could feel her reactions coming from deep in her belly. Her lips parting, her pupils widening. Her heart rate sped up. And of course he could feel that, quite easily. One arm was circling her waist. His hand rested just below her left breast, on her ribcage, above the heart.

'. . . *sicher, und mag ich mit Frau Vollenhaus sprechen?*' he was asking, smiling casually. His eyes flickered over Lisa's, and she hated the amusement she saw there. Then, indolent, experimentally, he splayed his fingers over her ribcage and began to caress her, tracing his fingers lightly against her skin, stroking the underside of her breast almost imperceptibly.

It was like an electric shock. Lisa gasped, then bit her lip to stop herself moaning aloud. A wave of lust rocked through her. She was trapped, and he knew it, and he did not propose to spare her. She tried to pull herself away from him, violently. But his arm tightened hard around her, his grip was iron. He looked at her, grinning, and shook his head very slightly.

There was the sound of footsteps in the corridor. A heavy-set woman was coming. Sam smiled again, luxuriating in his opportunity, and bent his head to Lisa's, brushing his lips over hers. Kissing her, but not quite. And Lisa felt herself, despite all her will, surrendering, her mouth opening under his, her lips full and soft and yielding to him. Sam gently mixed his tongue against hers, running it against her upper lip, teasing the outer reaches of her mouth. Lisa felt her knees buckle. Helplessly she pressed herself against him. Her nipples tightened in her bra. Her heart thudded against her ribs. Oh God, she thought, I'm done, I'm so done . . .

'Sam! It is so good to see you again, my darling.' The woman was speaking English, heavily accented. Lisa reluctantly broke away from the kiss and nestled against Sam, shy, way too shy to actually look him in the face. 'And who is this lovely creature?'

'This is my girlfriend, Emily. I want someplace to hide out, Marianne,' Sam was saying. 'No passports, no bullshit. I got cash. Her husband's a player. There are people looking for us.'

'And nobody knows that game better than you.'

'Exactly. Can you help a guy out?'

The woman smiled. 'How many times you got the cops off my back, Sam? Of course.' She looked at Lisa, and Lisa thought she saw a cold twinkle in the brown eyes sunk in the ageing face. Marianne Vollenhaus had seen lots of sun, lots of booze and lots of cigarettes, and it showed. Good make-up and an expensive hair-dye job could not hide the years of damage. Her eyes lingered on Sam, and Lisa suddenly realised the older woman was jealous. God, and she was forty-five on her best day. Had she carried a torch for Sam Murray? For how many years?

Marianne looked her over. 'Come this way. You pay me, Sam. Discount for you. How long you wanna stay?'

He shrugged. 'Three nights? We should be tired of each other after that.'

'Just one hundred euros, then.'

'Come on, it's more than that.'

'Not to you, *liebchen*,' she said.

Sam handed her two hundred and kissed her on the cheek.

'*Vielen Dank. Du bist meine Süsse*,' he said.

Frau Vollenhaus led them up a flight of wooden stairs covered in a well-trodden green runner. Lisa wondered if this was a brothel too. Old habits probably died hard, right? They moved into a corridor, which was narrow and poorly lit and smelled strongly of smoke. It was a dive, but at least it was relatively clean. She liked the surroundings. It was a house to get lost in.

'Here.' The older woman stopped outside Room 52 and handed Sam a giant metal key with a long steel tag. 'This is a good room. Tucked away, like you say.'

'Thanks, Marianne.'

'Call if you need anything. We can make

sandwiches, bring you beer. There are places to eat down the street.'

Sam pulled Lisa to him again, and she almost trembled. This woman was about to leave. She was going to be alone in a room with Sam Murray. And nobody there to stop him.

'We won't want to be disturbed. Thanks, though, Marianne. For everything.'

'Yes, thank you,' Lisa added. Marianne looked back at her, and her smile did not reach her eyes.

'I will leave the lovebirds to it,' she said, and turned and plodded back the way they had come.

Lisa almost wanted to beg her to stay. Sam had the key and was turning it in the door lock, nice and easy. It opened, and he carried their bags into the room. There was a good queen bed, a nice size for a small European hotel. The place looked clean, and had a desk and a chair. She glanced into the bathroom; it was white-tiled and functional, and the towels were at least big enough to wrap around her midriff. She strongly suspected this was one of Frau Vollenhaus's best rooms. There was not a lot of extra space around the bed; not many places to hide.

The door closed behind them and clicked shut with a thud. Lisa was intensely aware that they were now alone together.

She swallowed drily. Sam Murray was watching her, with his arms folded across his chest. His eyes were on her. She felt herself growing moist and slippery between the legs. Her heart pulsed: panic, lust, a mixture.

'Well,' she said, trying to be casual. 'That

seemed to go fine. I mean, she buys I'm your girlfriend . . . '

'Lisa,' Sam said. And the heavy tone of his voice meant he knew that she was lost.

'Sam . . . ' She lifted her eyes to him, protesting. 'Don't . . . '

'It's no good,' he said softly, intently. 'Is it?'

She opened her mouth, to argue, to say something. But nothing came out. Just a strangled sound, almost guttural.

'Come here,' he said insistently. 'Now.'

Lisa walked round the bed towards him. Almost stumbling. She couldn't look him in the face, she couldn't force herself to meet his eyes. She was shy, her breath was ragged. That kiss . . . her mouth, her heart rate; her body had told him everything he needed to know.

There was no place to hide.

She was in front of him now. Her clothes felt heavy on her skin. Her jeans were clinging to her, the cotton of her bra was chafing against her nipples. He put his hands on her shoulders, and ran them down both sides of her ribcage, and Lisa heard herself gasp aloud with desire.

'Look at me,' Sam said.

She raised her eyes for half an instant, then dropped them again. She was aroused and painfully embarrassed. He had her; she was so naked before him. She could hardly take the suspense.

'It's going to be difficult for us to have a relationship if you can't even look me in the face,' Sam said gently.

Lisa breathed hard and forced herself to look

263

at him. A wave of wanting swept her from the crown of her head to the tips of her toes.

His dark eyes fastened on her. They drank in her face, then lowered, taking in every inch of her body. Lisa felt stripped naked, assessed. And not as a trophy wife or a social pawn. As a woman; with nothing to offer other than herself.

Sam reached out and put one hand under her chin, making her look at him. She reddened in the face. He smiled and pulled her to him, slowly but insistently. Lisa's body was enfolded in his arms. She felt very slight, very slender, against the muscles of his chest and his thick biceps. She was emotional, shaking. This man had given up much for her. A whole life. He was protecting her from God knew what horrors. And now she was here, in his arms.

'Ssh.' He held her to him, calming her as though she were a skittish mare. 'Stay here. Just relax. I'm not going to force myself on you, Lisa. This will happen if you want it to happen.' He looked down at her and grinned, maddeningly confident. 'And we both know you want it to happen. But I'm going to have to hear you admit it.'

'Admit it?' she managed.

'Yeah. Admit you like me. You want me. You want me to make love to you. And you're basically falling for me.'

'You're wrong for me,' she muttered. 'This is wrong. We shouldn't.'

'That's right, we shouldn't. But we're still going to. Aren't we?'

She couldn't bear it. His blood, the warmth of

it around her. The faint scent of sweat and his aftershave. The feel of his muscles and his chest. He was so masculine, she felt weak.

'Yes,' she murmured. 'Yes . . . I don't want to talk . . . '

'Mmm. You fought this pretty hard.' He was enjoying teasing her, and she hated herself for finding it erotic. Lisa pressed close, and felt him hard against her. He lowered his head, tightening his grip around her back, closing his mouth over hers. And this time, his tongue was insistent, probing, flicking. She half groaned in the back of her throat, surrendering to the kiss. Her tongue answering his, delicate, offering herself. His hands raised and caressed the sides of her throat, his thumb and forefinger sweeping lightly over her skin. Then his left hand moved to her belly, and lay there, open, feeling her hot and melting under his touch. Heat literally pulsed from her skin, where the blood was pooling . . .

And suddenly Sam thrust his hand under her T-shirt and unsnapped her bra, with what she knew was practised ease. Her breasts, freed, were warm and full in his hand, her nipples tight, hard as he caressed her; very subtly, not pawing at her, exploring her body, trying to give her pleasure. Lisa shook and arched under the touch. She reached down to her jeans, her hands shaking, but he stopped her.

'I'll do it.' And he did; his hands undid her buttons, freed the jeans, tugged them halfway down her knees. Her panties clung to her; she was wet, like she hadn't been in years. He slipped the T-shirt off over her head, tugged her bra aside. And now he was kneeling over her, staring at her body like he wanted to drink her in.

'God. You're stunning,' he said, and his voice was thick with desire. Lisa felt it hit her like waves of heat coming from him.

'I want to see you,' she whispered. She reached for his shirt, but his left hand held her back.

'Not yet.' He stroked her, running his hands across her breasts, down to the flat of her stomach, then moving them to her hip bones, stroking down the sides of her haunches. Not touching her between the legs. Just feeling her thighs, her legs. Waves of heat crashed through her. Josh had never taken his time; with him she'd felt like an item on the to-do list. And the boyfriends before had fumbled and grabbed. Sam's touch was assured. His eyes were on her like sex was just the start, as though they were together on the edge of a cliff, about to see if they could fly . . .

She gasped. He bent his head and kissed her, hard, on the slope of her breast. She felt his right leg pulling her jeans completely from her. His tongue was licking, circling at her skin. Lisa moaned and lifted her body a little, trying to angle it under his mouth. He was clothed still, and she was completely nude. She felt vulnerable, submissive, exposed. Sam was toying with her, and the eroticism of it was overpowering. Fumbling, she tugged at the waistband of his jeans, but her fingers were shaking. They were tight on his skin; she could feel rock-hard muscle under the denim.

'I thought about you,' Sam said, and his voice was harsh with lust. 'Ever since that night in the garden. I wanted you, even back then. You're different from any girl I've ever known.' He leaned down, undid his jeans, kicked them off. She grabbed awkwardly at his thin, long-sleeved T-shirt; it was Armani, a dark aubergine, and it clung to his muscles and picked out his eyes. Almost frightened, she pulled it off over his head. His body was tanned, developed, strong. Sculpted, like Italian marble. The thick muscles of his chest and biceps slid around under the skin.

He moved over her. She felt his hardness on top of her. He was looking into her eyes. His face lowered so his lips were millimetres from hers. Lisa opened her mouth, in abject submission. She was burning up. He was the only thing she could think of.

'I never took a woman that didn't want it,' Sam said, pressing his chest on hers.

'Jesus.' Lisa choked. 'You don't need to give me the manifesto.'

'No. But I want to hear you say it. Explicitly.'

'You want me to beg,' she managed.

'Yeah.' His lips brushed tantalisingly over hers. 'I want to hear you say it.'

Lisa squirmed. His hands stroked gently, patiently. He never touched anywhere important. It was teasing, sweet torture. His eyes above her said he knew what she was feeling. But he did not insist. He waited for her to say it.

'I want you,' she half choked. 'I did from the beginning.'

Sam didn't say anything. His body lowered on top of hers. And she opened to receive him.

His mouth locked on hers. His hand cupped her breast, caressing her. His legs moved in between hers, his knee thrusting her thighs apart. Lisa half reared under him, thrusting herself up to him. And as he kissed her, Sam took her, gently at first, then hard, deep . . . and her desire burst over her like a dam breaking, flooding her skin, waves of lust rushing to her groin, to her fingertips, to the top of her skull, and she moved with him, accepting him, his hands all over her, feeling every inch of her, and the sensations were so intense. It had never been like this with Josh, not once . . .

And as she arched and writhed beneath him, Lisa suddenly understood, with helpless clarity, that she had fallen in love with this man. That like it or not, she was his.

★ ★ ★

'I'm going out now. To file my story,' Sam said.

He pulled on one of his tight sweaters, lightweight, great for travel, and buttoned up his jeans. She was sitting on the edge of the bed, a T-shirt on, no bra. The sight of her breasts swaying a little under the cotton, her small bud nipples outlined, got him hardening slightly in his pants. Which was incredible, considering he'd just come twice in under an hour.

But then she was incredible. Her beautiful face still reddened from the glow of sex. He loved how the blood flushed to her cheeks when she got aroused. She was literally hot. And her hair, tousled from the bed. Her kissable mouth slightly open. God, she was the sexiest thing. What an idiot Steen had been, to think he could improve on perfection.

Lisa Costello was so brave, so beautiful. Sam knew that he had fallen deep. Craig would kill him: journalistic ethics, aiding and abetting, all kinds of laws and moral codes . . . all smashed to pieces, and he didn't give a goddamn. Lisa was his woman. Simple as that. She was his woman, in a way no female had ever been before. And there was an idea fermenting in the back of his mind that one day soon he would make her his wife. But right now it was enough to look at her, remember her gasps and moans, savour how wet she'd gotten, how exquisitely responsive she was. And that they were together, and she was his.

'You really have to go?'

'If we don't want them to add my name to the wanted list. Look, I'm driving to Switzerland, it's ten minutes away. Then I file, I come back here. It won't take long. We could use the money, too. They give me twenty-five thousand per instalment now.'

'But you can't get at that money anyway, you said. Once we use the ATM they can trace you.'

Sam pulled his passport from his jacket. 'I've got this, and we're in Liechtenstein. Home of discreet banking. I take this to my branch, make a withdrawal, nobody knows anything. It's the best way to get money. We should have some cash, we're getting low.'

'OK,' Lisa said. Reluctant. He looked at her,

and she blushed. She was so exposed to him now. They both knew how she had gasped and clutched at him. God, she was the hottest lay he'd ever had. The faint stirring deepened. He should get the hell out of here. 'How long will you be?'

'I'll try to keep it to under an hour.'

'All right. Anything I should do? Go out, buy supplies?'

'Go out?' He stared at her. 'You only leave the room with me. And only when we have to. The fewer people who catch sight of you, the safer we are. Don't answer the door to anybody but me. And I'll have the key so I'll just let myself in.'

Anxiety crossed her features; he hated to see it.

'Why would anybody else come here?'

'They wouldn't. I'm sure it'll be fine. You just hang out here, shower, whatever you want. I'll be back as fast as I can.'

'I hope so,' she said.

Sam looked at her, and felt that unfamiliar clutching around his heart again. God help him, he really was falling in love. Maybe she'd been right about the hookers. This was so incomparably different, this was what sex should be. He'd never pay a woman again.

'What, you think I'd stay away from you? As soon as I come back, I'm putting you right back on to that bed.'

He walked past her to the door, leaned down, and cupped her breasts in his hands, feeling her nipples harden almost immediately, her breath quicken. A surge of testosterone rushed through

270

him, and he kissed her full on the mouth, then walked out before he forgot everything and just took her in his arms again.

As Sam strode down the corridor, he picked up his pace. He had to do this, and he hated it. All he wanted in the world right now was to be back in that room with Lisa Costello.

★ ★ ★

Felix hung up the phone and spun his car around, smiling. You had to be lucky in this game, as well as good. Course, the more contacts you had in the field, the luckier you got. And luck was his first name.

The motel network. Old-fashioned, really beta-level spy stuff. But it worked. They'd been seen, together. Acting a john and his hooker. Paid in cash, but left together, in the same car. Felix shook his head. Sam Murray would never make a spy.

It told him a bunch of things. That they were together, that Murray was in the tank for her. That they were running. He also assumed Murray believed her. The form book on this guy didn't lie; he wouldn't throw away a million dollars just for a piece of pussy, no matter how sweet. A million bucks bought a lot of pussy. No, Sam Murray was a boy scout trapped in the body of a libertine. He was wading in to rescue the innocent woman. What a fucking idiot. It would be a special pleasure to kill him.

They'd headed north. Another classic mistake, running for shelter instead of staying laterally in

271

one place, moving only slightly, making the hunt harder. Clearly Sam wanted to take her out of Italy. Switzerland had good banking, but Felix knew now that he'd gone one better. Gone to Liechtenstein. He already had names, numbers and locales for all Sam Murray's best contacts; Lisa Costello didn't have any. The girl was fucking friendless. At least that cut things down for him.

And Sam knew nobody in Switzerland, but he did have a contact in Liechtenstein, a former madam. Exactly the kind of bitch you'd run to in serious trouble. And secure banking. Sam had gone there to hide his woman. Felix had the address, and he had the time. And now he was sure he was going to get this finished. The woman was his. No journalist was going to stand in his way. This time, no loose ends — he would kill Sam Murray as surely as he would kill Lisa Costello. And the madam and her staff, just to make sure.

★ ★ ★

Marianne Vollenhaus sat at her desk. The receptionist, her cousin's daughter, had left for home early, that gum-chewing bitch. Marianne sat alone, daring the phone to ring, daring any of these stupid fuckers to complain. She was angry. Her mood was black, bleak rage. Sam Murray had passed her on his way out, and smiled at her with such heartbreaking casualness. It was totally obvious that he didn't want her. Years in LA, providing him with girls, laughing into the small

272

hours, drinking, doing lines together. She had liked him then, wanted him. It could have been love, if he'd encouraged her. And they'd kissed and fucked once, a few years back, when he was half-drunk and she was at her lowest weight and eager. But he hadn't mentioned it the next day, and he'd stayed away from her.

And now, even the friendship they'd maintained hurt her. He was here with another woman, younger, prettier and thinner. Marianne hated her. And the girl was upstairs, in her house, waiting for Sam. She wished she had never set eyes on him.

The bright, up feeling from the coke she'd snorted earlier had started to leave her, and she was jittery and cold. She thought about the girl. There was something familiar about her face. And she could tell from the set of Sam Murray's shoulders that he was lying about her. Something he wasn't saying . . .

Marianne drummed her fingers on the paper blotter and concentrated. She would get it soon. It would come to her, like these things always did.

★　★　★

Felix moved his car into the right lane. The customs guard asked for his *papieren*, and he gave him one of the fake passports he'd carried into Europe. Good ones. The man thanked him, and he was through the border post, into Liechtenstein, a pointless postal stamp of a country. Good for fuck-all except banking and

273

hiding. And hunting, he thought, and smiled.

Vaduz was an easy place to drive through. He was almost there. He put his hand in his pocket, checking his weapons. There was the stiletto, the needle, the syringe. He wasn't sure what he would use on the girl. His gun and silencer were sitting in the glove compartment, and they would get pulled first. But he wanted back-ups, for close-combat work. He glanced at the satnav. He was three minutes away.

★   ★   ★

Marianne clenched her fist and put down the porn mag she'd been flicking through. Of course, of fucking course. The girl — the slut. It was Lisa Costello, the gold-digger who had killed Josh Steen, one of Marianne's best former clients. Under other circumstances, she might have had a soft spot for Lisa. Girls who knifed the men who traded in them . . . Marianne might have turned a blind eye. Sure. Fuck 'em.

But in this case, the whore was here with one of her personal favourites. Not that she loved Sam; she never allowed herself the weakness of love. But she liked him, and she wanted her feelings returned. Which they were not.

For that, right now, she blamed this girl. And the girl was going to get it.

She considered calling *US Weekly*. But that was Sam's magazine. Marianne was vaguely aware that he had some kind of big story there. She didn't want to screw him over. It was the girl she wanted tracked. There was the *Enquirer*, of

274

course, but why hand the big story to Sam's rivals? LAPD?

Marianne had enough contacts in her little black book to get listened to. But she had an ex-hooker's natural distrust of the cops. She traced a pattern with her long red nails on the desk. It would come to her. Exactly the right place to shop Little Miss Lisa. Because if she couldn't have Sam Murray, Lisa Costello certainly wasn't going to.

* * *

Lisa lay in the room half nude for a few minutes, gazing at the door. Finally she reached for her clothes and pulled them on, half-heartedly: panties, leggings. She even slipped on her socks and shoes. She didn't want Sam to find her naked when he got back. Her body was lightly dewed with sweat. She had no idea how to deal with the torrent of feelings rushing through her.

The bad ones were easier to identify. Guilt. Josh wasn't two weeks in his grave and she'd just fucked her brains out with a guest at their wedding. The thought horrified her, and warmed her too. Josh had screwed Melissa back then; he could hardly ask for fidelity. But that was what death did for you, it gave you respect and sanctity. And she had seen his body, covered in wounds. He still meant something to her, lots to her. She was sorry they hadn't worked out. It had looked good once. And now . . . she had barely met this guy, Sam, but felt like she knew him, had known him for ever. And the way he looked at her, not wanting anything from her other than herself, the woman. That was so attractive. He was so attractive. Was it retro, was it unfeminist, to fall for a man who was trying to save her life? Physically risking his liberty for her? And yet she had . . .

The way he looked at her. Dear God, she burned from it, even now. The aftershocks of her orgasms still rippled gently through her groin and body. No man had ever turned her inside out like that. His hands, his tongue, his cock inside her . . . his strong chest moving over her, his dark eyes locking on her, his mouth clasping on to hers . . . the memories stirred the heat in her body. But if she was waiting patiently when he came back . . . Lisa was afraid; she could not afford to lose herself in a love affair with a second man. Sam must not find her stretched out and eager. She'd have to fight to keep her identity straight.

She rose, trying to ignore the tendrils of desire trailing across her skin, and went to check their luggage, just for something to do. Sam said they needed money. How much had they got left? She herself had a couple of hundred euros. Curiously, she rifled through Sam's small case. He had about forty-five, plus some coins. She shivered; obviously that line about needing more cash was real. God, it was strange, going from being Josh Steen's fiancée, rotting in a gilded cage in Beverly Hills, never thinking about money from one day to the next, to running here, some basic hotel in the middle of nowhere,

276

counting the notes and coins in a shitty little bankroll . . .

There was a sound in the corridor. Lisa's head lifted. Somebody walking fast. It sounded purposeful, not like a guest padding along gently to their room. She knew instinctively that it wasn't Sam. His footfall was familiar to her already.

It was someone else. The footsteps slowed. He was coming to her door. Lisa's pulse raced, her heart started to thump. She put the euro notes in her pocket and moved quietly to the window, opening the latch.

There was a knock on the door, loud and confident.

'Room service,' the male voice said. 'Compliments of Frau Vollenhaus. Can I come in?'

★ ★ ★

Felix stood outside the door. Excitement crackled through him. Any minute now he'd have this goddamn case put to bed. The stupid journalist had left his target. She was entirely by herself. Easy. God, sometimes it was just as easy as pie. Walking in to find reception deserted except for the old whore, hanging up the phone. Who had she been talking to? Felix didn't know, but he could guess. Shopping Lisa Costello to the highest bidder. Honour amongst thieves, but none amongst whores. Not one ounce of professional courtesy. It was so simple to take out his silenced gun and have her tearfully confess everything, whimpering and choking,

277

begging not to be killed. But what did that old bitch have to offer? Not even an enjoyable fuck with a gag in her mouth. He shot her, and dragged the corpse back into her office, stuffing it in a closet there. His dick was hard from the power. Those old familiar rhythms of the kill. Then he moved into the corridor where he knew Lisa Costello was, and the man, Murray, had left her all alone. That was a nice bonus, after all the shit he'd been through. It was a much easier, cleaner job without male protection. Five decades of feminism meant fuck-all when a woman was faced with a man who wanted to do her harm; they found that out the hard way all the time. He could overpower a female, any female, in seconds, whether she'd done some pathetic self-defence class or not. Guns were for when time was short. Felix quite enjoyed the basic domination of the trapped woman, smashing them to the ground with nothing more than his fists, or his hands locked around their necks. Really, the biological disparity between men and women was absolute.

He enjoyed it. He was hard and he wanted to fuck. And Lisa Costello, gold-digging trophy wife slut, was in that room all on her own. She'd spent years wringing it out of that sucker Josh Steen; maybe it was time for a man to have a little fun with her. Either way, she was dead, but he saw no reason why he shouldn't slam his dick into her first. And gag her while she was being raped, because who wanted to hear the choking moans and the cries? She could turn on the waterworks all she wanted, but her pretty head would be shoved on the bed and he wouldn't see it. He smirked. He'd wanted that gorgeously shapely ass since Thailand. It would be a particular pleasure to nail her. And as soon as he'd come, with his cock still inside her, Felix thought he'd push her down on the bed, on her belly, falling on top of her, and strangle her, not withdrawing until he felt her go limp . . .

The thought stirred his groin. He loved this job sometimes. He couldn't wait to call his client with the news. This was the door, Room 52. She'd be dead within ten minutes.

Felix raised his hand and knocked.

9

Sam walked down Oberdofstrasse, in Flasch, Switzerland. It was the nearest town to the border, and he'd come here before, wanting to call outside of the principality. There used to be a little phone kiosk on this street, right by the bookmaker's. Yeah — it was still there. He investigated; it took cards. He had picked up several in Rome. A good reporter was never without them.

Uncharacteristically nervous, he shoved one in the slot. It wasn't that he gave a fuck about what they did to him. But Lisa; he wanted to protect her, and she was a weak spot now, his Achilles' heel. They could get her through him. Sam did not want to let a thing go. This call would be a delicate balancing act.

'Let me talk to Rich Frank. It's Sam.'

'Oh my God, Sam.' Sarah, the breathy assistant, sounded like she was having a coronary. 'I can't believe you actually called. He's been climbing the walls. Hold on, OK?'

'OK, but tell him to be fast. I'm working phone cards here.'

'Wait up.' A moment's piped music down the phone, and suddenly he was greeted by the dulcet tones of big Rich Frank, barking at him like a rabid dog.

'Sam fucking Murray. What the flying fuck? Where the fuck have you been?'

'On the trail,' he replied coolly. The nerves vanished. Rich Frank was a clown, and Sam could play him. 'I was making the story, so I was too busy to file one.'

'Fuck you!' screamed Frank. 'We had to fill the last issue with stock photographs and quotes from her schoolfriends! At a quarter mil a story, I need something!'

'I got you something,' Sam said. 'I met her.'

'Bullshit,' Frank breathed, and Sam could see the dollar signs in his eyes. 'You met her?'

'Yeah. In the Vatican. St Peter's Square, where the Italian police have no rights.'

'I fucking love it.' Rich Frank was breathing heavily like he was having an orgasm. 'What a story. She's some operator. The Vatican. What did she say?'

'You want the headline? That she didn't do it. And I'm thinking, guess what? Maybe she didn't.'

'Don't tell me you're thinking with your dick again, Murray,' Frank said crudely. 'She's a killer. Remember that.'

'Why don't you let me file the story? I got some juicy stuff. She called the airline to let them know about the girl in the closet, Rich. She wasn't marked, no sign of a struggle. She thinks she was drugged. From what I saw that night, it could be true. She was lit, but she wasn't fall-drown drunk.'

'Man,' Frank said. 'The readers hate this chick.'

'They'll love a mystery better. I'll report, they can decide. Water-cooler stuff; controversy will shift those copies, you know it.' Sam toughened his voice. 'I'm reporting it the way I saw it. You know any other eyewitnesses?'

'No. No,' his editor said eagerly. 'When can I get it?'

'Tonight. Soon as I get confirmation the next two fifty's in my account. No, Rich, don't complain. You need to work with me on this.' Sam grinned. 'Have them wire it right now, or we'll miss next week's deadline too, won't we?'

'God, you are a fucking prick.'

'Yes, sir. Guilty as charged.'

'You motherfucker,' Frank said, and Sam thought he detected a note of admiration. 'You got me over a fucking barrel. If this story ain't what you're cracking it up to be, this'll be the last payment like this you get, and you'll never work again, either.'

'You don't get to make those decisions, Rich, so you can stop beating your chest. Shape you're in, it's likely to give you a coronary. Send the cash.'

Rich Frank grunted and hung up on him. Sam smiled again, and called his bank as he walked back to the car. An obsequious flunky promised to text him as soon as the money landed. Meanwhile, he would start writing; he didn't need a laptop, it was all in his head. This was important, maybe one of the most important stories he'd ever write. How to keep them guessing, defend Lisa, keep her out of it. It wasn't just hackery now. Every word would be pored over by the FBI, watching for clues. And not just them. Josh's killers would be out there,

282

watching. And waiting.

They wanted to get her. Had done from the moment they set her up. The thought of the killer in that bedroom, looking down on Lisa, made Sam's heart clench with fear on her behalf. How vulnerable she had been. He must have been sure of himself as he wrapped her slender fingers around the rich ivory handle of the dagger. And he, Sam, had made it easier, hadn't he? Setting up Lisa Costello as the girl America loved to hate. The perfect suspect. And now he was trying to untangle the mess he'd gotten her into.

He reached his car, and stepped inside. The article could be written and faxed from the hotel room. The key thing was not to stay away from Lisa.

★   ★   ★

The knock. The voice. There was something in that voice. She didn't have long to analyse; it just hit her in the stomach. An American accent. Did your typical Liechtensteiner, or Swiss-German, speak like that? Was he somebody Frau Vollenhaus had hired from the old brothel days? She had to doubt it.

Lisa looked around the room, panicked. Fear welled up in her like a swollen river overflowing its banks. But it was no good. Sam wasn't here, and the other guy was. No point in waiting for rescue. Five minutes from now might be too late.

She swallowed, hard. She had outrun the combined police operations of Thailand and

Hong Kong. Now it was time to run from a killer. She had a couple of hundred euros in her pocket, but no way to get more, and no way to contact Sam. And there was a guy who wanted to kill her mere feet away from her . . .

That idea concentrated her mind. She shoved the window upwards and looked down disconsolately at the sheer drop below. At least there was nobody outside her window. But the fall would break her legs, if she had the guts to endure that much pain. And he would come to find her, and he would kill her . . .

She looked to the right and saw the young elm tree spreading below her. It wasn't substantial, wasn't hoary. Would it hold her up? The slim branches waved prettily in the wind, their light green leaves attractive against the sun. No comfort for her there. And yet, she instantly processed, it was this or nothing. The angle was bad, and the tree was several feet away from her. But it was her best and only hope.

She heard a fresh round of banging on her hotel room door.

'Hello? Mr Murray? Ms Costello? I'm afraid we need to come in. We'll be getting the key; could you let us in instead? Hello?'

The voice was American, clearly nothing to do with Frau Vollenhaus. It was a man, and a man who was there to kill her.

Lisa touched the euro notes in her pocket. Sam was gone. She was on her own again. The man was at the door, he was coming. She stepped up on to the windowsill and shifted her body gingerly outside of the frame, holding on with both hands. The tree was still there, and she was still paralysed . . .

There was a shove on the door. Hard. Lisa saw it shaking in its frame. She turned her eyes to the slim young tree, angled to the left below her. Closed them and murmured an inchoate prayer, then bit the bullet and jumped . . .

She was grabbing at the branches as she fell, clutching at them. They were too slim to take her weight and her hands were slipping. Scratches ran up her skin, making her gasp with pain as twigs and the trunk hit her. But the tree was slowing her down, breaking her fall; she was still hitting wood and leaves, and then she was on the grass at the back of the hotel. Bleeding. But alive.

Would he have heard? Would he have heard anything outside that door? She was not sure. She didn't want to wait to find out. The hotel's back garden was a piece of scrubby lawn backing on to a road. Immediately Lisa walked across to it, moved between the cars and began to run. She had no idea where she was going, and that seemed important. If she didn't know where she was going to end up, how could the man who was hunting her? Her cell phone was right there, in her back pocket. In a few minutes she was going to find someplace to hide and call Sam, let him know what had happened. The last thing on God's earth she wanted was for him to come back now. They were split up, and she was terrified. But she desperately wanted to protect him. Dear God, she thought. I'm in love. And at a time like this . . .

But the man, whoever he was, could still be coming. It would only take him minutes to head back down the stairs. And he'd have a car, and he'd come looking for her, the minute he realised she was gone from the room. Lisa choked back a sob of terror, and tried to put herself into his head. If she was a bastard killer, how would she hunt?

For now, she just kept running. Down side streets, turning left, right almost at random. Heading into the centre of town. Once she got far enough away she would find somewhere to hide. Not a hotel, not anywhere he might have spies. Somewhere he wouldn't think of looking. A party place, perhaps. Nightclub, casino . . .

A Shell garage loomed up ahead of her. Lisa walked across the road, tempted by its bright lights and welcoming display of cigarettes and candy. So nice, so normal. But none of that was for her. Not any more. She walked around the side of the building, and stood in the dark shadows at its back. Not visible from the road; nobody was looking. Behind her was a patch of tarmac and empty beer cans and water bottles. There was some scrubland beyond, fenced with barbed wire. She looked around her cautiously, but he was not there.

Lisa breathed out. She was still alive.

★　★　★

Sam turned the car and saw the hotel looming up ahead of him. He was getting aroused again just by the thought of Lisa there, waiting. So

286

beautiful. So brave. He almost couldn't think too much about it. It was hard to say he deserved a girl like her. But they were locked in this together, and he was fiercely glad about it. She needed him, and now he needed her too. His mobile rang, startling him; it was Lisa. He grinned. Impatient, was she? Didn't like him staying away too long? That was a real good sign for a man. But he was right at the hotel. His finger hovered over the answer button. Maybe he should put her to voicemail, make her sweat for a few more seconds.

★ ★ ★

Felix knocked on the door one last time. Nothing. He'd thought there was some slight noise from within. The girl, perhaps, hiding. Under the bed or something. It was really amazing what people thought would help them, the stupid things they did in extremis. Getting into closets or crawling under piles of laundry, as though it was a childhood game of hide and seek, and he would just pretend not to see them. But perhaps you tried anything if there was no other choice. No matter how dumb.

Still, she wasn't answering. And he had a corpse downstairs. There was no time for niceties. This was a standard hotel door, shitty lock, zero security. He took out the skeleton key he kept with him for emergencies; tried it. No joy. It worked better in newer hotels. Fine. This would happen the old-fashioned way. Felix pulled out a very thin piece of metal, specially made for him by a guy in Geneva. It was fiddly, and took a few minutes, but could get you most places without a deadbolt. He slid it in the lock and jiggled, working quickly. Within two minutes he heard the satisfying tumble and click. The door eased from the hinges. He turned the handle. He was in. He walked inside, his blood pumping, ready to kill, ready to fuck her. He shut the door tight, looked around.

She wasn't there. That fucking bitch. The window was open. He didn't bother checking under the bed, or in the closet. He could hear a target breathing from across the room. This one was empty. He rushed to the window and looked out. It was immediately obvious what she had done. The tree; the shitty little tree. Some of its branches were broken, damaged; he could see the white pith where she'd bent and cracked them. There were footprints on the wet grass, faint, but he was good at spotting that sort of clue. The girl had headed to the road. He cursed aloud and ran the sums in his head. A noise in the room, maybe five, six minutes ago, tops. He'd wasted two minutes knocking. So she'd had five to run. That wouldn't get her too far, unless she had a car. The journalist hack was in their hire car. Did Lisa Costello know how to boost? He shook his head, disgusted with himself. How come he was even asking that question? She was a trophy wife, a rich bitch, he told himself. Not some fellow pro. And yet . . . he was starting to worry about this woman. Because she was either very lucky, or very good.

But he was Felix, and he was luckier. Assume

she had not taken a car. That meant she was somewhere, somewhere close. She didn't have a damned teleporter; she couldn't magic herself over the border in under five minutes. She was out there, panicked, and running, with no man to protect her.

Felix withdrew from the window and ran out the door and down the stairs. An old man barked something at him in German, but he wasn't listening. Lisa was out there. And he was coming.

$\star$ $\star$ $\star$

Lisa leaned back against the wall of the garage. His phone was ringing, ringing. Her eyes scanned the road again, watching the beams of the car headlights sweep past in the darkness. Any one of them could be carrying the man who'd killed her husband. The man who might now be going to kill her. Goddammit! Answer the phone!

'Couldn't wait, huh?'

It was bizarre; even here, even now, he was turning her on. That languid, sexy voice. A dreadful pang of loss, to be away from him. She wanted his protection, his comfort. Just his strong arms round her.

'Sam. Don't go to the hotel.'

His tone changed instantly. 'Lisa, what is it, honey? What happened?'

'He came. The killer. I'm sure it was him. Banged on the door and tried to get in. I jumped out the window. He's probably after me.'

289

'Did you break anything? Where are you? I'll come pick you up. Right now.'

'I shouldn't tell you.' She choked back a sob. God, how she longed to say it, longed for him to drive right up in that wonderful, safe little car and come sweep her away from here. 'He found me. How? Maybe he's got these phones bugged.'

'Impossible.'

'A long-range transmitter . . . it can happen. Josh was telling me about that stuff. Always warning me about what I said.' She smiled through the tears. 'Beware of you reporters.'

He was quiet a moment. 'You're right. Don't say. Contact me, honey. You know how. Lisa . . . '

'I know.' She wept to herself, placing one hand over the base of her phone so he would not hear her crying. 'You don't have to say it. I think I feel the same.'

'Run safe. You'll be back in my arms soon.' He said that with complete confidence, reassuring her. Another pause. 'And you, guy, if you're listening to this, you know who I am. My name's Sam Murray. I'm the man who's going to kill you.'

There was an inexpressible chill to his voice. Then a click, and he hung up. She was standing there behind the garage. And she was totally alone.

★ ★ ★

Sam swung his car away from the hotel and circled the block. It was important not to let his brain freeze up in a panic, important to think, not become paralysed by thoughts of Lisa, frightened and stranded out there. His target was the assassin. What would the assassin do?

He wouldn't stay in the hotel. He would break in to the room and see that she'd run. She had no idea how to cover her tracks, so she'd probably pointed out her direction. And he'd follow. He'd have an area to sweep. He'd be tracking her, trying to climb into her head the way Sam was trying to climb into his . . .

His phone rang again and he jumped on it. 'Baby?'

'It's not your fucking baby, asshole. It's Craig.'

'Craig.' Sam had gone around the block again and was approaching the hotel. He needed clues, he needed to see where that guy had gone. He dropped his lights and parked half a block away, across the street in the lot of a small convenience store. Then he slipped out of the car, adrenalin pumping through him. This man had weapons and he had none, but he was under no doubt that he was the hunter, that he was the guy who would be doing the killing. It was intense, how visceral and immediate it was. This person was threatening his woman. Lisa Costello was his woman now. He knew it in his gut. And he intended to kill him for it.

In one phone call, in less than sixty seconds, this mission had stopped being a story proving her innocence. It had become something far more basic. Survival. And revenge. Years of dissipation and selfishness fell away from him. He was the kid again who'd applied to the FBI, the top recruit who'd aced the training. That man he'd buried, who'd crawled right up from the depths of his psyche, and was instantly ready to go.

'I can't talk to you now. I have a problem,' Sam said.

He started to head across the road. There were no extra cars parked out front. Doubtful the killer had come on foot, which meant he knew Lisa had run and was already out there looking for her. It was a gamble, but Sam made the decision instantly. He ran across the road, conspicuous now if anybody was looking.

'You need to talk to me.'

'I really don't. Bye, Craig.'

'Wait!' He could hear the surprise in his old partner's voice, that Sam Murray was no longer seeking his approval. 'This matters. We went to Thailand and we did forensics.'

Sam kept moving, but he was no longer about to hang up. The door of the hotel was ajar. He pushed through it. Frau Vollenhaus was not at her desk.

'Go on.'

'We found male hair and cells in the bathroom, partial prints, semen on the headboard of the bed. Spray from masturbation, standing position.'

A shiver of disgust rippled through Sam. He saw the scene exactly as Craig did. No need to ask questions.

'Can you eliminate Josh Steen?'

'It's real old. Degraded. Fifty — fifty at best, but it's in the lab. I'll keep you informed. A good defence attorney would make some nice hay for her . . . '

'Thanks, Craig.' Even as his eyes scanned the room, part of him thought about the story. Now it wasn't just Lisa's testimony. Now it was outside evidence. This would be explosive. Not that he cared about that much. But it would clear his girl. This would be easier if the entire world didn't hate her. 'Listen, that killer. He came to find her. I'm running with her.'

'Fucking idiot. What the fuck did I tell you?'

'I don't give a goddamn, Craig. She's innocent and I won't let her be jailed or go to the chair. And I won't let her be killed, either. Somebody found us in the middle of nowhere, tried to break into her room while I was out filing a story. She ran. I don't know where she is. He's here and he's coming for her. Tying up loose ends.'

'So what are you going to do?'

Sam moved behind the reception desk. No sign of Marianne. There was an office just behind that area. He walked in, glanced around. The closet was open, very slightly ajar. He could see dark cloth, and knew what he'd find.

'I'm going to kill the guy. He just murdered the owner of the hotel we were staying at.'

As he spoke, he opened the closet door. Marianne's body tumbled out, slack, a dark hole in her forehead, dark dried blood ugly on her face. Sam reached down and pressed his fingertips to her neck. The body was still warm. He hadn't been gone long. He had no wish to be caught with the body. He moved out of the

293

reception area, went upstairs.

'What?'

'Shot her dead. Stuffed her in a closet. I just saw the corpse. Lisa doesn't have a gun, Craig, and nor do I. This is real.'

'For fuck's sake. Tell me where you are. And don't do anything dumb. We'll get local cops down there, pick you up . . . '

'Right. Like a pro like this can't beat some Keystone Europeans. Come on, Craig. You know I can't tell you. If I let her be picked up before we've proved her innocence, she could be strapped to a gurney in San Quentin waiting the needle.'

'But the semen . . . '

He was in the corridor now. The door to their room was open. Sam scanned the lock. It had been expertly picked, with little damage. He went to the open window, looked out. She'd used the tree; that was quite a jump. He felt a surge of pride at her bravery.

'A judge could throw that out. You know our legal system as well as I do. It's a crapshoot. No, she's been convicted by the tabloids and the great American public and they're just going to have to acquit her.'

'Jesus, Sam. I give up our evidence to you and you're not giving me shit.'

'This isn't trading, Craig. It's her life. I'm past trading now. All that's done. Her court is America, and that's where I'm going to try this case.'

A heavy sigh. 'I knew it. You've fallen in love with her.'

He thought about denying it, then realised he couldn't be bothered. Let Craig think whatever he wanted. 'Yes. And my judgement isn't clouded. She's innocent. You know that now.'

'I'm FBI. You're aiding and abetting. I have to track you now, buddy. I don't have a choice.'

Sam had turned the corner and was running down the stairs, full tilt, back to the lobby.

'Craig, don't take this the wrong way, but right now you're the least of my worries.' He hung up.

The instinct to race back to the car and drive, drive was overwhelming. But Sam made himself pause. His gut was the wrong guide now, because he cared too much. The question was what did he need. And the answer was clear. A gun, he needed a gun.

Marianne kept guns. Back in LA. Most of the madams did. A jealous husband or unsuspecting boyfriend, a john who was high and wanted more, a pervert who got off on harming working girls, even killing them. It was black out there, in a black business. He didn't think she'd have dropped that habit out here. Once you were in the life, you always had to be afraid that someone would come and find you.

In LA she kept the guns in a concealed drawer under her desk. Sam vaulted the reception desk and felt around, tapping. It was there: a hollow space to the left, the thin plywood meeting his knuckles with a different sound from the rest of the desk. He looked above and saw a drawer. It was locked. A quick scan around the area revealed no key. He shouldn't be here; a guest could drop by at any time, and a couple of feet

295

behind him was the mistress of the house with a bullet in her forehead. Sam couldn't wait. He smashed his elbow through the thin wood under the drawer, and caught the small Smith & Wesson as it tumbled through the hole. It was loaded. He felt around inside the drawer with his fingertips; she had kept a spare clip too. Thank you, Marianne, he thought. He examined the gun briefly as he moved to the door. The model 4040, popular with women because it was a standard 9mm, single-stack magazine and slim grips. A good choice for her, he thought, and felt a pang. What a waste her life had been. He and Lisa had to do better.

The slightness of the gun would make it harder for him to shoot; he had strong, powerful hands and long fingers, not designed for something delicate and fiddly. But it was a hell of a lot better than nothing. He palmed it a little, trying to get used to the weight and the grip. Thinking about returning the favour for Marianne, using her own weapon. Even without Lisa in the mix, he'd have been pleased to do it.

And now here was the car again. Soon he would have to dump this and get another. No Avis, though, no nice normal car hire. Something untraceable. Something cheap. But for now there was no time. The killer was out there, looking for Lisa. And Sam had to find him.

10

Lisa looked at the phone in her hand. It was a lifeline, and she didn't want to throw it out. But she had to. How did these things work? They tracked you, right, they could track you with GPS. She'd just made a call. Maybe he knew where she was right now. She needed to lose this phone. And she had no idea when it would be a good idea for her to get another.

Reluctantly she moved forward to the edge of the garage. Cars drove past intermittently. That was the trouble with the night-time: you were so obvious when there were fewer people around. But she had to get rid of this thing. She dropped it in a trash can mounted on the street corner, venturing into the full view of the street lights . . .

And then she saw him.

Afterwards, she wasn't sure how she'd known. But it was immediate. The face . . . yes, the face was slightly familiar, although she could not place it, yet it hit her that they had met before. It was more the way his eyes were on the road. How he swept the street, not just looking. Scanning. Not on the road, but all around it.

He was maybe forty. Dark, thinning hair. Normal build. She only flashed on him as the car went past. But she felt a great sense of evil. His car stopped at the lights, and she saw his profile, a Roman, aquiline nose. The lights changed; he drove through. She stood fixed, staring after him. Like she was paralysed. And then he spotted her.

Lisa knew instantly. Just a slight turn of the head, to pick up something in his peripheral vision. But his eyes glanced back, and they picked her up. And although his car was driving forwards, he had got her, he had found her.

In another second he would be stopping. Terror and nausea welled up in her heart. She started to run, back behind the garage, leaping over the barbed wire in the darkness. There was a little street behind her. She raced down it, sobbing.

★   ★   ★

Fucking hell, there she was. That was her, that was his little bitch, staring at him like a lovestruck teenager, and he loved her for it, the nice easy target giving herself away. She was no pro, she was nothing. She was a ripe apple waiting for him to jostle the tree, just a little, just slightly. Like he said, he was lucky.

Felix wrenched the wheel to the left and parked the car. The extra second it took to do that would lessen attention. No woman could outrun him anyway. He was a male at the peak of his fitness. She was a soft society belle. He wasn't concerned. He jumped out of the car and turned around, running in the direction she'd come from, by the garage. She wouldn't be dumb enough to run down a main street. He went behind the garage, saw a patch of scrubby land with a depression in the barbed-wire fence hiving it off. Yeah . . . that's where she'd gone. Short cuts, side alleys. The smarter ones tried those first. He leapt over into the scrub, and put his hand into his pocket, withdrawing his Glock, the other hand effortlessly attaching the silencer. There was a street ahead of him, narrow, lined with shops, leading up to the older quarter of the town. He forced himself to stop a second, and listened. His acute hearing was one of his greatest assets. And there it was, faint but still perfectly audible. The light, sharp footfall of a woman running. He turned his head, pinpointing the sound. She was on higher ground, to his left. He ran towards her.

★ ★ ★

Sam drove around the streets, feeling helpless. The cars and trucks on the roads looked normal to him. There was nothing unusual. Even in a country the size of a postage stamp, they could be anywhere. His girl, and her killer. He had a gun now. He had evidence that could clear her. And none of it was any use.

Think, think, damn you, he told himself. He'd be following her . . . and she was on foot. A car . . . he was looking for an abandoned car. If he saw Lisa, the killer wouldn't take his time parking it . . .

Sam drove a little further, and then he saw it. Right by the garage. A black Mercedes, a car that stood out in this part of Vaduz, away from the financial centre. It was parked, but the angle . . .

that was wrong, it wasn't neat, it smacked of a hurry . . .

He stopped his own car at the side of the road opposite and got out. Behind the garage was a stretch of waste ground, and past that, a narrow street leading up towards the castle. Sam scanned to his left. Wide, floodlit roads. In front of him was a large roundabout, and past it more well-lit hostelries. To the right he saw a squat Lutheran church, with nothing but a parking lot and more bright lights. OK. If this was the car, then logically she'd have run in the only direction where there was cover. And that was across the waste ground. Sam started to run, and adrenalin surged through him. It was so easy to do it when your hormones carried you through. He thought of Lisa, scared and helpless, and this man bearing down on her. He visualised his finger on the trigger, squeezing, merciless, making the problem go away.

He entered the narrow street and raced uphill, looking to his right and his left, trying to hear anything, see anything. But there was no sound. They would have gotten ahead of him, though. It wasn't much of a clue, the car and the landscape together, but it was all he had, so he kept running.

★ ★ ★

Lisa moved as fast as she could. She tried to keep in the shadows, to run by the sides of buildings. All the locked doors in the street! God, if only it were day, and she could duck into

300

one of them! But there was nowhere. At the top, it widened out again, and now she was running between chalet-style houses, a little closer together than in the modern town. But still, no place secure to hide . . . nowhere to go . . .

★ ★ ★

Felix pounded up the street. Her footfalls were getting closer. So far he'd been lucky; there was only one way she could have run. The town itself was herding her, helping him. But at the top, a few hundred yards away, it opened up. Easier to see her, but more places for her to go. That wasn't so good. He paused for a second, catching his breath. It would save time just to hear her . . .

Only he didn't pick just her out; he heard something else. Something annoying. Somebody running, and the weight and thud of the feet said it was a man. He was being pursued. A goddamn distraction now, when he was so close. Who the fuck could it be? The journalist . . . Murray? He didn't think his skills were up to much. But it was possible. A cop? Presumably even Liechtenstein had some of those. And there likely wasn't much for them to do. What if some elderly *hausfrau* had seen him from her window, running, disturbing the peace. Called it in. Or worse, some guest had noticed him at the cheap, tacky little hotel, maybe found the fat bitch who owned it . . .

That was possible; like it was possible she had a man, a husband or something, somebody who objected to him doing the world a favour and slamming a bullet into her brain. Felix debated briefly what to do. Should he wait, take the guy out? But no, that might lead to Lisa getting away. She was one slippery little bitch. There'd be plenty of time to kill this fucker later. He'd leave him the body to find, stripped below the waist, exposed and humiliated in death. Maybe put a shot right through that pussy, since he wasn't going to have time to fuck it. Yeah. A surge of anger and testosterone raced through him. This man was going to cheat him of his rape; well, he'd leave a cute little surprise for him, something to give him nightmares for the rest of his strait-laced life.

Felix listened again, stripping one sound from the other. The lighter footfalls were heading west, above the hill. He followed.

* * *

Sam ran, higher, pushing himself. He was fit, but working at his maximum. He gasped for air. Liechtenstein was no place to run and hide; the houses were spaced too far apart, it was prosperous and well-lit at night. He thought of Lisa, trapped like a rabbit frozen in front of a car. Christ. He had done it, he had left her . . .

He took out the gun, held it ready in his right hand as he sprinted. And then he heard it. The sound. Way above him. A man, a man running. Running after his girl. Sam breathed in deep, and forced himself to go faster, much faster, to attack the pavement, the gradient of the hill. His

302

lungs screamed for mercy, but he ignored them. His heart was thumping and pulsing. None of it mattered. Only Lisa mattered. Right now, he thought, if he lost her, nothing else in his life would ever be worth shit ever again.

★ ★ ★

Lisa tried to slow her breathing. Panting like this would give her away. She looked round wildly. She could hear the guy coming. God, at that pace she could not outrun him. He was a man, stronger than her. She was going to have to hide, hide and pray. The houses here were mostly Swiss chalet style, relics of the fifties, with ordinary cars parked out front or in their garages. They had balconies, decoration. Inside, families were sleeping. They didn't look the type to be fitted with burglar alarms or security lights.

She thought about where he would look. He'd run around and conclude she had hidden. And then he'd try to find her. Where was the best place to hide? That was the first thing. Quickly she noted the carved balconies, with their curves and turrets, protruding from two houses facing each other across the street. Made by the same builder, long ago. Those would be good, obvious places to hide. Then there was a copse of trees a little to her right. Perhaps a smart girl would run in there, even climb up into the branches. Open garages, too, offered some darkness, some refuge. All great places to hide. She could not use any of them.

Parked up by the side of the road leading to

303

the castle was a truck, a freight lorry of some kind. Forcing herself to walk very quietly towards it, Lisa looked underneath its wheels. There was a deep, dark shadow between the two front wheels, a narrow slot where a body could curl. She was small, slim. She muttered a silent prayer, then lowered herself to the road and the dirt and noiselessly slipped under the truck. She made herself tiny, curled up. Her head was turned, her eyes fixed on the blades of grass on the verge, the thin trickle of water running along the gutter, right by her head. It was the only sound, apart from her heart crashing against her chest, the terrified breathing she was fighting to still.

And then there came another sound. Hard, intense footsteps, a man running, pursuing her. She heard him race to the top of the street; then they stopped, and she heard him panting. This was the man who had killed her husband. Now he wanted to kill her.

★ ★ ★

Sam kept running. The other guy had stopped. That meant he was close to Lisa. He wanted to yell out, scream, shout, but there was no breath left in his lungs to do it. He moved at a steadier pace. He needed to recover his pulse, to be fit to take this guy on. A professional, a hired killer. And he didn't want to clue him in to where he was.

Sam had almost reached the top of the narrow street, where it opened up into the old town. He

304

listened: silence. The guy wasn't running, Lisa wasn't running. So she was hiding, and he was looking for her. His sharp mind processed that the killer had probably heard him in pursuit, but decided to finish off Lisa first. So he was very serious about this mission. He wanted to get it done.

But guess what. Sam wanted to get it done too. And having the man here, in the open, hunting, was an opportunity. Sure, he was afraid for Lisa. But you couldn't kill what you couldn't see. And this guy was waiting to be removed. He just didn't know it yet.

Sam moved into the shadows and looked ahead of him, carefully. In another minute he would be around the corner.

★　★　★

Felix scanned the ground. It was summer, so no obvious footprints to help him out, in snow or mud. She had stopped running maybe sixty seconds ago. She was hiding. He was very aware of the cop, or whoever it was, coming up behind him, but if he moved fast, no amateur would track him unless he wanted to be caught.

The ugly chalet houses had nice accommodating balconies. That was the place to go. And Lisa had to feel her odds were good, because there were five or six of them within climbing distance. Any one he picked was likely to be wrong. But she didn't understand how this worked. He moved to the nearest house, put his strong hands on the lip of the woodwork and effortlessly, like a gymnast, hauled himself over the top on to the flat wood of the balcony. She was not in this house. Wooden shutters were closed on the bedroom window right behind him. Noiselessly — Felix had started out as a cat burglar, and nobody did quiet motion like him — he moved around the side of the balcony and started to climb up to the roof of the house, hand over foot, his sinewy body finding a purchase on the least little outcrop, windowsill or ledge. If it wasn't smooth glass, he would find a way to climb it. From high up on the roof, he would be able to draw his gun, and at his leisure spy every balcony, every tree, every pool of shadow within a five-mile radius. He had infrared goggles in his jacket pocket, along with ordinary binoculars and a foldaway scope. He would see her, and his shooting would be dead-on accurate. When Prince Charming turned up, Felix would see him too. And take him out.

At last. A surge of pleasure rippled through him, to have her somewhere in his vicinity, to have a good gun and a crisp target. He reached the top of the roof and straddled his legs across it, settling in a shooting position. Then he pulled out his mobile phone. His fucking client. He sent a text, grinning to himself as he pressed the send button.

Found her in Liechtenstein. Taking her out. Not in job. Wire another million, no tears. Nice doing business. F.

Another million? Why not. He deserved it; this was a pain in the ass. It ought to have been specified that Lisa Costello, naive and unwilling

306

bride, was part of a package deal. Now he'd had to waste weeks of his life and get stressed and anxious over loose ends, when it had nothing to do with him. Of course he wanted more money. Whatever they'd agreed. And the client would pay. It was justified, and no client ever wanted you turning around and hunting them instead.

Now. He twisted on the roof. The naked eye revealed nothing. That was fine; it was dark. She might have been in black clothing. Felix didn't think she was clinging to the wall on any of the house balconies. Well, that would have been just too easy. If she was there, or hiding in scrubland, or in the woods, he would find her. He put his hand in his pocket and took out the infrared goggles. These were top-notch, an experimental, lightweight version designed for the US Special Forces. He put them to his eyes. There was nothing on the balconies, not even a mouse. He saw a fox streak off towards the woods, but there was no human there, in the trees, or on the ground. Frustrated, he turned in a complete circle . . .

There was a figure . . . hanging back against the wall of the pharmacy at the top of the narrow street. His heart sped briefly, but it was not her. It was a man, the man. He lowered his goggles and used the binoculars again. The guy was edging around the corner of the building; he disappeared from view, then came back in sight again. Felix knew the gait, the build, immediately. It was not necessary to see the face. That was indeed Sam Murray. The fucking hack writer. Jesus. He must have the hots for this broad. Didn't he know what he was getting into?

He was about to find out. The plan was to get Lisa, but she must be in a garage or something. He couldn't see her. Murray was right there. He fitted the sights to his pistol, angled it, and fired.

★ ★ ★

Lisa twisted her head under the lorry. She didn't want to move too much. This man was an assassin, looking for her. Movement would attract him. She believed it. But she wanted to see. She had heard him arrive, then tiny, quiet sounds. Not coming near the truck. She looked on the road, right ahead of her. There were no feet, no boots. So she'd been right; he'd climbed up to one of the balconies, and he was hunting her there . . .

And then she saw something. And crammed her fist into her mouth. Sam's shoes, his plain John Lobb shoes, the ones she'd recognise anywhere, coming around the top of the street, standing in the road. She could tell, instantly. It was Sam. He'd found her . . . God knew how, but he'd found her. And now here he was, come to fetch her back. Only the killer was around . . . maybe on a balcony . . . above Sam. With a gun.

If she moved, she might die. He'd shoot at her first. It did not matter to her. In the heart and belly of her, she wanted Sam Murray to live. She pushed back with her hands, angling her legs out towards the front of the truck, jackknifing herself

308

out on to the verge. She clutched the thick, mud-covered wheel of the truck, lowering her head, hoping the elevation of the cab would protect her.

'Sam!' she shouted, as loud as she could. 'Sam! He's on the roof! He's got a gun! Get back!'

There was a soft, vicious sound: *phut*. Then a strike. She heard the bullet land in the road. Then another, like a hornet whizzing past her head. He'd fired in her direction, but she was too close to the front of the truck, and it landed harmlessly in the grass behind her.

'Baby, get down!' Sam shouted. 'Get the fuck down!'

She hit the dirt, sobbing. This man had killed Josh and now he was going to kill her, and Sam too, the only man she thought she'd ever really loved, the guy she'd just found . . . It was a matter of time, that was all.

And then she heard the gunshot. Not *phut*, *phut*. A terrifyingly loud bang. A scream. Several screams. A dog barking. The killer had a silencer, but now she realised that Sam had a gun too.

'Be careful!' she screamed. It didn't matter; obviously the killer knew where she was now anyway. 'Sam! I love you!'

Jesus. Lisa buried her face in her hands. She was targeted for assassination on a remote street in the middle of nowhere, and now was the time she chose to admit her love?

But the English sarcasm didn't help much. She was desperate for him to know, right now, in case these were the only moments she had left.

What if this unknown man killed her, and she'd never said it?

* * *

Sam reacted quickly. He gave himself that. The shot rang out over his head, then Lisa, his Lisa, was shouting, warning him that the guy was above him, and he spun on his heel, and even though he heard the shot at her, he was not distracted. He saw the figure up above him, and he fired . . .

Boom! The shot rang out in the night. Immediately, lights switched on in the windows of the houses in the street. He didn't care. Let them wake up, let them all wake up. Let them call whatever passed for a cop round here. Spook the guy into running. Anything, so long as he got away from Lisa. Sam didn't need to look up to know that he had missed. There was no cry from the fucker, no gurgle, no scream. When he did raise his eyes, the gargoyle on the roof had disappeared. It was obvious that he had gone to get Lisa. Amidst the shouts and the opened windows, and the sleepy burghers of Vaduz becoming alarmed . . .

Sam moved, fast, into the open street. Lisa's voice had come from the end of the road. He looked. There was a giant truck. Jesus, had she actually slid under the truck? No wonder he hadn't got her. He guessed that was the last place round here a pro would look. Smart girl, he thought, and felt a fresh rush of love. He scanned the street leading up to it. Where had

310

that bullet come from? Which house? No time to think. He made a guess, in his gut, and moved around to the right, and there the fucking guy was, not paying attention to his back, just moving towards the truck like a man on a mission from hell. And Sam stopped thinking and pulled back the trigger and shot . . .

★　★　★

Felix heard the gun. Curses boiled up in his head. This jerkoff, with his loud-ass little weapon. Dimly, part of his brain registered the small gun as unsuitable for a man; it was a woman's weapon, he shouldn't have it. It must have come from the dead fat woman at the hotel. But it could still kill. He was halfway down the roof already before the shot was fired. Stupid little Lisa had shouted out to save her man, given herself away. The truck; that was smart. Betraying herself was idiotic. If she had let him take time to kill Sam Murray, she might have gotten away herself. But she had no concept of buying time, and he wasn't here to explain tradecraft. He ran towards the truck. Pretty sure she wasn't armed. The Liechtensteiners were shouting things in German; he didn't give a fuck. By the time the police got here, he'd be long gone.

Another shot. Christ! He was almost at the truck. That one caught the back of his fucking jacket. The journalist could shoot. He turned around, cursing, and dropped to one knee. Aimed, pointed, fired, all in a single motion. Right at the guy's head. But he dived to the dirt

311

and rolled on to his back, was firing again. There were screams now, shouts all around them. Felix ignored them all. He was in a firefight. Fuck! The next bullet whistled past him, so close it almost singed his ear.

'Sam Murray! Stop, we can do business.' No response. 'Put your fucking weapon down, maybe I'll let her live. Maybe your magazine pays more than my client. Don't be an asshole.'

It didn't matter how much the magazine paid; he had taken the fee for Lisa's death and it was dangerous for any assassin not to deliver. They sent your colleagues after you. He would kill Sam Murray the second he opened his mouth to talk. Maybe kneecap him first, let him lie there waiting for it while he walked over and finished the woman. He had no fear of the fat civilians in their nightshirts and dressing gowns.

'Sam, you want to make me an offer? She's a pretty girl, Sam. Don't you — '

Bang! The fucker had hauled himself to his feet and fired yet again, and Felix suddenly realised, to his horror, that he was bleeding, fucking bleeding. His goddamn shin. It hurt. He looked down, saw blood pumping through his jeans. A second later the shock wore off, and violent pain seized his entire body. He forced himself on to his belly and returned fire. Once. Twice. But the journalist was fast, real fast. He dived to one side, then leapt to his feet and was running towards Felix, gun drawn, and Felix began to feel real fear, terror, mixing with the pain. He lifted his hand and shot again, but nerves were making his grip shaky. The gun

312

wobbled. He saw the shot ricochet harmlessly off a tree.

Sam Murray was running towards him, gun drawn. The locals were shouting. Murray's grip was firm. He was not shaken. Hatred pulsed through Felix. Goddamn fucking bastard, in his way, between him and the gold-digger. The agony in his lower body intensified. For a split second he dragged his eyes downwards. There was another hole, in his stomach. Holy fucking shit. He was going to die.

Murray's footfalls were closer. He was standing over Felix, pointing the gun down. This fucking amateur, looming over him. Felix spat towards him. Blood bubbled from his mouth, mixing with the spittle.

'Who hired you?' Sam Murray demanded.

Felix coughed. 'Go fuck yourself.'

'I want to know. It's her life, the rest of her life. You're hit in the stomach. You don't have long.'

Felix groaned helplessly from the pain. 'Hospital,' he said, and started to cry.

'I can get you to a hospital. They can give you morphine, maybe. That's not fixable, man.' Murray crouched over him. Felix had looked into the eyes of his targets before, but not like this, never like this. The journalist's eyes had softened. There was pity there. Pity from the asshole who'd just killed him, because Felix knew Murray was right; it wasn't fixable. Frightened, he felt his heart pump, felt the blood leaking out with every beat.

'Do the right thing. You're dying. Who hired you? Were they close to Josh?'

Felix cackled. 'Very fucking close. She'll never guess. She was easy to set up. No idea what they thought of her. Dumb bitch.'

Murray shrugged. 'Maybe she just didn't care. And she's not dumb, man. She's alive. She's free. You killed her husband and now you're dead. She fucking won, remember that.'

The words burned in Felix's brain. *She won.* The bitch won. That half-naked, drunken slut lying on the bed; she had beaten him, found this fucking guy and beaten him. Two steps ahead all the time. Rage surged through him. Fury and despair leaked into his mouth till he could almost taste it, along with the blood. Shuddering, he cocked his gun and fired right up at Sam Murray; he was close, you wouldn't have to be good, just lucky . . .

But Sam's eyes narrowed, and he jumped back, twisting his body away, and his pistol was moving in response. Even as Felix fired, hearing the screams of the locals dimly in the background, he felt a *whoomph* in his chest and then more pain, much more pain. He craned his neck to see the wound in the left side of his chest and he knew it was his heart, and bad, dreadful thoughts, horrors, crowded in on him. He tried to pray for mercy, for forgiveness, and then the blackness rushed up on him.

★ ★ ★

'Lisa!' Sam shouted, frantic. One glance told him the assassin was dead. 'Lisa! I killed him! Get up, get up!'

He looked around wildly. But there she was, running out from behind the front grille of the giant truck. She was alive, unhurt. Relief flooded him, such violent relief it shocked him. 'Come here!' he yelled, and she was already racing towards him.

A fat man burst out of the doorway of one of the chalet houses to his right. He was wearing a nightshirt and a hastily pulled-on pair of corduroy trousers. He was also carrying a shotgun. He brandished it at Sam, then cocked it, ready to fire. '*Mörder!*' he bellowed. '*Ich werde die Polizei rufen!*'

Sam sighed and fired one shot into the air. Then he levelled his pistol at the guy's chest.

'Back off, buddy,' he said, calm and clear. 'We're leaving. Just back off.'

Lisa had reached him. She looked at the man, frightened. He was shaking now, but still gripping that gun.

'Baby. Run through his pockets. Get anything. Phone, watch, rings, wallet. Anything. Be quick.'

She was already crouched over the corpse. Sam saw her narrow shoulders shaking as her hands dipped into the bloodstained pockets of the guy's clothing. Poor kid; she still was a kid really. She shouldn't have to see so much death, shouldn't have to see anything like this. Now the still-bubbling, warm blood of his fresh kill was running over her hands. Blood on both their hands, he thought grimly. It couldn't be helped, but that didn't make him feel any better.

In his peripheral vision he saw another couple of men approaching down the street, warily, but

315

they were still coming. He was only one guy. He was certain that if he and Lisa were caught, separated by the cops, put into cells, they would both be dead within twenty-four hours. He didn't fool himself based on the death of one hired killer. Whoever had picked this man had the resources to send more. Lots more. And it was easy to hit a stationary target.

'Lisa,' he said, his voice as calm as he could make it. 'You done?'

She stood up, covered in blood; her hands looked like something from a horror flick. It was on her top, her trousers, splashed on her shoes. All over her skin. Wherever they went, she would be utterly conspicuous.

'Yeah. I got what he had.' She lifted her hands, and he saw a jumble of stuff. A phone, a wallet. Superb. There would be clues, at last, real clues.

'OK. We have to go, we have to move. Come on, sugar.' Sam spun around, gesturing with his gun at the men who were approaching them. '*Wir verlassen*,' he shouted. '*Bleiben Sie weg oder ich scheißen!*'

The men fell back. Lisa was next to him. He took the stuff from her and packed it into his pockets. She could be killed for it. Then he took her hand and started to run with her, straight down the hill, back the way they had come.

'What did you say?' She was panting, racing after him. She smelled of blood and sweat. He wondered how hard the assassin had chased her. But she had survived, his clever little beauty.

'I told them to stay back or I'd shoot. It won't buy us long.' He slowed to a fast walk and she

316

did the same. 'We have to get out of this street. They'll be waiting for us at the bottom with police.'

'He shot at you . . . '

'Doesn't matter. We can't be caught now. We'd be trapped. Understand?'

Lisa nodded, tight-lipped. Sam glanced around him. To his left, a little below him, was a pharmacy, the large neon cross outside it switched off at night. It had a flat roof.

'We're going up there, across the roof, down the other side. You first.' Sam gestured. They only had seconds. To his relief, Lisa did not argue. She ran towards the sign and jumped, trying to loop her arms around it. He lifted her up by the waist, and as she grabbed, he pushed up against the soft curves of her ass and she got a purchase and hauled herself up. The sign shivered a little in its mountings, but held steady.

He could hear the sounds of shouting, footfalls at the top of the street, and in the distance the whine of a siren. Lisa was crouched on the roof, waiting for him. Sam moved to the other side of the street and ran, pounding his feet as hard as he could, then leapt against the wall, his hands grabbing at the sign, his feet pushing up hard, scrabbling for purchase against the smooth granite of the pharmacy. Nothing but the sheer strength of his muscles held him up there. His thighs screamed; the lactic acid burned through them. But there was nothing else, no other way out. And suddenly, with one last desperate push, he swung himself up and over, through the wall of pain, and landed on the roof, hard, feet first, and she was in front of him, alive and safe.

'Here.' He grabbed her hand and led her to the edge. There was a drop of twelve feet to the ground; effortlessly he swung her over, then grabbed the rough edge of the flat roof with his hands, grazing his palms, and dropped himself down. They were now in the next street over. The police siren was coming closer.

'This place is tiny. They'll find us,' Lisa warned.

'The hell they will. We're stealing a car. Then another. Come with me.' He glanced around and saw a dark blue, beat-up Skoda parked on the street. The driver's door looked rickety to him, a little loose on its hinges. Lisa watched as he bent over the lock. He took the handle in his hands, set his shoulder against it, and wrenched the door open with sheer strength, unlocking the other side. Then he carefully placed it back in position. It was broken now, but it only needed to last him a few hours. Lisa scrambled into the passenger seat while he ripped open an interior panel and wired the thing. It sputtered into life, and he briefly checked the gas, wrenched the wheel, and set off down the street, back to the wide roads and the anonymity of Vaduz centre, heading towards Switzerland.

As he drove, forcing himself to keep his eyes dead on the road, Sam saw the police cars, grey and blue, heading past him into the old town. This was serious now. They had both been seen, there would be descriptions, APBs. It was early morning, and he thought he could drive over the border without being stopped. There were enough euros for a motel, but they dared not stop in one for a little while. Anyway, he wanted to get away, take Lisa somewhere far from here, somewhere they weren't looking for a couple. The shape of a plan was starting to form in his mind, emerging out of his consciousness like a city from the mist. He thought he knew exactly how to run with her. After that, the hunt was going to be on. Sam Murray did not enjoy being the prey. He far preferred to be the predator.

11

The party was in full swing. Artemis Studios was throwing a bash for their tentpole movie of the summer, *Animal Instinct*, and they had spared no expense. Peter Mazin, now Hollywood's biggest producer, moved amongst the studio executives, accepting their tributes. They all hoped they would be the ones to land his next release in development. But then again, there was a slight air of doubt that hung in the air, and he could feel it. Doubt that Mazin could deliver on Steen/Mazin projects. The insolence drove him crazy. Josh was dead; didn't they get that? He was not coming back. And these guys were gonna have to deal with Peter and his new-found power, whether they liked it or not.

Peter looked across the room, over to where Hannah was conversing with Michael Alamo, the business affairs supremo of Artemis. Normally he would have been proud of her. The perky, fake, paid-for tits. Her supremely round, high and fuckable ass. She did Pilates four days a week, and he loved the way it made her look. Her caramel-honey-blond hair, long and luscious, was around her shoulders, and she wore a dress by Herve Leger that combined body-conscious, sexy fashion with the social-permission-to-wear of haute couture. Indeed, assessed purely aesthetically, Hannah Mazin was the ultimate trophy wife, a possession other men would drool over and envy.

Had Joshua Steen envied him? Had he done anything about it?

The perennial question rolled back to Peter as he watched Hannah move. Josh's victory was that he would always be suspicious. Their life in bed together — and Hannah was enthusiastic and skilful; she knew, at least, the bare minimum required not to be divorced as a Hollywood wife — would always be tainted by the spectre of his suspicions, that Josh had had his way with her, but taken that secret to the grave.

Hannah looked hotter than hell. But these days he could barely speak to her. Jealousy gnawed at him like a starving dog with a bone. How could he articulate those doubts?

Peter looked again. She was nursing a champagne glass, the same one she'd been working on for hours, and chatting lightly now to some Middle Eastern-looking diplomats. Her body language, leaned back, defensive, said she was no more interested in them than Peter was. She was playing along, doing her duty.

He tore his gaze away from his wife and regarded the room set before him. There were fairy lights, strung from the ceiling in satin ribbons. There were displays of Diptych candles, arranged in trios around the space, keeping the atmosphere fresh and the light soft and beautiful. There were huge, heaped stands of fruit, and further stands choked with orchids and foxgloves. The table decorations were low-slung baskets, or soaring vases, full of the hottest designer arrangements. A-list stars milled around, and waiters circulated with the extremely precious vintage champagne. As Peter moved across the floor, neatly suited Artemis executives in their bespoke Savile Row threads came up to him, and asked if they could book in an appointment, have a word. Meanwhile the wait staff moved through them like obsequious ghosts. He glanced to one side and saw the bank of television cameras there. Not that it fazed him — Peter Mazin was used to the cameras — but it was certainly useful in gauging the studio's pulling power. Fame, money, influence . . . all rolled into one.

Peter allowed his gaze to drift to the entertainment they had provided. Girls, gorgeous girls in their twenties and early thirties, walking by in hot pants, their blond hair blown out and falling to the waist. The party was stuffed full of them. And as the older men gawped and drooled, hitting on them, flashing their wallets and allowing their hands to creep down, patting and caressing those perfect asses, he was suddenly hit by a bright surge of disgust. That was Josh Steen all over. And tonight Peter was feeling like he'd never be rid of him.

You couldn't get away from the story on the news. E! Television led with it every night. Leaks from the police investigation, stories from the forensics out of Thailand. Lisa Costello, still on the run. And now that cocky bastard of a journalist, Sam Murray. Hadn't heard too much from him lately. The magazine was spinning that he was on her trail. But Lisa Costello was a gorgeous woman. Peter wondered exactly how closely he was on her trail. Until somebody fried for this, Josh would hang over this party, and all his parties, like a bad smell.

His fingers clenched around his glass. Goddamn it. He didn't think it was possible to hate the guy any more. And Lisa Costello, spinning the story out. He despised her as well. Pretty girl, but so fucking what. They were ten a penny in Hollywood. And his eyes drifted across the room again to his wife.

★ ★ ★

'Here,' Sam said.

They parked the car and stepped out. He had driven them to a field outside of Zurich, halfway up a mountain. A few handwritten signs in Schweizerdeutsch had indicated something on the winding drive into the middle of nowhere, but otherwise nothing; sheep and goats grazing, a couple of houses, small local shops. And now they were standing looking at a way out.

It was a makeshift hangar, a small concrete building with a corrugated-iron roof. Inside were parked two tiny prop planes. A third, slightly larger, was stationed on a small tarmaced runway in the centre of the field.

'I was always going to wind up here.' Sam squeezed Lisa's hand. 'My friend Hans Durben, I knew him in college. He was the ultimate hippy. In the end he came back to Switzerland and teaches guys how to fly. He gives rides to tourists in the summer. Everybody knows him; all the air traffic control, everybody.'

'My God,' Lisa said. Her eyes gleamed; he could see the hope in them. 'I can't believe it.'

'That plane right there seats four. He can take us anywhere short-haul in Europe. They'll be looking for us around here. Nobody will suspect anything further away. And baby, once we land, running is over. We're going to find the guy who killed Josh.'

'You already took care of him.'

'He was just the dagger in somebody else's hand.' Sam smiled at her, looking into her eyes. She was so brave, so perfect. Anybody else would have cracked long ago. She had gone through the mill and survived. 'People want a head in cases like these. And I'm going to give it to them. Just not yours.'

A skinny man, young, with a phenomenal scraggy brown beard, emerged out of the hangar, shading his eyes. Then he gave a great whoop of joy and rushed over to them, giving Sam a bear hug.

'So I guess you remember,' Sam said. 'Hans, this is — '

'I know who she is,' Hans said. He had a deep baritone voice, rough from smoking, and a weather-beaten face. 'I've been expecting you.'

'We were idiots. Should have come before.'

'You were an idiot. How would she know?'

Sam grinned. 'True.'

'Mr Durben, you think you could do this for us? Give us a ride, I mean?' Lisa asked nervously. 'We don't have passports . . . '

'Not legitimate ones, anyway,' Sam said. 'You could get into a lot of trouble.'

'And when have I not?' His German burr was wonderful to Lisa, comforting, reassuring. This scraggly, unkempt man looked like a goddamn angel to her right now. 'Getting into trouble is what I do. We'll leave now, she's got a full tank. Nobody will guess anything. I fly every day and they all know me. Where were you thinking?'

'Well, Interpol will have our stuff. Even if they're no good,' Lisa said. 'I went to Rome because I thought the police might be laid back.'

'So try Spain. Lots of Brits over there. Some hair dye, some shades . . . nobody'll look twice at you.'

Spain. She wanted it. Sun, anonymity, maybe swimming in the ocean, paella . . . God, it sounded perfect. She looked hopefully at Sam.

'I love it.' He nodded. 'Let's go.'

'There's a small airfield in Puerta Ventura which I fly to regularly. Best of all, I have a cottage there.'

Sam's grin widened. 'You're kidding. You do?'

'Cheap beachside place. One bedroom. Bit run down, but it's got a telephone and a TV set.' He looked directly at Lisa. 'Not exactly what you're used to, sweetie.'

She smiled back warmly. 'Hans, believe me, I'm getting used to just about everything. And this is the best thing to happen to me in weeks. I can't thank you enough.'

'Sure you can thank me enough. I assume you didn't kill him?'

She shook her head.

'Then Sam here will find whoever did.'

'Thanks for the vote of confidence. It's not that easy.'

Hans puffed out his cheeks, like he was blowing away an aggravating fly. 'Sure it is. No false modesty, Sam Murray. You don't fool anybody with this writer shit. You were always the best hunter in our class. You'll get him.' He glanced back at Lisa. 'And then you'll be one of the richest women in America.'

Lisa blinked. 'What?'

'You married him, didn't you? Hasn't the thought occurred to you? If you did not kill him, you are his heir. Once Sam here clears your name, it's away from the beach hut and back to Bel Air for you, honey.' Hans smirked. 'And I want my own jet. A Gulfstream IV. Plus a year's supply of fuel. Make my fortune giving rides to people like you.'

Lisa's face coloured slightly.

'I — I hadn't thought. About anything. Just getting free of this.' She managed another smile. 'But listen, if I can give you a jet, you'll get a jet. Now, can I hitch a ride on this?'

'Your chariot awaits,' Hans said, bowing at his scrawny waist.

They followed him over to the plane and Sam helped Lisa up. He looked preoccupied, bothered. But he was always thinking. She concentrated on strapping herself in. It was funny how extreme situations changed you. She had always had a fear of flying. Much worse when you were in a prop plane. And as for some rust-bucket like this . . . three months ago she never would have agreed to climb into it. Now, all she was thinking was get going, get going . . .

Hans turned the ignition. It sputtered into life, the little beauty, and they were trundling down the runway, bumping up and down, and Lisa didn't care; she willed the thing on, and suddenly it gathered speed and took off, gossamer light, into the air, and they were soaring, and she looked at the disappearing ground beneath her with nothing but the purest delight, because she was alive, and free, and Sam was with her, and she trusted the guy flying this plane, rust-bucket or no; and hope, real hope, started to grow inside her.

Because back down there, somewhere far behind them, was the corpse of at least one of the bad guys. A man who had tried to kill her. Who had killed her husband. And whom Sam Murray had taken out.

She looked across the narrow seat at his profile. He was staring out of the window. He had actually killed for her. He had saved her life, risked everything for her. And she understood now that she never wanted to leave him.

★ ★ ★

They touched down two hours later. There hadn't been much conversation; it was too noisy for that. They landed at dusk on a small airstrip not far from the sea, which glittered and sparkled as they came in to land, impersonal and soothing. Hans helped them out of the plane and waved to the control tower, such as it was; he had parked the plane at the far edge of the bays, where they could not be easily seen.

'How do we get to your place?' Sam asked.

'Follow me,' Hans replied. 'You can walk it.'

He led them down a half-made white road, full of rocks and little pebbles, with olive trees clinging on grimly to the hills beside it. There were crickets humming in the sparse grass, and the fresh breeze from the sea blowing in over dunes to their left. The houses were small and compact, most looking as though they'd been built in the sixties; ugly little breeze-block things, but Lisa didn't care. It was warm, welcoming; it seemed like the end of the earth to her, the last place anybody would ever look for them.

Hans pointed out a few landmarks. 'That's the local church, San Juan Battista; don't go there, everybody will see you. And that place down there is a farm. You can get eggs, just throw a euro into the basket and take half a dozen. Sometimes they put out fruit too and bottles of oil. It's all good, and you won't have to see anyone. And right there, the chemist. But they gossip. There are two grocery stores in town, not big. They gossip too. Best thing, give me some money and I'll walk in and shop for you, bring you a week's stuff.'

Sam was touched. 'Jesus, Hans, that's good of you, man.'

'And that Gulfstream will be good of you guys. So we're here.' He gestured at a tiny house, yards from a half-deserted beach. It had a small yard fenced in with concrete, and was built of unlovely red brick with a flat grey roof. There were cacti growing in the scrap of garden, and Sam noticed his friend had made a half-assed effort to plant some pampas grasses for variety. The pink and white paintwork was peeling and the window frames were grubby, but it looked solid enough.

Hans led them through a decrepit iron gate and retrieved a key from under a large rock behind one of his cacti. The front door opened easily enough, and though the place smelled of dust and salt air, it was clean and compact. There was a tiny electric stove, a fridge, and some cupboards with dry goods — pasta, tins of tomatoes, some sugar.

'Don't keep anything. It's too hot. Even bottled water doesn't keep, you gotta buy it new. Speaking of which, Sam, give me some money.' Hans held out his hand and Sam peeled off some bills.

'Thanks again, man.'

'Don't sweat it. This is fun. Sam Murray, on the lam. I love it. You two lovebirds stay here.'

Sam blinked. 'I didn't say we were lovers.'

Hans rolled his eyes. 'I ain't blind, dude. Never was.'

He walked out and they were alone. Lisa glanced past the tiny kitchen.

'You want to check it out?'

He nodded. 'Sure.'

She frowned. 'Sam, what's the matter?'

'Nothing. Everything's fine.'

'No it isn't, or you wouldn't be acting so strange. Don't give me the silent treatment.' She was a little angry, and it made her eyes sparkle.

'What's bothering you?'

'Just something he said, back in Switzerland.' He shrugged. 'About what happens if I clear your name.'

'What about it?'

'He's right.' Darkness settled over Sam's face, and she hated to see it. 'You would be the heir. You'd be entitled to every cent.'

Lisa shrugged. 'Doubt it. We were fighting at the wedding. Lots of witnesses. His mother would claim he'd have divorced me. She and Josh's sister, they'd ask for the money.'

'Did he leave them anything?'

'Fifty thousand each. He didn't like them too much. He kind of tolerated them. Deep down, I don't think Josh really liked anybody, not even himself.'

'Then they'd have zero case. Any judge would throw it out. If he left it to you, it's yours.'

'He told me he did. I never asked to see a copy of the will. Look, why does that bother you? I don't get it.'

'Don't you?' Sam asked. His eyes glittered. 'We could come out of this. And you'll be the heiress to fifty million dollars and I'll just be a working schlub of a celebrity reporter. An ex-celebrity reporter. With a bit of money and some clothes in a backpack.'

Lisa blinked. 'So what? Why would I care?'

'Maybe you wouldn't. But I would. You'd be back amongst the super-rich. Christ, do you know what your story would be worth? Five million for the book rights alone. More for the movie.'

330

'I wouldn't sell rights to it. Josh's murder is not entertainment.' She was shocked, a little chilled by the anger in his face. 'Sam, for God's sake. If he left me rich, that's hardly my fault. What the hell would it have to do with us?'

He shook his head. 'In my whole life, I've never depended on a woman for anything. I don't want to have to start now.'

'Who says you would?' She was getting angry herself. 'How does it affect you?'

'What, you'd be content to come live in my one-bedroom apartment, when you could buy the entire complex with your spare change? Face it, Lisa, money fucks things up.'

'That's crazy,' she said.

'Is it? Is it really? Then why were you walking down the aisle with a man you didn't love? A guy you didn't even like? Why did you stay trapped in a relationship that was stifling all the life and all the joy right out of you?'

She tensed. 'OK, well. A lot of women are in bad relationships and they stay in them when they should leave. Rich, poor. We're afraid sometimes. We've been trained that way. And has the thought crossed your mind that maybe you could live in my house? I could sell Josh's place and we could get a new one. Anywhere you like. Here. In Spain, by the sea, if that's what you want.'

'Share your money? Live off you, live off a woman?' Sam passed a hand through his hair. He looked distracted, harried. She hated to see it. 'You know, Lisa, the only good thing about this whole goddamned mess is I've gotten my

331

self-respect back. Now you want me to give that up again too.'

'Really. And I thought I was something good that came out of this for you. I thought you loved me.'

'Of course I do.'

'Then what the hell is the macho bullshit? I had enough of that with Josh.'

He flushed. 'Don't compare me to that man. I'm not trying to buy you.'

'And guess what? I'm not trying to buy you.' Lisa shrugged. 'If he left me all his money, how about we give it away? Then your ego can be satisfied and we can spend the rest of our lives working diligently. Instead of, I don't know, on a beach enjoying ourselves, taking care of family and friends, that sort of thing.'

Sam had the good grace to grin. 'I'm not telling you to give it away.'

'After the last two weeks, you might say I earned it.' Lisa smiled back at him, trying to warm him. 'Look, I had my own ambitions. I wanted to be a florist. Run a chain of designer stores. But if Josh left me everything, it's kind of stupid to ignore that. We can go to the Cayman Islands, somewhere private and discreet. Mauritius. The Seychelles. We can get a beach house, swim, make love.' She shivered. 'I don't want to run any more. I don't really want to do anything. If we wind up rich, I'd like to just quit.'

'Just quit,' he said slowly. 'I don't think I've ever heard anybody say that before.'

'Because nobody ever does. I was with Josh, remember. I knew him, I watched his friends.

They all had more money than you could spend in a lifetime, but they stayed right in their offices, working themselves to death, stressing out, competing with each other. They looked for ways to waste it. If something was cheap, they would never buy it. I asked him why he bothered once. He just looked at me like I was insane. It's what they do. But you only have one life. I'd like to relax in it. Drink some good wine. Walk barefoot on a beach under the palm trees.'

Sam exhaled. 'I hate how much sense you're making.'

'That's because you need to relax.' Lisa took him by the hand. 'I've been with one chest-thumping macho man, I don't need another one. Besides, maybe Josh didn't leave me anything. Then it's back to selling flowers. Still think I'd be good at that.'

'I'd have something. From this story.'

She kissed him. 'Great, then you buy the tickets to Mauritius. I really couldn't care less.'

Sam grinned and put his arms around her. She loved how he felt, the muscles, the strength of him. Josh had postured and thrown money around, but Sam had defied the law, run after her, killed for her. In his arms she felt safe. Loved. *Happy.*

'You're a crazy broad. I guess he told you that.'

'Frequently.'

He kissed her, and a wash of heat liquefied her groin. Her nipples sharpened, she became instantly slick, wet between the legs. Sam's grip tightened around her. His kiss deepened, possessive, and he pulled her to him. He was hard already. She felt the desire beat up between them like it was a living thing.

'How far away is that grocery store?' she managed.

'Not far enough. He'll be back any second.'

Lisa was so turned on she thought anybody that came in right now would see it.

'I'm going into the bedroom. Can you deal with him? Tell him I wanted to sleep?'

'Sure.' Sam bent his head to her and kissed her again slowly, luxuriously. 'After he's dropped off the food, he's going back to Switzerland. We'll be all alone here. And you won't be doing much sleeping.'

★ ★ ★

They emerged from the bedroom three hours later. After the lust had finally subsided, they fell asleep, bodies tangled together, limbs draped over each other. Sunset was falling over the sea, and golden light streamed through the windows of the little cottage. Lisa walked to the kitchen door and opened it, standing in the tiny front yard, looking out towards the dunes.

'My God,' she said. 'It's magic. It's so peaceful.'

The sea sparkled in the light. To the left, a local was walking his dog, shouting at him as he chased something she couldn't see. Apart from that, the beach was deserted. Miles of white sand and scrubby grass, bleak and beautiful, she thought.

'He left us some great food. Look.'

She turned around. Sam was laying a meal out on the table: French bread, thick slices of peppered ham, some local soft cheese wrapped in wax paper, tomatoes, salt, and a bottle of Rioja. There was also a bag of ripe peaches; her mouth watered just looking at them.

She groaned. 'God, I'm so hungry. Being targeted for assassination takes it out of me. And so does making love to you.'

Sam broke off a large chunk of bread and spread it with soft cheese. 'Then come here and eat something. I don't want you drained. We're going back to bed in a couple of hours.'

She moved to a rough wooden chair and sat down. The table looked to be carved from pieces of driftwood nailed together, surface smooth from the sea, the shapes of the planks gnarled and knotted.

'A couple of hours? Why not sooner?'

He put ham and tomatoes on the plate with the bread and poured her some wine into one of Hans's plastic cups.

'Because for the next two hours I'm going to be filing the story of both of our lives.'

She bit deeply into the bread, then took a mouthful of ham, intensely flavoured and salty, and the glorious sunburst of the tomatoes, so rich and ripe they were almost a dessert. Sam was demolishing bread and ham, and swigging down wine. He pushed her cup towards her.

'This is so good. Drink.'

She obeyed him, blushing slightly. It was; rough, full-bodied, perfect with the simple food.

335

The warm glow of the wine spread through her, and for a few minutes, she was bathed in contentment. She ate quietly, with Sam sitting opposite her. Her body was relaxed from sex, incredible sex, her responsiveness more than she had dreamed it could be, and the sun was on the sea, the food was wonderful, she was alone with Sam, she was safe. The pleasure of eating had been dulled for her in the luxury of the trophy wife existence. But no more, because she was learning what it was like to be hungry. And to cherish every wonderful thing that life delivered her. Like Sam.

After they had eaten several chunks of bread and cheese, and Lisa had sipped down a half-glass of wine, she felt mellow enough to ask, 'Are you going somewhere then? To file your story?'

He nodded. 'I don't think we should use this house. Landlines are too traceable. There's a small town a few miles down the road. I'll go there, get a phone card, file from a booth somewhere.'

She swallowed drily. 'So I wait here for you to come back?'

Sam held her gaze, and she felt her belly give way beneath her with sheer lust.

'Uh-huh. Right. You wait here, alone. Because that worked so well last time.'

Lisa attempted to ignore her relief, her desire. God, but there was something so basic, so masculine about a man who wanted to protect her. She felt like every cell in her body was crying out for his touch.

'But that guy is dead . . . '

'He's dead. The guy who hired him isn't. And he may already have somebody else on our trail. You don't know who watched us at that airport, who tracked our flight. I think we're alone here, but I'm not basing a goddamned thing on what I *think*. Not any more. It's a miracle he didn't kill you. You're coming with me, and if you have to stand next to me and be bored for an hour, tough shit. You can buy a magazine in a grocery store. While I watch.'

Lisa felt the blush rise from her neck till it consumed the whole of her body. She was on fire, alight with desire for him. In the beginning, she'd said yes to Josh, whenever he asked, out of a sense of duty, gratitude. But towards the end, he had had to negotiate for every session in bed — she was resentful, tired, controlled, full of avoidance. She'd thought she was like so many women, that she hated sex, that it was the price of her relationship.

It wasn't like that with Sam. She could hardly wait to get his clothes off. She would ask for it if she had to, beg for it. When they slept together, she could see her own hand sneaking over his hip bone, down towards his cock, finding it, stroking and cupping, teasing, intending to wake him from sleep, to get him hard enough to fuck her. God, but she was like a schoolgirl or something. She had to get a grip. Relate to him normally, not like a teenage girl in the front row of a gig by her favourite boy band. But it was hard. Her words were combative, but her feelings were soft, warm, almost helpless in his presence.

337

'You don't have to watch me,' she said.

'Yes I do.'

She looked down at the table, tried to compose herself. If they were going to be together, she would have to learn how to handle these feelings she had for him. She'd have to be normal. Not dissolve into water just because he was strong, when so many men were weak.

She looked up. He was watching her, smiling slightly. Goddammit. She hated to be so transparent to him.

'Are you ready?' he said, grinning.

'Yes. Ready.' She stood up. 'If you insist.'

He came around the table and pulled her to him. He was hard again. She gasped, pressed herself to him. But he held her away, one hand on her chest, by her shoulder.

'Later,' he said, softly, in her ear. His hand ran lightly down her back, his fingers tracing a little pattern on the slope of her ass. Lisa's knees buckled. He was torturing her now, and he knew it. His smile was full of triumph, dominance.

'Oh God,' she muttered. 'You're cruel.'

'You wait. I have to do this. Unless you'd like to stay on the run for ever. We need to get ourselves back home. We can't fight them with the police on our backs. We need to go back, and we need to hunt.'

'But I'll be arrested. And if I'm trapped in one place . . .'

'There's no warrant out for your arrest. They dragged their feet on it. And now there's unlikely to be one. I know the FBI guy working this case. I kind of gave it to him. He found that semen.

But I agree, we can't let you be tied down. We're going to enter the US illegally. The key thing is that everybody should know you're innocent. You were convicted by the tabloids; you'll be cleared by them too.'

She nodded. 'Then let's go.'

He kissed her again, on the lips. 'One more thing, sugar.'

'What?'

'Are you prepared to go public with me? If I file this story, I've got to tell them everything. Especially tell them that I'm with you. That I love you.'

She panicked a little; her heart sped up, but she was held firmly in his arms, and the beat-beat-beat of her pulse gradually slowed against the steady rock of his chest.

'But then they won't believe you. They'll think you've been seduced.'

'Nah.' He shook his head. 'If I lie, they won't believe me. A prosecutor will expose us, and then everything I wrote, the public will discount. They hate being lied to. You want to talk about the wisdom of crowds? You just can't get past them. Our only chance is to spill everything. To lay out the facts and ask them to judge. It means you confessing you love me, even just weeks after your husband was brutally murdered. It means that for years to come, probably, you'll be famous. We'll be like Bonnie and Clyde.'

'But they killed people.'

'And so did I.'

Lisa shuddered. 'Self-defence.'

'Still. My feeling is we don't have a lot of

choice. I have to tell all, give them the kind of exposé they'll read once in a lifetime, but not as Sam Murray, dirt-disher extraordinaire. I *am* the story now. I'm in this. And so are you. And once it's out, there's no going back.'

'There's never any going back,' she said slowly. 'If I've learned anything, I've learned that.'

'So you'll do it?'

She tilted her mouth up to his. 'I'll do it. And not just because right now I think I'd do anything you asked. I'll do it because I want to go home. Because I'm tired of running. Because I'm tired of people I've never met seeing me as someone I'm not. You tell them, Sam; write your story, make it the best damn story you've ever written. And scare the hell out of whoever ordered Josh killed. Let him know that his widow is coming for him.'

12

Craig Gordon's phone buzzed in his hand.

He looked down at it, grateful for the interruption. His fucking bosses were making him eat so many shades of shit. They were still working on the DNA of the semen, down in the lab. It had deteriorated pretty good. Possibly too much to eliminate Josh. They were clinging on to that like it was a straw.

'But it still could be his semen?' Emma Fitzgerald, his superior, had asked.

Craig had shrugged. 'Could be. Unlikely pattern. We'd have to disclose in discovery.'

Fitzgerald was scowling with annoyance. 'This doesn't help us. It doesn't finger anybody else.'

He looked at her coolly. 'The facts are often messy. You can talk to Justice, but I think even the hardest-assed DA in the world is going to hear 'reasonable doubt' on this one.'

'How about the man?' Jed Palminteri, his bureau chief, was thinking out loud. 'The hack? He's on the run, got a big story. Your reports indicate he could be with her.'

'Yes.' Fitzgerald seized on the thought. 'This makes his career. What if he saw her before the wedding night? He's written several pieces on her.'

'Most tabloid writers have, ma'am. They weren't flattering pieces.'

'Good cover,' she said.

341

'So he kills the groom, masturbates over the body and then sets up the wife?'

'It does make a great story.' Palminteri nodded sagely. 'You've seen his name all over TV. He's half a celebrity now.'

'I think it's a bit complex, frankly, sir. Lot of risk. Zero opportunity. No forced entry; this was a professional-style hit.'

Fitzgerald's eyes narrowed. 'But hotel staff reported to you that he'd bribed porters for access to the scene. That's how he got those exclusive photos. What if he bribed them before the actual murder? What if he didn't need to force? Had a skeleton key in his pocket?'

Craig bit his cheeks to stop himself responding. Stupid fool. She was just fishing like a junior detective in the third grade.

'Nothing in the evidence to suggest it, ma'am.'

'Well, Special Agent, you were in the Academy with Sam Murray. Are you sure you're being objective?'

Now she'd gone too far. 'Ma'am, I've never covered up for a perp in my life.'

'I wasn't suggesting that,' she said quickly, although she clearly had been. 'It's just that liking people can sometimes colour our judgement . . . '

'He's not my best bud. I haven't laid eyes on the guy for over five years. We talk on the phone about cases sometimes. He's given good leads on this one, leads that have panned out. The passport, the girl in Hong Kong. It'd have to be a pretty big conspiracy. I say reasonable doubt.'

They'd stared angrily at him, not liking the

sense he was talking. And then his phone vibrated in his hand, loudly, like an angel of mercy, pulling him out of this conversation.

'Excuse me. Might be a lead.' He made to get to his feet.

'A lead? What kind of suspects are you working on?' Palminteri demanded. 'You do understand the heat we're getting?'

'Well, sir, if it wasn't the wife, we're going back to basics. Friends, relatives, business partners. Steen fucked about a lot. Husbands. The hit was professional, so we're going through bank records right now. Looking for evidence of payments. If that fails, we start a round of questions. But I don't want to tip off the killer that we've eliminated Lisa Costello. That way he'll feel secure; he might get sloppy.'

'Agent Gordon,' Fitzgerald said severely, frowning again. 'Let's get this straight. We have not eliminated Lisa Costello. She fled the scene and committed assault. Her bloodstained clothes are in the bedroom and her prints are on the murder weapon, OK? Some semen doesn't take all that away.'

Craig said nothing, because legally it did, and they all knew it. No grand jury would indict with evidence like that. And if they did, the case would fall on the first motion to dismiss. His phone buzzed again. A text. With a landline number.

'I should go. Sources.'

'Report back before the end of the day. We need ongoing oversight,' Fitzgerald said, the bitch. Craig stood and walked out. She could

343

have oversight of his ass leaving the goddamned building . . .

Outside he bent his head and glanced at his phone.

Holy shit. It was him. It was Sam. He looked behind him, to be sure the door to the office was shut. Of course every communication here was intercepted, but there was safety in numbers, and he had a cute little bug inside his phone that scrambled stuff very effectively.

Time was short. He dialled the number. What was that country code? Spain; the guy was in Spain. How the fuck had he got there? The CIA was reporting noises in Liechtenstein, near Switzerland, and that was just a few hours back. Did he have a fucking teleporter?

Sam picked up on the first ring. 'Craig. I've been waiting here for five minutes.'

'Getting my ass chewed out because you blew their nice neat theory away.'

'And I'm gonna blow it some more. I wanted you to know first.'

Craig sighed. 'From you, those are never good words to hear. What the fuck is it now?'

'I'm calling my editor and filing a story. I'm going to tell everything. Including the semen you found in Thailand.'

'That's classified. You can't do that.'

'I'll cite hotel sources. I have to. It's the key evidence that clears her. I'm real sorry, but I have to.'

He knew it was true. Another sigh. 'Goddammit. OK.'

'You heard about where we were?'

'The dead guy in Vaduz? You want to talk about that? They brought up your name, Sam, they're looking at you. This better be good.'

'Get a sample from him. It'll match your semen. He was an assassin. Tried to kill Lisa. Chased her. She hid. I was trying to file another story. I left her alone, it was dumb.'

Craig digested this. 'And who took him out? You?'

'Yeah. He was a pro, but not expecting opposition. It caught him off guard that I could shoot. I got his phone.'

'I need that phone. I need to get you to somewhere.'

Sam ignored this. 'He sent a message to his client before I showed up. I'm forwarding it to your phone. I'm going to do what I can with it.'

Craig was practically salivating. 'Don't mess me around, Sam. We can analyse everything about that phone right down to which store sold it to him and when. You don't have the resources.'

'I'll get the phone to you when I'm through with it. Look, Craig, don't ask me to come in, OK. You know I can't do that and nor can she. You wouldn't. Don't treat us like kids.'

'I have to advise you to surrender yourself to the authorities, Sam.'

'Right. And I have to ignore you.'

Despite himself, Craig grinned. 'Smart-ass.'

'The papers may call you for comment.'

'They won't get any.' A beat. 'On the record.'

'Good man. If I were you, I'd look close to Josh Steen, real close. The killing, the fact that

345

they sent the same guy after Lisa. That's one worried perp right there. He wants the girl dead because he wants it tied up. And he has money to hire a pro twice. I'm sure right now he's looking for this schmuck's replacement. Anyway, go get yourself the corpse; you can check out his clothes and shit, see what else you can find.'

'I'll get right to it.'

'When I call, let me know what you've found, and I'll get the phone to you.'

'Sam — '

'Don't argue. We're past that.'

Craig gave in, with a good grace. 'Guess we are. And you've cleared your girlfriend and got one of the bad guys.'

'Cleared? Really?'

'They said she's not out of the woods. They know she is really, but they can't let that dream go. Don't bring her by to tour Virginia is my advice. Not yet.'

'You should work on them. She's sick of running. She wants to go to an island and drink cocktails with umbrellas and sleep in a hammock.'

'She can take a number.'

'Yeah, well, yesterday she nearly took a hit. The client will be sending a replacement out now. He'll be panicking. I want some safety for my girl.'

'Then send the phone. Help me catch him.'

'Help me get her cleared.'

They were at an impasse. Craig rubbed his head. In the past he'd led this friendship. Now Sam Murray was setting all the pace.

'I'll send it to you when I'm done. You have to act in your framework, Craig, I don't. I'm going to solve this case.'

'I hope you're right, buddy. Because once they figure out you killed the hitman, you're on the hook for murder too. Ever think about that one? She's not the only fugitive right now.'

'Just keep your phone on. I may need you at short notice.'

He hung up. For one second, Craig Gordon experienced a surge of envy. Yeah, he loved his wife, and he was goddamned great at this job. Loved the Bureau since he was a rookie. But just once, he'd like to be Sam Murray. On the run with a gorgeous woman. Hong Kong. Thailand. Italy, Liechtenstein. Spain. Shooting assassins. Solving the big case. All over the TV . . .

But it wasn't his life. Sam had always taken the risks. Craig just had to run the case from the ground up, same way he always did. He headed back to his desk to go through those financials again. Peter Mazin was first up.

★ ★ ★

Rich Frank was sweating. The A/C in his office had broken down again. It was still going, but it was chugging along, sputtering, barely effective. He almost didn't mind that. The heat gave him a great excuse to have moisture beading on his brow, on the rolls of fat on his neck. People didn't need to know he was also terrified.

Build 'em up, knock 'em down. It was what a good journalist did in their business. But that treatment was supposed to be reserved for the latest spoiled celebrity, not his own goddamned paper!

They'd ridden high on Sam's exclusives. Even switched from a weekly schedule to ad hoc publishing as each new one came out. But then the stories dwindled. And now the board of directors was screaming at him on the hour, every hour.

'We got a great front-cover lead. Two British royals, marriage troubles. No, it's sourced from a butler.' He tried to sound confident. Fuck Sam Murray! Fuck him and his demands for millions of dollars and wire fucking transfers! He could have that and a brace of Brazilian-waxed hookers if he'd call and give Rich something he could use. But no, now he had Eli Wassman, the money man, the guy who decided how much they all got paid, on the fucking phone from corporate HQ in Manhattan. And he had to sell him your basic celebrity splitsville cover.

'That's not a cover. Not this week. This week it's page ten, and only if it's true. And sourced.'

True! And sourced! Rich passed a hand over his fat brow. What did the asshole think he was running here, the *New York Times?*

'Nobody wants some old-hat film stars, Rich. We need Lisa Costello on the cover. We need *news.* Where's Sam?'

'Deep undercover,' Rich lied. 'Working on the biggest story you'll ever print.'

'Well he'd better work a lot *faster.* I got advertisers ready to sue us. We promised a gigantic exclusive last week. Do you have any idea how much we jacked up the rates? It's practically the Superbowl! Things like this can keep our paper afloat for years. Don't fuck this up.'

Rich panted with nerves. The job was his life. All the whores and the blow and the easy lays in the clubs, everything went away if *USA Weekly* kicked him out. Even his fucking Ferrari was a company car.

'Look, Sam's taking his time. It ain't my fault . . .'

'Rich. Don't give me excuses, give me a story. A major fucking story. Or we'll find someone who can.'

'I'm on it,' he managed, and slammed down the phone. It rang again immediately.

'What the hell is it now?' Rich Frank screamed at his secretary.

Sarah wasn't fazed, she was used to his moods. Her voice came through his phone, calm and collected.

'It's Sam Murray.'

'Bullshit,' Rich shouted.

'You think I don't know Sam's voice? It's him, on three. Pick up.'

His heart thumping like a teenager at a pop concert, Rich depressed line three's button, his hands shaking. God! Could it be? That selfish, drunk jerk had hauled himself off his ass to save the magazine?

'Rich Frank.'

'Hey. It's Sam.'

It was him, it fucking was. Rich's pent-up fear and frustration exploded into rage. 'Sam! You

349

prick! Where the fuck have you been! I got corporate rooting around inside my ass with a flashlight!'

'I've been busy,' Sam said. Deadpan, the arrogant fucker.

'Yeah, well. We've all been busy. Trying to keep this rag afloat. Do you understand that? Hundreds of people could get *fired* if we don't get a cover.' Including me, he didn't say. 'The whole damned building waiting on you, Mr Superstar. So don't give me any crap. Tell me you got something for me.'

'I got something for you.'

Suddenly Rich didn't want to kill Sam any more. He wanted to kiss him. 'You little beauty. You are a superstar after all. I'm gonna make you rich, Sam Murray.'

There was a beat.

'Send me the money by wire. All of it, everything else you owe me.'

'Fuck you,' Rich said immediately. But there was something in Sam's tone, some weird note, something that didn't sit right with him. A sombre kind of voice, the way you spoke when somebody got sick. It didn't seem like Sam was kidding. 'That's not our deal and you know it,' he added, although less certainly.

'Never mind our deal. Here's why you need to send the money. This will be the last story I ever write for you. Whatever you owe me, pay me now. There won't be another chance.'

'You're gonna kill yourself? Jesus, Sam . . . '

'No, I'm not going to kill myself. Somebody else might kill me. They tried to already.'

350

They tried to? Rich couldn't help it, his mind leapt to the story. There was no point beating himself up; newspapers was what he did.

'Rich, here's the thing. I am about to start talking. You'll set up a tape. You'll transcribe. This will hit newsstands and be the biggest story in American journalism since O.J. Only you'll have an exclusive. Maybe it's not Watergate, but it's all over the TV, and it's the kind of thing that makes a career for a guy like you. You want to sit in that stuffy office all day with the fucked-up A/C?'

Rich jumped out of his skin and looked around himself, as though Sam Murray might be hiding in the air vents.

'Or do you want to be the guy on the other end of the phone? Do you want to sit in the boardroom? This story is your ticket, Rich. And if I file it and you don't pay up, I'll talk about that. To a rival paper. Let every hack in LA know that *USA Weekly* doesn't stick to their deals. Maybe you'll screw me over, but you'll never get another story.'

'Fuck you, Sam,' Rich hissed again. But he was worried suddenly. Worried this guy meant it. Worried that he might be about to blow the exclusive of a lifetime.

'You'll wire the money as soon as I hang up. Put it this way, Rich. If I don't get confirmation from my bank within the hour, I will call up Larry King, live on air, and blow your exclusive. However close publication is, TV and radio can always match it. *Capisce?*'

'*Si*,' Rich Frank moaned miserably. 'God, I

351

hope you're right, Sam. I hope this story is good enough for the fucking Pulitzer.'

'It's better than that. It's good enough for *Entertainment Tonight* and *20/20*.'

'Did you catch her?'

'Catch her?' Sam laughed. 'You could say that. Why don't you wire up a mike. I'll dictate, you go straight to press. Call a conference if you like, have the staff sit around that dumb oval table in the office. You can wire the money while I talk and they type. And if I don't get it within one hour of hanging up the phone, my next call is to CNN. And I start saying this shit all over again. No exclusive means no sale.'

Rich clenched his fist, he was so pathetically grateful. 'You got it. Wait right there.'

'I can call back.'

'No!' he practically screamed. 'Stay where you are! Malcolm! Michael! Tim! Colin! Get the fuck in here! Get tapes! It's Sam Murray!'

There was the sound of chairs scraping back on linoleum as the hack pack rushed into the boardroom. Rich almost pushed Sarah inside, then turned it over to them, placing his phone in the centre of the table, on speaker.

'Get this typed and on to the cover. Sam, you still there?'

'I'm here.' Beat. 'Some of the stuff I'm saying is going to shock you. I don't want to be interrupted. I'm going to hang up frequently and call back so I can't be traced. Got it?'

'We got it, we got it,' Rich pleaded, sweating some more.

'Then you better get on to the transfer. Here

352

we go.' Murray cleared his throat. 'This is Sam Murray, reporting from the road on the Lisa Costello case. It's not going to be a usual story. For one thing, Lisa Costello is standing right next to me. For second, she didn't do it. And for a third, I'm in love with her.'

A murmur ran right around the table. Rich glared daggers at everybody, and Sam's disembodied voice continued to float around the packed boardroom, this time without competition.

'This is the story of a movie mogul murdered. A trophy wife blamed. A friendship betrayed. It's the story of the real killer, a supposed friend of Josh Steen's, who really hated him *and* his fiancée. And it's the story of a hired assassin wielding a royal dagger, then flying across the world to finish the job with the woman he set up. Only that assassin is now dead. And I killed him.'

'Christ!' said Martha Varney, the features editor.

'Don't fucking interrupt,' Rich said intently. 'I want this typed. I want it printed. Don't edit a word.' He stood up from the table.

'Where are you going?' Varney whispered.

'Where do you think? I'm going to pay the guy his money,' Rich answered.

And for once in his life, he didn't resent it at all.

★ ★ ★

Sam finally hung up the phone forty minutes later. He had talked, and the words had flowed

353

easily out of him. Lisa was standing next to him, her beautiful eyes prickling with tears at times. That was hard to see, but he ploughed on. With almost every word he felt their burden getting lighter. It was a rough story. They'd both been wrong. The lecherous, lazy tabloid hack. The trophy wife who didn't have the guts to get out. They weren't perfect. But they had not deserved this.

He'd told them everything. How Lisa had gotten drunk, provided a nice opportunity. Tricked Alice and hurt her and tied her up. Stolen a passport. Fled to Europe. He described hunting her, falling in love. Flinging his ethics out the window, his safety, his chance of a payday. He talked about the FBI. He talked about second chances. Their love, and how it surprised him, how he'd never thought he could feel like this. The sensation of being trapped. Driving over the border, late at night, in a car. Lisa the 'hooker', sharing a motel. How hard it had been not to touch her.

And finally, the assassin. He'd flicked through the man's phone. Sam thought he was called Felix. There was a garbled message from a woman, maybe something he'd forgotten to delete from voicemail. It sounded like that. Sam said he knew the name of Felix's client, but was leaving it out. It was important to scare the fucker. Important to keep him guessing as to what Sam knew. The story was hot enough without it.

Sam could hear the gasps, the oohs and aahs of the journalists, many of them his friends. It

354

was truly an incredible story. A once-in-a-lifetime thing. It blew the lid off the perception of Lisa, it told a tale of life on the run, incredible wealth, desperation, the sense of being hunted, falling in love against the odds. It blew up every fantasy, every perception of the easy life, the trophy wife who had it all. It shone a torch into the darkness of the world surrounding Josh Steen. It told America that Lisa was innocent, totally innocent. And that somebody was trying to kill her — a package deal with her husband.

TV was going to talk of nothing else. And this would be one of the biggest-selling issues in the history of magazines.

When Sam was finally done, he said, 'Rich? You sent the money?'

'Oh yeah,' said the disembodied voice. 'It's there. Go check. Thanks, Sam. You know what this means.'

'See you later, Rich. At times it was fun.' He put down the receiver, turned around. There she was, tears in her eyes, his Lisa, his woman. He had defied the whole world for her. And he would do it all again, in a second.

'Don't cry,' he said. 'We don't have time for it. Hold on one more second, OK?'

He picked the phone up again and called his bank. Yeah, they were happy to confirm the money was there. Amazing how deferential they sounded after a huge payoff. He issued orders quickly, used to the routine by now; the money split, landed in numbered accounts, a bit of it to an account under a false ID he'd set up when

355

still training as a Fibbie and had used now and then ever since. Never needed it as much as he did today.

The whole set of transactions took him five or six minutes, and when the last call was done, he replaced the receiver and felt a hundred pounds lighter. He exhaled; he looked out, past the whitewashed houses, to the sea, dark and massive under the twilight sky. A huge part of his life was over. He was the story now, and he could never be a journalist again. And he didn't care. Lisa was the future. She had changed everything, and now there was no map. And he found he loved it.

'Now what?' she said.

She was shivering. The temperature had dropped with the sun. He turned around, took her into his arms. Held her closely, heating her with his body. He wanted to make sure she was not cold. He wanted to protect her from every bad thing, ever. Or at least die trying.

'Now we go back to the house. Make love.'

'I like that part,' she said.

'And then tomorrow we take a ride to Barcelona. From there we fly back to LA.'

'How the hell do we do that?'

'I have a connection in Barcelona.' He hoped to God Roderigo was still active. Christ knew what he could come up with otherwise. 'We'll get fake passports. He makes the best. We cut your hair, dye it again, get you some sunglasses, you fly in.'

'That simple?' she asked, pressing against him.

'Best things in life usually are.' He slipped his

hand into hers. 'Let's go home.'

Home. God. They didn't have one. Right now he wasn't sure he could ever offer her one again. Maybe this was the dumbest move in the world. Flying back to the States, where they fried you for murder. Where law enforcement knew exactly what it was doing, and had the time, the money and the patience to catch you. As of this second, he was a millionaire. So far, so good, on the run. He could make that cash last a lifetime. It wouldn't be luxury, but they'd have each other, and a new life.

This was a risk, a fucking giant risk.

But they would take it anyway.

★ ★ ★

Yuri shifted a little in his seat. It was buttercup leather, a sleek modern chair that complemented the cowslip walls of the Beverly Hills sitting room. The lady of the house had decked this all out in a fantasy of white and shades of yellow; Paris meets California sunshine. Exactly the wrong kind of room to do dark deals in. It was incongruous, and he enjoyed meeting the client here. He insisted on entry to their homes. Unsettled them from the very start, and put the balance of power exactly where it should be in their relationship. With him.

The client hated him in this room. Hated him period. No problem. He was used to it. If the idiot hadn't hired Felix Latham instead of him, he wouldn't have this problem now.

'This job will be very expensive. Not that these

357

things are ever cheap. But times have changed since round one.'

'I get that.' Cold and clipped.

'You have two targets; at this point they're both famous, and *USA Weekly* is about to hit the stands in a special edition. Rumours on the wire are that it's a doozy. Sam Murray, special correspondent, admitting he's in love and on the lam. Also clears Lisa Costello.'

'How can it clear her?'

There was no point hiding what would be common knowledge soon enough. He had always enjoyed delivering bad news. He *was* bad news.

'The FBI found semen stains on the honeymoon bed, at an angle that meant Josh Steen couldn't have made them. Hair in the shower, too. And they got Felix's body over in Europe. DNA confirms. That clears Lisa Costello nice and neat.'

There was a sharp intake of breath. 'Semen? Hair?'

He grinned. 'Felix was always sloppy. That's probably why he got dead. You shouldn't economise with the important stuff, OK.'

'I don't care about cost.'

'Yeah. Good. You need this done. They have Felix now. They'll track his ID soon. Then bank accounts, everything. Sam Murray is the one that would bother me. The girl . . . ' He shrugged. 'She's a slippery little bitch. Impressive. But he was working for the Bureau once. Good rep, just selfish, lazy. Looks like he's trying to put that right.'

358

The client shifted. It was never a happy point in their lives when they came to see him.

'Can you find them?'

'I play in bigger leagues than Felix Latham. I got access to Interpol computers, I have contacts at the telecoms exchange. Got people in the FBI, the police. I pay all of them. Takes money. Lots of money.'

'Is that a yes?'

Snotty. 'That's a yes. I can find them. If you got the cash.'

'It's what all you people say.'

He was supremely relaxed. 'We both know that if you had better options, you'd have taken them. In my business it's about money. There are no awards ceremonies. No Oscars, no kudos. Just money. Your problem meets my numbered bank account. For this job the price is ten million, five million each.'

The eyebrows lifted in genuine shock. 'You're kidding.'

'You can buy a lot cheaper, but nobody more reliable. I'm high-end. It's what you need.'

'But the cops will find that kind of money transferred out. They'll track it.'

'A succession of small payments.' He smirked. 'Relatively small, at least. Various accounts. I have some slush businesses. I'll instruct you on how to pay.'

'OK.' It was almost a sob. 'Don't come back for more; there isn't any.'

He leaned forward. 'Believe me, I know your finances. If you had more, you'd be paying it. It will take me several days to track them. They've gone to ground. Then I'll kill them. It'll be fast.'

'Do you have any idea where they are?'

The question was pathetically eager. It was fun to answer honestly. 'Not till I've tracked them. But my best guess is that they're coming here.'

'Here?'

'To find you. Expose you. They don't get out from under until you've been charged. Sam Murray is going to hunt you.'

A blink of fear. 'How the hell can you tell that?'

Finally he threw out a bone. A touch of reassurance. 'Because Sam Murray is my prey now, and I'm watching him.' He got to his feet. 'I'll be in touch tonight. Start transfers immediately.'

'I've been let down before.'

'Felix Latham has missed targets before,' Yuri said. 'My record is perfect. These two won't spoil it. You get what you pay for.' He walked out.

★ ★ ★

It was early in the morning. The rising sun reddened the sea, sending ochre and ruby flashes across the windscreen as Sam drove along the coast road. He'd called Hans, found a neighbour with a car they could borrow, no questions asked; God knew how he'd get it back, but maybe Hans would take care of that. He couldn't worry about it. That was life on the run. You took things. Risks. Passports. Other people's cars.

They would turn inland soon. Lisa was

360

bundled up against the window, sleeping. He was glad of it. They had made love for most of the night. Breaking to eat, and then lying together until she made him hard again. He could scarcely believe what it was like with her. When they fell asleep, he'd woken in the night, wanting her, and had pulled her to him, taken her when she was half asleep, woken her thrusting inside her, his mouth clamped on hers. And she'd kicked and scratched and bitten; she'd squirmed beneath him, gasped and sobbed until he had her bite down on a pillow. Such torrents of passion. She was so excited by him, she made him feel ten feet tall. Love. It was weird. And exhausting. But he could handle little sleep. He'd sleep on the plane. If they got on it.

She was beautiful when she slept. Soon he'd start looking for towns, somewhere big enough to buy a couple of mobile phones, throwaway shit. Then he'd need to wake her. She wasn't staying in the car alone. She wasn't doing anything alone.

No way to live. He thought of his contact, hoped to hell the guy was still around. There really wasn't a Plan B.

★ ★ ★

Yuri made his first call before he was out of the drive. He didn't worry about waiting for the customer to wire the money. They were desperate, and rich. They'd pay up. He hated wasting time. Felix Latham, what a fool. That guy had a rep that was spotty at best. But he was

361

a pro. Taking out the killer of an assassin, one that was famous, the story of the month . . . this was a great job. And ten mil was a payday, even for him.

He rang a number. One of his best.

'It's me.'

'Yeah.' They didn't waste time in chat. None of his people wanted to know him very much.

'I want what you got on Murray and Costello.'

'Fuck, you don't want much.'

'You get paid. Are they in the United States?'

'Not to our knowledge. What's the rate?'

'Quarter,' he said. 'That's going to include follow-ups.'

Now the voice was much friendlier. 'You must have a hard-on for them.'

'Time pressure. Murray's got sources in your office. That's how he wrote up the semen thing. I want to know who he's talking to; I want a wire on that phone. Everything he says.'

'You want me to tap the FBI?'

'Quarter million dollars. You fucking work for the FBI. You're IA. You can't be touched. What the fuck, don't play games, Woody.'

'Call you back,' the guy said.

That's how you do it, Felix, Yuri thought, satisfied. You don't mess about with the second string. Hunt the man. Find his contacts and follow the thread. You don't go looking for them. You wait. Let them come to you.

He thought about his client. Ten million. A lot of money, even for these people. But he would deliver, like he always did, and his place would be assured. The kills would be worth much more than five each. He didn't think about retiring. He loved this job, because he loved power. There was no god, there was no morality; it was a bullshit social construct. Fame and money and sex, they were all real. And what he did gave him access to all of them. The client got rid of a problem. He got everything else. He imagined how he would do Sam Murray. With something of a flourish, maybe. He loved poisons, and there were some that would twist the vic into a human pretzel during the agony of his contortions, turn his tongue soot black. Yuri thought he'd do something like that. Call it a professional courtesy to poor stupid Felix. Besides, it would look real good. A calling card. The woman, on the other hand, he would just kill, clean and quick. A bullet, or snap her neck if there was no opportunity to shoot. She was caught up in this from the start. Nothing personal, usually, about his killings; Yuri thought emotion was sloppy, all emotion. Compared to Sam Murray, Lisa Costello was going to catch a break.

13

'Wow,' Lisa said.

She looked up from under her cheap sunglasses. They were standing with hundreds of other tourists around the church of the Holy Family, the *Sagrada Familia*. The ornate, almost otherworldly building soared into the sky, every square inch covered in neo-Gothic carving; the interior was richly modern architecture.

'Centre of the city. And one of the most famous sights in Spain.' Sam put his hand on her shoulder, his fingers caressing her through her T-shirt. 'You can't go wrong surrounded by crowds of tourists. They don't pay attention. You get lost.'

'You're going to meet him here?'

'If I can find him. Yes.' Sam pulled out one of his cheap mobiles, punched in the number. His heart was in his mouth, but he didn't want her to see it. There wasn't much of a Plan B. He'd think of something eventually, perhaps, but if they wanted to get back home, they needed to find a way past the INS.

Lisa watched him. Something was up. That might be a strange thought given their lives this past month, but she knew this man now, knew him with all her heart. And he was worried. More than the run-of-the-mill anxiety they lived with every second; this was big. He was dialling numbers, waiting, hanging up.

'He's not there?'

'None of my contacts are good. They're mostly just dead numbers, suspended accounts. That means he's either dead or he's packed it in. It's not hard to reach these guys if you're in their loop. Nobody has the numbers but people they trust. They don't answer, means they've disappeared.'

She moved closer, put a hand on his arm. 'Don't worry. We've come through worse than this.'

'I do. It's not easy to get into the United States. We could maybe sneak on a ship, but I don't have weeks to cross the Atlantic.'

'So we stay right here until you find someone else who does passports. There's more than one guy.'

'I could, but it might take weeks. You should get back to the States now. The story will hit the newsstands; there'll be a lot of sympathy for you. Whoever had Josh killed will be afraid and acting out. Easier to find. And I need to be there to track Felix. We have a window, and I don't want to miss it.'

Lisa looked at Sam and felt a fresh surge of love. All his mind, all his intellect was bent on her, clearing her name. He was prepared to take any risk.

'The FBI guy told you they have you down as a murder suspect. I could be in the clear, and you could be arrested. Tried, shipped back to Europe, flung in jail for life. Why do you think I started running? Do you want to take that chance?'

He moved in. Held her, kissed her. God, it was incredible, the way she melted into his arms, just every time. She had never been loved like this. It was as though every cell in her body was under an electric charge.

'We have to get free. Both of us. That means this. That means a hunt. I'm not running for ever. Takes energy away from you.'

'OK,' she whispered. He was settled; he'd decided for her. Lisa didn't try to change his mind. She was sick of running, sick of the shadow life. If Sam was going to take the risk, it was his choice, his privilege.

'You solved it.' He kissed her again. 'You're brilliant. The FBI guy. That's who we'll call.' He sighed. 'I got to trust somebody sometime. And I trust Craig Gordon.'

'The FBI?' she asked, shivering. 'They'd arrest us right away!'

'Craig wouldn't. Not if I can get him to treat us as sources.'

'But there are warrants out. Wouldn't that be illegal? Blow his career?'

'Yeah. It could.'

'From what you said, this is not a risk-taking guy,' Lisa objected. 'Family man, plays by the book. If you go to him, we'll be in custody within the hour.'

'I trust Craig, like I said. And you have to trust me. He's our man on this. It's a crisis, and we have a bargaining chip.'

'We do?'

Sam held up the slim black phone. 'Felix's cell. You see, Craig Gordon knows this guy was the killer, and he wants the man who hired him. He needs this evidence; he doesn't need us. So he'll defy protocol and his bosses. Because that's what helps him get where he wants to go. Taking the actual killer down.' He grinned at her. 'Once he understood you didn't do it, he lost interest in you. Maybe not other people there. That's how the Bureau is. You're important, you're a scalp, a name. But Craig only wants the guy who did it.'

★ ★ ★

Woody Harmon could hardly believe it. His phone was buzzing already. Not his regular phone, the new one he had set up to track Craig Gordon. It was easy to rig, designed to ring only when unrecognised numbers called. No secret around the J. Edgar Hoover Building that Craig Gordon, out in LA, was running this case and had a line to Sam Murray. But Murray had vanished. That was what most of them thought. The investigation was wrapped in the kind of security they usually reserved for corrupt politician cases, the real sensitive stuff.

But Yuri had said Sam would call. And he fucking had. Within twenty-four hours. Yuri scared the hell out of Woody, fifteen years in the Bureau and an ex-beat cop. Not like he hadn't seen his share of criminals. This guy, though, was something else. He was a slice of pure evil. And you didn't fuck with him. He paid very well, and Woody was long since tired of sweating his balls off for the federal government for fuck-all. But he was afraid that he'd be delivering whatever

Yuri wanted if he was offering a quarter and a can of Coke. The man was half psychic. He always knew, he always fucking knew.

Woody's heart pulsed as he lifted the phone to his ear. Depression and adrenalin pumped through him. He didn't want Craig Gordon killed. Guy had a rep for being a good agent, real solid. But he was much more afraid of being killed himself. He'd sold out long ago, and there was nowhere to go but forward. He would report this conversation faithfully; he knew that much. You didn't lie to Yuri. He didn't like it.

* * *

The plane was a small jet, Delta out to San Diego. A mixture of tourists and returning businessmen. Nobody paid them much attention. Lisa busied herself with a magazine and her bag of duty-free. Her hair was back to blond now, a dark caramel shade. It suited her skin tone, didn't draw attention. Sam marvelled at her calmness. She was really getting used to this now. Another flight, another fake passport. She looked for all the world just like any impatient passenger waiting to board.

They were at the last check. He handed their boarding passes over to the airline staffer. She glanced at them, dipped them into a machine, gave him the stubs.

'Have a good flight,' she said.

'Thanks.' He didn't like to speak too much. Paranoia, in case his voice was recognised. Lisa flashed a smile and filed down the gangway tunnel with the rest of the cattle in economy. Yeah, it was going to be a long flight. Craig had come up with the passports, let him know where to collect them. There were tickets waiting too. Sam was incredibly grateful. For all his confidence with Lisa, until the guy actually came through, there always had to be a little doubt.

But trusting Craig wasn't the same as trusting the Fibbies. For the first time, a third party knew in advance exactly where they were going. It wasn't just the cramped seats that would bother him. It was what was waiting once they arrived.

★ ★ ★

Yuri spun his Maserati down the Pacific Coast Highway and tried to think. It was not the position he wanted, not quite. That gibbering little coward Woody had tried to placate him.

'But that's it, that's all he said.'

Yuri spat. 'I want more. The names of the passports. Where they're being picked up. A flight number. The airport.'

'Call came from Spain.' He was pathetically glad to be able to supply at least that nugget. 'He wasn't on long enough to trace further. Throwaway phone, unregistered.'

But of course. Sam Murray was no fool. And apparently neither was Craig Gordon.

'You're certain he said nothing of names. Contacts?'

'No, Yuri. Craig just told Sam he knew where to go, and the stuff would be there. It was like he knew he was being traced.'

'He didn't know shit. Gordon was just taking precautions. He's a rules guy. Probably looks both ways and doesn't jaywalk.'

'I guess.'

Yuri ran the scenarios in his mind. He could get Woody to send over a list of all field agents, CIA, active in Spain. But that would take time. By the time he had done any serious winnowing of candidates, his two birds would be on a plane. And that was if Craig Gordon had even used an agent. It could be a hooker, a mutual friend, a local cop, a goddamned priest. Anything. He never looked for needles in haystacks.

'And nothing about where they landed?'

'Zip.'

'Keep on him. Start an internal investigation.'

His contact blanched. 'Based on what? He's a well-known boy scout.'

'Based on I fucking told you to,' Yuri insisted.

'People will talk.'

'Then make it a supervisory thing. Keeping an eye on the Steen case. I don't care how you dress it up, Woody. He's the guy Murray reaches for. Track him.'

He'd hung up.

And now he was driving south. There were some basic assumptions you could make eight times out of ten. That Murray and the girl would want to come home as soon as possible; that was why they'd called Craig. That they'd want to come back to Cali and find the real killer. So the tickets would be for a flight from Spain to California, leaving a maximum of six hours after the phone call. He had run through the list on his computer. The two most likely flights were Barcelona to San Diego and Seville to LAX. They landed within an hour of each other.

Yuri was going for LAX, because Sam Murray seemed like a pretty direct kind of guy. If that was wrong, no matter. He knew where they were coming. He knew who they were talking to. They were coming to him.

★ ★ ★

Craig Gordon travelled very carefully to the airport. First he was a passenger in a cop car, then he got out, changed to a bus; lastly he disembarked at a hotel and one hour later caught the courtesy shuttle. He scoped the crowd the entire time. He was not being watched, or if he was, they possessed more skill than he did, and he couldn't worry about somebody that good.

His normally calm pulse was fluttering. It had been a decade since he'd seen Sam Murray, at least in person. They'd gotten closer in a few snatched conversations lately than at any time since he was a student. Would he recognise the guy? All he had was an airbrushed byline picture. The girl, now. He'd recognise her, the little celebrity, and he wanted to be the only one who did. That meant getting her off the plane and out of the airport quick as possible. In Europe they'd been able to hide. In America, she was a star.

He wanted her alone. She needed debriefing, and then he would take the assassin's phone and catch whatever fucker set this all in motion. It was his duty. It was also the only way out from

371

under. He wanted this case off his back. Nothing else was getting done while America obsessed. But Hollywood and millions of dollars did that to you.

The airport was nice and crowded, the same way it always was. He kept his ID tucked away, and milled around the arrivals portal with all the other families, children wailing, girlfriends waiting eagerly. Every thirty seconds or so he casually scanned the crowd for trouble. Sam Murray expected a second hit, and so did Craig. Maybe a third or more. Whoever had killed Josh Steen was a big player.

The monitor screens said the flight had landed a little early. Great. He wanted to get them the hell out. Technically speaking he was committing a crime himself. But every field agent did that daily. That wasn't the problem so much as their safety. He allowed himself to feel a little sorry for the girl; this must really have sucked for her, especially when she'd believed she'd killed her husband.

But she was made of sterner stuff than your average gold-digger. He was starting to feel that she wasn't a gold-digger at all. That she'd gotten trapped. And that was still legal in all fifty states. Maybe she'd be good for Sam Murray. And if she was going to take him on, she was a braver girl than most . . .

Shit. They were here, they were here. Adrenalin rushed through him, making him alert and tense. No need to worry; he'd have known Sam Murray a mile further away, just from how the guy carried himself. Craig scrutinised his old friend for a second. Murray had killed an assassin. That changed a man, profoundly, taking a life. He turned his gaze to the girl. She had her head lowered; clever. She was not meeting anybody's eyes; she looked to be following Murray using her peripheral vision.

'Jack!' he said. He waved and shouted. 'Hey, Jack! Over here!'

Sam's head turned immediately. The guy had a good ear for voices. He lifted a hand, not replying aloud, and put the other on Lisa Costello's elbow, steering her. Craig was interested to note that the girl still did not look up. She pretended to fiddle with her carrier bags. No luggage, he saw; not even a hand case. Smart, These two had learned how to run.

'Hi,' he said, controlling his voice with an effort as they reached him. 'Hope your flight was OK. Follow me outside, guys, I got a car waiting.'

'Sounds good,' Sam said quietly.

Craig walked as fast as he could without calling attention to himself. It was hard not to turn around and grip the girl by her wrists. Every second he expected exposure. He was lucky; the passengers were steering their carts, chatting, complaining of exhaustion, paying parking charges. Everybody in their own bubble. That was America. It was useful.

He got them to the car, put the girl in the back.

'Sit in the middle,' he said easily. Away from the windows. She was most recognisable. That simple thing would camouflage her. She did as she was told, again keeping her head low. He saw she had a slight figure, good curves. She did not strike him as a tough cookie. But she was managing to survive.

Sam slipped into the passenger seat. Nobody said anything as Craig fired up the car, drove out of the lot. As he passed through the security barrier, without being prompted, Lisa reached down as if to tie her shoes and Sam looked in the glove compartment; they were keeping their faces from the security cameras. He had a moment of admiration. These two were semi-pro.

'Been a while,' he said, at last, when they were out on the road, heading to the freeway.

'Yeah. Thanks, Craig.'

'Hey.' He didn't want Sam Murray slipping too easily into friendship mode. 'Don't say that. I'm going to get full value out of you two. As witnesses. Starting right now. I want the phone, Sam, that was the price of your ticket.'

'That was the deal, yeah.' Murray fished in his pocket and brought it out. 'Felix Latham. Mid-ranking hitman. Took out lower-level politicians, some Mafia guys. Lately in Hollywood. Suspected of killing Susan Steinberg last year.'

Craig blinked. The Steinberg case had received almost zero publicity, because they couldn't prove the car accident wasn't one. But he'd been sure of foul play from the start. She was the wife of a Hollywood actor, long-standing marriage, in her fifties. The guy wasn't famous any more, but his residuals gave him plenty of cash. Plus he owned real estate. Six months after her death, he had remarried, a young, beautiful French girl. Craig suspected that either the husband or the new wife had ordered the hit; California was a community property state, and divorce would have cost him twenty mil.

'Is that right?'

'It's what my people are telling me.'

Craig didn't argue. Sam Murray had good sources. They both knew that.

'I'm thinking that's the key. The Steinberg case.' He read the text out aloud. 'That's what the guy sent before he died, and I think this was a love crime, hate crime, call it whatever you like. Why be so elaborate? Kill in the marriage bed? Why set the girl up? That's personal. And who would want to hire a guy that had offed a society wife? Somebody that wants the person dead.'

'Josh Steen fucked a lot of wives.' Craig glanced in the back. 'Excuse me, miss.'

'I'm past it,' Lisa said drily.

'Been thinking for a long time it could be a husband.' His eyes moved to the rear-view mirror again. 'You probably know the killer. Almost for sure. You being involved, that was deliberate. They hated Josh and didn't like you either. I done a million of these things. It's the money that's got everybody blind, but I think this was sex.'

'He's right,' Sam said. 'Can you list the husbands for us . . . the ones you knew of?'

She shook her head. 'I tried to ignore the rumours.'

'Un-ignore them. Tell us who you heard about, even if it seems unlikely.'

'OK.' Lisa sighed. 'Melissa Olivera. Tracey Jackson. Lori Mandel.' She paused. 'Some said Hannah Mazin.'

Craig shook his head. 'Looked at all those guys' bank accounts. Nothing unusual that could mean payment to a hitman. It's got to be somebody else.'

'Really?' Sam was surprised. 'Craig, I've been digging. Now I'm here, I was going to start the hunt for real. Peter Mazin was at the top of my list.'

'What?' Lisa asked. 'Peter?'

'Of course Peter.' Sam turned around in his seat. '*Cui bono*, you know? Think about it. Peter Mazin didn't like you; you told me that much yourself. He was always second string while Josh was alive. Now he gets to control the whole company, at least while the estate's in escrow while they figure out if you're the Black Widow or not. He's suddenly the star. Nobody in his way. And if Josh was putting him down at work and fucking his wife behind his back . . . '

'Yeah. And he's got the cash to hire a guy like that,' Craig agreed. 'I like him for it too. But I crawled over him. There was nothing. He isn't the client. He hasn't paid anyone.'

'OK,' Sam said slowly. 'You're sure?'

'I'll check him again. But yeah, I'm pretty sure. I didn't find anything in that group you mentioned.' He turned on to the freeway. 'And now I have questions, lots of questions. And I'm gonna be taping.'

'As long as we get to get out of the car when you're done.'

'You do. But that's it. Your get-out-of-jail-free card. After that, you guys are on your own. You should consider law enforcement.'

'Before we find the killer? You realise there'll be somebody else coming for us, right? Chances he stops at one hitman? We're out there. We're tracking. He has to be coming for us.'

Craig didn't reply. What could he say? Murray was right. It freaking killed him that there was nothing on the money trail. These two were in danger, real danger, and he didn't think they'd done anything wrong. And law enforcement would pen them in to be slaughtered.

'I could try for protective custody. Witness protection even.'

'For that you need a suspect, right?' Lisa Costello asked. 'And we don't have a suspect.'

Craig nodded. 'Then let's go get one. Answer all my questions.' He reached down to the gear box and retrieved his Dictaphone, started to record on it.

'Interview by Special Agent in Charge Craig Gordon with witnesses Lisa Costello and Samuel Murray. Are you Lisa Costello?'

'Yes,' she said clearly.

'Describe your discovery of the body of Joshua Steen. Be comprehensive. We don't know what details may prove important.'

She didn't flinch, didn't quail. He kept his eyes on the road with difficulty. She sounded rather magnificent, with her voice clear and loud for the tape, defying him, almost, defying them all.

377

'When I woke up, I had been drugged. At the time I thought I was hung over . . . '

★ ★ ★

Yuri turned away, annoyed. He had made the wrong call. It was a long shot anyway, but he did not relish getting things wrong. He had the secure cell out, calling Woody, pumping him. Useless sack of shit.

'Where's Craig Gordon now?'

'What do you mean?'

'I mean where is he? Right now.'

Woody sounded confused. 'He's working out of LA.'

'I know that. I mean specifically. Is he in the office? On patrol? At a scene? I need his location.'

'IA doesn't work like that.'

'They do now. Call his office. Get it for me. In five minutes or less.'

★ ★ ★

Craig dropped them off on West Third Street. Sam had a connection at Parc La Brea, a large, anonymous rental community, gated and full of identical townhouses and tower blocks. He didn't ask which apartment. He didn't want to know. What he did want was to get back to the office. There was so much stuff, so much evidence on that tape now. It really was a hell of a story. He almost envied them, the love affair sounded so wild. That came through even the

378

dry facts that Murray admitted to. There seemed enough here to clear them both. But only the stuff at the start could help him. What was hiding in Lisa Costello's account of that rich, spoiled, playboy wedding . . . and what Sam Murray had seen when he went in to take photos.

The killer was somewhere, somewhere in this story, and Craig Gordon's job was to ferret him out.

★ ★ ★

'Yuri.'

'You're late,' he responded. He was angry. He was driving back towards the 405. 'I said five minutes. You've been an hour. This is not a game.'

'I did my best!' he whimpered. 'Yuri, he met them. He's not saying where. He brought a phone into the lab. Felix Latham's phone. They're taking it apart.'

A fresh wash of disgust for Latham. What a second-rater. Yuri's client was now in trouble. Of course, that wasn't his problem; he was here to take care of Murray and Costello.

'Where are they? Where did he meet?'

'The readout comes through from triangulating the phone bug. But it's not legit and it's not real time.'

'Answer my question,' Yuri said, with soft menace.

'At San Diego airport.' Fuck. 'And then they drove to LA. Looks like he dropped them in the region of the Beverly Center. After that the route was pretty direct to the office and he was calling in to prep them for the phone.'

'Did he say anything of interest?'

'Yeah. That he wanted to look at Peter Mazin again. Said Sam Murray was convinced it was him. They've been through his accounts; Craig said they were starting over.'

Unwelcome news.

'OK. Stay on him. Have your team on surveillance.'

'I'm setting that up right now. It's easier to explain now. He met these two and didn't bring them in. That's cause for IA to get involved. He's being watched.'

'Good.' Yuri hung up and took the car off a slip road. The Beverly Center. If he were Sam and Lisa, he would not be shopping. They would need shelter, need to wash after the flight. Then food. His calls would be hotels and residences. Then the Wal-Mart, or the Farmers' Market. Probably the latter. Sam Murray would know better than to be trapped inside a concrete building.

He smiled. Woody gave up lots of good information. It would not be too difficult to track them now. For one thing, Craig Gordon had brought his information in. The FBI and cops would be fanning the city, searching. Yuri could watch their nets as well as cast his own. The web was closing around the prey. It would not be long now. Plus, they had to be exhausted. And tired people made errors. In Yuri's world, there was no room for that.

By the time they had stepped out of whatever bathroom they had found, he would be there. And he would be hunting.

⋆ ⋆ ⋆

The apartment was exactly as he had left it. Sam kept a furnished studio at Parc La Brea, high up in one of the tower blocks, rented under an assumed name. He'd used it for girls, sources, friends who came to visit. It was useful, and only smelled a little of must. The furnishings were bland and comfortable. They cleaned it for him once a month, and the whole set-up was so corporate and huge there was no danger of personal engagement. As long as the rent kept coming, nobody cared.

He had rarely been so glad to see anywhere. Lisa stumbled through the front door after him. She was drained from the flight, yawning, almost punch-drunk. The tension and fear took it out of you.

'What now?' she muttered.

'Wash and sleep.'

'We don't have time to sleep.'

'I think we have to.' He didn't do well on planes either. 'You can't function beyond a certain point. Shower, sleep for ninety minutes. I'll set an alarm. And then we go hunt. I'll buy a laptop, another disposable phone. Make calls. We need more information. I'm calling people about Peter Mazin. We'll add all the other husbands in.'

'But Craig said — '

'Craig's a cop. I'm a celebrity tracker. In this

381

case, that's more useful. I know these people, Lisa, I know what makes them tick, what drives them, why they hate, why they want revenge. Craig's missing something, that's all I know. This was a love crime. And it was Peter Mazin who did it. Now we have to get close to him and we have to prove it.'

'And if Peter Mazin hired a second assassin?'

'Then that guy will be reporting in to him. I know some good hackers. Most celebrities' cell phones are hacked by the papers. You need a second source to print, but there's not that much privacy out there. Now we're home, it's going to be easy to tail him, even if I don't do it in person.'

'But the killer would be hunting us.'

'And we're hunting him. It's crunch time, honey. Somebody wins, somebody loses.'

She shuddered.

'Go and wash.'

'I want you,' she murmured. She moved closer to him. 'I want to make love. We're here, right now. God knows when we'll get another chance.'

He hardened immediately. Damn, she was insatiable. He responded to her desire.

'We should sleep,' he said. That was the right thing to do, from a survival standpoint.

'You have to shower. So do I. Shower with me.' She put her hand between his legs, stroking him through his clothes. He felt himself rear under her touch. 'We can sleep afterwards.'

He said nothing. He grabbed her by the wrist and half pulled her to the shower. She stumbled after him. Sam turned on the water. Lisa reached for his T-shirt, but he stayed her hands. Slowly, patiently, he stripped her. The shirt first. Next he tugged off her jeans, impatient. She had on a little thong and a lace bra, coffee-coloured. He was so aroused, it hurt. But she was panting, almost squirming under his touch. They were alive, and together, and he had to take her. He eased the straps down her shoulders, watching her large, natural breasts fall out of the bra, her nipples already erect under the warm steam. Sam reached forward, controlling himself. He remained fully clothed. Apart from the snatch of cloth at her thighs, she was naked. He would not allow her even that scrap of modesty. He brushed his fingers over her nipples, felt them harden, solid under his touch, her body jerk like he had given it an electric shock. It was tough to control himself. The girl was literally panting. God almighty, how he loved her. She was so his, so helpless, so responsive. He hooked his thumbs into the lace at the side of her panties and tugged them, not off, just halfway down her thighs, framing her body for him. She moaned, but did not move. He ran his fingers between her legs. She was wet already, wet and open to him. Sam put his hands behind her shoulder blades and pulled her to him, she nude, he fully dressed. She pressed her body to him. He could feel the heat of her skin, her belly, through his clothes. His erection pressed against his zipper.

'Please, Sam.' She was begging. 'Oh God! Please!'

The hiss of the warm water struck his ears. He wanted to have her. His mouth fastened on hers, feeling her tongue, probing, pleading. He ripped his clothes off and scooped her nakedness up into his arms, pressing kisses to her neck, her collarbone, taking her under the shower. She shivered with desire. Warm water drenched them both, washing away the sweat and the tiredness. There was a small bottle of shower gel resting on a tray by the wall. Sam placed a little in his hands, and rubbed it over her wet skin, cleaning her, thoroughly, agonisingly slowly, cupping her breasts, her ass, soaping between her legs. She cried out. The water sluiced over her body, washing the white bubbles from her. He could delay no more. He moved closer, taking her in his arms, thrusting inside of her. Her knees weakened; she half slumped in his grip. He held her upright while the hot water washed over them both, thrusting into her, taking her like he would never stop, like he would never let her go . . .

★ ★ ★

'I don't understand,' Peter Mazin said again.

He glanced at the door to his office. It was shut. He could imagine what the staff were saying outside it. His secretary, his development girls, the junior execs, the other flunkies. They would be whispering like a gaggle of schoolgirls. He looked at the FBI agent before him with something approaching hatred.

'I think you do. At first I missed this in your accounts. We found no discrepancies,' Craig Gordon said. His eyes were cold. Mazin felt an

384

unaccountable fear. It was like this guy could see exactly what he thought of Josh Steen, look deep into his soul, peel back the politeness, see the hatred and rottenness inside.

'Because there aren't any, Agent Gordon. It's not like we haven't been over this.'

'Not from your personal accounts. But there are a series of small transactions from various joint marital accounts. Some have been made to shell companies.'

Mazin sighed. 'I have hundreds of standing orders. Payments my accountants set up. I never see them from start to finish. That's just how we work. You have to understand that people with money,' this was a deliberate insult to the working schlub, and he was pleased to see he took it this way, 'don't exactly balance their own chequebooks.'

'Possibly not, sir.' Gordon's face was granite. It could have been on Mount Rushmore. 'But there's a pattern. And put together, the amounts combine to several million dollars.'

'I see.'

'I have to tell you, sir, that the FBI works on information received. It is our understanding that there was a strong rumour that Joshua Steen had an affair with your wife, Mrs Hannah Mazin, amongst others.'

'Bullshit.'

'That's the rumour. Also that you were not happy with Mr Steen taking the limelight in your company. It goes to motive, sir. Can you tell me about your relationship with Mrs Steen?'

'Josh's mother? Didn't know her.'

'No, sir. Mrs Steen. His wife.'

'You mean Lisa Costello?' Mazin could not stop the sneer crossing his face. 'Standoffish, a snob. A gold-digger. Never mixed with my wife. That was not a real marriage, Special Agent. They were fighting on the wedding day.'

'Yes, and apparently Mr Steen slept with one of the bridesmaids.'

'So people said. Lisa had good reason to kill him.'

'He was killed in a professional hit. We have recovered semen from the assassin that has now been matched with the DNA of a known hitman. We are currently tracking down his bank accounts. If those payments match . . . It may be better for you if you co-operate, Mr Mazin. Because we will find any matches. It just takes a while.'

'There won't be any matches.' Peter was practically shouting. 'I didn't order a hit on Josh. For Christ's sake, I'm a goddamn producer. I'm fucking sick to death of hearing about him!'

He flushed bright red. Fuck it, and now he had blurted out his anger with Josh. To an agent who suspected him.

There was a long pause. Craig Gordon was regarding him steadily.

'I didn't do anything wrong,' Peter said sullenly. 'I want a lawyer.'

'Duly noted, sir. I haven't Mirandised you. As yet you're not under suspicion of anything. Please don't leave the jurisdiction.'

Gordon got to his feet. Peter stared up at him. 'That's it? That's all you've got to say?'

'For the moment, yes, sir. Thank you for your

386

co-operation. We may come back to you. Have a good day, Mr Mazin.'

Peter looked after him, open-mouthed, as Craig Gordon walked out.

★ ★ ★

Yuri moved through the stalls of the Farmers' Market. He had been here an hour already. None of the guesthouses or hotels had given him any joy. It had to be a rental place, and searching through those would take time. Or they could be at the house of friends. He would wait. They would come out for food eventually.

Lisa Costello would be the first kill.

★ ★ ★

The bedside clock was buzzing harshly. Sam Murray opened his eyes with difficulty and hit it to shut it off. He was lying enfolded in Lisa's slender arms. She stirred, groggy. Hell. It was hard to get up. After sex with her, he was drained at the best of times. Today her wet, slippery, squirming body had aroused him so much she'd milked him dry, and Sam had carried her, damp, to the bed and practically fallen asleep in her embrace the moment his head touched the pillow.

He could have slept for hours. Years. But there was no time. They needed to move from here. Craig Gordon knew where they were. The Bureau might have wheedled it out of him. They could not stay still.

'We got to get up. Come on, baby.'

387

'Where are we going now?' She rubbed her eyes. God, but she was beautiful when she was sleepy. He noted that she did not prevaricate, did not argue. She was a soldier. She moved when he said move.

'We need clothes, food. We didn't bring anything. Got to get supplies. I'll find another place to stash us.' He grinned. 'I know a few hookers I trust. You don't mind?'

'Don't mind anything from your past. They're more honest than half the trophy wives I knew,' Lisa said.

'The Farmers' Market sells cheap T-shirts, shorts, stuff like that. It'll do for now. And we can eat. I want to be open air.'

'Sure. I like the market.'

'We'll change in the bathrooms there, walk down to the Beverly Center, catch a cab. I know this chick in the Hollywood Hills. Then we start making calls on Peter Mazin . . . '

He turned and looked at Lisa. She was standing in the middle of the room, naked; enough of a sight to arrest him just by itself. But there was a look on her face he hadn't seen before. A terrible, fearful look. Understanding. Disgust.

His heart thumped. 'Lisa! What's the matter? What is it?'

She faced him, and he half quailed at the look in her eyes.

'I know who did it,' she said. 'I know who killed Josh. It's so obvious. It was always staring us in the face. You worked it out and then you looked right past her.'

'Her?' Sam repeated, and his mind swung

388

straight to the same place, and realisation ripped across him in a tidal wave of shock.

'Hannah,' Lisa whispered. 'It was Hannah Mazin. She slept with him. She might have loved him. But to Josh she was just another whore. He enjoyed her more because she was married to Peter; he was asserting himself over Peter . . . but he didn't want it open. He was going to marry me . . . he loved me, maybe, after a fashion. As long as he didn't have to stop screwing around.'

'Jesus, Lisa.'

'What you said . . . hookers . . . and I said they were more honest than the trophy wives . . . '

'Hannah didn't want second place. She wanted Josh.' Sam shook his head at his own blindness. 'It burns these people; they're myopic. Maybe she could deal with rejection, thought she'd get him back. But when he was actually going to *marry* you . . . that was too much for her. Going to the big society wedding. Watching you in your dress. The photos. The TV shots. My exclusive. She couldn't stand it. She wanted him dead and you to suffer for it. And with Josh out the way, guess what? Peter Mazin becomes the alpha dog. By default.'

'I think you should call Craig.' Lisa picked up her clothes from the floor. 'Have him check her money too. Do we still go out, go to Hollywood?'

'We need fresh clothes. We smell, we get noticed. And food. No, we go on as planned. It might not be Hannah. It's just a theory that fits right now.'

'It's Hannah,' Lisa said, and her eyes were dark with rage. 'It's Hannah.'

389

14

Peter Mazin waited as his garage door swung smoothly up to admit his Ferrari. Hannah's Aston Martin was parked next door, and the housekeeper's BMW in the third garage. The second row of garages, right behind, kept the customised Hummer he used for hunting, the SUV they took on weekend trips, and the gardeners' pick-up truck. They had never had any kids, never wanted any. Hannah didn't bug him about it. Until Josh . . . until the goddamned thing with Josh, he thought she was the perfect wife.

He parked the car and jumped out. She would be in. He knew her routine. Their house lay stretched out, perfect, in front of him. Ten thousand square feet of prime Beverly Hills real estate, the lawns smooth and lush from the sprinklers, the air fragrant with roses and hibiscus. The house itself looked like a Williamsburg Colonial from the outside, all cream and apple green and fresh-painted wooden shutters. Inside, it was wired up with more modern electronics than a NASA launch pad.

His heart raced, unsteady. His breathing was ragged. He almost wanted a drink, at eleven o'clock in the morning. When it had hit him, he'd come straight home, making an excuse to the guys in the office. Combine that with the

FBI visit and what would they think?

He knocked on the door. Juanita, their housekeeper, raised her eyebrows to see him.

'Mr Peter! You home early.'

'Is Mrs Mazin in?' he asked formally.

'Yes, sir, she upstairs.'

'Juanita, I want a little alone time with my wife. Can you get rid of the staff?'

He looked deadly serious. The housekeeper swallowed, broke eye contact. 'Yes Mr Peter. I send them away.'

'And the gardeners. And you too for an hour. You could pick up the dry-cleaning, OK?'

'*Si, senor,*' she agreed, ducking from his path. Peter Mazin was a mild-mannered guy, but you didn't mess with him when he was angry. The older woman was alive with curiosity. Who had that little Anglo slut been fucking now? she wondered. But it was more than her cushy job was worth to let it show. She bustled off to the kitchen to get rid of the maids, listening to him walk upstairs, his footsteps heavy on the polished oak stairs.

★   ★   ★

Lisa moved through the market. Sam was right behind her. He didn't have his hand in the small of her back, but he might as well have done. She had picked up jeans and some tourist T-shirts almost as soon as she'd entered the market, and Sam and she had moved into the bathrooms and changed right away, stuffing their old clothes into carrier bags and dumping them in garbage

391

bins. The feeling of clean cotton against the skin was utterly luxurious. They headed back and bought another set of clothes, socks included. One to wear and one to wash. Amazing how you cherished the small things when you were running for your life.

The market was dark with sunglasses on, but she dared not remove them. Even in shades and a baseball cap she felt conspicuous. It only took one astute shopper to spot her and Sam and she would be running again, this time with less safety than ever. There was no European anonymity here.

'Let's eat.' Sam steered her towards a stall making juices. God, Lisa thought, fresh-squeezed Californian juice; it was one of the great things about this city. She had missed it so much . . . her body craved it, the vitamin C, the sheer lightness of it . . .

*	*	*

Yuri replaced the trinket on its stall. He didn't jerk or move fast. He had seen them. Briefly, in his peripheral vision. But it was them. He had no doubts, none at all.

His mind moved to the car. It was waiting outside, parked near the exit of the Writers' Guild building across the street. There was a latex mask, a good one, and glasses inside the glove compartment. He would drive it down the block to the Beverly Center and lose himself in there for a while. There was a second car waiting by a pharmacy across the street. He would be in

San Diego by nightfall, and Mexico tomorrow, and then lie low for his customary two months.

Power and pleasure suffused him. Damn, but he was good at this. They had come to him, as surely as if he had them tied to a golden string. Time to let his nervous little client off the hook.

Keeping them in his sightline, he pulled his cell phone from his pocket and punched in her number.

⋆ ⋆ ⋆

Hannah Mazin was sitting in her dressing room. It was a vast expanse adjacent to their master bedroom, her closets and shoe racks and mirrors lining it wall to ceiling, the whole thing painted a dusty pink with silver accents. She faced her antique French gilt dressing table, regarding her pretty face in the ancient mirror covered with age spots.

Peter looked at her. She regarded his reflection, did not turn round. He thought her eyes were glittering, feverishly bright.

'There's money missing from our accounts. Millions of dollars.'

Hannah slowly raised her bone-backed hairbrush to her head. She did not deign to answer him.

'The FBI came to see me. They don't want me to leave the country. They know about you and Josh.'

It was the first time he had said those words out loud.

'I don't care,' she said then, and her voice was

393

high-pitched, half mad. 'He deserved it. He used me. Threw me aside. Chose that bitch, that fucking little English bitch.' She giggled. 'I showed her.'

Mazin felt like vomiting. His wife. His own goddamned wife.

'I want a divorce,' he managed. 'On grounds of adultery. You get nothing, Hannah, that's the pre-nup. I want you out of my house.'

'I'm not going anywhere,' she said. 'Not till she's dead. She'll be dead soon.'

'You did it,' Mazin said. 'You . . . you actually did this. You murdered him. They found you, Hannah. They'll kill you. That's why the agent left my office. He knew it wasn't me. It was you.'

'They won't kill me. They won't dare.'

'You're fucking insane.' Mazin started to back away, down towards the stairs. 'Go right now, take the jet, get over the border. Maybe you can make a life. Otherwise they'll fry you, Hannah. When you hired that assassin, you murdered Josh. And you did that in the USA. They'll try you and execute you, right here. And you'd deserve it.'

Her cell phone rang. Mazin jumped out of his skin. She took the call; she actually took the call.

'Good,' she said, after a second. 'You have all the money. Kill them.'

She hung up and looked at Peter.

'That was Yuri. He works for me. They are at the Farmers' Market and he's going to shoot them now.'

'You can't do that,' Peter Mazin stuttered. 'You've lost your mind. I'm calling 911.'

394

Hannah Mazin smiled gently. She reached into her little drawer and turned back to him. He gasped in shock. She was holding a revolver, a tiny little thing with a gleaming pink handle.

'No,' she said. 'You're not.'

Then she shot him in the chest.

★ ★ ★

Sam tossed back the juice. Orange and lychee and watermelon. God, it was good. It slipped down his throat, hydrated him. He watched Lisa gulping hers. They'd get a burger someplace, then get over to the Hills. He wanted Craig Gordon. Hannah Mazin, she was the one. He was close to freedom, at last. He sensed it . . .

Sam saw him almost too late.

His left hand went out reflexively. He shoved Lisa by her neck. She yelped in pain, the remains of the juice splashing her new shirt. He heard the *phut*, the whizz of the bullet.

Behind him, somebody screamed. He was splashed with blood. Then everybody screamed.

Another bullet. The guy was closer now. Pain exploded in his upper arm. He knew he'd been shot.

'Gun!' somebody screamed. 'Gun!'

The juice stall was upended; everything crashed to the ground. The market was full of people shrieking, running, mothers grabbing their children.

Sam saw the assassin. He was a Slav, blond and white-faced. He grabbed Lisa, yelping in pain from his arm. 'Run!' he shouted. 'Get out! Out!'

Christ. Jesus Christ. He didn't have a gun. This man was not Felix Latham; this man was serious.

'It's her!' somebody shrieked, even louder than the roars of the crowd. 'That's Lisa Costello! The killer! That bitch has a gun! Get her!'

He was a burly black man in a Lakers T-shirt. Sam tried to push him off, but the guy had eighty pounds on him. He moved in front of Lisa as she scrambled for her footing in the panicking crowd.

The man's head exploded. Sam retched. Skull ripped open, blood and brain matter everywhere. He had gotten in front of Lisa, and taken her bullet.

'She killed him!' a woman wailed. 'She killed that guy! She shot him!'

'LAPD!' came a cry. And another. 'LAPD! Drop your weapon!'

There were two cops. Full blue uniforms, guns drawn. 'Get down!' one of them shouted. He wasn't looking at the Slav, shoving his way through the crowd, gun held discreetly next to his chest. He was looking at Lisa. His gun was drawn on her. It was cocked. Lisa tripped and stumbled.

'Get down!' the guy roared. 'I said, get down!'

Lisa had no control. The press of the crowd was too thick. The cops were nervous, Sam could tell. He thought they might shoot. There were two of them. And the killer was coming, shoving inexorably through the press of bodies.

'It isn't her!' he shouted. 'She's unarmed! It's him!'

He pointed at the Slav. The man's eyes narrowed. Sam saw he hated being pointed out in the crowd.

'Get back, sir, *right now!*' yelled the larger cop. He trained his gun on Sam. The smaller one was already aiming at Lisa as she struggled for balance. She wasn't listening to them; she was running. Christ. They were going to kill her. Sam felt the chaos around him slow and stop, slow motion, like his heart, like life would be without her, and he knew if he interfered they would kill him, and he knew the assassin was readying his gun; he could see it. The cops weren't looking, and suddenly it was all absolutely clear to him, and he turned and punched the large cop in the solar plexus. Then he took the guy's gun, a huge, no-messing automatic, and he pointed it over the heads of the screaming crowd and he fired. The Slav stared at him, stunned, a bright red hole blooming in his forehead, and the second cop turned away from Lisa and jammed his gun into the small of Sam's back, and Lisa fell to the ground and looked up and cried out, 'Don't kill him, I love him! I love him!' Sam dropped the gun and felt the first cop manhandle him to the ground, kicking him so hard in the ribs that they broke, and he crunched in agony, trying to look around for Lisa, and then the blood loss from his arm overcame him, and he fainted.

★ ★ ★

Hannah Mazin watched the scene unfold on CNN. She was numb with anger. Peter's body was still warm in the room behind her. The servants would be up soon, but she still had the gun.

The scrolling titles on the bottom of the screen made no sense to her. The news feed was muddy, indistinct, shots from a helicopter showing the Farmers' Market sealed off, FBI vans and police cars parked around, lots of yellow tape.

Lisa Costello apprehended, it said. *Fatal shootings on West Third St. Casualties unknown. Samuel Murray under arrest. FBI investigating.*

Apprehended. Under arrest. That wasn't dead, was it? That wasn't fucking dead. She scanned the lines but nothing more came out. Where was Yuri?

'And now we have a report from Susie Chen, our reporter on the scene,' said the anchor excitedly. 'What's new, Susie?'

'Joanne, police sources are informing CNN at this time that the journalist Sam Murray of *USA Weekly* shot another man dead with a gun belonging to a policeman.' said pretty Susie to camera, looking earnest. 'These are unconfirmed reports right now. We are hearing that this second man was found to be carrying a gun. There are suggestions that he may have targeted Lisa Costello for assassination.'

'Well that's a very significant development. Are the police saying anything for the record?'

'Not yet. We are hearing though from several law enforcement sources that this may have something to do with the recently publicised theory that Josh Steen, former husband of Lisa Costello, was in fact slain by an assassin; you remember that major story that's been all over the airwaves this past week. A corpse has been taken to the medical examiner . . . One thing we know for sure is that Lisa Costello and Sam Murray are both in custody at this time, both alive. Sam Murray sustained a gunshot wound and is on his way to hospital under police guard, but it's not thought to be life-threatening . . . Lawyers are already scrambling to be the one to represent Ms Costello, and it would seem the strangest murder case in America for years has just taken another turn . . . '

Hannah understood that. The writer, the tabloid hack. Somehow he had killed Yuri. Her money was gone. Lisa was with the FBI. Peter, behind her, was dead. They had tracked her.

She thought of Josh for a few moments. Thought of his dark eyes boring into hers. Thought of her body leaping eagerly, God, so eagerly, to his touch. His mouth on hers.

Almost without thinking, she raised the gun to her temple, and she fired.

Epilogue

'You can go,' Craig said.

'Jesus.' Sam could hardly believe it. 'I can? Are you sure?'

'They're satisfied. Listen, don't fuck up again. My advice is to get out of this jurisdiction. Nobody likes a wise-ass.'

'Right,' Sam said. He didn't know what else to say. Craig had dealt quietly and patiently with his lawyer, with all the authorities. It was less than a week, and the DA had informed him there were no charges. Self-defence, and two notorious assassins dead. He was a free man. Apparently a hero too. A celebrity.

None of that mattered. Nothing did, without Lisa.

'Where is she? Did they charge her?'

Last he'd heard from his lawyer, they were still thinking about it. Multiple charges were possible. Abduction. Assault. False passports. Flight. Theft . . .

'No. Couldn't do it. Nobody hates her any more. Didn't you hear?' Craig's grin split his face. 'America's feeling guilty for believing the hype. Believing a tabloid hack like you. The general consensus is she did nothing wrong.'

'Where is she?' Sam asked. 'I want to see her. I want to talk to her.'

'She's waiting for you. Come on.'

His friend led him out of the interview room

and down a corridor. They were together in the middle of the Beverly Hills Police Department. Cops stared as they walked past, and Sam didn't give a damn. Craig shoved him into an open room. And there she was, in a white T-shirt and a pair of jeans, her hair blonde, blow-dried and healthy, and nothing on her face but lip gloss, and to him she was the most gorgeous woman in the world.

He wanted to fall on her. To take her where she stood. But Craig was still standing there.

'Press are waiting outside. You guys are the big story today. Innocent vics, all that stuff. They got TV crews, most of the tabloids. I can smuggle you out in a car if you want.'

'That'd be great,' Lisa said immediately. 'Thank you, Craig.'

'You want to hire some bodyguards. You'll be harassed by the public for six months at least. And the money, there's always the money. Abduction is a real threat.'

'My lawyer's setting it up now. Thanks again.'

Craig Gordon looked from one to the other. 'I'll give you guys a minute,' he said, and shut the door.

Sam walked over to Lisa, took her in his arms, and kissed her like he never wanted to let her go.

'What did he mean, the money?'

'They cleared me,' Lisa muttered against his chest. 'I inherit. The family's suing but the money's mine. And the lawyers say I'm keeping it.'

Sam stiffened. 'How much?'

'A bit over two hundred million dollars,' Lisa whispered.

'Holy shit,' he said.

'We can give it away,' she offered, and he felt her heart speed up against his chest. 'I don't want it to come between us. I don't want anything to come between us.'

Sam laughed and kissed her again, feeling her lips melt into his, feeling her body lift helplessly to him.

'Give some away. Keep some. Buy Hans his jet. Who cares. Let's get the fuck out of here and get to an airport. You want to go to the Caymans?'

'Are you going to be there?' she asked, kissing him again. 'Anywhere is good if you're there.'

'Yeah. I'm going to be there.' He couldn't believe the happiness that was flooding him. 'Every day for the rest of our lives.'

'Was that a proposal?' Lisa asked, and she circled her arms around his neck.

'It sure was.'

They kissed gently for a minute, in each other's embrace.

'I'd love to marry you,' Lisa said. 'I think I can do better second time around.'

'Would be hard to do worse.'

They laughed. Craig Gordon knocked, and opened the door, and they followed him out through the office, holding hands, still running, running from the press and the hangers-on, running to the airport, running to their new life.

We do hope that you have enjoyed reading
this large print book.

Did you know that all of our titles
are available for purchase?

We publish a wide range of high quality
large print books including:
Romances, Mysteries, Classics
General Fiction
Non Fiction and Westerns

Special interest titles available in
large print are:
The Little Oxford Dictionary
Music Book
Song Book
Hymn Book
Service Book

Also available from us courtesy of
Oxford University Press:
Young Readers' Dictionary
(large print edition)
Young Readers' Thesaurus
(large print edition)

For further information or a free
brochure, please contact us at:
Ulverscroft Large Print Books Ltd.,
The Green, Bradgate Road, Anstey,
Leicester, LE7 7FU, England.
Tel: (00 44) 0116 236 4325
Fax: (00 44) 0116 234 0205

Other titles published by
The House of Ulverscroft:

PASSION

Louise Bagshawe

Orphan William Hyde and professor's daughter Melissa Elmet fell passionately in love as teenagers at Oxford. But, after her family intervenes, their secret marriage is annulled. Heartbroken, Melissa retreats into her shell, and the life of a shy academic. Will, on the other hand, rejected and embittered, joins MI6 — then becomes a millionaire in New York, with a model girlfriend and only dark memories of Melissa. Their lives are completely different. They'll never meet again. And then the killings start. Only Will notices the link to all four high-profile murders: Melissa's late father, the secretive professor who died working on a confidential project. And now he fears that the next hit will be Melissa — unless he can get to her before they do.

GLITZ

Louise Bagshawe

The four Chambers girls are rolling in money, care of the fund set up by their super-rich Uncle Clem. Social climber Juno, scruffy academic Athena, wannabe actress Venus and trendy It Girl Diana take their extravagant and glamorous lifestyles for granted. But then Uncle Clem announces his engagement to Bai-Ling, a woman young enough to be their baby sister — and the Chambers girls know the party could be over. They must stop the wedding — by destroying Bai-Ling. But could Uncle Clem have a bigger plan up his sleeve? Will the four of them unite against the threat of Bai-Ling, or is it every woman for herself? Without the money, who will learn how to stand on her own two feet — and who will fall?

GLAMOUR

Louise Bagshawe

Three powerful women. Once best friends. Now deadly rivals . . . Texan honey Sally Lassiter, English rose Jane Morgan and Jordanian Helen Yanna meet at an exclusive girls' school and become best friends. They form a bond which will never be broken . . . Years later, the three girls are grown up, co-founders and millionaire co-owners of the exclusive *Glamour* chain of stores. They are fabulously wealthy, instantly recognisable, adored and revered. Or are they? The *Glamour* empire is on the verge of collapse and the three women are embroiled in a bitter feud . . .